FORGED IN FIRE

JULIETTE CROSS

For Julie Reece.

AUTHOR'S NOTE

Dear Readers,

Please note that FORGED IN FIRE was my very first novel, and THE VESSEL TRILOGY my first series to complete and publish. I realize these characters and this plot is *quite* different from my most recent works. So please bear that in mind.

This is where I started as a writer. Needless to say, my style and skill has changed over the years.

While I did revise with a few changes and additional scenes, this was a light revision with new covers for the rerelease. That being said, I do love Jude and Genevieve so much as they were my first hero and heroine.

So I hope you'll read on with that in mind. Both of the MCs are quite flawed and the sinister villains pretty damn malicious. I hope you'll enjoy it for the roller coaster ride it is, and for a heartfelt HEA.

Standing next to Mindy in the elevator, I wished I'd said no and stayed home. My idea of the perfect birthday celebration was pajamas, pizza, whiskey and coke, and a *Lord of the Rings* marathon. Not the club scene.

I knew I was too young to be this jaded about college nightlife, but I couldn't help it. The party scene simply felt old and tired.

Maybe it was because I was an *old soul* as Dad always told me. Maybe it was because I'd suffered a tragic loss at a young age, making the past-time of drinking till you drop seem rather a waste of time. Or maybe I just didn't want to sweat out the night in a packed club while strange guys groped me.

Either way, it didn't matter. I loved my best friend, and she'd refused to let me sit home on my birthday like I'd wanted to. So here I was.

I glared down at her, since I was about a foot taller. She beamed back with a syrupy-sweet smile.

"Oh, come on, Gen. Don't be so grumpy. Tonight, I want you to *relax*. Nothing else to worry about. Just have fun."

Her baby blues pleaded with me to loosen up.

"Nothing to worry about," I exhaled a deep breath on a semi-smile. "Fun. Got it."

"Awesome. Now let's go celebrate!"

We were total opposites in just about every way. She was petite, slender, and tan. I had inherited my height and dark hair from my dad. But my milk-pale skin and ice-blue eyes came from my mother.

"Stop brooding," muttered Mindy.

"I'm not."

Right before the elevator doors opened, Mindy shifted and glanced sideways under long lashes. A telltale sign of guilt I recognized from our long friendship.

"What? What did you do?"

"Nothing," she protested too innocently. "Just that I forgot to mention that Steven is coming with us."

The elevator dinged. The door opened.

"You did *not* set me up on a date tonight," I grated out.

"No, I promise! Not a date. He just wanted to come along. As a friend. That's all."

I eyed her with suspicion. "Whatever. But I am not on a date. This is my night, remember?"

"Yes, of course!"

She hooked her arm through mine as we entered the lobby of her mother's upscale New Orleans condo. I was still surprised by what an unemployed divorcee could afford, but then there was always an endless stream of wealthy men in this city willing to bestow treasures on attractive, charming women.

We waltzed into the lobby, arm in arm, clip-clopping across white marble to a set of gold brocade sofas. Her boyfriend, Dazzling Dave, jumped up along with his buddy, Slippery Steve. Monikers I gave them and kept to myself so it wouldn't hurt Mindy's feelings.

"Ladies, ladies. You two look divine."

He gave us his signature smile, beaming his super-straight

and over-bleached teeth. Yet again, I longed for my pj's and Jim Beam and Viggo Mortensen.

"Hi, David," Mindy gushed, instantly gluing herself to his side.

Steven stepped up, eyeing me from top to toe. "Hello, Gen. You look awesome. Ready to celebrate?"

"Hey, Steven. Thanks. Ready as I'll ever be."

I tried not to grind my teeth as we pushed through the glass doors into the night. Steven and I had a failed blind date nearly a month ago. I hadn't realized that watching a Will Ferrell comedy in the dark was a contact sport—not until I went out with Slippery Steve.

The ride downtown from the Garden District in David's convertible definitely lightened my mood. Cool night air hinted at autumn. Canal Street buzzed with life. Neon lights blazed from one end to the other, highlighting everything from liquor stores to Commander's Palace.

Partygoers laughed, sauntered, and half stumbled along the sidewalks. The din of honking horns chorused energy and life. I had no idea where we were going. Mindy had kept it all hush-hush, wanting to surprise me.

The New Orleans business district bustled during the daytime, but now the streets were near empty. All the shops and offices stood dark and closed. David parallel parked on a side street, folding the top up with a click on the dash.

"Let's go, ladies."

"Come on, Gen!" Mindy squealed as she scooted out.

I smoothed down my dark hair, unable to keep from laughing at her enthusiasm. "I take it you're excited?"

"You're going to love this place. Promise."

One block over, David led us down a few steps into a basement club underneath a fluorescent-green sign reading *Tartarus*. A broad, beefy guy took my license at the door, scanning it without expression. He blinked twice, then handed it back to me, saying in a monotone voice, "Happy birthday."

"Thanks, Sunshine." I gave him my brightest smile.

His mouth quirked at the corners, then straightened again to a grim line. I loved throwing people off-balance.

Mindy pulled me, literally, bouncing into the club. The beat pumped right through my body, vibrating to my bones. Laser lights flicked and twisted around the room, pulsing to the rhythm of the house music. While Tweedledee and Tweedledum went for drinks, I pulled Mindy out to the dance floor.

Making our way through the throng to the middle of the dance floor, Mindy and I moved our bodies to the rhythm pulsating around us. I loved this feeling of elation when I relaxed my inhibitions. I spent so much of my time behaving calm and controlled at school and at work, but here, I could let loose and dance with my best friend.

No matter that we were crushed between sweaty bodies reeking of cigarette smoke, hard liquor, and musky cologne—I felt free. I laughed. Mindy threw her head back and laughed with me.

A tall sandy-haired guy beelined for us. He passed Mindy and started dancing behind me. Why is it that every Timberlake-wannabe thinks he can grind on a girl when she's having a perfectly good time dancing without him?

I maneuvered closer to Mindy, rolling my eyes so he couldn't see. She smirked with a sympathetic tilt of the head, but the guy was not taking the hint. He put his hands on my hips, pressing even closer. I restrained from kneeing him in the balls, wanting to keep my birthday as trouble free as possible.

"No thanks." I pushed his hands away.

By some divine fortune, he didn't put them back, but leaned close, warm breath on my ear.

"You're really hot."

I nodded. "Yeah, you're right. It's really hot. Need something to drink."

I pointed toward the bar, pulling Mindy along with me. A quick glance back at gyrating boy had me stumped. He stood perfectly still, staring after us as if confused. Then something weird sent a shiver down my spine.

A sinister red gleam flickered in his eyes before I turned away, a weird reflection of lights or something. Still, it unnerved me. When I glanced back from the bar, he had started dancing with another unlucky girl.

"Creeper!" yelled Mindy in my ear.

"Appletini for you." David passed Mindy a glass of green liquid. "And rum and coke for the birthday girl."

"Thanks," I said, not complaining that it was bourbon and coke that I liked, not rum.

Mindy and I were still underage, but that didn't stop most of the young-adult world stuck in that purgatory between eighteen and twenty-one. Honestly, who came up with the law to allow college students to enter a bar at eighteen but not be served alcohol? For once, I'd love to see an undercover police officer shut down one of these clubs, flashing his badge and attempting to arrest the vast number of underage drinkers allowed into the place.

"Happy Birthday!" screamed Mindy over the music and clinked her martini glass to my tumbler.

I smiled back as we took a drink. Steven grinned at me too widely, and I don't know why. It's not like one drink would suddenly make him attractive to me. He wasn't bad looking, he was simply unappealing in personality.

I leaned back against the bar, propping my elbows up behind me. Scanning the scene, my eyes passed by a corner, then did a double-take, zoning in on a tall figure in the shadows on the other side of the dancefloor. The flashing lights streaked over him then plunged him in the dark.

Hitching in a breath, I couldn't look away from his silhouette. He stood against the far wall, still and watchful. Dark jeans, black button-down, crossed arms, and brooding handsome face fixed directly on...me.

Never before had my heart leapt into my throat. I tried to

swallow, to make it go back into my chest where it belonged. To no avail, mind you.

"Here, beautiful." Steven handed me another drink when I'd barely finished the first.

"Thanks," I muttered with a tight smile.

Mindy cozied up to Dave, whispering something in his ear. Steven was saying something to me, but I didn't hear him. I couldn't take my eyes off the dark figure across the room.

The music pumped hard and loud, wavering between old-school classics and modern tunes. Mindy suddenly squealed with delight. I knew why without asking. The Cure's song "Fascination Street" started thrumming all around us.

As much of a Barbie Doll as she was, Mindy had eclectic taste in music, and anything by The Cure required complete adoration. Taking my drink with me, I followed her back onto the floor, squeezing through the sweaty bodies.

Unfortunately, Steven did too. Persistence—I suppose that is a virtue in some people. Right now, it was just annoying. I sipped on my drink to avoid talking to him and moved to the slow beat.

Mindy and David shuffled off together, locked in an embrace. I feigned interest, pretending to listen to Steven yammer about who-knows-what, but all I wanted was to peer behind him and try to get a better look at the enigmatic stranger in the shadows.

He hadn't moved, still watching from his solitary post. I couldn't see if his gaze was on me, but I could *feel* it. His eyes glinted with an eerie light as the lasers flashed across the club. Again, an ominous sensation washed through me, tapping on my psyche to look around and listen. To beware.

Shit! Here came sandy-haired gyrating boy again, more earnest than ever. His hands found my hips, quickly moving south.

"Back off!" I shouted over the music, elbowing him in the ribs.

Not too hard, but hard enough to make the average guy get the hint. He didn't.

"Dude, did you hear her? Back off!" Steven stepped in.

For once, I was thankful he was present. Steven grabbed the guy's shoulder, but Sandy-hair pushed Steven so hard he fell through the crowd into the DJ's stage.

Other dancers sidestepped and turned back to their partners, probably thinking him drunk. Sandy-hair swiveled to me. A cold expression shuddered across his face.

I stepped back, but he caught my wrist in an unbreakable grip and yanked me hard against his chest, knocking my drink to the floor, pinning my arms under his. He grinned.

Primal fear bloomed in my chest. Something was very wrong here. Like earlier, a flash of red skimmed across his eyes.

Was I already tipsy?

"Let her go," a deep voice rumbled directly behind me.

Sandy-hair tore his gaze from mine. One glance at the deep-voiced person over my shoulder, and shock skittered over his expression. Or was it fear? He bared his teeth like a cornered animal, then let me go, backing away toward the exit of the club.

I twisted around, looking up, way up, into the face of the dark stranger standing a head taller than me. I was five eight and wearing boots. Dark eyes, so dark they were nearly black. An unreadable expression set in harsh lines.

I couldn't form a coherent thought, much less a sentence. From far away, he was stunning. Up close, I couldn't even breathe. He gazed down at me for what seemed like an eternity while lights and music pumped around us. Captivating. Hypnotizing.

Was he putting me under some spell? Why couldn't I think straight? My mouth hung agape as I tried to regain composure.

Finally, he spoke. "Are you all right?"

No, I was not okay.

"Yes. I'm fine," I whispered, clearing my throat.

All of a sudden, it was very hot in here. Where was that drink?

I checked him out while he seemed to be doing the same to me. He appeared to be somewhere in his late twenties or early thirties, but something in those dark depths made him seem so much older.

His olive skin reminded me of warmer climates, somewhere far away from here. Wavy dark brown hair hung loosely across his forehead and to the nape of his neck. He hadn't shaved recently. My fingers curled into my hand at the thought of touching his scruffy yet sharp jawline.

I realized I was staring, no, gawking at him. A ghost of a smile flickered across his face. Without saying anything else, he pivoted and headed for the exit. Which was quite a pleasant view, I might add.

By this time, Steven was back at my side, scowling.

"Where's that dude? I'm gonna smash his face in!"

Yeah. Whatever.

I couldn't figure out exactly what just happened. But I was glad the dark stranger had shown up, for more than one reason.

There was something very wrong with Sandy-hair. Maybe he was on drugs. Molly—MDMA—could make people very touchy-feely, so I was told. The way he glared at me, the sheer menace in those strange-colored eyes—disturbing to say the least. He could've been on a bad trip.

I waved the bartender over and downed another drink the moment it was in my hands, trying to chill out. Glancing back at the dance floor, I saw David half carrying Mindy toward the bar with a rip in her jeans at the knee.

"Mindy! What happened?"

"Fell and twisted it." She winced with each step. I pulled up a stool.

"Let me go get the car," said David. "I'll pull it around."

"No," Mindy whined in her lilting drunk voice. "Stay with

meeee." She hooked her arm tighter around his neck. One too many appletinis.

"I'll go." I set my glass on the bar. "Wait here."

Mindy grabbed my arm. "Sorry." She pouted with glazed eyes. "Didn't mean to ruin your birthday."

"You didn't." I smiled, eager to get home and end this shit-show of a night. "Be right back."

"I'll come with you." Steven took David's keys and followed me. We pushed through the crowd toward the entrance, passing by big-and-beefy at the door.

"Later, Sunshine," I called with a wave.

He nodded with a thin smile. Not a soul walked the street. I found it sort of strange to have a bar located in the more industrial end of town. But it was an eccentric place. Maybe that's what they were going for. Exclusivity, to make it more appealing.

A gust of wind whooshed by, lifting my hair. I wrapped my arms around myself as we angled down the side street toward the car.

"You cold?" asked Steven behind me.

"No." But something made me shiver. "You have the keys?"

"Yeah, right—"

I heard the keys jingle and fall to the pavement, then a thump. I spun to find Steven slumped against the wall. Unconscious. Before I could register what happened, my body slammed up against the brick wall behind me. Pinned in place by none other than Sandy-hair, his hand grasping and squeezing my throat.

"Keep still." Voice low and gravelly. "Don't scream."

How could I, of all people, get myself into a defenseless position? I knew how to fend off an attack in a hundred different ways, but he already had me in such a tight grip.

He crushed me against the wall, choking the life out of me. Staring up at him, I hoped to memorize his face for a police report later. *If* there was a later. Spots hazed my vision, though I definitely recognized those hate-filled eyes, blazing blood-red down at me. *What the hell?*

"Such a pretty one." A guttural murmur. "Such a shame to have to kill you."

Kill me? *What!*

I squirmed, trying to pull free, raking my nails on his arms then gouging at his wrists. Useless. He didn't budge, didn't even flinch.

A sinister hissing laugh in my ear. Lightheaded. Dark spots at the corner of my vision. I couldn't see anything anymore as my limbs felt light. I drifted. I thought how sad my father would be that I died in such a violent way as I slipped further into oblivion. I thought of my mother.

Suddenly, I gulped air back into my lungs. I was free of him, sliding down the wall, feeling my way along the cold brick behind me. A dark shape loomed, grappling with my attacker.

Finally catching my breath, chest still heaving, I focused to see a shadowed figure lifting my would-be killer by the throat off the ground, holding him midair. His words confused me even more.

"Stop human-hopping, and come out to play."

I knew that deep voice from the dance floor. The dark stranger. Sandy-hair held on to my would-be hero's arms. He laughed that wicked laugh again.

"Make me," he hissed.

"I was hoping you'd say that."

The stranger placed his free hand on my attacker's forehead, still holding him aloft. He whispered something I couldn't hear.

Sandy-hair screamed in agony. His body blurred. A second head twisted, separated from the first.

What the fuck?

The second one was malformed and hideous with deep-set eyes, no nose at all and gnashing fangs. The stranger pulled the monstrous head, slowly ripping a writhing, ghastly creature from inside Sandy-hair, letting the human host slump to the pavement.

The monster screeched and hissed as my dark rescuer chanted inaudible words. Tiny hairs on my arms rose with a rippling chill. An aura of flickering golden light swept wide above his head and shoulders, beaming off his back.

I rubbed my eyes, sure I'd been slipped some mind-altering drugs in the club. He whispered more vehemently, words I couldn't quite hear in another language, though they sounded familiar.

The creature screamed, twisted, unable to free itself. The size of a small child with bony, spindly limbs and gnashing teeth, the thing beat and scratched and clawed the air. I heard the final words of the creature's captor, his aura flickering like a wisp of flame.

"Go back to hell."

In a bright flash of reddish-gold light, the beast disintegrated into smoke and powdery black ash. A strange smell—sulfuric, acidic—wafted into the air, leaving a metallic taste on my tongue.

My rescuer dusted his hands off on his jeans, totally calm and collected. He sighed, walked over to Sandy-hair and checked his pulse. A sharp nod, then he walked toward me where I still sat against the wall, wondering if I was dreaming or having some extremely realistic nightmare.

Squatting in front of me, he lifted my chin, examining my throat.

"How do you feel?"

I blinked, trying to ignore the heated sensation of his touch on my skin and wondering if I'd truly lost my mind.

"Well, I was nearly choked to death, and I just saw you pull a monster out of another man, then use some voodoo-mojo or something to crush it into dust." I stopped to cough, rubbing my throat, my voice raspy. "I'm feeling fine. How are you?"

I knew I should be a little less snarky to the guy who just

saved my life, but what an insane question. His extremely distracting lips lifted into a smile.

"Better, then." He grinned. "Good."

He had some sort of accent, but I couldn't place it. I took advantage of our proximity to examine him closer. Above his top button, below his collarbone, I could see the black etchings of a tattoo.

I recognized the Celtic interlacing from my mother's artwork. The tattoo must be very big, and I wanted so much to see the fine details. He reached out his hand and pulled my necklace out from underneath my shirt, his fingertips brushing my collarbone. I sucked in a sharp breath.

The action surprised me as he moved farther into my personal space.

"Can I help you?"

He observed the medal dangling on the chain. "St. George. The dragon slayer." One dark eyebrow lifted in a question.

"My mother gave it to me."

"She is a smart woman."

"Was," I corrected.

Those midnight eyes gazed directly into mine, searching. "I'm sorry."

Sorrow whirled in those depths. I felt overheated again so near him. My heart hammered away. He hovered so close, too close, just staring at me like…like what? He seemed to be trying to solve a puzzle. Finally, I found my voice.

"Thank you." I swallowed, my throat tight. Glancing at Sandy-hair still unconscious, I nodded toward him. "What was that thing? The thing inside him?"

"A lower demon. A rogue, apparently. Why would he want to kill you?"

"A what? Are you kidding me?"

He shook his head once. "Not a joke, I'm afraid. I don't understand why he wanted to kill you."

His voice was so calm, so normal. A lower demon nearly

killed me, and he was playing paranormal detective. What was a lower demon? And what did that make my rescuer?

Steven stirred nearby. I'd forgotten all about him.

"Your boyfriend is unharmed. However, he'll have a headache."

"He is *not* my boyfriend," I enunciated very, very clearly.

Another ghost of a smile crossed his face. My insides melted into a pile of goo.

"Come. Your friends will worry."

He offered his hand and lifted me up. His hand enveloped mine, warm and rough with calluses. I needed to let go, suddenly overwhelmed by the sensation of his touch, his nearness.

I was never overwhelmed. I was Genevieve Drake, the epitome of calm and collected. Steven moved again. Damn him.

Then the stranger did something I'd never expected. He lifted my hand to his lips, brushing a soft kiss along my knuckles. His lips lingered, spreading warmth from my hand to my arm and throughout the rest of my body.

What an old-fashioned gesture. I shivered. Not from the cold. His eyes never left mine.

"Happy birthday." He let my hand slip from his.

What? How did he know? Unable to hold his gaze any longer, I glanced down, chanting a brief mantra in my head. *Get —it—together.* I took a deep shaky breath, finally summoning the courage to ask for his number.

When I looked up, he was gone.

2

I checked the rearview mirror. Sandy-hair had gripped me low on the throat. Four little bruises marked the left side of my neck above my collarbone. A fat bluish thumbprint was higher on the other side. Thank God for Mindy's supersonic concealer, making them nearly invisible.

"Good enough," I said to my messy reflection.

After a birthday celebration that had left me battered, bruised, and extremely confused, I'd fallen into bed last night without setting the alarm. Mindy had been so wrapped up in her darling David and his heroic ability to carry her through the club, to the car and up one tiny flight of stairs to our apartment that she lavished kisses on him all the way home before collapsing into an appletini coma.

Steven had been more difficult to deal with. He insisted that he'd been hit on the head in the alley until I convinced him otherwise. No way was I admitting what really happened. When he mentioned that he'd taken some sinus medicine earlier that night, I persuaded him to believe he'd just had a bad reaction mixing medicine with alcohol.

I grabbed my backpack and red hoodie from the backseat, stuffed my iPhone in my shorts pocket and took off. I practically

14

sprinted across campus to Professor Bennett's classroom, slipping into my hoodie as I went.

Ugh. Professor Bennett. Well shaven. Well groomed. Graying at the temples. Designer black-rimmed glasses and polished loafers. Wears a different blazer with dark jeans every single day. His professor-ish trappings and illusion of perfection apparently gave him the right to lord over the rest of us like we were slovenly, uneducated peasants.

Perhaps it was his attitude that made me dress more unkempt than usual for his class. The rebel in me couldn't help it.

I was tying my hair up into a messy bun as I entered the classroom. He'd already launched into one of his perfectly articulated lectures.

"Greetings, Ms. Drake. So good of you to grace us with your presence."

I plopped down in the front row.

"You're very welcome, Professor Bennett. I do aim to please."

Straight face. No smile. From either of us.

"Since you seem ready to go this morning, how about you take the first stab at explaining last night's reading from Milton?"

Oh crap. Homework. I'd glanced over it yesterday over lunch but hadn't taken any notes or anything. I opened my Norton Anthology.

"Page?"

"Page 908," came his sharp response, "where Lucifer first speaks."

I reread the excerpt from *Paradise Lost*.

> Here at least we shall be free;
> the Almighty hath not built here for his envy,
> will not drive us hence:
> here we may reign secure,

and in my choice to reign is worth ambition,
though in Hell: Better to reign in Hell than
serve in Heaven.

There was a bit of rambling from the devil before and after, but this was the crux of the speech.

"Well, it seems that the Fallen Angel is pouting about being thrown out of heaven, but he's also happy to have a place of his own where God can't tell him what to do. Sort of like kids going away to college."

A few snickers behind me. Professor Bennett's mouth tightened into a line.

"True, Ms. Drake. But what do you think of the quote where Milton expounds on the topic when he says, 'The mind is its own place, and in itself can make a Heaven of Hell, a Hell of Heaven.' How are these ideas related to Lucifer's fall?"

Damn, he was really punishing me for being late. I pondered a second or two.

"I suppose the idea that hell has become Lucifer's kingdom or domain where he can reign however he sees fit is similar to our minds. We can choose to use our knowledge or intellect to create beautiful things like art or terrible things like war."

"Not exactly—"

"*Or*," I cut him off before he shot me down, "it could mean that we use our minds to make beautiful things ugly or ugly things beautiful with the way we view the world, treat others, or just live our own lives."

How's that for only having taken Philosophy 101? Professor Bennett was getting his bearings to make some smart reply, but I had a question for him this time.

"What I want to know is what's so great about reigning and being in charge? Lucifer goes on and on about how power in hell is better than being a servant in heaven. But who wants all those responsibilities? I don't get it. I'd rather do my own thing and not worry about everybody else."

"Not everyone is like you, Genevieve," said Carol next to me, the stuck-up blonde who was the daughter of a senator or congressman or something.

Poor them.

"True, Ms. Drake," said Professor Bennett. "Power is a responsibility."

"Yeah," agreed my study partner Malcolm, "just like Uncle Ben said, 'With great power comes great responsibility.'"

"Who's Uncle Ben?" asked Carol.

Malcolm rolled his eyes.

"From *Spider-Man*? Come on. Seriously?"

"So," I continued, "if the devil has all this power in hell, why does he need to possess people? He can do whatever he wants in his own domain. Why mess around up here?"

"Ms. Drake, you're confusing Milton's fiction with demon mythology. Both of which aren't actually real. You know that, right?"

"No, I don't know that. How do you know?"

An expression of self-satisfied smugness plastered itself on his perfect face.

"It is known in *all* intellectual circles. Demons do not actually exist. Angels do not actually exist. This is a tale to discuss on the intellectual plane, not for determining the reality of the devil's actions."

Carol giggled. I wanted to slap the blonde right off her. Wouldn't take much since she dyed it like once a week.

"But what if you're wrong?" I pushed.

"I'm not, Ms. Drake. Shall we move on? Carol, would you read the next selection?"

Just like that, dismissed by the all-knowing Professor Bennett. First off, I believed in angels. I knew my mom was among them somewhere up there. And second, I was damn sure demons existed, because I saw one get ripped out of Sandy-hair's face last night.

Even if I was still reeling from the experience, I wasn't so dumb as to ignore what I saw with my own damn eyes.

Poor Professor Bennett. He really didn't know what he was talking about, even with all those academic letters behind his name.

I practically jumped for joy when class ended, shoving my books back into my backpack. Malcolm caught up to me outside.

"Way to go, Drake. Master of disaster." He laughed.

"So glad I could entertain."

"Always. Study group tomorrow night, right?"

"Yep. Meet you at the library as usual, say six o'clock?"

"Sounds good. See ya then."

He loped off in the other direction as I headed for my car. No way could I handle translating Cicero today in Latin class. Too heavy after last night. It was okay. Professor Minga loved me in that class. I was calling my own sick day after the lovely debate on Milton.

Professor Bennett's words still milled through my mind as I walked across Loyola's campus to my car.

The weather was changing. I zipped my hoodie and hiked my backpack up higher on my shoulder. Hugging myself as I walked, my mind drifted to my mother. Must be all this talk of Milton.

As an artist, my mother admired Gustave Doré, who illustrated scenes from Milton's sad tales. She painted his drawings with her own impressionistic style. While Doré's originals were all black and white, my mother's were smeared with vibrant, wild color. Doré's artwork evoked a kind of stillness, but not my mother's. You couldn't view one of them without feeling something—horror, awe, pity, joy.

For some reason, her rendition of Doré's "Numberless Bad Angels" kept popping into my head. My mother's painting showed a smoky-blue heaven with a twisted line of fiendish-looking angels trailing behind Lucifer, who was depicted as a beautiful, fair-haired angel. All the others flew in a long shadow behind him.

I'd always wondered why mother showed the worst of the worst in this way—glowing and glorious. Maybe she was trying to imply that evil hides behind a beautiful face. I don't know why, but the image never left me.

I can see her now in the garage studio, standing in front of the canvas in paint-stained jeans. She dipped the brush and stroked in swift, curving motions. Music played in the background. She was partial to Wagner and Bach, but any classical composer could plunge her into another world.

The day she created the host of fallen angels, the distinct melancholy tune of Mozart's "Requiem Mass" lilted through the room. I sat on the stool in the corner, watching for hours.

My mother seemed to be guided by the music itself, slowing or speeding up with the tempo. Wispy strands of fair hair hung around her face as she lost herself in a world of blues, pinks and gold, of shadow and light, of dark angels and a darker demon with a beguiling face.

"Let it go," I whispered to myself, sighing and walking faster.

I'd parked illegally on the street, knowing full well I'd probably have a ticket on the windshield when I returned. Campus cops were like sharks in bloody waters, sniffing out offenders with notorious stealth. You never saw them but sure as hell felt bitten when they got you.

Dreading to see that I'd been attacked by one of these predators, I rounded the corner, and my heart stopped.

Propped beautifully against my silver 350ZX was my rescuer, the dark stranger from last night. Faded jeans fit snugly on his hips, and a gray T-shirt accentuated a perfect upper body. His black hair fell just right across lovely dark eyes. With casually crossed arms, he watched me approach.

Heart, please stop pounding that way before he notices.

This was no accident. He'd found me somehow. Should I be afraid? He didn't look dangerous. Well, not in a serial-killer sort of way. Hell, he looked good enough to eat. Totally faking bravado, I stopped in front of him with one hand on my waist.

"Are you stalking me?"

He didn't answer, eyeing me from bottom to top. His gaze paused at my throat, his jaw clenched, then he finally made its way to my eyes. Still mute.

I hated awkward silences.

"Didn't your mother ever teach you it's not polite to stare?"

That seemed to jar him a bit. He straightened, his expression grim at best.

"I apologize. I was—"

"Checking me out. Yeah, I got that loud and clear."

Damn, I was brave. He cleared his throat, hiding a smile now.

"I was going to say, examining you." He gestured to my neck.

"Examining? Why? Are you a doctor?"

"Of sorts."

"What sort of sort?"

"I have a doctorate."

No way. He seemed too young to have a PhD.

"A doctorate in what?" I asked skeptically.

"Philosophy."

"Your expertise?" I asked, noting the rather sarcastic lilt in my voice. He didn't bat an eye.

"My thesis was on how weapons reflect the savagery and sophistication of a culture and society."

That accent again. Definitely European. But what country?

"Well, a PhD in weaponry may give you some idea how to inflict injuries, but it doesn't qualify you to *examine* and diagnose them."

"True."

Ha! One point for me.

"So…" I let the word hang. "How could you possibly have a PhD in anything at your age?"

"I'm older than I appear."

A slow, slow devastating smile. A fluttering in my stomach felt like a frantic flock of blind birds. *Re-lax, Gen.* Thank God he spoke, because for the moment, my lips had completely forgotten how to form words.

"I simply wanted to determine whether you'd recovered from last night's attack," he said, pushing off my car and coming closer.

Oh no. He was going to touch me. *Genevieve Elizabeth Drake, do NOT faint.*

He reached out and gently folded back my hoodie. He lifted my chin and angled it so that he could see the marks I knew were purpled along the left side. Why was I letting this stranger get so close? Even if he was picture-book gorgeous. I pushed his hand away and stepped around him to my car.

"I'm fine," I mumbled, pulling the keys from the front pocket of my backpack. "What I want to know is how you knew where to find me. And why are you following me? It's a bit creepy, even if you did save my life last night."

We'd now switched places. I leaned back against my car. He stood there, *examining* me again, thumbs hooked in the front pockets of those yummy jeans.

"Yesterday was your twentieth birthday, wasn't it?"

Okay. Double creepy.

"How did you know?"

My question confirmed whatever idea he had in his head. I could see it in the nod and drop of his perfect cleft chin.

Two girls flitted by, engrossed in a conversation. One nudged the other when they caught sight of him, ogling shamelessly. They giggled. Couldn't blame them, but it pissed me off for some reason. He gave them no real notice, turning back to me.

"I think we should go somewhere private to talk."

Said the creepy man to the little girl with a lollipop and a white van waiting around the corner.

"Um, I don't think so." I crossed my arms. "I don't know

you. And no matter what you did for me last night, at this point, I don't trust you."

He shifted weight to his other leg. "As you wish. We'll talk here."

"Not that I'm ungrateful, but why were you following me last night? Into the alley?"

"I wasn't following you. I was following the demon."

Wishing that he hadn't just confirmed that last night wasn't a figment of my imagination, I sighed.

"Fair enough. How did you know it was my birthday?"

"Last night, I wondered but thought it impossible. I had not thought to meet another like you in all my time as a…" He paused, glancing around and lowering his voice. "As a *Dominus Daemonum.*"

I shook my head. "Okay, hold up. Met one *what* before? And what the hell is a dominus da-whatever-you-said?"

Dark enchanting eyes kept me still, even with my saucy attitude. A face chiseled in stone regarded me with care.

I would never admit it, but I was afraid to move. Something in those almost-black depths warned me what he spoke of now would change my life forever. What's more, I knew those words. They were Latin. But the translation in my head didn't make sense.

"The *what* is a Vessel," he finally said. "And a Dominus Daemonum is a Master of Demons."

"Do you mean like a…a demon hunter?"

He nodded. No smile.

"That is what I am," he said.

"And what's a Vessel?"

"That is what you are."

"Okay," I said, drawing the word out in that you're-either-insane-or-stupid tone of voice. "Tell me what it is exactly that you *think* I am. What is this *Vessel?*"

He stepped closer. His presence suddenly became enormous and heavy. My heart picked up pace. Those dark eyes stared down, bewitching me again. His words were more terrifying than any demon at that very moment.

"A Vessel," he said, his voice brushing against me like velvet, "is a unique being that demons may seek for centuries but never find."

I scoffed, forcing a laugh from my completely constricted throat. "This is crazy. Absolutely insane. I can hardly register what you're saying to me, because it's just so…so fucking insane!"

I threw my hands in the air, exasperated. A guy walking by sped up, probably thinking he was witnessing a lover's quarrel. I wish.

He stepped closer and peered down at me with something like sympathy in his eyes. I swallowed hard.

"Whether you can register what I'm saying or not is irrelevant. Whether you believe me or not is irrelevant. Truth is truth."

"*Verum est verum,*" I whispered automatically.

His eyes narrowed. "You speak Latin?"

"Some."

"Not surprising."

"Why is that not surprising?"

"Because a Vessel would be drawn to the old tongue. You'll need it as a tool to defend yourself."

I closed my eyes, shutting him out. I needed a moment to come to grips with all of this. At the same time, I wanted to know more. Something inside itched to understand everything. I opened my eyes. He waited patiently. Watching.

"So," I sighed, "why would demons want a Vessel? What does that even mean?"

I knew I didn't want to know the answer. But I've always been too curious for my own good. His placid expression tensed with agony for a split second before straightening into a mask of indifference.

"Because once a demon bends a Vessel's will to his own, he

can possess her at any time and control her without interference from the Vessel herself or from a Dominus Daemonum. Her power becomes his power. The demon can commit untold horrors. There are no rules or limits barring what can be done when in possession of a Vessel. Hence, the demons' attraction to her."

My heart beat a feverish pattern in my throat. How I found my voice, I do not know.

"Rules?"

"Yes, there are rules."

"For demons?"

"For demons. For everyone."

There was more to that statement.

"If I'm a Vessel, why haven't they been after me my whole life?"

"Because a Vessel will *aperio* on her twentieth birthday."

I frowned. "Are you testing my Latin skills?"

He didn't respond, just waited patiently. I had no patience, rolling my eyes.

"What does that mean that the Vessel will *open*?" I emphasized the word so he'd get that I was smarter than he thought. The left side of his lips lifted a fraction, barely a half smile. "And why on my twentieth birthday?"

"Aperio refers to the very moment you become exactly two decades old."

I pondered this a second. My mother used to tell me how the full moon brought me early into her arms. I was definitely born at night. In the recovery room lit only by the luminescent globe high in the night sky, she sang to me a lullaby. She had painted this scene as she remembered it. The moment was frozen forever in shades of indigo, blue and pearly white over the mantel at home.

"I can only speculate about the age," he explained. "In numerology, twenty represents a call for spiritual upheaval, political revolution, or economic reform."

"That can be bad or good, depending on what the upheaval or revolution is about."

"Yes. A priest I once knew, an enlightened man, said it represents the source of all energy in the world, but he thought it ominous because it also represented the universal fight."

"Universal fight? What's that?"

"War." His voice dipped low, soft, his obsidian eyes capturing mine.

I didn't breathe, couldn't.

An autumn breeze fluttered past, lifting wisps of hair around my neck. I heard leaves scraping along the pavement behind me, but I was transfixed, unable to break away. Someone passed on a bike.

His gaze broke from mine to follow the biker, then he continued. "In Hebrew, this number is represented by the letter *caph*, in the form of an opened hand, meaning to seize and to hold."

"I don't understand."

My mind reeled, trying to process everything he was telling me in his easy tone as if talk of universal turmoil was an everyday occurrence. Who am I kidding? Of course it was.

"Genevieve," he almost whispered, stepping into my space again. He really needed lessons on personal boundaries.

His scent invaded me, circled me in a woodsy heat that was all his own. "All I know is that at this exact age, the Vessel opens, and the opposing sides vie for her—the Dark and the Light. The demons will come for you. The light is already within you. Who wins will be determined only by you."

"Are you kidding me? Who in the hell would choose to go with demons?"

His face darkened. His eyes grew distant, colder. His voice dropped even lower, a rumble of rolling thunder. "Many have. Many would." A tingling chill crawled up my spine.

"But I don't feel any different. Wouldn't I know if I was a so-called Vessel?"

"You will."

He was as certain as the sky is blue. I could see that in his determined expression. But I wasn't so sure. I played along for the moment.

"Okay. So if what you're saying is true, then why did that demon want to kill me last night? Why didn't he just want to… to possess me?"

The thought made bile rise in my throat.

"I don't know." He glanced at the marks on my neck again. "That puzzles me exceedingly."

I scoffed.

"Puzzles *you* exceedingly? Are you kidding me? In the past twelve hours, I've been groped by a red-eyed demon on a dance floor, nearly strangled to death in an alley, watched an actual demon being pulled from another man's body, and *now* I've been casually informed by my new stalker, a Dominus whatever, that I'm like chocolate cake to every demon alive and all of them want a piece of me."

He came back from that faraway place, studying me with a smirk on those pretty lips.

"Chocolate cake. That's quite a metaphor."

Was he flirting with me?

"It was a simile," I snapped back, not even blinking. "I have to go." I clicked my key fob to unlock the door.

"There's more we need to discuss."

"Not today. Thanks for the pep talk. It's been real. Too real, but I can't take any more of this right now. I don't know what to believe." I tossed my backpack in the passenger seat and slid behind the wheel. "That's another thing. How do you know so much about me? How do you know my name? I don't even know yours. I can't keep calling you—"

"Dominus whatever?" he asked with the smallest of smiles.

"Yeah. Right."

"My name is Jude Delacroix. Call me when you catch your

breath, Genevieve." He passed me a business card. "I need to prepare you before the next one comes searching for you."

The card was stark white with his name in all caps and a phone number. No fancy symbols or details of any business.

"Man of mystery, eh?"

"I only give it to those who know who I am and what I do."

"Hmm. You could add some devil horns with a big X on it or something. Give it some pizzazz."

He was trying so hard not to smile. Somehow that made me giddy. He stood up and closed the door. I started the car, then heard a light tap of knuckles on the window. I lowered it.

"Call me, Genevieve. Soon. There's not much time to waste." His mouth straightened into a somber line.

I nodded, unable to speak. I'd run out of smart comebacks. I shifted into gear and sped away. My mind reeled with the current state of affairs.

If I could possibly swallow everything Jude had told me, I had several issues to consider. One—I was a Vessel, some mystical thing I'd never heard of before in my life. Two—demons would be hunting me and soon. Three—my new would-be protector was probably the hottest man alive.

3

After a day of catching up on sleep and fetching Doritos, Easy Mac, a cold pack, four Advil, a brush and makeup for the invalid that is my best friend, I was ready for work.

I slipped on some workout shorts with a white tank and headed toward City Park. Cruising down St. Charles Avenue, I turned onto a side street and squeezed into a parking spot across from my dad's dojo, Drake's Karate Institute. Times like these reminded me why I bought a small, fast car—a necessary commodity in New Orleans where traffic was endless and parking was nonexistent.

Walking through the waiting area, I saw Dad leading a high-level class through the kata. Their slow, precise movements were more like a dance than a karate technique. I hurried into the locker room to pull on my white gi.

A rhythmic sound came from the back alley. *Thwump, thwump.* The door stood ajar. I peeked out to find Erik throwing Chinese darts at a target in the long narrow niche that served as a break area. Besides a wrought-iron table with two chairs, there was the bullseye on the wall.

Erik had been working for my dad since we opened the dojo ten years ago. I'd grown up around him after my mom died and always thought of him as an older brother. His lean, lanky figure was deceiving. I'd sparred with him on a number of occasions and been beaten by his wiry strength more than once.

"You know my dad hates it when you use those things."

Erik nodded and smiled, spinning a silver dart through the air to hit right on the red rim of the dartboard. His neatly trimmed brown hair and perfectly fitted gi seemed a juxtaposition with his constant rule-bending.

"I know, I know. 'It's not a true art form,' says the wise mage," murmured Erik with a lopsided smile. He shrugged. "It's just for fun."

He picked up a four-pointed star that curved at the tips.

"Let me try," I said, tying my black belt tight.

He passed me the star. I mimicked his asymmetrical stance, one foot in front of the other, then sent the dart sailing through the air. Bam! Right on the bullseye. I grinned.

"Sweet! You've done this before?"

"Nope. I'm a natural, I guess." I sauntered back to the door. "Gotta get to class."

"Hey, Gen. Can you close up for me tonight? I've got plans and need to get home and shower and stuff."

"Ooooo, hot date? Anyone I know?"

Erik blushed. He was so cute—the shy, intelligent guy with a sweet smile. The sort of guy who made me want to slap other girls upside the head to take a closer look.

"Gen, come on," he said in that I'm-too-old-for-you-to-tease-me voice. He was about five years older than me, though he acted like he was eighty sometimes.

"Fine. Keep your secrets. I'll close up. Have fun," I said, making a catcall before ducking back inside.

My Kyu class, made up of mostly minor yellow and green belts, flew by uneventfully except when eight-year-old Devon tried to sweep me to the floor. I countered quickly, leaping out of the way.

"You're really good for a girl." He grinned up at me with his two front teeth missing.

"For a girl, eh?" I popped into a fighting stance. "I'll show you what a girl can do."

I attacked, but with no intent to harm him. We sparred for several minutes. He defended well.

"Very good, Devon. You're improving. Pretty soon you'll have your orange belt." I gave him a wink, and he fled from the dojo in a state of glee.

I piled the grappling mats back against the wall where they belonged, pulling the Windex and cleaning rag out of the corner closet.

"Gen, I'd stay and help lock up, sweetie, but I've got to get to the bank before they close."

My dad stood in the doorway with his keys and bank bag in hand. Though in his late forties, he was still in top physical condition. I suppose he should be from training students in martial arts every day.

Though he was the picture of health, I often saw a sadness in his eyes. Don't get me wrong. He laughed all the time, usually at me and my stupid jokes. But he missed my mother. I knew he did—even ten years after her death. I hated when I caught glimpses of that far-off expression, a sort of longing. Like I saw in his eyes right now.

"You're not headed to your poker game, are you, Dad?" I teased.

The distance vanished. His face lifted into a smile.

"No, Gen. I'm not gambling with company money."

"Just checking." I swished my rag around before spraying the mirrors.

"See you Sunday, baby girl."

"Bye, Dad."

I heard him bolt the door from the outside after he left. I made short work of the mirrors, stopping once to pull down my gi's collar to check out my healing bruise. The markings from last night's attack were more visible after a sweaty workout, having rubbed off the concealer from this morning.

After passing the vacuum in the waiting room, I changed into a pair of jeans from my locker and stuffed my phone in my back pocket, having locked my purse in the car.

As soon as I walked outside, I felt it—that intangible foreboding when you should be alone, but you know you're not.

I glanced up and down the street. No one. I must be paranoid. Still, I quickly bolted the door, bracing my keys between my knuckles so they pointed out like daggers from my fist.

The sun had fallen, but a dim glow still lingered on the empty street. A dog barked somewhere. No one else was around. My car was right across the street. I took three long strides, then a man's voice stopped me.

"Where you goin' in such a hurry, sweetheart?"

I spun around. Three men closed in around me. They were all different except for one commonality—piercing red eyes.

I gulped hard against the cold reality that the demon hunter Jude wasn't lying. And what happened at the club wasn't a crazy hallucination. Demons were real. And three of them were standing in front of me, stalking closer.

The one who spoke was taller than the other two, muscular and tan. Brown hair hung long around his shoulders. He looked like he stepped off the cover of one of an old romance novel.

The one in the middle was a shorter, stocky guy with a build like a pit bull. The third was a slender Black man with a predator's gait, circling to block my way to the car. He had a tattoo that trailed up his throat, piercings in his face and gauges in his ears. He wore a spiked cuff on his wrist. He seemed the most dangerous.

Unlike last night's incident with Sandy-hair, I was more than ready this time. Still, the three of them stalking closer sent a shot of adrenaline through my body. I wasn't sure I could take them, but I sure as hell wasn't going down without a fight.

"Can we play with her first?" asked Pit-bull boy.

I shifted my feet into a defensive stance. *Dream on.*

Fabio shook his head. "No. He wants her unspoiled," he said, letting his freaky red eyes linger over my body. "Pity."

Gross.

"You guys all think alike. One of your buddies said the same thing before he tried to kill me last night."

The leader frowned. I glanced back at the guy behind me. He hadn't moved, legs apart and hands at his sides. Flexing his arms, he was a tiger waiting to pounce.

"One of our buddies?" asked Fabio.

"A demon-boy like you."

"Tried to kill you?"

"Redundant much?"

My bravado almost convinced even me. Why, oh why hadn't I listened to Jude? Shucking off the trembling sensation in my gut, I focused on who would do what first, trying to find my moment to act.

Fabio turned his head to say something to Pit-bull boy. I took that second of distraction to make my move. Leaping in two bounds, I punched him at the base of the throat, jabbing two keys into his windpipe. He bent forward and grabbed his throat. I spun and double-elbowed him in the ribs and face.

Pit-bull boy lunged for me, leaving his groin open and vulnerable. Stupid move. I kicked him fast and hard like I would a soccer ball. He fell with a groan.

"Bitch," he growled.

"You have no idea."

I spun fast. Scary spiky dude was nearly on top of me. Ducking his attempt to grab me, I sprinted for the car. I wouldn't have enough time to open the door, hearing his steps right on top of me. Turning, I kicked up toward his chest. He caught my leg and twisted. I fell face-first to the pavement. He landed on top of my back to keep me still.

Hell no!

I elbowed up into his ribs over and over again. He shifted a little, and I thought I was almost free, but Fabio was there.

Spiky flipped me over, holding my legs, while Fabio sat on my chest to keep me still. "Feisty one, aren't you?" He grinned as blood dripped from his nose and down his chin.

He wiped his upper lip with the back of his hand. I think I broke the cartilage in his nose. *Good.*

"No worries. He likes a little fight. Makes things more interesting."

"Listen, Fabio. Don't you dare bleed on me. No telling how many diseases you have."

He gripped my throat. Oh, come on! Did they have any other move?

"I see someone has been here before me," he said, rubbing his thumb over Sandy-hair's bruise. "Who was he? Why did he try to kill you?"

"Get off me, you smelly bastard!"

I pushed, but he was heavy, almost unmovable.

"Oh really? What are you going to do?"

Someone cried out. Pit-bull boy? Fabio glanced over his own shoulder, still holding me down. Spiky released my legs.

I heard scuffling and the sound of steel on pavement. Thankful for the diversion, I planted my feet and rolled my hips up hard. Fabio tipped sideways, releasing his grip on me to catch his balance. I rolled over and scrambled to my feet. He was up and in front of me just as fast, blocking my way.

"Going somewhere, sweetheart?" He pulled a long knife from a hidden sheath inside the front of his jeans. "Why don't you come quietly, like a good girl?"

Seriously?

A sudden high-pitched scream drew our attention. Behind him stood Jude, in all of his masculine glory, holding a long sword thrust deep into the chest of Pit-bull boy.

A sword? Just like in the alley last night, everything seemed surreal.

His victim screamed while Jude chanted something under his breath. He held his other hand out, palm flat in the air toward Spiky, who railed and beat against an invisible wall he could not pass.

As Jude chanted, a faint reddish-gold light haloed his body, similar but brighter than the first night I met him. Electricity snapped in the air, raising gooseflesh on my skin. Then it happened again. The flaming light took form around Jude's body. Wisps of gold swept into rippling arcs around his frame. So beautiful.

Was this real? I knew I was standing there like an idiot, mouth agape, but I couldn't move. My brain tried to process what I was seeing.

Jude continued chanting inaudible words, his fiery aura growing brighter. Pit-bull's body combusted into orange flames, shriveling and shrinking into a charred husk. With a wave of his hand, Jude swept the remains of ashy bone into the wind.

He turned his head with eerie calm, fixing feral eyes on Spiky, who stopped beating on the invisible shield still protecting the demon hunter. Spiky staggered backward and ran.

I finally came to my senses, spinning a hard kick up toward Fabio's head. He swiveled back to me, slicing out with his knife. It cut through my tank along my abdomen. Searing pain burned across my stomach. I screamed.

Jude stalked toward us, swinging his sword in an arc, fixing a murderous gaze on Fabio, who stared wide-eyed at Jude for two seconds, then disappeared after Spiky.

I stumbled, but Jude caught me in his arms before I hit the pavement. He lifted and carried me toward my car. His aura had vanished, and his eyes flashed storm-black. I marveled at how easily he held me.

I'm not a small girl, never have been, but Jude lifted me like I weighed nothing. Funny the things your mind thinks of in traumatic situations.

Blood seeped through my white tank. A wet trail trickled

along the line of my waist to my back. I couldn't think straight, feeling my mind pull away.

The worst injury I'd ever had was a broken arm from falling off the trampoline when I was seven. I had cried all the way to the hospital, still hurting when we left. That night, my mother settled herself beside my bed and painted Van Gogh's "Starry Night" all the way around my cast. My arm became a piece of artwork for everyone to admire. Pain cradled in love.

"Where are your keys?" Jude's gruff voice pulled me back to the present.

"Dropped them," I mumbled, the blood or the pain making me light-headed.

I'm not sure how, but he managed to bend and scoop up my keys without ever letting me go. I glanced over his shoulder, seeing nothing but a blackened spot of soot where Pit-bull boy had fallen.

Jude put me in the passenger seat, buckled me in, then disappeared for about ten seconds and slid into the driver's seat, tossing the sword in the back. As if he'd owned the car all his life, he shifted from first to third gear in seconds. We zoomed down St. Charles, heading into the heart of New Orleans.

"You missed the turn for the Medical Center," I murmured, watching a pool of crimson seep across my tank, coloring my blue jeans purple. "You're going the wrong way."

"We're not going to the hospital." He punched into fifth with violent force. "We're going to my place."

4

My reservations about this guy suddenly escalated from wary to holy-hell-I'm-being-kidnapped.

"Jude—" I focused on breathing in slow, steady breaths. "I'm hurt pretty bad. You need to take me to the hospital."

His eyes never left the road as he hung a hard right onto Canal Street.

"I know how badly you're injured." His voice was eerily calm, but there was a dangerous vibration in his low rumble. "I'm going to take care of it myself."

"Listen, Dr. Demon-hunter. Your philosophy degree doesn't qualify you with the skills to stitch me up."

"I have many skills, Genevieve." A searing glance. "Including the ability to tend your wounds."

"Why won't you just take me to a hospital?"

"Because the two demons who got away know you're injured. They'll be searching for you."

"How would they know which hospital I went to? Let's head to one farther out."

"It wouldn't matter. They'd find you."

"How?"

His eyes slid to mine, scanning my body in a millisecond.

"You're like a beacon now, shining in the dark. They can sense you."

Feeling faint, I let my head fall against the headrest, trying desperately to understand all this. Did this mean I would always be looking over my shoulder? That I would live in a constant state of fear?

Careening down Decatur, he barely missed a group of tourists in front of Jackson Square. I winced at the growing pain in my stomach. My vision blurred. We passed under a street sign, Ursulines, taking a sharp left onto Dauphine. He squeezed into a spot on the first block.

I barely realized we'd stopped before the passenger door opened, and I was in his arms again. Not that being in such a position hadn't crossed my mind once or twice, but somehow I had envisioned something more romantic and less, well, bloody.

He carried me through an open brick archway into a dark alcove, stopping at a tall, wrought-iron gate. Leaning against the wall for about two seconds, he fit his key into the lock. The gate swung open and clanged shut behind us.

We passed through a smallish courtyard, water gurgling somewhere. My head felt heavy, falling onto his shoulder as he opened the door to the house. The small foyer led straight up a flight of stairs into a spacious living room.

He set me down on a plush, tan sofa. A shiver ran through me as he strode down a hallway.

The décor was stark but beautiful in warm colors of brown, red and gold. An old fireplace was set in the far wall, the cherry mantel in Baroque style with an elaborate roaring dragon curling along the top of the fireplace. French doors stood behind me, most certainly leading to a balcony overlooking the court-yard. I pivoted onto my side to get a better view, wincing with pain.

"Damn." I hissed in a breath, lifting my red-soaked tank.

A six-inch slash cut through the skin and muscle from my belly button down to the top of my jeans. Jude settled beside me, placing some kind of kit on the mahogany coffee table. Adrenaline spiked, my pulse racing. From seeing the injury or Jude's sudden closeness, I wasn't sure.

"Lay back. Relax."

"Do you really know what you're doing? I don't want to get butchered. Or an infection." My voice quavered, not as confident as my words.

"I know what I'm doing."

"I don't even know you," I protested. My stranger-danger antenna kept popping up, then lowering at random. This guy could be a killer. Hell, I knew he was. I just watched him stab a guy to death on the street.

Of course, he was apparently possessed by a demon and was trying to kill me at the time, but that didn't mean this guy was truly on my side. Then again, there was that strange aura of fire. What was that all about?

"How did you know I was in danger with the demon guys?"

"It's my job to know."

"It's your job to know when I'm being attacked by demons?"

"To know when someone is in danger from demons. To expel them."

"So, am I the only one in this city in danger, or are you following me?"

"Genevieve, you're currently a magnet for every kind of spawn of hell." He heaved an exasperated sigh, observing my injury closely, dark brow knit in concentration. "I knew it wouldn't take long for them to find you."

"That's not an answer."

He dabbed my wound clean, not meeting my eyes.

"Try to stitch it closely please. I don't want an ugly scar across my stomach."

"Would you rather continue arguing while you bleed to death, or would you like me to close the gaping wound in your abdomen?"

I scowled, reclining back at the same time. My pride clamped my stupid mouth shut.

He pushed my tank up a little higher. I shivered at the intimate touch. He spread his left hand along my ribs and stomach, flattening the wound evenly. While the pain of the wound overrode most all other sensation, I couldn't help hold my breath with him touching me and leaning so close.

"Relax."

His deep, soft voice eased the tension from my rigid body. Ironically, a good bit of that tension came directly from his touch. After wiping the blood clean around the wound and dabbing antiseptic with a gentle hand, he took out a needle and vial, then leaned close to the cut.

"Good thing this was done with a knife."

"As opposed to?"

"Claws. Teeth."

"Yeah, good thing."

What planet was I living on? Geez. He gave me one of those looks saying I had no idea what I was in for. He was right. I was in way over my head, and I wasn't afraid to admit it at this point.

"This will sting, but I need to give you a local anesthetic to dull the pain of the stitching."

I nodded, biting my lip and closing my eyes. I tried not to think about his hand splayed across my rib cage. The sting of the needle jarred my wayward thoughts. I didn't cry out, squeezing my eyes shut tighter.

After a minute, the pain subsided. A numbing sensation traveled over my body from the wound. When I opened my eyes, Jude was watching me with dark intensity. My heart hammered against my ribcage. Surely, he could feel it.

The power of his gaze scattered every sarcastic remark from my brain. No one had ever looked at me so fiercely. Except maybe that demon in the alleyway. Only, that guy's gaze had been edged with violence. Jude's was more akin to hunger.

"What are you waiting for?" I asked hesitantly as well as a touch of fear, though I wasn't quite sure what I was afraid of. I knew he had no intention of hurting me.

"I'm waiting for the anesthetic to take effect," he said, still and observant.

"It's working. You can start." I tried to keep my words calm, steady.

The tension between us felt thick, tangible. His next move made it even worse. He unbuttoned my jeans and folded the flaps under to reveal the end of the cut more clearly. My heart decided she was done with this and just about stopped altogether. But then he leaned over and set to work like a surgeon—all focus and precision. I didn't feel an ounce of pain. Now whether that was from the anesthetic or from the gallons of adrenaline flooding through my body, I'm not sure.

"These are dissolvable stitches. Keep the area clean, and it will heal well."

I felt the slight tug as he tied off and snipped the ends. I wasn't interested in stitches right now. I wanted answers.

"You murdered that guy."

Of course, the guy was trying to kidnap me, but murder seemed an extreme punishment. Jude's brow creased together as he snipped the other side close to the skin. He continued pressing and taping a thin bandage along the cut in silence for a moment.

"That is one way to see it."

"There's another way?"

"Of course. I expelled a demon from this world, keeping the monster from doing further harm to the human populace."

"Human populace? Who says that?"

He glanced at me as if he didn't understand the question.

"Okay, whatever. But you didn't expel him like you did with that little demon at the club."

"Lower demon, not little. There's a difference."

"You *killed* Pit-bull boy."

His mouth quirked on one side as he put his surgical things back into the kit, seemingly unperturbed by the accusation.

"You have interesting nicknames for people, Genevieve Drake. I'm intrigued to know what name you might have for me." Dark, exotic eyes focused their full attention on my face, cheeks, lips, then finally on my eyes.

Breathe in, breathe out.

"Stop changing the subject," I snapped.

"You don't understand." He draped one finely muscled arm along the back of the sofa, effectively enclosing me in, his broad chest hovering over mine. I wasn't cold anymore. The shivering was long gone. "Pit-bull boy, as you called him, was fused with the human. There was no other way to expel the demon."

"Fused? Like permanently?"

"I have never seen a fused demon separate from its human host. The only way is to expel them both."

"By death."

A slow nod.

"So you mean, Fabio was just a helpless dude flipping his pretty hair, working his model day job when along came a demon, jumped in and fused to him?"

His mouth quirked up on one side. "The host must accept the demon's presence, which requires more time than the average possession by a lower demon, but yes, that is correct."

"So Sandy-hair, I mean that guy at the club on my birthday, he wasn't fused."

A shake of his head.

I chewed my lower lip. "So now Fabio is basically condemned to death. Once you get a hold of him, that is."

"And I will," he countered quickly.

"But that's not fair."

"Life isn't fair, Genevieve. Surely you know this by now."

My mother. I knew that truth very well.

He shifted on the sofa, bringing his body an inch or two closer. My heart responded, pounding harder.

"No one is purely innocent who is fused to a demon," he continued. "A demon, lower or high, can't enter any being that is not, shall we say, receptive to the dark lure. That includes a Vessel."

He said the last with such emphasis I felt the weight of his words heavy in the air. Almost like his very breath held power, forcing me to comprehend something still out of my reach.

A strange energy passed between us while he continued to lean over me, observing me closely. Obsidian pools swirled with shards of amber, glinting impossibly with sparks of light. I couldn't have seen that.

I was suddenly struck by the notion that this man was unlike any I had ever met—not because he was pinch-me gorgeous, not because he was a demon hunter or slayer or whatever, and not even because he was the product of some sexy European cross-breeding. My eyes traveled to the slope of his shoulders, remembering the aura of light stretching wide as he chanted the demon back to the netherworld.

He watched me, waiting. Infinite patience, this one. Those blind birds were fluttering around in my stomach again, bouncing off every wall, making themselves stupid-dizzy.

"So, tell me," I found myself nearly whispering. "How did you become a Dominus Daemonum? Where does one fill out this kind of job application?"

"One doesn't."

"So, how did you—"

He abruptly stood up—the spell broken—and then disappeared down the hall. Okay. Note to self—Jude is touchy on his demon hunter origins. I heard a cabinet open and close. A medicine bottle popped open, pills rattled, and a faucet turned on for a few seconds, then off. He returned with a glass of water, passing it to me with a small blue pill I'd never seen before.

"What's this, Morpheus? Will this take me down the rabbit hole into reality? Because I'd totally like to wake up from this nightmare."

He didn't seem to get my *Matrix* reference and pushed his pill on me again.

"Never watch sci-fi?" I asked.

"Yes, Genevieve. I've seen *The Matrix*. Unfortunately, this isn't Hollywood. And reality is quite a bit less glamorous and more dangerous. Now, take this. It will stem the pain."

"I need to get home. My roommate, Mindy, will be worried. She might call the police or something."

He motioned for me to take the medicine again.

"Are you trying to drug me?"

He cocked an eyebrow.

"Yes. I saved your life from demons. Twice. I drove you away from danger and took you into my home, then stitched up your bleeding wound so that I could poison you with a tiny pill."

Smiling, I noted more to myself, "You're kind of funny."

"Take the pill, Genevieve," he grumbled, though his tone had softened.

I did as I was told without further argument. For once.

Seemingly satisfied, he glanced down at his T-shirt, stained from my blood, and walked into what must be his bedroom off the living area. I could see the foot of a bed and a black dresser with nickel hardware. I sat up as he disappeared near the dresser, feeling the skin stretch tight over my stomach.

Facing the dresser, he stripped off his soiled shirt. I tried not to gasp and failed miserably.

Covering the entire expanse of his broad back was the scene of St. Michael the Archangel defeating the devil. Great feathery wings spread wide, spear held high, an expression of deepest calm and utter concentration fixed on the archangel's face as he speared the serpent. Strangely, I'd seen that expression before. On him. The beauty of the artwork sucked the breath right out of me. I cannot imagine how many hours he lay under a needle, bleeding for this amazing ink.

As he turned and pulled on a white T-shirt, I saw another massive tattoo of an ornate Celtic cross encased in a vine of thorns spanning his chest and abdomen. Chiseled abdomen. *Oh my.*

The horizontal design fell right below his pectorals; the vertical part of the cross divided his chest in half up to his collarbone and disappeared down into his jeans. I saw it for only a second. Long enough. I quickly lay back down, throwing an arm over my eyes to cover my reddened face. I didn't need a mirror to know I was blushing.

I knew lots of people with random tattoos—butterflies, hearts, tigers and dragons. I knew others with carefully chosen ones—poetic verses, philosophical quotes, religious symbols. Personally, I was a blank canvas, never finding something I wanted branded on my skin for life. If I did, it would be small and inconspicuous. Jude's ink screamed to the world—justice with a sword, the smiting of evil, and faith encased in pain.

Who was he?

I envisioned him as he was that night in Tartarus—the stunning, sexy guy across the smoky club, shrouded in mystery. The vision changed. In reality, he was far more mysterious and bewitching. No less sexy or stunning, mind you, but each discovery added another question mark to who or *what* he actually was.

My mind drifted farther. I yawned. That blue pill lulled me to a dreamy place where a black-eyed man with an aura of fire whisked me away into the night.

5

"**M**other?"
	I was having a dream. A nightmare. Warning bells rang loud and clear even in my unconscious, sleep-induced state.

I stood in her studio, watching her paint white walls in hues of red. I called out. She wouldn't answer, wouldn't even acknowledge my presence. Her blonde hair fell long around slim shoulders, shrouding her face, as she streaked the room in scarlet shapes—winged angels falling from the sky, mouths gaping and twisted in horror as they fell into a blood-red abyss. Somewhere, staccato, operatic voices chanted in Latin, urging her onward. I called her name again. She swiveled. Soulless eyes widened, the color of her dripping brush, staring from a ghostly pale face. Her mouth opened to speak or scream, I wasn't sure.

I awoke in the dark, bolting upright. A cold sweat dampened my scalp and neck. I nearly choked on my own fear. Pain rippled across my stomach where my stitched wound throbbed.

"Ow!"

I sucked in a breath and pushed a fleece blanket off me, vaguely wondering when Jude had put it there. What time was it? Glancing down, I realized I was barefoot and wearing an oversized gray T-shirt that was definitely not mine. I panicked for a moment, wondering how the hell I'd slept through *that*.

Some blue pill. I calmed when I realized I was still in my bra and jeans. Okay. Not too mortifying, I suppose.

The vision of my mother had faded, yet the music still played in my head. No. It was coming from down the hall.

Jude's bedroom door stood open. A desk lamp revealed an empty room, a made bed. I followed the operatic music, easily recognizing *Carmina Burana*. I didn't know the music from my mother, however. Professor Minga had made us translate the Latin lyrics as a class project last quarter. Songs about wine, women and lascivious behavior, ironically composed by a randy gang of defrocked monks in the 12th century. My classmate Mary and I had laughed, imagining "monks gone wild" with their brown robes and tonsured heads.

I padded farther down the hall, edging closer to the source, realizing his home was much bigger than it appeared from the outside. I passed several closed doors. A sliver of light peeked from a crack in the last one on the left. I tiptoed closer, pushing the door open as the final and most famous song of the piece blared from within. I translated as the words streamed in dramatic Latin verse.

O Fortune, like the moon, you are changeable.

The door creaked ajar, revealing Jude wearing nothing but a pair of loose-fitting, black workout pants. He swiveled and spun across the wood floor, swinging two great broadswords in fluid movements. It was a long empty room with no furniture but an iPhone docking station and tiny, powerful Bose speakers in each corner. The back wall was windowless with brick facing, typical of older homes in the Quarter, but I barely registered any of this since my eyes were glued to the dark god moving across the floor with his eyes closed.

He seemed to be working through a memorized routine, almost dancing, with sharpened steel in each hand. As he moved, sinewy muscles rippled, accentuating the contoured lines of his body and dynamic works of art covering his skin. A faint golden glow shimmered along his limbs, shoulders, back. Raw energy pulsed in the room. All the while, a choir chanted the Latin song about fate.

Fate, monstrous and empty…

He swung his left arm low, slicing through an invisible enemy, shifting right to swing at another. The heavy weapons appeared like something out of *Gladiator*. I'd watched that movie a thousand times with my dad, mesmerized by Russell Crowe's epic sword-fighting skills. No offense, but Crowe had nothing on this man.

The size and bulk of the weapons should weigh a man down with dull, heavy strokes. Not Jude. The Latin chorus steadily grew louder, leading him into a rhythmic dance of sweat and steel. Always in control, he'd never shown an ounce of emotion on his face until this moment. The pain etched into his brow as he fought an unseen rival broke my heart and fascinated me at the same time.

You are malevolent, well-being is vain and always fades to nothing.

As the music built to a climactic frenzy, words of despair screamed in perfect harmony. I trembled at the sight of him, as if he was in the midst of a great battle, doomed to fail.

Since Fate strikes down the strong man…

Then it happened. My senses sharpened on every level— sound shattered my eardrums, heat burned my skin, sweat and fear coated my tongue, and the sight of him whirling like a warrior in agony slapped me into another time and place altogether.

The room shimmered. For a split second, I saw Jude, thinner, perhaps younger, bare-chested with no tattoos and much longer hair, braids at the temples. Clad in some kind of natural-leather pants and covered in blue war paint, he wielded a single sword, surrounded by thatched-roof houses engulfed in flame.

The fire roared into the night, mingled with the screams of women and children. Grim faced, Jude clanged metal against metal. His weapon bore down upon the head of a beautiful, fair-haired man dressed in a Roman tunic. His enemy grinned back at him with malice. The overpowering feeling of hatred mingled with fury stemming from Jude filled my veins as if I were there battling the sneering foe, not him.

I sucked in a loud, gasping breath, like coming up for air after being submerged too long underwater. The vision came and went in a blink, tearing through me like opening a wound. I trembled from the strange, almost painful sensation of being thrust into the horrific memory of the man standing before me.

I knew without a fraction of doubt that this was part of being a Vessel. Whatever vision I'd conjured, the power came from within me. I quivered in my bare feet from the aftershock, rage—not mine—still coursing through my frame as I stood in the doorway.

Jude faced me, frozen, eyes wide open, betrayal flitting across his face. He held the swords low in each white-knuckled fist. The music crashed to a halt at the end of the song.

Silence.

His chest rose and fell rapidly. He glared at me with that obsidian gaze before finally snapping out of his trance.

Walking to the wall at my right, he popped open a cabinet. Inside, a case for swords in various lengths, widths and designs was stacked in sheaths from top to bottom. Breathing heavily, he used a towel to wipe the first blade before placing it home.

I suddenly felt overwhelmed by the vision and by Jude's current state, glistening skin and all. I struggled to regain composure, still shaking with the lingering taste of rage, *his* rage, sharpening my senses. Still, I couldn't help but notice his ink— harsh and beautiful, delicate and jagged, soft curves with razor tips. Just like him, a paradox of beauty and predator. Alluring and lethal at the same time.

"What did you see?"

I flinched. How did he know? "What do you mean?"

"Don't be coy, Genevieve," he ground low and deep, his back to me as he wiped down the second sword and put it away. "It's written all over your face."

Swallowing hard, I couldn't tear my eyes away from his back and the perfect way his shoulder blades gave way to strong lines rippling with each movement, sinewy muscle disappearing into the waistband of his pants.

He toweled off then slipped a black T-shirt on. "I can sense the change. You're becoming aware."

"What do you mean by 'becoming aware'?"

"You're beginning to see past the *alucinatio*."

I frowned. "Past the 'illusion'?"

He nodded.

"Do you mean like glamour? Like vampires?"

"There's no such thing as vampires."

"Oh, sorry, I forgot. Those monsters are mythical. Right."

He walked over to his iPod station, ignoring my sarcasm.

"So who exactly can use alucinatio to hide their true selves?"

"Not hide, but mask. Any of the *Flamma*."

"Wait. That means *fire* or *flame*."

"Yes, this is the name given to those who are, shall we say, touched by fire."

"Now I'm even more confused. Who are these Flamma exactly?"

"Any intelligent, sentient being other than human."

"That doesn't really answer my question. I'm even more confused."

"I'll answer almost any question you have, Genevieve. Be specific."

I didn't miss the slip of the word *almost* in there, but I was on a mission. "Define Flamma. Touched with fire by whom? God, the devil, angels, demons?"

Black eyes measured me carefully. "All of the above."

Again, I found myself wavering between fantasy and reality, wondering how the hell all this was happening to me.

Jude had unplugged his iPhone, turned off the machine and walked closer.

"So tell me, what did you see?"

I closed my eyes, struggling with the truth. "I saw you."

"And what was I doing?"

"You were fighting someone, but you were younger than you are now."

I kept my expression as blank as I could, not wanting him to know what I really saw, what I felt coursing through me. Bitterness, rage, and utter despair. Was that who he truly was?

He stepped even closer. I hated when he did this, inching inside my comfort zone, scattering my brain cells to never-never land. To make matters worse, a sweaty Jude was a hotter Jude—literally and in every other way. His molten gaze flickered over my face, down my body then back up.

His voice was soft and deep when he asked, "And what did you feel in that moment of Sight?"

"Everything."

My heart pounded harder. Poor little thing never could keep up with my erratic emotions.

"Define *everything*."

He held my gaze, throwing my own sassy remarks back at me. I stared back, trying to appear like an open book, while turmoil swirled inside.

"I felt heat. I felt as if the music were beating inside my chest, almost to bursting. I saw you. I heard metal on metal. I felt…everything. But it's gone now."

He stared a moment longer. Finally, his rigid shoulders slackened ever so slightly.

"Yes. You're becoming aware. It may happen more often than you like from here on out. When you're fully awakened, you will be able to see the Flamma no matter if they try to hide behind illusion or not. You'll even be able to foresee them, perhaps, depending on your gift with the Sight."

Foresee them. Like psychic?

"I don't mean to sound dense, but what does heightened sense have to do with being a Vessel? What good does that do?"

"A Vessel needs her own weapons against the enemy. And

she has many. Your heightened senses are a warning that you are near one or more of the Flamma. Ninety percent of the time, that will be a demon."

"But you're not a demon."

His eyes sharpened, sending a cold shiver up my spine.

"When you feel your senses heightening," he continued, ignoring my comment, "observe who is around you and what they are doing. You'll feel all your senses, all six."

"Six?" Was he kidding me? "Um, I know I didn't do very well in biology, but as far as I know, there are five senses."

"There are six."

"Of course there are."

In true Jude fashion, he ignored my attitude and barreled ahead. All business.

"The sixth encompasses intuition, which comes in many forms—sensing their signature, or you may have a vision, what we call the Sight."

"What's a signature?"

"All Flamma have a distinct signature that you can either feel, see, sometimes even taste or smell."

"What's your signature?"

His granite features didn't crack. "If you don't know yet, you will." Electricity prickled in the air. I remembered the aura of flame, the constant heat rippling off him, wondering if I'd already felt his signature but hadn't recognized it.

I was completely overwhelmed—visions, becoming aware, signatures, Sight, Flamma, more crazy Latin terms. He was withholding all kinds of information I needed.

"So why didn't you tell me any of this about being a Vessel before?"

"And when would that have been? In the dark alley where I first met you? On campus, in front of a dozen coeds, after you refused to go somewhere private to discuss these events?" His voice remained eerily steady, so calm, yet the flash in his dark eyes made me want to retreat. Fast. He stepped even closer. Of course. "Or when the last three demons were trying to assault you? Or perhaps when I was stitching up your injury? How is it, by the way?"

I scowled back at him. "Fine," I snapped, realizing I sounded like a petulant child.

Silence again. There seemed to be many of these moments between Jude and me, where we said nothing but the quiet was heavy, weighted.

I had an English teacher once who called this a pregnant pause, a stillness filled with thoughts growing rapidly that would at some point give birth. I wondered when that time would come between Jude and me, when we'd stop withholding information and spill it all.

His phone buzzed with an incoming call. He answered it, eyes lingering on me.

"Yes."

Pause.

"Good."

Longer pause.

"This evening. I'll meet you there."

He slipped his phone back into his pocket without any sort of explanation. Not that he was obliged to tell me anything anyway, but I really wanted to know who would be calling him at whatever ungodly hour this was. What kind of friends did a demon hunter have?

"It's time to get you home. I'll escort you to ensure you arrive safely."

"How will you get home if you drive me home?"

"There are other modes of transportation."

"Modes of transportation? Who talks like that?"

He made no reply, walking toward me. Knowing he was about to squeeze into my personal space as he liked to do, I ambled back down the hall to get my things.

"Your phone is still on the coffee table. I sent your room-mate a message. She texted you thirty-eight times to find out where you were, threatening to call your father."

"Oh no! Mindy!"

He was right. She had texted me exactly thirty-eight times. Her messages were repetitious: *Where R U? Who R U with? Why aren't U texting me back? I need more Easy Mac. David isn't coming over till later. Why won't U answer me? Is your phone dead? If your phone's dead then U can't get this message. OK, you've never not answered me. WHERE R U? OK, if U don't answer me, I'm calling the police. No, I'm calling your dad, which is worse and U know it!*

Her string of messages finally ended. Then a brief reply from my phone: *I am okay. Do not call my dad. I am in good hands and will explain to you when I arrive home in the morning.*

This was a bit stiff coming from me, but she must've bought it. The message after read: *In the morning? Are U sleeping at a guy's house? OMG! Are U at Malcolm's? No, U wouldn't be with Malcolm, not like that. Did U run into that hot guy from Tartarus? The one U told me about? Details! I want DETAILS! David's here now. See U in the a.m.*

I literally felt the blood drain away from my face as I read this last text. Please tell me Jude did *not* read her response. I wanted to crawl under a very large rock in a very deep hole in a very dark cave and never come out.

I wish I'd never told Mindy about meeting Jude that night. Of course, I withheld nearly our entire encounter, but I had to tell her about the dance floor incident since Steven wouldn't shut up about it on the way home.

The sad thing was, my thoughts of the "hot guy from the club" had morphed into something entirely different. Yes, he was still hot—hotter, actually—but the attraction was tempered now with a sense of dread. Or maybe cautious respect. You know, the way you respect a rattlesnake or a grizzly bear.

"Are you ready?"

I yipped.

"Jumpy?"

He eyed my phone in my hands. I quickly tucked it into my

back pocket. I swear he smiled, just barely, but I saw it. Heat flushed into my cheeks.

There was a sheathed sword strapped to his back.

"Are you going to walk around like that?"

"Of course. I never go anywhere without a weapon. Demons don't sleep, Genevieve."

"Don't you think people will find it a little odd? Halloween isn't for another two weeks."

"No one will see it."

"What do you mean?" Hooking my thumbs in my front pockets, I considered. "Can you make it invisible or something?"

"Yes. All Flamma can cast illusion." By all, he was including demon hunters.

"Were you wearing a sword the night I met you?"

"As I said, I never go anywhere without a weapon."

"I suppose I couldn't see it then because I hadn't 'become aware' or whatever."

Somehow, this made me feel safer knowing I could now see what might be coming for me around any corner.

It was nearly six a.m. as I followed Jude down the stairs and through the courtyard. Misty morning light barely lit the path to the wrought-iron gate. When I tripped over an uneven brick, Jude caught me around my upper arm, steadied me and kept me close the rest of the way to the car.

His touch was firm but gentle. The heat radiating through his fingers banded around my arm, making me feel safe, protected, and something else. I slid into the passenger side, once again letting him take the driver's seat. I wondered how often this would happen in our bizarre, demon-hunter-helps-demon-hunted relationship.

6

"You need to turn—"

Jude had already made a left before I could tell him exactly where to go. I stopped giving him directions. He made the next one—correctly—without a word from me.

"You know where I live?"

A stiff nod.

The fact that he'd stalked me to my home at some point should make me nervous. It didn't, and that was worrisome.

"So," I said, swallowing a little pride. "I've given it some thought, and I think you're right. I do need preparation or training or whatever as a Vessel."

Amusement played across his dark features, though he never took his eyes from the road.

"Of course," he agreed with no hint of smugness, though I knew he was just hiding it well. Grand illusionist, this one. "When would you like to meet?"

"When are you available?"

He stopped at a red light. Obsidian eyes shimmering with flecks of gold held mine for a moment. He picked up his cell phone from the console and clicked on the calendar app.

55

"What time are your classes scheduled on Monday?"

Ha! He didn't know everything about me.

"I'm open from noon to four."

"Noon, then."

He plugged in our meeting time and date, then set the phone back on the console. Okay, I'm not normally a sneaky or nosy person, but I couldn't help it. He'd left his weekly calendar open, so I saw the appointment he had scheduled for tonight: Kat—Jackson Square—10:00.

Kat? Jude had a girlfriend? The green-eyed monster inside me narrowed her feline eyes, growling and spitting at the prospect.

What was I thinking? No matter what my initial impressions of this guy were, I knew he was not dating material. Kitty better retract her claws and get over it.

"Are you feeling all right? Do your stitches hurt?"

How did he notice my shifting mood so fast? He was like an emo-detector.

"I'm fine. Just tired," I lied.

He pulled up the drive of our small duplex. David's car wasn't in the driveway, thankfully. I didn't feel like dealing with the saccharine-sweet couple at the moment.

I suddenly felt on edge. Now that Jude had successfully saved my life, twice, I felt protected with him. As much as my pride bristled at being dependent on him or anyone else for that matter, the thought of being alone terrified me.

I'd been wondering if I should even come back here, imagining a red-eyed demon breaking in, abducting me, and killing Mindy in the process. Yeah, she was little, but she was feisty. No way would she cower and hide if my life were in danger.

"Can I call you if I have, you know, visitors?"

"You will be safe. While in this building, no demon will be able to detect your presence."

"Wait, you can cast illusions on a place?"

"Some Flamma can."

He smiled. My heart fluttered. I wish he'd smile more often. On second thought, I was glad he didn't.

"What do you mean some? Why not all?"

"The power of using illusion depends upon the strength of the user."

"So, I'm guessing that hiding whole buildings takes a pretty powerful user."

"Correct." His steady gaze pinned me in place, dropping to my mouth before skating away. When a flame of heat crawled up my neck, he quickly stepped out and came around to open my door.

"Guess that makes me a lucky girl that you wandered into Tartarus that night," I said as we came to a stop outside the door of the duplex.

He grew very quiet and still, gazing down at me. Unreadable thoughts flitted behind heavy-lidded eyes. When he spoke, his deep voice had dipped another octave.

"Do not go anywhere alone outside of this house, Genevieve." His command was serious, his voice rumbling with danger. "Do you understand me?"

Ordinarily, I didn't let guys order me around like that, but my survival instincts told me to simply nod in agreement. So I did.

The deep frown creasing his brow softened a fraction. "I'll see you at noon on Monday."

I nodded again. The curtains by the door fluttered. I ducked my head and skirted past him. After bolting the lock behind me, I spun around to find Mindy propped on the sofa with a stupid-wide grin plastered on her face.

"O! M! G! *Who* was that? Was that him? Was that the guy from the club? He is *so* hot. No, he's beyond hot! What happened? Where did you see him again?"

She spat out a string of questions. When she finally paused to suck air into her little lungs, I attempted to explain.

"Yes, that was the guy. I was—"

Her squeal pierced my ears. "Did y'all have sex? Please tell me you did!"

"No! Geez, Mindy, I just met the guy!"

"Well, I know, but damn, did you look at him? It's like *Vampire Diaries* showing up on your doorstep."

"There's no such thing as vampires, Mindy." And who did I sound like right now?

"You're right," she said, perking up with a devilish smile, "but he is *definitely* real."

I sat down on the loveseat, wincing as the bandage rubbed the stitches.

"Oh no. Are you okay? Does your stomach hurt or something?"

"Actually, I was mugged right outside the dojo."

"You're kidding!"

I'd already come up with this excuse, an easy one for her to believe. Mindy and I'd been mugged once during Mardi Gras.

We had wandered too far from our group on Canal Street to find a bathroom. Finding an available restroom in New Orleans during Mardi Gras was like scouring the Sahara searching for a swimming pool. Of course, we turned down a remote alley in our ridiculous nothing-can-harm-me, life-is-perfect giddiness. What can I say? We were sixteen and reckless and stupid. This scruffy-looking guy pushed us into a niche in the wall and demanded money. I checked to see if he had a gun. He didn't. I grabbed Mindy's hand and ran. He chased us until we reached the next street, where tons of people milled up and down.

Till the other night at Tartarus, that was my first and only brush with death. Sadly, I sensed there would be more in my future.

"Yeah," I continued. "I locked up the dojo for Dad, and this guy jumped out of nowhere. In the struggle, he cut me. Luckily, Jude came and ran the guy off."

Okay, actually, none of that was a lie. I just left out minor facts—three guys, not one; demons, not humans; attempted kidnapping, not mugging. And, oh yeah, Jude killed one and scared the bejeezus out of the other two with his badass demon-killer mojo.

"Oh my God! Seriously, Gen. Are you okay? Did you call the police?"

"No. My dad has enough to worry about. If he knew this, he'd never let me out of the house alone again."

This was definitely true.

"Let me see." She hobbled over on her wrapped ankle as I lifted my shirt.

"It's not as bad as it seems," I lied, so happy the wound was still covered by the bandage.

"Yikes! It's really big. Thank goodness your hottie showed up. Why *was* he there?"

I ignored her reference to Jude being mine. That was beyond laughable. Could a demon hunter like Jude actually ever belong to anyone? However, I had come up with a decent lie for him being there.

"When I met him the other night, I'd told him where I worked. He mentioned he was a black belt."

"Of course he is."

"He was looking for my dad."

"Of course he was."

"He wants to do some moonlighting at the dojo."

"Of course he does."

"Stop it!"

Mindy had that wicked gleam in her eyes. "You stop it. He's totally into you. And now he's saved you from some crazy creeper on the streets? It's like a requirement that you two now have some kind of passionate love affair."

She sighed, leaning back with a purple throw pillow clutched to her chest, gazing up at the ceiling.

There was no harm in letting her believe her delusions.

Better to let her think that than know the truth. The very idea of Jude being *into* me sent chills through my body all the way to the bone—terrifying, mind-numbing, body-shaking chills. I picked up the other throw pillow and chucked it at her face.

"Ow!" She giggled.

We laughed the way girls laugh about hot guys. I popped two heaping bowls of buttery popcorn, made us some Coke Zero slushies, then we settled onto the sofas with fleecy blankets for an all-day marathon of *Lord of the Rings*. Mindy got her way last time with *Harry Potter*, so it was my turn. What I'd wanted for my birthday all along anyway.

I tried to deny that I had an ulterior motive, but I couldn't. Every time Aragorn swung his sword, the vision of another warrior came to mind. Darker, fiercer, and more beautiful beyond compare.

"Thank you again, Malcolm, for giving me a ride," I told him as we packed our books to leave study group.

"No problem. I was happy to."

He beamed at me. I wondered for a second if this was a bad idea. Not that I thought he wasn't tough enough to frighten off a demon. Malcolm played rugby and filled out his six-one frame quite nicely. Much bigger than Steven, anyway. He would make that demon Fabio think twice before approaching.

I wondered if perhaps I'd given Malcolm the wrong impression. We'd always met up with Mary at the library for study group. I hoped he wasn't reading into this.

I knew when a guy was crushing on me. And Malcolm definitely was. He kept our relationship sort of flirty-friendly, but I'd just crossed that boundary like an idiot in my own selfish need to get out of the apartment.

We left our study nook near the reference shelves—a graveyard of research materials time had forgotten—with Mary.

"I'm so sick of Milton. I'll be glad when we move on," sighed Mary.

"Same," I agreed right as my stomach growled."

"Hungry, guys?" asked Malcolm, holding the library door open for me. "Let's get something to eat." He'd had finished off his Skittles and DP an hour ago.

"Not me," said Mary, adjusting her glasses and shifting her I-heart-Poe satchel higher on her shoulder. "I've got work in the morning. And in addition to Bennett's torture device he calls a midterm on Monday, I've got one in Sociology too. I need sleep right now."

"How's the coffee biz?" asked Malcolm.

"Same ole, same ole. Everyone needs caffeine in a pretty cup with sugary foam on top."

I was only vaguely tuned in to the conversation as we walked to the parking lot, my mind wandering somewhere it shouldn't be. I couldn't help myself.

"How about beignets, Malcolm?" I asked, only half-concerned this might be construed as a mini-date.

"Sure. Awesome! There's a new café over on St. Charles we could go to."

"Nah. Let's get the real deal. Café du Monde."

"The Quarter? On a Saturday night?" he asked, obviously surprised by my suggestion.

"Y'all have fun," said Mary, walking toward her car across the lot.

"See ya, Mary," I called, looking back to Malcolm. "Yeah. Why not?"

I tried to sound casual as I climbed into his Jeep Cherokee. I knew "why not". Saturday night in the French Quarter meant a number of things—noise, drunks, tourists, street vendors looking for tips, drunks, bachelor parties gone awry, drunks. Need I say more? It was far from what most students would want after several grueling hours of studying.

"I'm in the mood for a little ambiance," I lied.

"If that's what you want, Drake, let's go."

I settled back into the seat, belted myself in, and tried to ignore the niggling fact that I wanted neither beignets nor Malcolm's company. My mind registered only two facts in determining our destination. Café du Monde was perfectly positioned with a wide view of Jackson Square. And it was nearly ten o'clock.

7

Thirty minutes later, we were parked near Jax Brewery and walking the few blocks to Café du Monde. Café Maspero's had a line a mile long wrapped around the corner block of Toulouse. Those waiting for platters of fried seafood, overstuffed po'boys, and the best French onion soup in town sipped on dollar strawberry daiquiris as they waited. My mouth watered, thinking of cold, salty raw oysters with horseradish sauce, but Maspero's was two blocks away from Jackson Square. Too far away.

A cacophony of noise that was distinctly the French Quarter filled the night—sporadic laughter, plates and glasses tinkling, jazz music, car horns, random shouts, horses clip-clopping as they pulled tourist carriages along Decatur, and the distant horn of merchant ships on the Mississippi River. Café du Monde wasn't as crowded as usual. A bearded man played an upbeat rendition of "When the Saints Go Marchin' In" on his saxophone at the entrance.

"Hmph. Wish they'd hurry," I mumbled.

"What's that, Drake?"

"Oh, nothing."

I squeezed past the smiling tourists dropping dollars and

coins in his open case and beelined for a table on the outer edge of the awning. Malcolm followed. I winced as my stomach bumped the back of a chair right over my wound, but hid my grimace, not wanting Malcolm to notice.

"Didn't know you were a fan of this scene," he said from behind.

"Sometimes." I smiled tightly, scooting my chair away from bumping the table behind me. They crammed as many teeny-tiny round tables in this place as possible, and usually every one of them was full.

Malcolm gave me a nervous smile. We'd never been anywhere but class or study group together. I hated lying to him. Worse, I hated using him, but who was I kidding? I wanted to know who this Kat person was. I'd just get a glimpse, then I'd be satisfied. That's what I told myself, anyway.

"Order?"

An Asian woman in a white uniform wiped the remains of powdered sugar off the table.

"Two orders of beignets and café au lait," said Malcolm.

Within six minutes, we were served and enjoying the famous delicacy. Funny thing was, I usually did enjoy the ambience of the Quarter and its distractions. Tonight, my eyes were peeled for one and only one person.

My Vessel senses prickled along my skin. I smiled inwardly because I could actually feel the slow change. I was becoming aware, as Jude had said. I could feel my Vessel Sense on a primitive level, some secret awakening tickling along the outer edges of my mind and body.

There were Flamma out tonight, but I was either too far away or they were good at hiding. I couldn't find them in the crowds, but I knew they were there. Still, I felt no immediate threat zoning in on me.

"I swear, it was the coolest thing ever. Taika Waititi is a freakin' genius," Malcolm was saying. "So, you want to go see the new one coming out?"

"I'm sorry?" I asked, sipping my chicory coffee.

"You know, the new Marvel movie."

"Sure," I mumbled, scanning the Square across the street. "Awesome."

Malcolm bit into his fourth beignet, having finished his order and moved on to mine. After all of my faked enthusiasm for beignets, I could hardly eat a bite. I was draining the last of my café au lait when I saw him.

Striding across Decatur like a man on a mission, he wore black jeans, a black leather jacket and black boots. No matter his dark allure, something about him made everyone step clearly out of his way. I knew what that something was—eau de Jude.

Despite his magnificence, he emanated an aura of back-the-fuck-off wherever he went. My heart skipped a beat, even though I'd firmly resolved to keep my heart out of this. I'd decided Jude was entirely off-limits in the dating category, but he knew a hell of a lot more about what I was than he was letting on. I needed answers, and if that meant I had to resort to becoming the stalker in this relationship, well, then, so be it.

Oh hell, who was I fooling? Honestly, I just really wanted to see who this Kat person was.

I didn't see a sword hilt sticking up anywhere and wondered if my ability to see through the illusion had faded. Not likely. He marched directly toward the stairs leading up to the riverfront. Malcolm was still talking away, but I totally couldn't focus on whatever he was saying.

"Hey, let's go take a walk along the river. It's nice tonight."

"Yeah, sure," agreed Malcolm. His eyes brightened, and I hated myself a little bit more.

The riverfront at night was dimly lit, perfect for couples and lovers who wanted privacy on a moonlit stroll. A cool autumn wind nipped the air. The crescent moon hung low, cutting a sideways smile in the starry sky.

I felt sick deceiving Malcolm this way, especially when he slid a sweet smile in my direction, but my choices were limited.

Out of nowhere, he took my hand as we climbed the stairs as if to guide me, but we both knew that wasn't why. His palm was a little damp, and I let him hold my hand, let him believe what he wanted for the time being.

Ugh. I'm such a bitch.

Ignoring the uncomfortable feeling of my hand in Malcolm's, I tuned in to the dawning sensation creeping along my skin. I was close to Flamma. An ethereal tendril wove out of that secret place within, wrapping a warm layer around my chest, spreading over the rest of my body like a blanket alight with electricity. It was the oddest sensation I'd ever felt, though it seemed to happen without me doing anything at all. I had no idea what this meant, yet at the same time felt protected.

As soon as we stepped onto the stone walkway along the riverfront, I saw them, conversing closely near one of the many stone sculptures dotting the riverfront.

Though Jude was definitely a specimen to draw the eye, I couldn't help but gaze at the tall, slender woman standing next to him.

She must've been six foot. Blonde hair braided tightly in a thick line halfway down her back and a pale face with wide, pretty eyes. She was dressed from head to foot in brown leather, including a duster jacket that hit her knees. Jealousy burned in my chest. I suddenly felt small and insignificant in my faded jeans, white knit shirt and red denim jacket cropped short at the waist.

Malcolm guided me straight for them, but I pulled him to a stop.

"You're shivering," he said. "Are you cold?"

Malcolm wrapped me into a hug, rubbing my back. I didn't protest. Now I had an excuse to watch the two over his shoulder without moving into their line of vision.

My senses heightened. The smell of the muddy river mixed with salt water from the Gulf wafted over me. The cool, humid air clung to my skin. And sound amplified to a ridiculous degree. I honed in on the one sound I'd come for—the conversation between the model look-alikes not fifteen yards away.

"What kind of signs?"

"You know very well what the signs are, Jude."

The familiarity with which she said his name twisted something in my stomach. To my utter disgust and that of my caged green-eyed monster, whose hair stiffened straight in the air, the woman's voice was husky and silky at the same time. She had a bit of an English accent too, though watered down.

"And have you spoken to George about this?" Jude asked her.

Her eyes narrowed at the question. "No," she said tightly. "I don't need his permission to theorize, do I?"

"I never said you did."

Though she was apparently beyond miffed at the mention of this George guy, Jude had a very amused expression on that gorgeous face of his. The woman continued in a much more businesslike manner, which was more to my liking. "My region has been overrun by servants to a high demon, one of the highest. He's crafty, stays well-hidden and not always here on our plane. He's the reason I'm here in New Orleans."

"He's come here?"

I heard something I'd never heard before in Jude's voice—a combination of excitement and anxiety. The blonde shook her head.

"No. His henchmen are here, though. Something big is going on. I think he could be—"

Suddenly, she went rigid, pulling a dagger lightning fast from somewhere near her thigh. I froze. She sensed Flamma.

I glanced to my right and left, then back at them. Both Jude and presumably Kat were staring straight at me. Shock, then fury passed across those dark eyes I'd come to know so well. Without a second's pause, he marched in long strides directly toward me, his eyes cutting to Malcolm before landing furiously back on mine.

To say I wasn't terrified, as well as mortified for spying, would be a complete and total lie. Still, I held my ground, moving out of Malcolm's arms and pushing my chin up a notch. I was getting good at acting. I fleetingly wondered if I should switch my major to Drama, or maybe Politics.

Then he was there. Whoa. Way inside my personal space. And Malcolm's. Jet eyes staked me to the spot.

"Do you have a death wish?" His voice grated against my skin like sandpaper.

Malcolm pushed himself into the conversation. "Dude, excuse me. What are you doing?"

Malcolm made a hands-off gesture. He went to push Jude away but caught the look of death in Jude's eyes and stopped himself.

Holy hell! What was I thinking? I'd brought Malcolm up here based on my own selfish desire to get some answers and now I might be responsible for his untimely demise. I could see the headlines now in the Times Picayune: *Twenty-year-old Student Spontaneously Combusts into Pile of Ash, Source of Death Unknown.*

"Answer me, Genevieve. Why are you here?"

"You know this guy?" asked Malcolm, trying to cut in on the staring contest passing between us.

"We were just taking a walk," I said, trying to keep my voice from quivering. "This is—"

"Lie."

"Jude, seriously, I was just—"

"Do you have any idea how dangerous this place is for you?" He made a sound in the back of his throat that could've been a laugh if it weren't for the expression of rage warring across his face. He glanced at my jacket with a shake of his head. "Little Red comes wandering in the woods infested with wolves."

He was so close now our toes were touching. I inched back a step.

"Hey, dude! I don't know who you are," began Malcolm, putting an arm between us, "but you better back off."

Jude fixed a glacier-melting gaze on Malcolm, standing at least a head taller. I swallowed, but there was no moisture in my throat. How had I gotten Malcolm into this?

"Kid," Jude annunciated softly and slowly, a sure sign all hell was about to break loose, no pun intended. "You need to remove yourself and run along home now. Alone."

He sounded as if he'd just dismissed Malcolm back to his playpen, an errant child being put in timeout.

"What?" Malcolm lowered his arm and turned to me. "You know this asshole?"

"Yes. Malcolm, um, this is a friend of, um, my dad's. A work associate. From the dojo."

I was stammering like an idiot. To say he was a friend of mine would've been laughable. Though he only appeared to be in his late twenties, he exuded maturity on so many levels. He in no way looked like a friend I might know from school, and for being a good liar, my brain was misfiring at the moment and not helping me come up with anything better.

Jude did not extend his hand in greeting. He did not welcome the introduction. He did not move an inch. As a matter of fact, I felt his presence swelling beyond the miniscule area where we stood, like a colossus breathing down on the pitiful people beneath his feet. He in no way appeared cordial or polite or even remotely human, for that matter.

I had to get rid of Malcolm before this became seriously ugly. I put myself between them, pushing Malcolm gently back.

"Thank you for the beignets and the company, but Jude can give me a ride home."

"I'm not letting you go anywhere with this guy," he protested.

Wrong answer. I heard another scoff behind me that was supposed to be a sort of laugh but wasn't.

"I'm sorry, Malcolm. This is my fault. My dad is kind of strict. There's been trouble with the family business and stuff. I'll let Jude take me back home."

When did I become such a huge liar? Trouble with the family business? Was I embroiled in the mafia now? Malcolm didn't know my dad, except from a distance. For all he knew, he could've been in the mafia. And Jude more than looked the part of the enforcer. I insinuated in my tone there were things I couldn't say, because of course there were.

"I'll explain to you later, I promise. I'll call you tomorrow?" I added lower, squeezing his hand.

Malcolm put his hands on my shoulders. I swear I felt two points of heat boring into the back of my skull. I wondered then about my "sixth sense."

"Are you sure, Drake?"

I nodded. He pulled me into a brisk hug, then let go, giving the man over my shoulder a hard stare. I watched as he marched back toward Jackson Square, descending the stairs with one last scowling glance over his shoulder.

Taking a deep, shaky breath, I turned to face the executioner. I didn't speak. Just waited. He was doing that thing where he appeared to be dissecting my thoughts, observing every line on my face, trying to solve a riddle that perplexed him. Flinty shards of gold sparked in his eyes. A shot of relief washed over me. Any fraction of light in those obsidian depths was a good sign. Or so I thought.

"Why are you here?"

His voice had lost its edge. Well, let me clarify, the razor-sharp edge that could slice an oak into splinters. There was still the blunt steel swinging in slow, even strokes, threatening to cut me if I made a wrong move. I glanced toward the sculpture. She was gone.

"Who's Goth Barbie?"

His head tilted slightly to the left. His eyes narrowed, still glinting with golden stars.

"She's a friend," he finally responded. "Who's Schoolboy Ken?"

He evaded, a special talent he possessed by the butt load. Two can play that little game.

"He's a friend."

Jude smiled. A genuine smile with teeth and everything. My heart stuttered with the sudden shift in mood. His gaze traced the contours of my face, hair, shoulders, lower.

"At least you had the presence of mind to cast illusion. When did you discover you could use your ability?"

"Huh?"

Oh. I was pretty sure that was what the "warm blanket" was, but now I knew for certain. I felt it skimming along my skin, draping me from the inside out.

"Just now. It happened automatically, actually."

"Not automatically. Subconsciously. Your Vessel instincts are kicking in to protect you since your brain has apparently taken a leave of absence."

"Excuse me? Did you just call me stupid?"

"Stupid would imply you have no intelligence whatsoever. I am well aware that you are quite clever, so I would define this as either rebellious or apathetic behavior. Which is it?"

I made a disgusted sound, while smiling inside at his back-handed compliment.

"What is it exactly I've done to warrant the label of rebellious or apathetic?"

"You're standing in the middle of demon hunting ground. This den of debauchery lures demons for hundreds and hundreds of miles. You are a Vessel, a prize above all prizes for a high demon. The illusion you cast would certainly fool a lower creature, but not one in the upper hierarchy. So either you are being rebellious in disobeying me, or you are simply indifferent to keeping your soul intact. Which is it?"

I felt the blood drain from my face. Maybe I was stupid. No. But I wasn't being rebellious or apathetic about my well-being. My green-eyed monster lifted her head with wide eyes to remind me why I came, but I glared at her to keep her hissy mouth shut.

"Okay, you said to not go out alone. I wasn't alone. Malcolm was with me."

Did he really just roll his eyes at me?

"You might as well have been stripped naked, hanging from a balcony on Bourbon Street and screaming 'Come and get it.' That boy could have done nothing if you were spotted by any form of Flamma."

Now that was an image I didn't want in my head. I was slightly disturbed it was in Jude's. Switching gears quickly, thank you very much.

"Well, you didn't explain any of this to me. Perhaps if you were more forthcoming in explaining all of these rules I'd make better decisions," I said, feeling the color coming back into my cheeks.

"You are right about that. I will certainly be outlining the rules more clearly so you'll not misbehave in the future."

"Misbehave? Who do you think you are? My overprotective brother? Never had one. And I don't need one now."

He moved even closer. I started to step back. A strong arm shot out, gripping the top of my shoulder. His thumb pressed gently along the side of my neck over the cuff of my denim jacket. Surely he felt the quickening speed of my pulse. Was that his intention?

"No. I am not your brother." His hand shifted underneath my hair, his fingers curling around my nape. His possessive grip sent a shiver down my spine. "Nor do I want to be," he emphasized with a deep rumble. "However, I am your protector, whether you would choose me or not. If you value your life, or at the very least, your eternal soul, then you must trust me and do as I say."

Speechless, I nodded, unable to think clearly for the moment. His fingers tightened around the back of my throat, his thumb stroking my pulse in a strangely soothing manner. I can't begin to describe how distracting that was.

"Good." His gaze slid to my lips. I wished he wouldn't do

that. Or maybe I wished he would. Often. My thoughts spiraled in a million directions, unable to move in any coherent way. I tried to cut the tension crackling between us.

"Demons have a hierarchy? Like a class system?" I was aware I was nearly whispering, my questions sounding feeble and irrelevant.

"Yes. There is a hierarchy in heaven. There is a hierarchy on earth. There is a hierarchy in hell. That is the way of the world—every world."

"I don't know the difference between a lower and a high demon. You've told me little about them, except for the fusing thing."

He nodded in agreement. Small victory, but victory nonetheless. He still hadn't pulled away. His thumb trailed down over my collarbone. Since the moment he touched me, a pervasive warmth had slipped in over my own protective blanket, draping down over my chest and limbs.

"So, Little Red wants to play in the deep, dark woods," he mumbled almost to himself. His dark gaze feral, his grin flashing white teeth. "Let us go straight to the wolf's den, then."

His hand dropped to mine, swallowing it whole. The mantle of electric warmth continued to spread, sealing to my body like a glove. It didn't feel suffocating. On the contrary, the sensation comforted me like a cozy fire in the dead of winter.

Jude pulled me toward the stairs. I took two steps to his one. "Wait, where are we going?"

"I had an appointment tonight. You might as well come with me. Actually, this turn of events will be quite enlightening." He gave me a wicked grin. "For you."

The sudden image of a mischievous child dangling a minnow over a shark tank popped into my head.

"What kind of an appointment?" I didn't like the sound of this.

"As you said, I have not been as forthcoming as I should've

been," he said in an obvious tone of mockery, leading me across Decatur along the left side of the Square.

"You didn't answer my question."

Evasive bastard.

"Smile. You are about to get many answers to many questions. I am going to introduce you to a high demon."

8

"What! Are you out of your fucking mind!"

He led me down Royal Street, slowing his stride so I might keep up. "Some might say so."

"Why didn't you tell me there was a high demon in New Orleans? And why in the world would we be going to meet him?"

We took a right on Toulouse. He pulled me closer. I knew it had nothing to do with a desire for intimacy, but more to become my shield.

"My intentions were to educate you on the nefarious underworld that has surrounded you your entire life when we met on Monday. However, due to the fact that you foolishly decided to play spy under the guise of strolling with a lover under the moonlight, I have decided to accelerate your schooling. Training starts tonight."

Geez, could this get any more humiliating? I had to defend myself on at least one point.

"He's not my lover."

A sidelong glance full of threatening heat. What did that look mean? Ugh. I hated when my voice sounded sulky and petulant. I felt like a grade-A moron already, but Jude had a way of making me cower farther into my shell. He was so…intense.

I continued to brood in silence as we ambled down Toulouse, until a sudden harrowing sensation gripped my heart in a vise. I stopped, jerked my hand free and peered over Jude's shoulder, realizing exactly where he was taking me.

"I'm not going in there."

My voice had dipped very low, almost inaudible. My Vessel senses skyrocketed. A new layer of warmth sealed my whole body in a snap. I stiffened into an unmovable line in the middle of the street. Jude faced me, but my eyes remained on the entrance beyond.

"Genevieve, I won't let anything harm you."

I shook my head. "I'm not going in there."

A primitive fear scaled my body, yelling, screaming for me to run. Run now. Run fast and far away. My eyes wouldn't unlock from the doorway, over which was a sign in the shape of a battle-ax with emblazoned red letters reading *The Dungeon.*

Mindy and I'd been partying with our friends in the Quarter many, many times. Every now and then, we'd straggle down Bourbon Street to sing karaoke at the Cat's Meow, have a hurricane at Pat O'Brien's, or dance to a tribute band at Krazy Korner. But, never, and I mean never, had we veered off our path to this place.

I'd always given it a wide berth, and now I knew why. Even before the universe knew what I was, a part of me already recognized this place as an epicenter of evil. My Vessel Sense radar had blown off the charts within ten yards of the door.

"I'm not going in there," I repeated, knowing full well I sounded like a monotonous robot. I stood in the middle of the street, frozen, trembling.

Warm hands cupped my face, shocking me to gaze up at the owner. Jude blocked my view of the sign, forcing me to look only at him. His mask of metal melted into softer lines. His gaze held something I'd never seen before—a gentle, coaxing tenderness. I pulled back from the brink.

"Genevieve." He used the sultry voice. I was listening. "I will not let anything harm you in this place. No one will even touch you. I promise. Do you understand?"

For a moment, I only stared, feeling the sensation of his warm palms against my cheekbones, mesmerized by the flecks of gold in his eyes. At the same time, he poured another layer of armor, of illusion, over my own. I could drown in this sense of serenity. I was safe with him.

"Do you trust me?"

"Yes," I finally muttered.

"Good girl."

A small smile, then he took my hand and led me into the mouth of hell.

I glued myself to his back as we passed down a dark, narrow passageway into an open, empty courtyard. He let me move ahead, guiding me into the dimly lit bar with his palm at the small of my back, never removing his hands from my body. I guessed that he must only be able to cast illusion on someone else if he were physically touching them.

Immediately upon crossing the threshold from the courtyard, I felt a physical punch of fear slam into my soul as if my spirit might just up and vacate the premises with or without me. A large hand slipped under my hair, wrapping firmly but gently around the nape of my neck like he did before. I shivered, hoping Jude would assume it was from the dark decor of the club and not the effect his touch had on me.

Mindy's favorite new club, Tartarus, was like glitter-Goth compared to this place. Painted skulls adorned posts and bar tops. I wouldn't be surprised if they were real skulls. Wooden cages instead of booths sat in every room, where black-bedecked patrons did unseemly things to each other. Wait, what *were* those two doing?

A woman with long black hair covering her face sat on a

guy's lap her back to his chest, her hands on his spread knees, her skirt flared, covering where they were obviously slow-fucking in public. The guy had his hands on her waist, guiding her up and down, but his gaze flicked to mine. He winked.

Heat shooting up my neck, I faced forward and blew out a shaky breath. As we rounded each corner, sinister demons stared from artwork adorning the walls. The most disturbing one was the horned devil in black and white, holding a goblet of red liquid in one hand and a still-beating heart in the other.

The patrons paid no attention to me but watched Jude with a fierce scowl. I'd already targeted two passersby as demons with red-glinting eyes, including the biker dude behind the bar. Most were simply humans who lived left of center.

An albino-pale guy with a shaved head passed us, dressed completely in black from head to toe. He held something in one tattooed hand, a chain, which draped over his left shoulder. I followed the silver line connecting to a spiked choker wrapped around a petite brunette's throat. Ghostlike with black lipstick, she wore a red corset and skintight leggings. She actually smiled at me as she passed.

My VS reached out, touching on the girl's psyche for the briefest of seconds. In that moment, I knew the girl was not being kidnapped or oppressed in any way. Quite the contrary, she was filled with ecstasy in her current state as an enslaved creature.

Seriously?

I would never let a guy chain me like a dog and drag me around. Then I laughed inwardly at my absurdity as Jude guided me by the back of my neck up a narrow stairwell, leading me like a marionette.

My wandering reverie stilled as we mounted the stairwell. Bone-deep dread pounded into me. As we reached the second floor, a song blared at an ear-splitting level. I recognized "Burn" by In This Moment right away. Couples were sort of dancing, grinding in a slow, fluid motion—an odd paradox to the violent beauty of the song.

The vocalist, Maria Brink, didn't exactly sing the lyrics, more like said them in a singsong way. Words about suffering as a blessing, death as life, and burning right before your eyes. The air of this place scraped at my Vessel shell, trying to get in. I trembled but fixed my face like stone, locking my jaw. Jude stopped me, leaning close.

"Breathe, Genevieve."

His lips brushed the top of my ear. I hadn't realized it, but he was right. I'd actually stopped breathing.

On the far wall sat a throne below a mounted dragon's head. In the corner of the room was a wooden perch where a huge black raven stared at the crowd. For a second, I thought it was real, but it didn't move or blink. I wondered how long the lifelike statue had been there. The eerie words of Edgar Allan Poe filtered through my mind: *And the raven, never flitting, still is sitting, still is sitting…and his eyes have all the seeming of a demon's that is dreaming.* The urge to run kept shoving at me.

A throng of Dungeon groupies sipped from goblets in true Goth style surrounding the one on the throne. I wondered if I'd stepped into a vampire coven, but as we all know, vampires don't exist.

Maria Brink screamed the word "burn" in a long, agonizing wail as if she were literally on fire. The sensation of walking directly toward a dark creature who would snatch the chance to own me like an animal, like the girl on the leash, with a woman screaming about burning alive sent me into a state of surrealism. I might have an out-of-body experience at any moment.

The man, if you can call him that, wore black dress pants, an expensive-looking white button-down with silver cuff links. He held a clear glass with crimson liquid and whispered intimately to a corseted, red-lipped blonde propped on the edge of his throne. I noticed a pewter skull ring on his forefinger.

Silver studs pierced pretty much everything, lining his

earlobes all the way up the cartilage. If it weren't for all the metal crap in his face, he might've been attractive. The blonde's cleavage spilled out of her top when she leaned forward for his pleasure. The creature's eyes grazed her a moment longer before turning his attention to us.

Annoyance skittered across his eyes when he saw Jude. And something else.

Jude nodded. "Dommiel."

The man pulled himself more upright, taking a sip from his glass.

"Greetings, Jude," he crooned as if a Dominus Daemonum stepping into his lair were an everyday occurrence. He tipped his glass up in a toast, "To the saint of lost causes."

I didn't miss the underlying insult. I glanced at Jude, seeing his eyes wiped clear of any light, his expression like granite. Apparently, he caught it too. Jude had that look about him when he's examining every minute detail, trying to discover what's hidden beneath.

Fixing my gaze on our host, I shuddered. His eyes had flickered to me. Though I couldn't tell their exact color as he observed from the shadows, one thing was for certain. There was no sign of the fiery-red hue coloring the irises of the other demons I'd seen so far. There was also no doubt in my mind, body or soul that this thing was in fact a demon. A high one.

"Mmmmm. You've brought me a gift?" he asked, letting his gaze rove up and down my body. "Overdressed but quite delectable. Come on, Jude. I'll give you mine if you give me yours."

The blonde slid Jude a seductive smile, tilting her voluptuous body so he could see all she had to offer. Apparently, this proposition was nothing new to her.

Jude repositioned himself directly behind me, moving his hand to wrap around my right hip. It was an act of possession. Not in any romantic sort of way, mind you. This was the way Jude did things. Subtle moves to let you know where you stood in his book. Right now he was telling this Dommiel dude I was in no way up for grabs.

I pressed back into the wall behind me, the six-foot-five wall of muscle and badass attitude, just so our host knew how *I* felt on the topic of swapping. Dommiel smiled, revealing a row of perfect gleaming-white teeth.

"So, Jude. If you're not here to share, then for what purpose do I owe this pleasure?"

His words lilted like liquid, one word pouring into the next.

"There's another high demon in your territory."

An unpleasant frown deepened Dommiel's brow, hooding his eyes further.

"None of my brethren would venture into my domain without proper homage."

"None of them, Dommiel? You don't know your kin like I do."

Jude's voice rumbled low and deep, vibrating through his chest to my back. Dommiel clinked his skull ring against the glass in thought.

"You're lying, Master of Demons," he replied with poison in his voice. "It's against our rules. What do you want?"

Rules. I needed a seriously long discussion with Jude on more of these damn rules.

"Obviously, there is something you do *not* know."

Cold drifted over me, like a draft when you're cozy in your warm bed and someone yanks the covers off you. I sucked in a short breath, knowing Jude had lifted his shield of illusion. Fear reared its ugly head, threatening to swallow me whole. His hand tightened on my hip, a warning to keep still.

Dommiel watched me with interest. There was a shift in the air. He set his glass down on a table at an insanely slow pace. A dawning flickered over his features. His creased brow straightened to a blank slate, then contorted into a mixture of feverish anger and hard lust.

He growled deep in his chest. I don't know what happened

next, because things moved literally too fast for me to see. One second I was pressed hard to the front of Jude; the next I was behind him. He had Dommiel on his knees before him with a long dagger pricking the hollow of the demon's throat. Seriously, I was standing there fearing for my life, then I blinked and Dommiel was cowering before Jude.

The raven in the corner cawed. It *was* real! The groupies shrank back, losing their façade of Goth-cool, except for the one who wasn't human. A lower demon lurched forward.

Jude put his free hand palm out and chanted three words in Latin. The demon bounced off an invisible wall and fell to the ground in a stupor. Jude then gripped Dommiel's shoulder and pressed the dagger blade so that a drop of black liquid trickled out, staining his pretty white shirt.

Jude inclined his head to Dommiel. From this angle, I could see that first emotion shining bright in Dommiel's eyes, the one he'd hidden the second he saw Jude walk in the door—pure, raw fear. His lips bared in a snarl, revealing a row of pointed teeth, two canines much longer than the others.

What the hell? I thought vampires didn't exist! The grating tone in Jude's voice made me take a step back, and he was on *my* side.

"If you or any one of your minions come near her, touch her, think of her or even breathe her name in your sleep, I will hunt you down and send you back to the *real* dungeon in such miniscule pieces that they will never…" Jude paused, shoving the point an inch into the demon's neck. Black oozed out. "They will *never* put you back together again."

Dommiel made a choking noise but nodded obedience immediately. Jude dropped him, grabbed my hand and led me back out the way we'd come, still holding the dagger in his right hand. I didn't protest. I couldn't get out of there fast enough.

Before we'd descended the stairs, Jude had shielded me again. I felt an electric snap, diluting the fear I'd been swimming in since he'd removed it. He slid the dagger into a sheath under his jacket as we made our way past the courtyard and through the claustrophobic pathway into the street.

We walked two blocks without saying a word. I had no idea where we were going now, and I didn't really care. My mind raced, repeating the scene over and over. My emotions stewed into a whirlpool—fear, safety, anger, relief, then finally pissed-off-beyond-belief.

We'd passed Jackson Square onto Ursulines Street. The crowds thinned. Only a group of three ambled down the walkway, laughing as they went. The joyful noise of the city infuriated me more. Everyone was going about their happy little lives, not knowing that creatures of the underworld lurked at every corner, waiting to prey on them.

I jerked my hand away and crossed my arms, walking on in silence. I felt his eyes on me but refused to meet them. His safety blanket of illusion vanished, leaving me cold again, making me even more furious.

"Why are you angry?"

I came to a halt. "Are you kidding me? What were you *thinking* taking me into that, that cesspool!"

My instincts weren't so far off with the whole minnow/shark-tank analogy.

"I had to know if he was the one trying to capture you. There was only one way to find out."

"Like hell! I can think of a million ways, like go in by yourself and do your demon-hunter mojo thing and say 'Hey. Know anything about a Vessel?' Get your answers, then go on your merry way."

Not that Jude did anything in a merry way.

"He's a high demon, a master in the art of deception. I could never trust his words."

"Why did you show him that I was a Vessel? Now he knows who I am, what I look like. It'll be pretty damn easy for him to find me now!"

I felt what was coming. The inescapable physical reaction I

always had when a catharsis of emotions boiled over. Hot tears welled in my eyes then trailed down my face, though I refused to make a sound. Jude stepped closer. I stepped back. He stopped, unreadable thoughts swimming in his black eyes. He glanced toward Jackson Square, then back at me.

"Give me your hand, Genevieve." He held his hand out, palm up, waiting.

"I want answers. Why did you set me up like that? You used me like bait."

I couldn't keep the hurt from my voice. His hand was still outstretched.

"High demons can deceive all creatures, human and otherwise. They have difficulty disguising emotion. I brought you to achieve two things, which I did. One, to establish that Dommiel was not the one behind the demon at the club the night I met you or the would-be abductors at your father's dojo. His violent reaction upon realizing you were, in fact, a Vessel confirmed my assumption. Two, to make him understand that you are in no way a possession he is allowed to add to his collection. Give me your hand. Now."

Okay. That was a lot to absorb. I wiped my face with the sleeve of my red jacket, then I put my hand in his, feeling a sudden snap of Jude armor. We walked on.

"Could you really do that? Cut him into a bunch of pieces?"

A sharp nod.

"But he wouldn't die?"

A shake of the head. "Demons don't die. They move into different realms and shift forms, but they never die."

I sighed heavily, feeling the weight of the world bearing down on me. How was I supposed to beat these guys if they couldn't be killed? How was I ever going to have any peace again?

"However," continued Jude, his large hand tightening around mine, "there are places they can be sent and states to which they can be expelled where a millennium is not long enough for them to regenerate. And if he disobeys me and tries to come near you, he'll fucking regret it."

His voice had gone rough and raw, his pace quickening.

"I'm assuming by places, you mean the place down there," I said, pointing.

His mouth quirked in an almost-smile. "It's not actually in the earth. That's a myth."

"Well, I know," I snapped, though my Catholic upbringing had filled my head with Danté's version of hell. A dark, fiery pit deep underground. "Speaking of myths, what's up with the fangs? You said there were no vampires."

"There are no vampires. Raw emotion draws the true beast out. You'll notice the eyes and mouth transform at times like this, sometimes more."

"Wait. Hold up. Explain this to me, then. That's not what Dommiel truly looks like? He looks worse than that?"

He actually laughed, the sound buzzing warmly in my chest.

"High demons have a permanent humanlike form."

"Humanlike? Nice."

"This may resemble their appearance before the Fall. Their perversions in hell and on earth have distorted them. They hide the beast within to live amongst humans, corrupting their souls as they go."

"Great," I sighed.

"You wanted answers."

"Sort of like Dorian Gray, right?"

He paused, glancing at me, obviously considering my literary reference. "I suppose, yet their portrait is concealed right beneath the surface not hidden in a room in their mansion. They can also shape-shift into other forms, animals, elements. They all have their favorite creature they like to mimic, typically keeping one around."

"Like a familiar? Like with witches?"

"Genevieve, there's no such thing as witches."

"Yeah, well, he sure did look like a creepy-ass vamp tonight. And you said there were none of those."

"Appearances can be deceiving," he said, his gaze drifting to mine. "The truth is far worse than Hollywood's glittery version of undead monsters."

"So, Dommiel's familiar is a raven? I saw it in the corner of the room."

"Yes. Not a natural raven either. High demons create unnatural spawn."

I sighed again, feeling like I had an endless stash of puffed-up air that had to be released. I knew this world was real now, but I could hardly process it all.

We passed under a gas lamp and stopped. We stood outside of Jude's home. As much as I felt protected in his presence, I feared being alone with him in his house more than anything else right now.

We appeared to be a romantic couple, holding hands along the sidewalk, but he was right. Appearances can be deceiving. He wasn't exactly human. He was my protector, not a suitor for my affections. I wanted to know why he was protecting me but decided to save that discussion for Monday. It was late, and I was exhausted—physically and emotionally. But I needed to clarify one more thing.

"I can feel your layer of illusion when you touch me. Dommiel could see straight through mine, but not yours. Will I ever be able to hide myself from them on my own?"

I needed to know this. I needed to know there would come a time when I could protect myself. He didn't respond at first, gazing at my hand held in his.

"Yes. You're still in your awakening. I have no timetable, but, one day, you won't need me to shield you."

His eyes met mine, pools of pitch. No emotion whatsoever glimmered there. A shiver trembled through me.

"Come. Let's get you home."

Whew. No sleepover.

He led us back toward the street, letting go of my hand. I scanned the cars to determine which one might be his. My eyes landed on a mode of transportation with badass written all over it. I knew exactly what it was, because I thumbed through Erik's magazines at the dojo in between classes, secretly fascinated by beautiful, hot, fast machines.

"You've got to be kidding me."

If it hadn't fit him so well, I'd say it was cliché. A sleek, shiny black Honda CBR1100XX Blackbird. It had made that year's list for the top five fastest motorcycles in the world.

Suddenly I was holding a helmet. I hadn't even noticed Jude had gone back into the house for helmets. Too busy drooling over his pretty bike. He zipped up his leather jacket and straddled the motorcycle while strapping on his helmet. He nodded to the tiny seat behind him and grinned.

"Saddle up."

I am well aware that Jude Delacroix is not dating material. One does not bring a demon hunter home to Daddy or do dinner and a movie with the likes of Jude. I doubt seriously the word "dating" is even in the demon hunter vocabulary.

Jude seems to have one mission in life—seek and destroy. Oh yeah, and protect.

Now, a man has needs, and he is fully equipped to fulfill those needs with pretty much whomever he wants. I mean, seriously, God was a poet the day he made Jude. But I was slowly realizing that whatever a Dominus Daemonum was, it wasn't completely human; therefore, he didn't fit into the category of regular men.

Having given a full disclaimer on all the reasons why I shouldn't be attracted to him, let me now confess how utterly and totally euphoric I felt riding behind him on one of the fastest motorcycles in the world, my thighs gripping his hips.

On top of that, he continued to shield me with his illusion, wrapping me in an otherworldly shell. Mind-blowing—zipping through the streets of New Orleans with my arms strapped around his waist and my chest pressed against his back. The experience was exhilarating. The man was divine. And the ride home was all too short, probably because we exceeded the speed limit the whole way. He pulled up close to the door.

Begrudgingly, I shifted off from behind him and removed my helmet.

"Hang on to it," he told me when I offered it back, removing his own. "Bring it to class on Monday."

"You're picking me up?"

"Do you honestly believe I would let you wander through the Quarter to my place unaccompanied? Your ability to cast illusion is growing but would only fool a lower demon."

I nodded. I resented the fact that he was becoming my keeper, like a babysitter, but I also didn't have a death wish. After meeting Dommiel, I in no way wanted to encounter one of the big boys on my own. Black-belt skills wouldn't help me there. I thought of Dommiel on his knees before Jude.

"Dommiel was terrified of you."

"As he should be."

Geez. Okay, Mr. Modesty.

"You told Dommiel that one of his brethren had broken the rules by coming into his territory. I thought they all had to follow the rules."

"They do. It's a compulsion greater than their desire for evil."

"Then how is there another high demon roaming in his territory? How is our phantom stalker able to break the rules?"

"Even within their aristocracy, there is order of importance. Those on the lower levels are always subject to those higher up."

Stunned for a second, I asked, "Do you mean there are higher demons within the high demon category? There's like someone worse than Dommiel?"

I realized my voice had risen to a screechy level, though I didn't yell for fear Mindy would come bouncing out here in her pink undies just to meet and drool over Jude.

"Dommiel is an arch-demon, the lowest in their aristocracy. The fact that someone has disregarded him in his own domain means we are dealing with either a duke or a prince, not one on his level."

I knew my mouth was gaping, but are you fucking kidding me?

He gave me a small smile. His demeanor was so light tonight. Mine was leaden, weighted with all I'd discovered, all I still didn't know, and the fact that my world was irrevocably changed forever. My life as an English major at Loyola with dreams of becoming an editor for a savvy magazine suddenly seemed ridiculously stupid. Now my dreams were to keep my ass alive for one more day.

"Don't worry, Genevieve," he said, reaching out to slide a stray lock behind my ear. He let his palm linger along my jaw, his thumb brushing close to my lips. With a sudden movement, he pulled away and strapped his helmet back on. "Not even a dark prince is a match for me."

He gave me a wink. A fluttering burst inside my belly.

Poor prince, wherever he was.

I went to the door but couldn't help myself. I glanced over my shoulder to watch him zoom off into the foggy gloom, feeling a little pang of regret it wasn't a sleepover night.

9

Sunday was the day Mindy visited her mom and I visited my dad. It was the day we clocked out of college/apartment life and went home to get spoiled for a bit. This was also the first Sunday after my new discovery that there really were monsters in the world, and a good many of them were hunting me. Still, it was Sunday, a holy day, so I was off-limits according to the rules.

I'd texted Jude early this morning with a demand to know the "rules." This was how the conversation went.

Me: Explain the rules. Please.

Jude: High and lower demons cannot possess a human host (or Vessel) on holy days, which includes the three days before Easter and that Sunday, Jewish Passover, Yom Kippur, and the Sabbath.

Me: What happened to Christmas?

Jude: That's not truly the day of Christ's birth. December 25th was originally a pagan holiday celebrating the winter solstice.

Me: Oh.

Jude: Demons are forbidden from entering sacred

ground, including churches, synagogues, graveyards and other places that are blessed.

Me: What about holy water?

Jude: What about it?

Me: Does it burn them or something if you throw some on them?

Jude: There is no such thing as vampires.

Me: I know, but we're talking about demons.

At this point, there was a lengthy pause where I could hear the heavy sigh through cyberspace.

Jude: No. Holy water does not affect them. Nor do crucifixes or other sacred objects.

Me: Well, that sucks. Is that all?

Jude: Those are the basics. Other rules pertaining specifically to Flamma I'll explain as we go along.

Me: Cool. Have a nice day! ☺

Pause. Pause. Pause.

Jude: ☺

I almost lost it! Jude sent me a smiley face. With my newfound knowledge, I looked forward to a day of normalcy. I wanted to relax like I did before all this began. Even more, I wanted to do something without my babysitter/guardian tagging along.

So, I took a quick shower, noting how quickly and smoothly the wound on my abdomen was healing. I twisted my hair into a messy bun, put on my favorite jeans and the sunny yellow Victorian-tailored blouse that made me feel pretty and sweet, then headed to Dad's as I did every weekend. Without informing Jude.

Dad was grilling burgers on the deck. Erik stood next to him, sipping a Bud Light. Even in casual clothes, he appeared tailored. I swear, he probably ironed his jeans and T-shirts.

Erik had moved here from Ohio a long time ago as a researcher for the National Wetlands Research Center. My dad had sort of adopted him when he started working nights at the dojo, so he was always around.

"Hey, guys!"

"There she is. You hungry?"

"Starving."

Dad gave me a one-armed bear hug with a spatula in the other hand.

"How'd that hot date go?" I asked Erik with a smile.

Dad placed the patties on a plate on the grill sideboard. "What hot date?"

Erik blushed all the way down his neck. I laughed.

"It was fine, Gen."

"Mmm, fine. Sounds exciting."

"Sweetie, would you go get the lettuce and onions in the fridge? Today's nice. We'll eat out here."

"Sure."

As I marched into the kitchen, my VS whispered over something, then was gone. Not a warning that Flamma were near like last night outside The Dungeon. No, it was almost a soft tapping, searching for something. As soon as I sensed it, the feeling left me.

When I opened the fridge, I burst out laughing. Dad always delivered his birthday presents in odd places. On my fourteenth birthday, I had to follow *The Nightmare Before Christmas* ringer "This is Halloween" until I found my first iPhone wrapped inside my stuffed Jack Skellington propped on the fireplace mantel. That was a cool one. I kept the same ringer for a year.

Now, leaning in front of the platter of sliced onions, tomatoes and shredded lettuce, there was a large rectangular envelope with my name scrawled on the front in Dad's slanted hand. He sketched an apple next to my name. Weird. I took the platter and the envelope out to the deck and sat down with the guys.

Dad grinned. I smiled back as I opened the envelope. The card was sweet, with a cartoon daddy and daughter hugging on the front. Inside, the bold font read: *No matter where you go, you're always Daddy's little girl.* Underneath, he'd written: *I've been stubborn about this long enough. I'm finally letting you go. Happy birthday, my beautiful baby girl.*

I started to tear up at the sentiment, having no idea what this meant until I read the brochure that slid into my lap. On the front were photos of Times Square, MOMA, the Statue of Liberty, Broadway. The heading read *Come to the City that Never Sleeps*. I squealed with delight.

"Ow," said Erik, "bring it down a notch."

"Dad! Seriously! Like seriously, seriously?"

Mindy and I had wanted to go together for ages. She'd already been twice with her mother, but Dad would never let me tag along. I jumped up and squeezed him tight, nearly strangling him from behind.

"Thank you! Thank you! Thank you!"

I did a giddy little dance before settling back into my chair, perusing the pamphlet.

"Well, you'll be going with Mindy and her mother the week of Thanksgiving. You can even see the Thanksgiving Day Parade while you're there."

"Mindy knows? How did she keep this from me?"

That girl could never keep a secret.

"Actually, I asked her mother to keep her out of the loop until today."

Suddenly my iPhone vibrated on the table with a crazy, excited text from Mindy, including twenty smiley faces and exclamation points. Talk about timing. I giggled while texting her back.

Then it hit me. How could I possibly go to New York now? How many demons were traipsing around New York? I might as well serve myself on a platter with an apple in my mouth.

"What's wrong, sweetie?" asked Dad, his butter knife midair with mayo on it. "Why the sad face?"

I couldn't tell him the truth. Now I was reduced to lying to everyone I cared about. I felt even worse.

"Oh, I was just thinking about Mom, how she loved the Thanksgiving Day Parade."

I knew this would dampen the mood, but I had to say something. And I wanted to say something that was at least half the truth.

I hated lying, and I hated liars. Now suddenly I was one of them. But in all honesty, my mom did love the Macy's Thanksgiving Day Parade. I can see her now, doling out cinnamon rolls while the turkey was still baking, saying, *"Oh, look, Genevieve! It's Charlie Brown."*

"Thank you, Dad. This is an awesome present," I said, forcing myself to smile and take a bite of my burger that threatened to lodge in my throat.

Erik glanced at his watch. "Oh, so sorry. I totally forgot I have a field appointment with my supervisor today."

"Where y'all headed today?" asked Dad.

"Not sure. Again, sorry to run so quickly."

"You didn't even finish your burger," I said, pointing to his plate.

He grimaced as he rose from his chair. "I'll have to take it to go."

He wrapped it up in a napkin and was gone. After lunch, I did the dishes while Dad adjourned to the sofa to watch the Saints play the Falcons on television. I wandered through, not really feeling like watching football today. Dad stretched out on the sofa, shoes off, and propped his feet on the coffee table.

"That's right, Drew! You got it!"

Touchdown. While Dad watched Drew Brees take the team to a victory, I walked up the wooden staircase to the second floor. I knew exactly where I was going, where I'd wanted to go ever since I had that nightmare at Jude's house. My dad kept one room entirely devoted to my mother's artwork, our own personal gallery. And memorial. After she died, he refused to part with any of her paintings, no matter how much collectors had offered for them. And they'd offered quite a lot.

The room's décor was sparse but elegant. Underneath a Persian rug of burgundy and creams, a gold brocade sofa with matching chaise sat around an oval cherry coffee table. A porcelain vase painted with two lovers in Victorian clothing on a picnic stood on a glass side table. A large mirror with gold trim squared itself above the antique fireplace. Having been built before central air-conditioning or heating, many of the rooms in our City Park home had fireplaces, not all functioning. There were no other furnishings except for the wall-to-wall paintings.

Starting with the wall to the right of the fireplace, I perused my mother's art. She focused on remaking the masterworks with new vitality, energy, and emotion. Here she'd given her own rendition of Monet's water lilies in shades of violet, purple and white. She recreated Degas's dancers into otherworldly angels floating on the stage. The back wall was a random mix of reinvented works by Van Gogh, Matisse, and Renoir. All of them reflected an inner joy which might or might not have been present in the original.

The last wall waited for me like the midnight toll of a clock. Among some rather distorted renditions of Picasso's works was "Les Demoiselles d'Avignon."

The original had always given me the creeps, but my mother's version transformed Picasso's black period even blacker with the chopped, distorted limbs of prostitutes who stared wide-eyed out from the canvas. A horror show of twisted, mangled women, both beautiful and terrifying. More than this, there were two others that had always haunted me.

My mother's adaptation of Vermeer's "Girl with a Pearl Earring" held the gaze of a young woman looking on the face of fear. If you glanced at it, there was only a slight difference from the master's version. The Baroque shadows were now dark crimson. But on closer study, you'd see the haunted expression in the girl's eyes, as if whatever she beheld made her blood run cold.

She had frozen in fright upon seeing something, long

enough for the artist to capture her fear. Her eyes widened just enough and in such a way to make the viewer tremble. In the glassy reflection of both eyes was the reflection of a dark figure approaching.

The worst part of this painting was that the girl had a distinct similarity to my mother. My stomach squeezed tight.

As my eyes wandered over canvas after canvas, my fingers played with the St. George medal around my neck, a nervous habit when Mom came to mind.

I moved on to the last one, far more disturbing. It was the remake of Paul DeLaRoche's "Le Jeune Martyre." I'd seen pictures of the original in the Louvre. A beautiful, angelic martyr floated in a pool with her hands bound. She was radiant, emanating an ethereal light as her gossamer gown drifted wide like a cloud. A golden halo crowned her head in death. The lingering shadows on the fringe of the painting hid a man leaving the scene, the one who had doomed her to this untimely death.

My mother painted it *exactly* like the original. Not one change in hue, not one variation in line or form. Someone could've taken a picture of LaRoche's in the Louvre, framed it side by side, and no one could detect the cheat. What troubled me most of all was the fact that this was the last work she ever painted.

I sucked in a breath. VS screaming. Flamma present and behind me. I spun around. Jude leaned against the fireplace with his arms crossed, shoulders rigid. Black eyes measuring, calculating. The door was still closed.

"How did you get in here? How did you get past my dad?"

He remained still, watchful.

"There are other means of entering a building than the front door."

"Yeah, there are. It's called breaking and entering."

He made no reply. I felt invaded upon here in this private place. I'm not sure why it unnerved me so much.

"Why didn't you tell me you were leaving home today?"

"Actually, this is my home. My apartment is a temporary place where I live with my best friend, but *this* is my real home. And I didn't think I had to tell you where I was every second of the day."

"It's dangerous."

"It's Sunday. There are rules. You told me so. I'm safe."

"I'll cast this house in illusion as well. But you are never safe away from a protector. Be sure of that."

"Away from you, right? And why do you even give a damn? What does a demon hunter have to do with a Vessel anyway? Is there an ulterior motive I should know about? Are you even listening to me?"

His gaze had strayed to the paintings behind me, specifically to the martyred beauty in a drowning pool. The expression on his face shifted, became harder. He straightened away from the mantel.

"These were your mother's paintings." He stated it as fact, not a question. His face had become a granite mask.

"Yes. And this is a *private* collection."

I wanted to shield her work from his eyes. Why was I so defensive?

He walked toward me, boots echoing on the wood floor. His attention remained fixed on the canvas above my head. He stood a foot away, for once not in my personal space, finally dropping his gaze to mine.

"She was mad."

I flinched as if he'd slapped me. "You don't know anything about her. These are paintings, just..." Flustered and angry, I wanted to hit him.

He scanned the room carefully, finally coming back to "Le Jeune Martyre." "She was insane."

His words were scorched with a cold rigidity. No spark of light in his eyes now. Why was he saying such a heartless thing about my mother?

"You didn't know her."

"It's apparent. You had to have known this already."

"Stop saying that! Stop it! Just get out! I don't want you in my home. I don't want you invading my privacy. You've already taken everything else away—my future, my hopes, my freedom. Leave me alone!"

I yelled. I raged. I cried. I buried my face in my hands, letting it all out. My VS shrank away, and I knew he was gone without opening my eyes. I was more alone than I'd ever been in my entire life. More alone than the day we said goodbye to my mother.

I ran to my childhood room, closed the door, and fell onto my bed and wept. The world had dealt me a cruel, cruel hand, and I wasn't up for it. I grieved.

My old life was dead, and the new one was too much for me to bear. Thunder rumbled in the near-distance, reverberating off my windowpane. As sobs subsided onto my damp pillow, I drifted into a broken, dreamless sleep.

THE SOFT SOUND OF PATTERING RAIN AGAINST THE WINDOW woke me. The day had darkened, making my white room gray. I roused and trudged downstairs. The television still hummed with football commentators, but for another game. Dad had dozed too. I sat on the end of the sofa, gazing at the man who'd shaped my world.

Dad was a tall physical powerhouse. Not to mention that several of the single moms coming in to the dojo tried their damnedest to get his attention. To me, he was Dad—protection, safety, and love.

Though I knew he loved me dearly, he could no longer protect and keep me safe. There is only one person I knew of who could, and I'd sent him away.

Dad shifted and opened his eyes. "Hey, there," he said, voice groggy.

"Hey."

"Why so down? Still thinking of your mother?"

He knew I only went to the upstairs gallery when I missed her and needed to connect in some way. I nodded. He sat up, rubbing his face with his hands. His hair was sweetly tousled.

"Did you…?" I started. I stopped. Unsure whether I could ask this question.

"What is it? Go ahead."

"Was she, was she sick in the end?"

He sobered, angling toward me. Rain poured onto the deck outside, mirroring my emotions. "Gen, your mother was sick. Of course she was. Anyone who would do what she did must be."

"But what I mean was, had she gone crazy? Like, really and truly crazy?"

I had no more tears to shed on the matter. I wanted to know the truth. I was only ten when she killed herself. I'd gone through all the emotions a child does—blaming myself, blaming my father, blaming the world. Now I just wanted to know really and truly—why?

"Toward the end, she became restless, obsessed, painting all the time and never painting the beautiful things she used to. She was angry, afraid, and depressed. I took her to a psychiatrist, but nothing helped. Not even medication. In the end, she only saw one way to end her suffering."

He reached over and took my hand, giving it a gentle squeeze.

"It had nothing to do with you. You know that, right?"

"Yes, Dad." I nodded and tried to smile.

I gave him a hug to reassure him I hadn't fallen into my own depression. Sometimes he watched me with an odd expression. I wondered now if he was waiting for my mother's madness to rear its ugly head as if it were hereditary or something.

"I've gotta go, Dad. Class early in the morning."

He saw me out to the porch. I made a mad dash for my car,

realizing with a sharp pang that Jude's motorcycle was nowhere in sight. Nor was he.

The awful things I'd said started spinning through my head on the drive home. He didn't deserve my anger, my bitterness. The worst part was that he had been right, and deep down, I knew it all along. Why he became so cold while staring at the painting, I don't know, but no matter what, I was still the one in the wrong.

"Oh hell!"

I hit the steering wheel with the palm of my hand and headed for the French Quarter. The streets were empty with the downpour settling in. Lightning flashed. I pulled onto the curb a block down from Jude's place, the closest spot I could find.

Of course, I had no umbrella. I never did. Mindy kept like four in her car, all in varying shades and patterns to match whatever ensemble she happened to be wearing when caught in the rain. Me, I never had one. I ran as fast as I could, realizing the rain had pushed in a cool front. I could feel the air dropping by degrees since I'd left my dad's ten minutes ago.

I ran into the alcove and found the gate locked. I was nearly soaked through, shivering and wishing I could get into Jude's warm living room and wait there. Perhaps I should come back later. My emotions had caused me to react irrationally, defensively.

Discovering that my mother had indeed been ill, choosing suicide over fighting another day, left a trail of bitterness in my gut. I could never face the truth before now. Before Jude. I didn't even know what I was going to say to him. I just knew I needed to apologize. He didn't deserve my anger.

The temperature was dropping, and I had no idea when he was coming back. I had decided to leave when my VS tingled. I felt him approaching. He rounded the corner, swathed in shadow.

"Jude, I wanted to—"

My pulse sped up frantically. He stalked toward me in long,

smooth strides. Wearing black jeans and a white button-down, wet and clinging to his skin, he moved with determined purpose straight toward me. As if he knew I was there. As if he knew I was waiting. His eyes gleamed molten gold, and in them I read only one feral emotion—hunger.

Never had I seen this hue or emotion shining in his eyes. Not like this, edged with steel and violence. I knew he was something other, but in that moment, I truly feared where he'd come from and who'd made him.

I couldn't move. I waited, like a doe in the headlights.

He reached me, grasped my wrists, and pinned them to the wall above my head. He crushed his lips to mine and covered my body with his in one swift move. A whimpering noise escaped my lips, barely, before he devoured any other sound of protest or pleasure.

Demanding submission, he explored my mouth with lips and tongue. God, how I'd imagined what kissing him would be like. This wasn't it. Fire branded me from the inside out. All thoughts of anything else fled. Gone. All I wanted was this. All I could think, smell, breathe was Jude. His body pressed against mine, a visceral friction clawing between us.

One hand cuffed my wrists; the other gripped my jaw firmly, keeping me in place so he could do as he pleased. I could hardly breathe from the shock of the assault to my senses as he slanted his mouth over mine, tongue stroking deep.

His hand trailed down my body, over my soaked shirt, then under. A large hand squeezed my hip, caressing up the side of my waist along bare skin. He nipped at my lower lip as if he longed to consume me, bit by bit. I wasn't complaining. He released my mouth, biting along my jaw. So rough.

"So sweet," he whispered.

Words I'd never imagined he'd say. I panted, trying to catch my breath. He trailed scorching kisses down my neck. My skin burned, like being licked by fire. My Vessel sense flared into orbit, screaming for these sensations to stop. I wondered fleetingly how my mind and my body could have totally different opinions on the matter.

He shifted away just enough so his hand could trail over my rib cage, then higher. He clasped my breast—a proprietary feel, not a lover's caress. He pinched my nipple through my bra—hard—rolling it till it peaked for him. He growled and rolled his pelvis, grinding his hard dick between my parted legs.

"Wait, Jude," I murmured.

He apparently was as overwhelmed as I was. He lowered his hands to my outer thighs and lifted me up, pushing his pelvis to hold me in place, again showing me the extent of his desire, grinding against me on a moan.

His desire was more than evident. My thoughts scrambled from the sensations burning through my body. Too much. Too much. The dynamic of our relationship had changed in a blink.

Feeling faint, knowing I needed to reel this in as we were both overcome, I tried to lower myself. He pushed harder against me, growling. Dropping one leg, he hooked his fingers over the collar of my blouse and yanked it down over one shoulder, popping the top three buttons. Sharp teeth grazed the skin along my lower neck near my pulse.

"Jude!"

Warning bells clanged inside, trying to wake me up. I heard them. Too late. Pointed teeth punctured my skin. I cried out. Stinging pain ripped through me as he drank from the bite, sucking hard and fast.

"Stop!"

Panic seized me. I shoved at his chest, moving him only an inch, but enough to get both feet on the ground. He released my throat with a groan, his tongue licking one more time over the bite. I stared where my hands landed, splayed across his chest. Through the thin shirt and along the V of the open neckline, I saw…nothing. No sharp-edged, lovely lines of a cresting Celtic cross. My heart hammered like a rabbit who's been caught by the cat, waiting for the death blow.

"You have no tattoos," was all I could say, stupidly. The truth dawning second by second, the air growing colder.

"I have no use for that."

Not Jude's voice. Somehow, I found the courage to look up into his eyes. Molten gold glimmered, then bled into crimson.

"Oh God," I whispered in a trembling broken voice.

His lips contorted into a lopsided grin, exposing a full row of sharp teeth, two extending longer than the rest.

"No, baby. Guess again."

10

I couldn't move. Couldn't speak. Couldn't breathe. I was in the arms of the high demon who wanted me as his own.

"So lovely," he said, trailing a finger down my cheek. I flinched, feeling as if I'd been cut with an icy blade. "So soft."

My Vessel senses protested, registering every sensation on an agonizingly painful scale. A freezing fever began to spread from every point of contact—his thighs against my hips, his chest against mine, one hand at the nape of my neck, the other petting me where he pleased. The bite on my throat throbbed with chilling pain. A paramour of ice had me in his clutches, and I was helpless to do anything about it.

He looked like Jude, a distorted, monstrous version of him. An abomination of beauty and beast. Nausea swelled in my stomach. His touch produced a flash of memory.

I was seven years old and sitting next to a bubbling cauldron, wearing my witch costume for Halloween. Dad dropped blocks of dry ice into a pot with gloved hands. I dared to touch a piece with my bare finger, yanking it back in pain.

"Don't touch, sweetheart. It's so cold, it burns."

My eyes fixed on the not-Jude, demon eyes grazing over me

with a hungry expression that made me sick. I trembled. So cold, it burned.

"Stop," I choked out, panting.

Desperately trying to regain control, I called on my Vessel Sense, not knowing how or what to do. I closed my eyes, seeking that place that opened when I needed it, yearning for some form of protection. My VS responded. Like a beacon in the night, an inner light pulsed outward. I felt an expansion of warmth from my core.

The beast pressed his finger to my lips. I winced, jerking my eyes open, blue flames burning wherever he touched. The pulse died away as swiftly as it had come.

"Shh, pretty little thing. No need for all that. I'm not going to climb inside just yet," he said in a silky voice, threading both hands through my hair along the sides of my head. I feared he would crush my skull. Perhaps he just wanted to show me he could. "Too pure in there at the moment. But we'll take care of that, won't we?"

Red eyes narrowed; a beastly grin widened. He licked a drop of blood from one pointed canine. I trembled and couldn't stop.

"Perhaps you'd prefer a more pleasing form."

Dark hair lightened to gold, fiery eyes iced to sky blue, sharpened teeth smoothed to a fine row of pearly whites. A perfect face—angular lines, chiseled, not sharp.

"There, now. Better? I don't much care for wearing the hunter's shell anyway."

Fear prickled like needles through my veins. My body was stone. I'd seen this face before—beautiful, grinning, glacial, menacing. He was the one locked in combat with Jude in my vision of an ancient time.

Lightning struck nearby, brightening the face of my captor for a fleeting second.

"Who are you?" I managed to whisper in a quivering breath.

"You may call me Danté. You are far more lovely than I

thought. I couldn't wait any longer to meet my bride. The temptation was too much. I never have been one for patience."

Bride! My body cringed, wanting to fold inward upon itself. I stared in shock at the beautiful demon entrancing me with storm-cloud eyes. He trailed a finger along the bite mark at my neck.

"And now you're mine."

He angled his head as if he were listening for something. His gaze slid toward the alcove entrance for a split second.

"One more taste before I go."

"No—"

He crushed his lips to mine before I could form a thought—tasting, demanding, thrusting his tongue along mine. I struggled, tearing my mouth away to the side. Teeth sliced through my bottom lip. I cried out as he backed away, releasing me. I slipped sideways, staring at the beautiful specimen. He smiled, canines at full length again. Blood smeared his wicked grin. My blood.

"Be sure to give the Master of Demons my name. Till next time, my sweet."

He blew me a kiss, then his body evaporated into wispy gray mist, sliding between the bars of the wrought-iron gate and into the air.

I heard the slide of steel, a sword being pulled from its sheath. Through the alcove stepped Jude, the real one, black-eyed and fuming with iron weapon in hand. My body slipped against the brick wall, falling toward the pavement. He caught me. It seemed Jude was always catching me before I hit the ground.

"A prince," he grumbled, gravelly voice vibrating against me, cutting like shards.

He held me close, a fiery blaze against the bitter cold chilling me to the bone. At first I thought he was squeezing me, but he wasn't, even though the air was being sucked from my lungs. I gasped. Then I could breathe again. The next thing I knew, we were standing in his living room.

"Whuh…"

I was dizzy, but I didn't pass out. First, we were standing in the alcove, then we were standing in his house next to the sofa in less than a second. I trembled even more. He sheathed his sword and set me down on the sofa, dark eyes assessing. He slanted my chin to the side, catching sight of the bite.

"Fuck!"

"What?" I asked through chattering teeth.

I didn't know if I shook from the cold, the trauma, the arctic touch of the prince, or the abrasive, angry manner with which Jude was handling me.

"You've been marked." His voice cut the air. "What did he look like?" he demanded while grabbing the fleece blanket from the armchair and wrapping it tight around my shoulders.

I could hardly speak through the quivering. He stood up and did something near the fireplace. A sharp crackle, and a fire came to life.

"What did he look like, Genevieve?" He stood directly in front of me, gaze hard and focused.

"Y-you."

Jude went still—predator still, deathly still, grim-reaper-standing-on-your-doorstep still. His eyes roved over my open blouse, the loose threads where buttons once held it together, my swollen lips, the abrasions and bite on my neck. His voice dipped so low and so soft I could hardly understand him.

"Did he tell you his name?"

His eyes fixed on me in such a way I thought that if I moved a muscle, the tiger would pounce. I was afraid, knowing the demon boasted about who he was and wanting Jude to know his identity. I'd not forgotten the image of a younger, tattoo-free, rage-filled Jude locked in a warlike embrace with this same demon prince.

"Answer me."

"He said his name was Danté."

Black. Black. Black.

Irises, pupils, and the whites of his eyes blanched of all color but the deepest pitch. He seemed to be something so other, I feared he might transform into a supernatural beast right before my eyes. A blazing aura whipped in the air. Razor-edged energy cut and slashed in waves around his body, slicing outward across my skin.

"You're hu-hurting me," I whispered.

He wasn't even touching me. He closed his eyes, trying to rein in the turbulent rage filling up the room. I scooted back onto the sofa. He spoke, articulating three words in a deep, guttural, almost-animal voice.

"Do. Not. Move."

He vanished. If ever I was in doubt of whether or not he was human, the answer was absolutely, irrefutably *no*.

I sat there for I don't know how long, wondering if I should flee the premises. Who was I kidding? I was too terrified to go anywhere. Jude obviously had some otherworldly ability to do great harm, but that harm was always directed at the bad guys. The monster that caught me on the street would definitely harm me.

I tucked my knees to my chest, willing the scene away from my mind. I'd given myself over so willingly, thinking he was Jude. I hadn't objected for a single second.

All my lofty thoughts of considering Jude just a platonic protector flew out the window. I wanted him. Bad. My body had responded automatically to his lips—no, not *his* lips. I was going to be sick. I wiped the back of my hand across my mouth, wishing I could erase the demon's touch.

"Ow."

The cut was puffy and swollen, stinging. Minutes passed. Still no Jude. I knew he told me not to move, but this was ridiculous. I sat there, exposing way more than made me comfortable.

I crept into his room—stark, neat, and clean—and took a brown T-shirt from the top drawer. I felt a little embarrassed going into his personal things, but I wasn't going to stay like this till he came back. Heading into the hall bathroom, I jumped at my own reflection. A ghostly pale girl with a trickle of blood dripping from one of the puncture wounds stared back at me.

My pretty yellow blouse was bloodstained and ruined on the left side, not to mention the rip exposing me to the world. How many times was I going to end up looking this way—battered and bloody?

Stripping off the blouse, I dropped it in the waste bin and splashed my face and neck with warm water. Then I toweled myself dry, cleaning all traces of Danté's marks.

Unfortunately, I couldn't erase the bite mark at the base of my throat, hissing between clenched teeth as I tried to clean the area. I pulled on Jude's shirt, which smelled of him, and stared at the pale, blue-eyed girl in the mirror.

"What did you do?" I asked her, shaking my head.

To plummet from ecstasy to sheer terror so fast had my head spinning. My heart had expanded with the feel of Jude's lips and hands on me, retracting the instant I realized it wasn't him at all. I couldn't bear for Jude to know the truth—I'd melted into the demon's embrace, believing it was his arms that held me, his hands touching me, his tongue in my mouth. I cringed at the shame of it all.

The demon prince took Jude's form, knowing I would not run. He pinned my wrists, thinking I might protest Jude's advances. How elated he must've been when I was well and beyond receptive.

I moped back to the sofa and curled into a ball, wrapping myself in the blanket. Still no Jude.

The icy sting in my neck had started to subside, the throbbing pulse slowed, and the shivering had stopped altogether. I stared into the crackling flames, a warm gold around the hearth shadowing the room. One blue flame licked up from the bottom, drawing my eyes.

11

I hadn't realized I'd fallen asleep, but there I was, certainly in a dream world. A dark fantasy. There was no light of any kind, but I could still see. Silky folds of a white gossamer gown shimmered over my body, hugging at the bodice, the hem brushing my ankles.

My dark hair hung in long, soft waves down my back. Cool gray mist curled around me, parting as I passed. My bare feet skimmed over black sand, the path winding toward a shadowed castle.

I stepped up to wrought-iron gates, their spires pointing like knives into the sky. Wait, there was no sky, only a murky abyss above.

Something made a movement on a low niche in the black cliff to my left. A spindly creature of gray bone and dangling flesh scuttled farther into a crevice, white eyes watching me. A red spider crawled out of a hole in the side of its throat, then disappeared in a cavity somewhere around its rib cage. I had no reaction whatsoever, as if this gruesome sight were normal.

"Touch the gate," the thing whispered in a dry, raspy voice.

I did. The gates swung wide. My feet touched lightly over smooth, black stones. The fortress loomed large with pointed lines holding the stone in place. I stared up at the Gothic castle, beckoning me closer.

Flying buttresses jutted out at wide angles, like massive dragon wings. Gargoyles of varying sizes and shapes squatted on columns and niches along the wall—grotesque, pot-bellied, beady-eyed, sharp-clawed, gaping-mouthed, and watching. They were stone, and yet I felt their hollow eyes following my progress toward the black doors.

Why was I not afraid?

Edging closer to the entrance, I crossed under a pointed tympanum. The double doors stood three times my size, made of wood with iron nailheads and no knob or knocker of any kind. There was a gash in the dark wood as if some great beast had tried to claw its way in, but to no avail.

"Touch the door," came the hissing command of that thing back near the gate.

I did. The door swung wide.

Unlike the exterior, the inside welcomed me with warmth and beauty. The room had a medieval air with modern luxuries. Crystal chandeliers, gold candelabras, well-lit with white candles, and a massive fireplace with crackling flames illuminated the vast hall.

Plush carpets of every shade were tastefully fitted between plush sofas, chaise lounges, and overstuffed chairs in burgundy and black brocade. Black velvet throw pillows adorned every piece of furniture, inviting guests to sprawl and enjoy.

Piano music echoed through the great hall, but there was no one there. I stepped lightly into the room, my sheer gown caressing my skin with each step. The music lured me to a corner, where a white grand piano echoed the music of a melancholy tune—Mozart's Requiem. When I stepped up to see the musician, I was not surprised, nor was I frightened. Danté had his eyes closed, playing the notes as if he knew them by heart, as if they echoed from his very soul.

He slowly opened his eyes, still playing the keys, and smiled at me. I smiled back. Why would I do that?

"Come here, my love, and sit next to me."

I felt like a Stepford wife robotically following the commands of my oppressor. But in this instance, I obeyed his will with pleasure, sitting next to him with a ready smile.

"You are so lovely and fair," he said, still playing while gazing on my face. His voice lilted with charm. I wanted to hear more sweet words from those lips. "You will be the perfect mistress of my domain, and I will be the perfect master."

A glint of red twinkled in crystalline eyes, then was gone. I sat there, gazing on him with admiration. He was so beautiful. The golden light of the room cast him in an aura of perfection, blond hair waving perfectly to the nape of his neck, clear-blue eyes gazing on me intently, well-formed lips smiling just right.

"I have been alone for far too long, Genevieve."

He stopped playing. The fire crackled. There was no other sound.

"I apologize if I frightened you today. It was not my intention."

He cupped my cheek, sweeping his thumb across my lip. There was no cut or pain. I leaned toward his hand, closing my eyes at his touch. A compulsion I couldn't resist. Why?

"That's right, love. Deep down, you know where you belong."

When his lips pressed hard against mine, I felt the icy chill of death at once but could not make myself resist him. On the contrary, I wanted him as he wanted me, all along feeling the grip of ice crawling up my spine, bleeding into my bones.

"You are mine now," he whispered against my lips.

"Yes," I murmured, threading my fingers into his golden hair, leaning into his cold embrace.

The great black doors exploded open, knocking them off the hinges. A gusting wind carried chanting words, a familiar voice, snuffing out every candle and the roaring fire in one swoosh.

The prince's eyes flared blood-red. My body slid away from his with my arms still outstretched toward him. He stood, furious. A golden prince veiled in shadow. I felt myself being carried by the wind back out of the luxurious room, past the smashed doors, through the open gates and past the thing cowering on a precipice of the rocky outcropping, scuttling deeper into its crevice.

My eyes shot open. I gasped as if I'd been underwater. The figure of a man, Jude, was beside me, over me, chanting with large hands wrapped around my skull.

The cold fear that had been absent in my dream gripped my body so tight I started to cough and spasm. I jumped backward on the sofa, punching out at him, totally freaking the fuck out. A cold sweat covered my body and dampened my scalp. Jude held his hands out in a calming gesture.

"Shhhh. It's me, Genevieve."

"How do I know it's you! It was supposed to be you last time!"

"It's me."

He leaned closer into the lamplight from where he sat beside me. Black eyes swirled with flecks of gold; the whites of his eyes had returned to normal. The familiar hard, impenetrable mask shielded his thoughts. Yes, it was him.

"Well, damn it! I couldn't tell. We need a code word or something."

"A code word."

"Yes! Like Rapunzel or Rumplestiltskin or something."

"A fan of fairy tales?"

My breathing was almost back to normal. "Yeah, actually, I am."

"Then Rumplestiltskin it is."

I nodded, noticing an unusual smell on him—earth and electricity. He appeared calm and in control again.

"What happened? Where'd you go anyway?"

"You don't want to know."

"Okay, then how in the hell did you get there! And don't tell me I was seeing things. You just vanished."

He straightened himself on the sofa facing me and sighed in a sort of resigned way. "It's called sifting, moving between space, not vanishing."

"You mean like time travel?"

"No. More like travel between space and dimension."

"Space, like stars-and-the-cosmos space?"

"Space as in the unlimited or incalculably great three-dimensional realm or expanse in which all material objects are located and all events occur."

My heart still hammering from that insane dream and my body buzzing with adrenaline, I finally said, "You lost me there, Einstein."

He watched me carefully, seeming to recognize my fragile state, but he carried on with his explanation. "The plane in which all things exist in this dimension and other dimensions."

Jude seemed to revert to facts and concrete things when I was out of sorts. Maybe he didn't have much experience with hysterical females. Not to be cliché, but hell, I deserved to be hysterical after what I'd just experienced. And now he was blandly talking about time travel. Or space travel. It was hard to keep it all straight.

"So, you can move like superfast here on earth where people can't see you, and you can move in other dimensions, as in dimensions that are not earth."

"Close enough."

"Okay."

"I didn't tell you this sooner for fear it would frighten you."

"Well, you were right. It scared the bejeezus out of me! But no more than—" I broke off, gesturing toward the courtyard, not wanting to say the name of the demon prince.

His voice gentled, became much softer than usual. "There

was no other alternative. I needed you in a protected space. Quickly."

I was still curled into a ball, backed into the corner.

"Your house is protected? Like spells and stuff."

He cocked an eyebrow. "Spells? I thought we had our discussion about witches."

"Yes, yes. They don't exist. I got that. So what, holy water or something?"

"A cast of protection. Some Flamma have this power. You will too. One day."

I gave a curt nod. "I just wish it could protect me from nightmares. I don't want to have another one like I just had."

His face shifted from slightly relaxed, as much as Jude actually relaxes, to stone once again. "It wasn't a nightmare."

"What do you mean? It certainly wasn't a daydream. I was out cold. I went to this other terrible place."

"He marked you. You were soul-sifted to his lair. It wasn't a dream of any kind. Dreams are subconscious fragments within your mind. None of what you experienced took place in your mind."

"Wait a second…soul-sifted?" I thought my head was going to pop off. "My soul left…my body?"

"Having tasted your blood, the prince," he ground out, as if saying his name were too painful, "now has the ability to summon your soul, among other things. I should not have left you, but I was unable to… I needed to leave before things became volatile."

Before they became volatile? They were pretty damn volatile before he left.

"Please, I need you to tell me in plain English. Are you saying my soul left my body?"

He nodded. "When I returned, I knew what had happened instantly. I didn't think he would summon you so soon. I called you back at once."

I thrust both hands through my hair along the sides of my

temples, trying to grasp this.

"What would've happened if you hadn't brought me back? Would my soul be stuck there forever in that fucking Dracula castle?"

I think his jaw popped. Or he was literally grinding his teeth to the bone. "No. He needs you, body and soul. Soul-sifting you is a way for him to, how should I put this, woo you."

I actually snorted a laugh, but there was no joy in it. "This is dating in the demon world?"

"It's no laughing matter."

"Trust me, Jude, I in no possible way find any of this funny."

Perhaps it was the sudden crack in my voice or desperation in my eyes, but his tense vibe ebbed a tad.

"I thought demons couldn't do their dirty work on holy days. That's what you told me."

"No, I told you they couldn't take possession of another being on holy days, which he did not."

I stared at the fire in the hearth, trying to come to grips with a new fear I'd never imagined, that my soul could actually be pulled from my body without my permission. I tried to imagine what it would be like if a demon took possession of my body.

Would my soul be stuck inside with the demon too? Or would it go to some other place?

"When I was there," I started hesitantly, "I couldn't, I mean, I didn't have full control of myself. It was like I wasn't myself."

Jude sighed. "He's marked you. With your blood, he can manipulate you to a certain degree, have a certain amount of control through soul-sifting."

I nodded but made no other response, remembering the haunting way I fell so easily into Danté's arms.

"Genevieve, I understand this all must be difficult for you, but there are certain things I must know. Now."

His voice had dipped lower than usual, taking a more serious tone, if that was even possible. His eyes darkened ever so slightly. His posture stiffened.

"Which are?"

"Have you ever murdered someone with willful intent?"

"What! No! Not with *any* kind of intent. That's ridiculous."

"Have you ever physically or emotionally harmed someone with malicious intent, with hatred on your heart?"

I shook my head. "Of course not. What is this Jude? Why—"

With each answer, he seemed to relax a fraction. "Just one more. Are you still an innocent, a maid?"

What the hell? Is he asking me what I think he's asking me? A maid? Who says that in the 21st century? I didn't respond. This was *so* personal and none of his damn business.

"Are you still a virgin?"

"I sincerely don't think that's any of your business."

My lips clamped shut. I knew I was blushing, feeling heat flush my cheeks and neck. I was still tightly curled in a ball, feeling smaller and smaller by the second. He leaned toward me, eyes carefully measuring.

"Answer the question."

When he spoke to me that way, I could do nothing else but obey. I wondered if he used some sort of Stepford mumbo-jumbo like the Lord of Goth back in my dream. Wait, not a dream. I was feeling overwhelmed and exhausted again. I'd been feeling this way a lot lately.

"Genevieve."

A gentle coaxing. Tenderness from Jude made my heart beat a little faster. Finally, I nodded. His squared shoulders visibly relaxed. I became quite busy fiddling with a loose thread on the fleece blanket.

"Why do you need to know any of this? It's so…so personal."

Of course I was only referring to the last question, but I'd never admit it.

"I needed to know what we were up against. A Vessel with

untainted hands, heart, and body has a better chance of keeping the demons at bay, so to speak."

"Not funny, Jude."

I was suddenly glad I hadn't let Jeffrey Davis talk me into that age-old cliché, sex on Prom Night like he so very much wanted to. I'd always guarded that part of myself.

Perhaps it was because my mother had always taught me to be a good girl. Even after her death, I had wanted to please her. I gasped, realizing what Jude just said and what this meant, and for some insane reason, I was unable to filter the thought running through my head and out of my stupid mouth.

"Does this mean I have to stay a virgin *forever*?"

Why, oh why did I ask that question? The languid smile spreading across Jude's face had my heart hammering hard against my ribcage.

"No," said the man whose voice made things melt inside me. He leaned closer and traced a finger along my jaw, searing me with heat. "Not forever."

Before I could digest the intent behind those words, he stood and outstretched his hand.

"Now, come, let us get you into bed."

I know I must've drained sheet white.

He laughed a full, throaty laugh. The first time I'd heard it, and I somehow knew I'd need to hear that sound for the rest of my life.

"You are *sleeping* in my bed. Alone. I'll escort you to class in the morning."

I nodded, too tired to argue. As soon as I placed my hand in his, a shock of Jude armor enveloped me.

"Why are you casting illusion?"

He glanced back with a frown as we came to the side of the bed.

"Instinct, I think," he said, as if he hadn't realized he'd done it. Weird.

I climbed under the gray down comforter, lying on my side.

So cozy, but a frightening thought frosted my heart in ice.

"What if he summons me again?" I asked almost in a whisper as I snuggled my head into the pillow. The bed didn't smell like him at all. Just clean, unused.

Jude gave me a closed-mouth smile. "He won't be able to. I'm going to chant you into a dreamless sleep. You'll be safe."

Somehow, I trusted whatever Jude told me. If he said I was safe, then I was, so I closed my eyes. He switched off the pewter lamp on the side table.

One of his hands brushed aside my hair, then remained still, covering my temple and forehead. He planted his other hand on my shoulder.

"Will I be able to sift?" I whispered.

"Sifting is a power of the angels. Only they can give this power to other Flamma."

Eyes still closed, I asked, "But demons can sift too. He… Danté sifted."

Jude remained quiet for a moment, his fingers brushing softly at my temple. "High demons can sift."

My mind was already slipping into deep relaxation, but I managed one last question. "How?"

"They were once angels. They are the Fallen. Now, relax and go to sleep, Genevieve."

Jude whispered words in Latin, lulling me into serenity. I caught some of them—*haven, encircled within, wings of, hearth and home*.

The chant was songlike. It reminded me of the Gregorian chant my high school English teacher used to play while we took tests. The words didn't make sense to enhance a dreamless sleep, but none of this really made sense. All I knew was that whatever he was doing chased away the edge of fear, sadness, and confusion.

Perhaps I imagined or dreamed it, but as I slipped further into a quiet oasis of warmth, I felt someone combing my hair with featherlight fingers.

12

Mary had been right. Professor Bennett's exam on Milton was a torture device masquerading as an assessment of *Paradise Lost*. After ten short discussions and two multi-paragraph essays requiring textual evidence, I thought my brain was going to melt. Bennett was such a sadist. He loved making us sweat, and he was doing a damn fine job of it today.

The exam had already begun when I'd crept in a minute late. Malcolm had given me a sharp, annoyed glance before burrowing back into his test. That was when I remembered I'd promised to call him after the incident in the French Quarter and had failed to keep that promise.

Geez, Genevieve. Can you get any more inconsiderate?

Mary gave me a two-fingered salute as she dropped her test on the pile on Bennett's desk. Of course, Bennett wasn't even present. His annoying grad assistant relaxed lazily in the professor's chair, kicked back with his Converse shoes propped on the desk, flipping through some Marvel comic way too loudly.

I stopped contemplating the agony of the test. Instead, I started devising the best way to torment a certain insensitive grad assistant—the rack seemed the best option at the moment, perhaps disembowelment—when Malcolm finally made his way to the front, plopping his exam down and making a hasty exit.

I scribbled my last paragraph, not really caring if I was right or wrong. Somehow, Bennett's philosophy on angels and demons didn't matter so much anymore. I knew a hell of a lot more than he did, regardless of what grade he gave me.

I threw my paper on his desk and ran after Malcolm. He had just passed through the double doors opening to the commons area. I sprinted, punching through the door and hurrying across the leaf-littered walkway.

"Malcolm! Wait!"

His shoulders hunched as he stopped, turning slowly. I was panting by the time I caught him.

"Hey."

Awkward pause. "Hey."

Damn. He was pissed.

"Listen. I'm sorry I didn't call this weekend. There was just so much going on."

You seriously have no idea. Like so *much going on.*

"Sure. I understand."

But he didn't.

"I'm sorry if I was rude the other night. I wasn't ditching you, but I didn't want my dad to worry."

When did I become such an amazing liar? We started walking again, making our way to the far end of the commons toward a side street.

I glanced down, thankful again to Jude for allowing me (yes, fucking allowing me) to stop by my apartment so I could change before he dropped me off at school. It would be even more awkward having this conversation in an oversize T-shirt that obviously belonged to a large male. I didn't think I could explain that away so easily. Besides, I needed this high-necked hoodie sweatshirt to hide the ghastly bite mark purpled and tender at the base of my throat.

"No biggie." Malcolm shrugged. "It would've been nice to know what that was all about, though."

"Yeah. I know I owe you an explanation. It's kind of complicated."

Malcolm took hold of my forearm gently and stopped us both. He faced me, speaking low and even. "Try me."

The expression on his face made my heart hurt. He really liked me, and I wasn't so sure I couldn't like him. We'd been friends for nearly two years, and he was fun to hang out with. I mean, this was the kind of guy I needed to date—funny, good-looking, a gentleman, and completely lacking in the dark-secrets-and-rage-issues department. I sighed.

"I can't tell you exactly, but my dad gambles a bit on the side." Not completely a lie. He gambles, but not at a casino, just with his buddies on poker night twice a month. "And, there were some guys who thought maybe my dad had cheated, and they were pretty upset about it."

Well, the guys did accuse dad of cheating like every week, because he always won. They were so upset, they demanded he bring a case of beer if he beat them more than five rounds.

I stopped talking, because anything else I might say would be a complete and total fabrication. I made this sort of and-that-was-that shrug of the shoulders, hoping he'd fill in the rest with his imagination.

"So, that guy was like a bodyguard or something, to watch for any sort of retaliation?"

I gave a sharp nod. A breeze caught a stray lock of hair that had fallen from my messy bun. "Something like that."

Malcolm's eyes followed the strand whispering across my lips. I tucked it back into place. His winning smile was back where it belonged.

"You don't have to tell me anymore. I can see it's personal."

"Good. Thank you."

The sudden rumble of a motorcycle engine pulled our eyes across the street. Jude had been so curt and quiet this morning, dropping me off without a word, I'd thought he might give me a reprieve from the babysitting routine. No dice, apparently.

"Are you kidding me?" Malcolm grumbled, not even trying to hide his disgust. "Genevieve, does your dad think there are mobsters who are going to attack you on campus?"

The biting sarcasm was so unlike Malcolm. It didn't suit him at all.

"He can be really overprotective sometimes. Silly, I know."

Malcolm glared at the man in denim and leather astride the sleek, black crotch rocket. "You're not riding on that thing with him, are you?"

I suddenly felt sweat beading along my temples. I'd never had to evade and tap-dance around the truth so much. This charade was becoming exhausting. Finally, I just straight-up lied. "Yeah, Dad wants me to go straight to the dojo."

"Whatever, Genevieve."

Malcolm had moved away again, and for some reason, I couldn't let him stalk off in a fog of bruised male ego.

"Hey!" I caught him by the arm. "Why don't we go see that movie you were telling me about tonight? I could use a little R and R after that horrific midterm."

"Really? You want to?"

"Sure I do!"

A bit too enthusiastic, even to my own ears.

"Will your bodyguard have to come?"

"No! Of course not!" *Oh crap. Of course, he will.*

I flashed him a smile. His brown hair slipped, covering part of one eye, making him look adorable, and I found myself excited about a night out with boyishly charming Malcolm.

"Sweet. Pick you up at six thirty."

He leaned down and brushed a light kiss on my cheek. That felt a little weird but sort of nice. I decided I needed to see if there could be something between us. Malcolm was perfect boyfriend material. Right?

The motorcycle across the street revved.

"Six thirty," I repeated, then marched across the street.

I couldn't see Jude's eyes behind the helmet screen, but my VS sensed a definite unsettling aura in the air. I caught the helmet he chucked at me when I was a few feet away.

Pulling it on, I then cinched my backpack tightly over both shoulders and slid into place behind Jude, locking my arms around his waist. He cast that iron-clad armor on to me the moment I made contact with his body then mumbled something under his breath. All I caught was "kid" and "head" or "dead" or something.

"What's that?" I asked.

He snapped his head sharply to the left. "Nothing."

Then we went from zero to sixty in a blink. I squeaked and held on tighter. I swear Jude sped even faster. He was getting some sort of sadistic pleasure out of this, I was sure.

A cool front had settled in after the rain. My hands were trembling by the time we wound our way through the Quarter. At a red light, Jude took me by the wrists and tucked my hands into the pockets of his leather jacket. His right hand lingered on my wrist within the pocket, his thumb brushing back and forth over the fleshy part of my palm. My heart leapt at the sensation.

I dared not imagine this meant more than it did. Clearly, Jude felt some sort of protective responsibility for me and my well-being, though I still had no idea why. On green, his hands slipped back out to the handlebars. I pressed myself to his back, gathering what warmth I could. Okay, maybe it wasn't just for the body heat. I couldn't help myself.

When he pulled into his parking spot on Dauphine Street and stopped the engine, I was reluctant to move, so nice and warm against him. An odd silence drew out. Perhaps only a few seconds, but it felt long and stuffed with too many thoughts that would remain unsaid. Finally, I lifted off his body since I was glued to him and then off the bike.

Without a glance in my direction, he marched ahead into

the alcove. After making our way through the wrought-iron gate and into the courtyard area, he stopped and pointed to the left.

"I'm sorry. What?"

He wouldn't speak to me, and I had no idea why. He seemed pissed off. What was it with everybody today? I followed his line of direction to see Goth Barbie sitting Indian style on a small patch of grass near the water fountain I'd heard so often.

"Am I supposed to…?"

Before I could finish my question, Jude was already gone. He sifted out in an electric snap.

"Rude much?"

I walked toward her. Her hair was the same as the other night, braided in a long golden rope down her back. Her night-clothes gone, now she wore stretchy black pants and a red long-sleeved knit top. She seemed to be in deep meditation as I approached but gave me a brilliant smile when I stood only a foot from her.

"Hi, Genevieve. I'm Kat. Please have a seat."

She gestured to the small grassy space in front of her. Her voice was soft but husky.

I took a seat, mirroring her position. To my great dismay, she was even more beautiful up close. Creamy-pale skin with a dusting of light freckles across her nose and cheeks. Dark eyes, the same forbidding shade as Jude's. However, instead of flecks of gold, the inky color of her irises was broken only by small slivers of moss green. A burning churned in my stomach.

"I'm Genevieve, but I guess you already know that."

She smiled. "Jude asked me to come, to train you in what I know of the Vessel."

I frowned. Her part American, part English accent was as lovely as she was. "I thought Jude would train me."

She laughed, a full throaty sound. "Well, he doesn't have, shall we say, what it takes to train the gifts of a Vessel. One needs a softer temperament to find that peaceful place."

She smiled a secretive smile. The burning increased. How

long had she known Jude? And in what capacity? Friend? Lover? Like it was any of my business. Still, I couldn't help but hope they'd never been anything but platonic colleagues.

"So, what do we do?"

"Shall we start with questions? I'm sure you have quite a few."

Questions? Are you kidding me? Like a billion.

"Wow, um, where should I start?"

I was actually flustered as I gathered my thoughts together.

"How did I become a Vessel? I mean, why me?"

"That I do not know, I'm afraid. We all have our roles to play in this world and the next. This is yours."

Strike one.

"Okay. How many Vessels are there in the world?"

"At present, I am certain there are a minimum of six, maybe more."

"Where do they live? Are most in the US or in Europe or where?"

"Actually, none of them live here on earth."

"Excuse me?"

"They live in their demons' realm. Not here." Her voice dropped, a flicker of pain creased her brow before she went on. "The only time they surface is when possessed by their demon host. Now their demons reign over territories here. For instance, though I still don't know his identity, I know that one high demon rules in New York, where I work."

"As a Dominus Daemonum."

"Yes." She smiled again. "There are others in distant lands. You can bet that wherever there is disorder, chaos and war, a high demon probably rules there with a Vessel, if he has one."

"But, I still don't understand what it is a Vessel actually does. Why am I here? Other than being the target of every demon in the world, that is."

"When a Vessel is fully awakened and has come into all of her power," she started in a quiet voice, "she can use her gifts to destroy evil. Her visions of Sight can warn Flamma of Light. Her abilities as an empath can influence and manipulate the feelings and actions of others, including those of demons. Even more, she can banish demons to the farthest corners of hell."

I gasped. "Like you? Like demon hunters?"

She nodded. "Yes, but without some of the drawbacks of our position."

"Drawbacks such as?"

She flipped her braid and straightened her posture, her expression solemn. "The evil we fight can weigh us down over time." She glanced away, obviously uncomfortable. "A Vessel would feel none of that."

"But, how does any of what a Vessel can do help demons?"

Her gaze shifted back to me. "If you are corrupted by evil, all those gifts would become the gifts of darkness, to do terrible things."

A shudder shook me to the bone as something finally dawned on me.

"So, none of the Vessels are actually free of a demon host, as you say. They are all owned and possessed by a high demon?"

She nodded.

"Has any Vessel you've ever known been able to live free of a demon host?" My voice sounded low and choked with fear.

"None that lived."

I blinked hard and gazed at the fountain on our left. I'd never actually seen the figures poised in white stone above the trickling water. Eros and Psyche locked in a passionate embrace. He held her voluptuous nude form, partially horizontal, from behind—his right hand caressing her face that fell back to gaze up at him, his left wrapped around her rib cage and gently cupped her breast. Her arms encircled his head as he dipped low to gaze on her beauty, his wings lifted high as if he would take flight with her at any moment.

I jumped when Kat put her hand over mine in my lap.

"Don't worry, Genevieve. I never knew any of these other

Vessels. I don't think they had anyone to train them, to help them, before they were captured. Some survived and fought for several years, but eventually, they succumbed to the darkness or to death." I couldn't breathe, wondering how in the world I would survive. "But Jude tells me there is inner strength in you, and—" Her full lips tightened into a line.

"And what? What is it?"

She glanced up at the balcony overlooking the courtyard as if searching for the owner's stalwart form.

"He doesn't want me saying too much, but I think you have a right to know because I'm sure I'm right."

"Right about what?"

"There is mention of someone, a woman, a Vessel, in a prophecy. She will tip the scales one way or another in the war."

"In what war? Like the Middle East or something?"

She shook her head. "The war between the hosts of heaven and hell."

I blinked several times. "Excuse me?"

She took a deep breath and exhaled. "The hosts of the two realms have battled one another from afar, using humans as pawns, since the beginning. But there will come a time when the powers of light and dark will wage their war on this middle ground, on earth. This war will ultimately determine who reigns for eternity."

"And when will this war take place?"

"It could be any time. Today, tomorrow, in a year, in a hundred."

"Well, if it's a hundred, then it definitely can't be me."

"Why is that?"

Could she be that bad at math?

"Umm, I'll be dead by then. I mean, we have longevity in my family genes. I had a great grandmother who lived to ninety-six, but I doubt I'll live another hundred."

Her head angled to the right. Her eyebrows rose in a questioning way. The long rope of her golden braid fell across one shoulder. "Jude did not tell you?"

The way her words were spoken slow and low, my heart skipped a beat or two. "Tell me what?"

"All human Flamma are ageless. This would include you."

Now my heart was really pumping. "Ageless. What does that mean? Immortal?"

"Not exactly immortal. Your human body can certainly die, there is no doubt. However, we do heal faster. All Flamma, that is. One of the perks of fighting nasty demons."

My stomach muscles clenched, straining the stitches along my abdomen. Yes, definitely mortal, though I'd noticed the angry red line had already faded greatly beneath the stitches.

"Though not immortal," she continued with my rapt attention, "you will not age beyond your current years, and you will not die of natural causes. At least, that's what we've noticed of the Vessels we've been able to keep track of."

A choking laugh escaped my throat. "Are you telling me I could live to be a hundred? And still look like this?"

"One hundred, two hundred, three hundred, who knows? Just as a Dominus Daemonum."

I flinched. "You're immortal? Jude is immortal!" My voice escalated into a fever pitch.

"Not immortal. Our physical form can die as surely as a regular human. Our souls are a different story, of course."

She said the last with a sad sigh. I couldn't get past the idea that Jude was much older than I'd originally thought.

Holy crap! How old was he? This explained so much about his demeanor and strange vocabulary sometimes. Ageless. You'd think I'd be past shocking revelations, having encountered shape-shifting demons and sifting hunters, but still my mind reeled from the idea.

"How old are you? I mean, if you don't mind me asking."

She smiled. "I was born in 1803 in Manchester, England."

I laughed. "Seriously?"

"I realize that may be difficult to accept, but it is true."

"Difficult? You have no idea. So, how old is Jude?"

She glanced back up at the empty balcony. "Older than me."

"When was he born? Where was he born?"

"I don't know exactly. You should ask him, though I doubt he'll tell you. He's a bit secretive."

"That's an understatement."

I bit down on my bottom lip. What the hell? What else didn't I know?

This was a huge piece of information that he failed to pass along. I was grateful for the forthcoming, albeit ridiculously beautiful, demon hunter sitting before me. The idea that I could outlive my father was not too distressing as that was always going to happen, but the idea that Mindy and my friends would continue to grow old while I remained the same gave me a sinking sensation.

How could I keep friends for any extended period of time without them knowing? How could I ever possibly have a husband and children and watch them grow old and die, while I remained? The answer was clear—I couldn't.

My stomach clenched into a knot with all the tragic realizations passing through my mind.

I thought of Jude. Now, that forlorn, almost lonely expression he wore sometimes made total sense. How long had it been since his family and friends had died? I wondered if he'd ever been married. A stinging pang pierced my heart.

"Any more questions before we try our first lesson?"

I shook off this new revelation and thought for a minute. There was something I'd been wondering but was too afraid to ask Jude, mostly because I was afraid of the answer.

"Will I ever be able to protect myself from demons, specifically a high demon?"

Her dark eyes swirled with more green than black. So strange. From afar, the eyes of a demon hunter appeared normal, just dark. Up close, one could see the pools swimming with something not of this world.

"Yes. I think you will. I won't lie. Most Vessels are unable to continue the battle against the dark forces seeking you for their own, but I believe you will. Even now I can feel your essence beating brightly within your chest. It's almost blinding to my hunter senses. I'm surprised you aren't being attacked all the time."

"Actually, I am. Or at least, it feels like it."

My fingers went to the bite on my neck. She fell silent, then finally spoke softly. "Are you okay?"

Her eyes held so much compassion. I knew the vicious mark was hidden, but she seemed to know it was there all the same. I felt the sharp prick of tears behind my eyes.

"I am. I almost wasn't. He…he called me his bride."

I knew my eyes revealed the same fear I felt yesterday when Danté had me in his arms, leering down at me as if I were the mouse being batted around by the cruel, creepy cat.

She squeezed my hand. "I understand your fear." She swallowed hard, such deep empathy in her gaze that I wondered what she wasn't telling me. "But we will do everything we can to keep you safe."

"But, his bride? I mean, what the hell?" My voice lapsed into cynical humor.

Kat didn't laugh. "When a Vessel is taken in possession by a high demon, she becomes his—body *and* soul."

I shuddered, inhaling deeply and letting it go.

"Thank God Jude came in time yesterday. The demon, Danté, must've sensed him coming. He sifted out a second before Jude walked up."

She gave me a warm smile. "He will lay down his life to keep you from harm. Trust me on that."

"But why?"

"He has his reasons."

"Which are?"

"You should ask him."

I sighed heavily. More evasion. Well, not exactly. Perhaps Kat didn't really know and was just putting me off.

"Now then. Let's get started. Give me your hands."

She held out both hands, palms up. Warmth covered me like lapping waves on a sandy beach. She cast illusion over me. A very different signature than Jude's iron-plated vise and flaming aura.

"Do you feel it?" asked Kat.

"Yes."

The sensation of being immersed in warm water was strangely comforting, like a baby in the womb.

"One Flamma's cast can call to another's, so I think it best to start this way and see if we can draw yours all the way out. Okay. Close your eyes."

I did so.

"Now, I need you to imagine the safest you have ever felt, whether it's a specific memory or a place or a person. Doesn't matter. Picture it in your mind."

She paused. I thought for a moment. The safest I've ever felt? My mind wandered, then fell upon a repeated memory from childhood.

Mother would come into my room at bedtime and read my favorites by Dr. Seuss. Nestled into the crook of her shoulder with one arm wrapped around me and the other holding a book, I was safe and loved and completely innocent of the encroaching darkness and loss in our future. I could hear her sweet voice crooning to me. *"Today, you are you. That is truer than true. There is no one alive who is Youer than You."*

"Do you have it?" asked Kat, startling me from the memory. "No, keep your eyes closed. This is your safehouse. When casting illusion, especially to cast a strong shield, you must go to this safehouse. That is where you start. Concentrate on the memory now."

I closed my eyes again. My mother's golden-blonde hair

tickled my cheek as she leaned down. She snuggled in closer and turned the page.

"There are words, chants," Kat continued in a low voice, "chants for many different things. We hunters have our own for what we do, but there is one for casting illusion, for protection." She recited the words slowly in Latin, and I translated in my head. *Through time and space within your heart, there is a place where one must start, within this seed of hope there lies, a warrior shield to deceive all eyes.*

She paused, holding my gaze then said in a serious tone, "Repeat the words while thinking of your safehouse."

Thinking of my mother's lovely pale eyes and warm smile, I repeated the Latin chant line by line as Kat said them too. When I spoke the last line, I felt a concentration of heat pool within me, extending to Kat in a burning flash.

In my mind, I saw a starburst of light, like fragments of the moon, explode into glittering brightness. She gasped and squeezed my hands. My eyes popped open.

"What? Did I do something wrong? Are you okay?"

Her greenish-black eyes swirled. She shook her head once as if trying to awaken herself from a dream. Then shock melted into a wide, wide smile. She laughed that throaty laugh.

"Oh, Genevieve. I wouldn't worry so much. Your casting is already at full strength. How, I don't know. Simply amazing," she marveled.

I couldn't help but grin back at her. She inhaled a deep breath. "Your defense is more than ready."

"Really?" I heard my voice squeak. "So I could shield myself entirely from demons finding me now in public?"

"Oh, yes. If you shield yourself in this capacity, they'll only see a pretty girl, nothing more."

I was beaming.

"Now that your defense is in order, tomorrow, we will work on offense. Yes?"

"Yes."

As she told me farewell and sifted out of the courtyard, I decided I truly liked Kat. She was genuine and compassionate. I grimaced at her ability to disappear and go wherever she wanted. Like Jude. I wondered how someone got that power. That would certainly come in handy.

I stared at Eros and Psyche a minute longer, frozen in passion, then went to find Jude.

I was hoping he was watching television or something, but then I hadn't seen a television anywhere in his house. What I didn't want to do was interrupt another of his swordplay episodes in his training studio, all sweaty and half-naked.

Of course, that's exactly where I found him.

Thankfully, he had his shirt on this time and was kicking a punching bag in the center of the room. Okay, kicking was putting it mildly. Tool's "Schism" pumped through the room. At the end of each line "I know the pieces fit," Jude would kick the hell out of the bag. The bag fell all the way to the floor with each roundhouse, slowly righting itself before he'd smash it again.

"What did the poor thing ever do to you?"

He snapped up, broad shoulders tense, face guarded. He walked to the sound system connected to his phone and stopped the music. "How was the training?"

"Enlightening."

He moved toward me in a smooth, slow manner. I'd seen that movement before.

I watched this show on the Discovery Channel once where a lion walked into another pride to challenge the male leader and take over. His gait was sinuous, almost sultry, in his determined stride. I held Jude's gaze, refusing to be intimidated. Well, trying anyway. He stopped only a few inches from me, totally in my personal space, where he seemed to like to be.

"Enlightening how?"

"Why didn't you tell me that I was ageless?" I bit out the last word as if it were offensive.

"Because there are some things you are not ready for."

"How old are you?"

"Very."

"Ha. Something else I'm not ready for?"

"No. I just don't particularly like your attitude at the moment."

"Is there anything else you deem me not ready for?"

His eyes flickered down my body, slowing at my breasts and hips, and back up in a flash. "Yes. For now."

"You're infuriating, you know that? You're really good at giving orders, making demands, and dragging my ass to every hellhole in town, but you can't answer a simple question of mine."

"Not can't. I won't. At the moment."

I was fuming. My mind and mouth switched gears, continuing to attack. "Why didn't you warn me about Danté?"

I hadn't seen him move, but he was imperceptibly closer. I could feel the heat radiating off his chest, pressed only an inch from mine. "What do you mean?"

"I mean, you didn't warn me demons could shape-shift into the appearance of other people. Like you."

"They can't shape-shift into just anyone. And I didn't know the one who was hunting you was that sick *fuck*."

He spat the last word with so much venom. His irises had gone super-black, and I knew I was treading on dangerous ground, but some inner demon (pardon the pun) was poking me with a pitchfork and egging me on.

"You didn't tell me that he wanted me for his bride either. I mean, hell, he got to sample the goods and everything, and I didn't even know who it was that I was—"

His hands shot out, gripping my upper arms. I swear I saw flames licking around his shoulders, but I didn't budge. I couldn't if I tried. His fingers dug into my skin. There would definitely be bruises there tomorrow.

"What did you just say?"

I couldn't speak.

"Answer me."

His voice had dipped to that low, gravelly pitch.

Full of trepidation, I could barely whisper when I finally replied, "I thought he was you."

The storm raging in his eyes stilled. For a fraction of a moment, he held me there in his burning gaze. One hand wrapped the side of my throat, his fingers holding me in a firm but painless grip, his thumb stroking my pulse.

A whimpering sound escaped my lips before I whispered, "Jude."

He struggled with something, though I didn't know what. But I was caught in his feral gaze, both afraid and excited at the intensity of his tight expression.

Finally, his brow softened. His grip loosened. Yet there was an edge of danger flaring between us, igniting to a melting point.

The hand at my neck came up and tucked a loose lock of hair behind my ear. Slow and steady. I felt as if I'd been burned where his finger traced along my skin. Pleasantly so.

The same arm suddenly snaked around my waist, his hand pressed at the small of my back, pulling me flush against him. I gasped. The other hand dropped my arm, gripping my hip instead. His thumb pressed against my pelvic bone. I resisted the urge to squirm. He dipped close to my ear, his breath hot against my neck.

"Hold on tight, Genevieve," he whispered, pressing me hard against his body. His lip grazed the sensitive shell of my ear. A warm tingle bloomed between my legs. "I wouldn't want to lose you in the Void."

"Wha-what?"

My brain had stopped functioning for a second. The exquisite torture of his body against mine had caused all circuits to misfire. Then I realized what he meant a split second before it happened.

All air was sucked from my lungs. I wrapped my arms around his neck. A soft pressure seemed to fold me inward, pressing me into an enveloping darkness. We slipped fast, so fast, through a black void. Not all black. Unidentifiable images flitted by in flashes of white and gray. I had no idea what they were. Feeling the onset of motion sickness, I squeezed my eyes shut and clung to Jude. I felt the pressure of his unrelenting grip. Caged in muscular arms, I felt safe, despite the unnerving sensation of weightlessness as we crashed through time and space.

A soft whoosh, pressure gone, and all was still. I realized then I was panting with my forehead pressed into the center of Jude's collarbone.

"Breathe, Genevieve," he said huskily, brushing a firm hand up my spine. "You're home now."

I opened my eyes. We were standing next to my bed in my apartment, my beige goose-down comforter half hanging off the bed. Some of my clothes were junked in a pile, including the last T-shirt of his I'd borrowed. I still clasped him around his neck, fingers laced at his nape, my body pressed intimately to his. I let go at once, stumbling back awkwardly.

A crooked smile spread across Jude's perfect face.

"Why don't you give me some warning next time?"

"I did. I told you to hold on." Still smirking.

"More than three seconds' warning please," I said in a syrupy voice with a wide smile.

His smile smoldered, heat returning to his gaze. "Do you have class tomorrow?"

I shook my head, finding it hard to swallow when he looked at me like that. "I work at the dojo in the afternoon."

"What time?"

"My first class is at one o'clock."

A curt nod. "I'll meet you back here in the morning for training with Kat, then drop you off at the dojo."

I realized that he planned to escort me every place I planned to go for like fucking forever. I rolled my eyes. "You know, Kat said my illusion casting is perfect. Maybe I don't need an escort everywhere I go."

"Mmm. I am sure you think that."

"Seriously, Jude, I can drive myself to your apartment."

"I am sure that you can. Nevertheless, I'll be here at eight in the morning. You have my number. Call me if you plan to leave the apartment."

I nodded, glancing at my shoes for no reason at all. He stepped closer. I fought the urge to retreat. He tipped my chin up with one finger.

"Genevieve," he said, the scary vibe back in his voice. "Call me if you plan to leave this apartment."

"I will."

Maybe.

While still staring into my eyes, he sifted out with a snap. That was a little disturbing, to put it mildly.

I sank down onto my bed, thinking of Malcolm. I'd promised him a movie date. Date. Yes, it would definitely be a date, and I was still trying to figure out how I felt about that.

I certainly didn't want Jude tagging along, watching from the corners, making Malcolm want to spit fire. The idea of Jude hovering over us made me extremely uncomfortable. And I liked Malcolm as a friend. Maybe more.

Jude wanted to control my every move. For my protection, of course, but Kat herself said I was more than able to shield myself from demons finding me. But, what if that demon prince came back?

"Ugh!"

Okay. I'd have to tell Jude, but I was too cowardly to do it in person. So it had to be another text.

Me: *I'm meeting a friend for an 8:00 movie tonight at the theater on Prytania.*

Jude: *A friend?*

Me: *Yes. Please be discreet, if you come.*

A lengthy pause as I turned on the hot water in the shower. Finally, my phone bleeped again.

Jude: *I'll be there. You won't see me.*

I totally did *not* get a smiley face this time. "Okay, then. That's sort of encouraging *and* disturbing."

Taking a deep breath, I headed into the shower to get ready for my date.

13

"I still can't believe you threw popcorn at those girls texting in front of us."

"They asked for it." Malcolm leaned back in his chair and swigged his beer. "I mean, come on! How can you possibly do anything else while Thor is kicking ass onscreen?"

I laughed, enjoying the chill vibe of this bar with its mellow music and Malcolm's company. It felt so *normal*. After the week I'd had, it was welcome and wonderful.

We sat across from each other at a small two-top in the back of the bar. "You Belong to Someone Else" crooned out of the jukebox next to the pool tables, where a few steroid boys yelled and laughed a little too loudly at their own antics. With the exception of a few other groups of two and three, the crowd was sparse.

I'd felt Jude's presence all night—sometimes closer, sometimes farther away. Just as he'd promised, I never saw him. Even so, I continued to glance around, wondering how he hid from view so well, wondering what he thought or might say about my outing with my "friend." The anticipation of our eventual tête-à-tête had my nerves on edge.

"You're so much fun," Malcolm suddenly blurted, taking hold of my hand across the table.

"Thanks." The mood shifted from silly to serious. "You are too."

He rubbed his thumb softly across my knuckles. His hand wasn't clammy like the first time on the Riverwalk. His gaze held mine with a tender smile, his lips quirking up more on one side.

I'd never noticed his eyes before. They were a shade of bluish green that changed hue in certain lights. Here, in the corner under a yellow lamp, they shone dark green in a smoldering gaze I wasn't used to seeing on him.

I glanced down at at the table, my heart pounding in my chest. Not from butterfly feelings about Malcolm, but from what a certain stalking demon hunter might think of Malcolm holding my hand.

"I'm going to…" I pointed toward the restrooms, smoothly pulling my hand from his as I stood.

He nodded. "One more round?"

"Sure. One more."

Malcolm headed to the bar, while I zigzagged around tables and through the pool area to the hall leading to the restrooms. I saw one of the muscle meatheads nudge his friend. Their attempt at low-talking was sadly inadequate.

"Nice."

"Think she'd want to play with my pool stick?"

A vulgar gesture, I'm sure, sent them all into raucous laughter behind my back. Drunken idiots. Why must guys do stuff like that? I wanted to scream at them, *Can you please ogle me in a less conspicuous manner?* But of course that would defeat the purpose. And there's no way they'd know what the word "conspicuous" meant.

I glanced to the right, avoiding the asshats. One of their friends slouched over the front of the jukebox with both hands splayed on the top. His broad frame and beefy arms tensed as I passed, swaying slightly from side to side. The hazy light from the jukebox shone on a sickly pale face, eyes squeezed shut. I walked faster, afraid the guy might be about to puke.

Zipping around the corner past the employee-only closet, I found the women's restroom last on the left. I stepped into one of the three empty stalls and did my thing then checked myself in the mirror while washing my hands.

Glassy, dilated pupils around black-lined eyes radiated come-hither—the effects of lots of laughter, three beers, and good company with a hot guy in a cozy place. It's true I'd had a good time. I always did with Malcolm. He was a good guy. The problem was I still didn't know what I was doing.

Did I really want to date him? Did I have time to date in between my demon defense training classes? Would Jude let me date?

I shivered at the flash of his dark eyes in my mind. Blowing out a heavy breath, I dried my hands and swung open the door.

"Oh, my God! You scared me."

Big-and-beefy jukebox boy straddled the doorway, both arms gripping the frame. His head drooped low as he stared at the floor, swaying slightly.

"Dude. The men's bathroom is behind you."

He didn't move. Well, except for the slow leaning of his body blocking my exit.

"Hey!"

I didn't want to push on him for fear he'd tip over and never get up. Then I'd have to do the polite thing and go tell his fuck-tard friends to come and get him.

"Hey," I repeated, reaching out to tap his shoulder.

The second I touched him, a huge hand gripped my wrist. He snapped awake, reaching for my other arm. Piercing, blood-red eyes bore into mine.

Gasping, I swung my other hand out of his reach then kicked out on instinct, aiming for his dick. Dad always told me to go for the most vulnerable spot I could reach. But he blocked with his other hand.

I twisted out of his grip, elbowing him in the chin and rushing against the farthest wall. Trapped in this too-close space, I quickly scanned the room for some sort of weapon. But of course there was nothing. It was a fucking bathroom.

He stepped fully into the room, closing the door and sneering with delight. It was then I realized my VS was no longer humming under my skin. Shit. Somewhere between the movies, beers, and Malcolm's sweet smiles, I'd lost concentration and let my shield slide away.

"So who's your master?" I asked the hulking demon in front of me, hoping, praying he was a lower man on the totem pole. "Danté?"

His massive head tipped at an angle. This guy was way bigger than I'd realized. He blocked the door completely. There was no way to squeeze past him. I squared my feet, preparing for his attack.

He noticed and grinned, unmoving. "Danté?"

"Yes. Danté. You know, one of the princes of darkness. I'm sure you know him. You guys all hang in the same crowd."

I sounded much more confident than I felt, a trembling now weakening my knees. And my voice. When he took another step toward me, I pressed back fully against the wall.

"My command comes from another master."

"Great," I mumbled. Two high demons after me. Then I remembered something. I pulled down the high collar of my button-down to reveal the bruised bite at my neck.

"Danté has marked me," I said, hoping this would be enough to make him back off.

Jude hadn't explained everything the mark meant, but I knew at the very least it was a warning to other high demons that I was taken. Not that I in any way considered myself property of a fucking demon. Still, I was willing to try anything to get this demon to back off.

His red eyes glimmered over the mark, then met mine again as he prowled forward, unperturbed. Definitely not the reaction I was hoping for.

"Danté will have to mourn your loss."

Fuck. My heartbeat fled into hyperspeed. His formal words were disturbingly out of sync with the muscular exterior. I reminded myself that it was a demon inside who spoke, not the man whose huge frame was crowding me in.

"What do you mean, loss?"

I shifted left, closer to a stall door. His hand flicked an oblong shape out of his back pocket. An ice pick! What the hell!

I wondered briefly if he'd snagged it from behind the bar, which led me to ponder when and how lower demons hopped into their hosts. I didn't wonder long as he stalked closer, caging me into the corner. My left hand slid up the stall door, gripping the top.

"True," he sneered, glaring with so much menace I felt my pulse pounding in my throat, "it does seem a waste to dispose of so lovely a Vessel, but my master must have no challenger."

He lunged. The ice pick jabbed straight toward my heart. I arched my torso back just in time, grabbing his arm with my right hand, thrusting it forward, and slamming the stall door as hard as I possibly could. He grunted but didn't drop the pick.

The surprise gave me a split second to bend and duck behind him, darting for the door. As I gripped the door handle, a sharp pain stung my scalp. Yanking me by my hair, my ass hit the floor and he dragged me back across the floor.

I cried out in pain, reaching back to claw his hand and wrist.

"No, no, my beauty. That won't do," he hissed.

He jerked my head to the floor, stretching my body out. With his hand gripping my hair, there was no way I could wiggle free. I rolled into a ball and kicked him squarely across the jaw over my head.

He yanked harder, knocking the back of my skull against the floor, clattering my teeth together. Stunned by the jarring pain, I couldn't move while he quickly immobilized me with a knee onto my stomach. I gouged the wrist with my nails, drawing blood but he kept his hand firmly entangled in my hair.

"Oh God, no," I whispered, feeling tears prick from both the fear and the pain.

The demon bent low, malevolent crimson eyes glaring at me.

"He won't hear you," he whispered, raising the ice pick again.

I froze, watching the swing of his arm, but it never hit its target. A sharp pull on my scalp, then I was free, his weight no longer on my chest.

Jude had the hulk of a man pinned against the wall. He'd sifted in superfast, a murderous expression tightening his face into hard, taut lines. A flexed arm shoved the point of his broadsword into the hollow of the demon's throat. I scrambled back to the wall near the door.

"Give me your name, demon." Fury and death shook his voice. The throaty malice of his command made gooseflesh rise on my arms.

I thought I'd seen Jude at his scariest after Danté had caught me in the alcove at his place. I was wrong. So wrong.

The demon laughed, but not for long. Jude threw the sword aside with a clang, snapping the demon's head back, cracking it against the wall, and clenching the demon by the hair with violent force.

The creature cried out. I felt some small vindication for the swelling lump on the back of my head.

Energy shifted in the room. A whirl of electricity crackled, emanating from Jude. The familiar aura of blazing flame licked around his shoulders, head, and arms. An unnatural wind stirred the air.

"*Verum vel infinitas infinitio nex.*"

Jude bit out the words. *Truth or endless death.*

I couldn't see Jude's eyes but guessed the black had flooded them entirely. The demon's angry scarlet eyes tried to resist Jude, but some force held him captive.

My VS responded to whatever was taking place, flushing my body with a wave of starry light.

"Garzel," grumbled the demon, his mouth twisting abnormally.

"Garzel," commanded Jude, "give me your master's name."

The demon beat its head from side to side, trying to break free. The demon's true form popped its horned head out from within the human shell. The left horn was broken, the right curved like a goat's.

Jude snatched the unbroken horn like the handle of a motorcycle, chanting low and literally yanking the creature violently from the human form. One hard tug and the nasty creature was out, held aloft in Jude's tight grip. The guy I'd thought was just puking drunk at the jukebox crumbled to the floor, completely unconscious.

The creature was much bigger than the first one I saw in the alley on my birthday. Long, gray skeletal limbs dangled from a bony body. An oversize chest cavity and emaciated pelvis held together by papery, leather-like skin wrinkled over the bony frame as it twisted and writhed, beating against Jude.

My demon hunter didn't budge an inch. Still as stone. One of the beast's arms contorted and shortened into a black bat wing, then elongated again into its regular, ghastly form with filth-encrusted claws.

"You cannot shape-shift away, Garzel," Jude rumbled then bellowed with power and rage, "Give me his name!"

I flinched at the violence in Jude's voice. Ripples of ethereal flame banked higher, reflecting in the demon's serpentine eyes.

"No," rasped the creature between tight lips, dribbling spittle.

The constant jerking of the demon had angled Jude so I could view his profile. He closed his eyes, not chanting but obviously doing something.

My VS throbbed in response. I gasped. Then all was silent and unmoving. No, not silent. Deaf. I could hear nothing, absolutely nothing. A vacuum consumed all sound until only the faint thrum of my heart beat within my ears. The ghostly light deepened to darkest blue, touching everything with an eerie shade of twilight.

Jude opened his eyes but never moved. The demon hung there midair, no longer flailing, just staring wide-eyed into the mirror along the wall. I followed his gaze, not believing my own eyes.

The glass reflected a creature straight from darkest nightmares, from mythical underworlds, from horror stories of the ferryman and the Grim Reaper. Shrouded in tattered gray cloth, corpselike remnants of the grave lifted in a wispy wind that wasn't there.

Long, black-boned limbs extended from the gray trappings of death. A skeletal head of black bone, oddly stretched and angular, held eyes of liquid red. The words *I walk through the valley of the shadow of death* came to mind. This being was the shadow of death personified, carrying with it the promise of eternal night. And damnation.

The being floated closer, then crossed through the glass, sliding out of the mirror from some other dimension, gliding into our space, filling it up with static darkness. My pulse tripped faster, throbbing in my ears.

The thing spoke in a whispering breath. *"Acherontis pabulum."*

A cold shiver shot up my spine. Ominous words. *Food for Acheron.* Confused and terrified, I could do nothing but watch.

"Garzel." Jude's voice was clipped and hollow and other. Sound resonated like something trapped in a jar. I shrank farther into the corner. "Give me your master's name, or I give you to the Collector," he stated in a dark rumble. "Your choice."

Jude didn't even glance at the hovering, ghastly specter floating only a few feet from him, but the gangly beast did, closing his blood-red eyes in resignation. "The Collector's kiss."

Jude still held the demon by one horn. "So be it."

Without pause, he released Garzel the same instant the black-boned wraith opened its arms for an embrace. Sucked swiftly to the angel of death, its hideous head tilted, pressing a gaping, fleshless mouth to Garzel's.

At once, I heard and felt a piercing sorrow wash over me. Overlapping voices cried and wailed in soul-deep anguish. I pressed my hands over my ears but still heard the tormented cries.

Hot tears streamed down my face though the pain I felt wasn't mine. Pain that was sharp and intimate, as if the voices broke all barriers, piercing straight to my heart and shattering it into tiny pieces.

Garzel's sinister eyes glared at me, an unspoken warning, just as the Collector inhaled. The demon evaporated into a black stream of vapor, sucked into the mouth of the grim creature.

Jude bowed his head to the Collector. It swept one black arm outward in a regal gesture of farewell, slipped back into the mirror, then vanished. Instantly, the blue-tinged room brightened, and I could once again hear the hazy sound of music and voices from the bar. I panted, my chest heaving, trying to wrap my mind around what I'd just witnessed.

Jude took two long strides and lifted me by my upper arms. His dark gaze shimmered with emotion—compassion, fear, frustration, anger. Definitely anger. He shook his head in slow motion from side to side, pulling me within a hairsbreadth of his chest. Black eyes scanned my entire face in a swift blink.

"Oh, Genevieve, Genevieve." My name slipped from his lips like a broken prayer. "What am I going to do with you?"

"Must something be done with me?" I choked out, body trembling, tears still coming, though I hated it. I wasn't usually a crier, but apparently near-death terror did that to me. Also, those terrible cries, their pain.

"Be calm." His voice soothed. He brushed the tears from

one cheek with his thumb. "Relax. The pain will disappear soon enough." He brushed the other cheek, both hands cupping my face in warmth and safety.

I closed my eyes. "I feel so empty," I whispered, a deep ache expanding in my core.

"I know. The feeling will subside. Relax."

"What was that thing?"

Opening my eyes, I caught him staring at my lips. One thumb brushed across my partly open mouth. I shivered again. His eyes met mine, unguarded, sparking with glittering shards of gold.

The anger now gone, another heated emotion swirled feverishly, touching the contours of his face with a melting quality. He wanted to kiss me. No mistake. I was shocked by the sudden intrusion of desire cutting through fear and unfathomable sorrow. His gaze held mine a moment more, his thumb stroking down the column of my throat.

Then his face shuttered closed, his mask well in place. Even while one hand gripped my waist when I swayed and tightened to keep me upright, he broke the intimate closeness.

"I'll explain everything, but we need to get out of here. Garzel may not have been working alone. I'm in no mood for any more tonight."

Loaded words.

"No, wait!" I said, realizing what he was about to do. I pushed out of his grasp. "I can't sift out! Malcolm. Damn. Poor Malcolm. I can't just disappear."

No longer touching me, Jude held a blank expression, void of the heat visible seconds before.

"Genevieve. Listen to me very carefully and do *exactly* as I say."

Hell. Angry Jude was back.

"Listening," I said with not a hint of snarkiness or humor. I might be brave, but I wasn't stupid.

"Walk straight through the bar, tell the boy you're not feeling well and you need to go home. You have exactly eight minutes. Go a second over, and I'll sift into his fucking truck and take you without warning. I'll be waiting for you in your bedroom. Eight minutes, Genevieve."

A whoosh of wind rocked me on my heels. He was gone.

"Eight minutes!?"

I dashed out of the bathroom, dusting off my jeans, and smoothing my hair as I sped down the hall around the corner, where I slammed right into Malcolm holding a beer in each hand.

"Hey, you okay? I was starting to worry about you."

"Um, yeah, well, I'm really not feeling well. So sorry, but can you take me home?"

Concern written all over his face, he set the beers on a stool, took my hand, and guided me back through the bar. I didn't even think about warning the muscle-bound dweebs their friend was unconscious in the ladies' bathroom. He was going to wake up with a nasty headache, but somehow I didn't feel that sorry for him. Jude had said demons can only possess those open to them, which meant in some small way, the guy had asked for it.

Malcolm opened the passenger side of his truck for me, hopped into the driver's seat then headed out. Thankfully, the bar was near City Park, not far from my apartment.

"I hate that you're feeling bad." Malcolm kept glancing at me with a worried expression. "Is it your stomach?"

I nodded, doing a damn fine job of using my anxiety as a disguise for a stomachache. Three minutes had passed. I watched the clock on the dash, tapping my foot at each red light.

"You okay?" he asked, noticing my fidgeting.

"I'll be fine. Just need a little Pepto and bed."

"You want me to stop and get you something?"

"*No!*" I yelled. He flinched. "Um, I mean, no thanks. It's not that serious. Just probably overworked and all… Thanks."

Malcolm nodded and by some miracle had me on my

doorstep with one minute to spare. As Malcolm faced me at the door, I was very aware that Jude was waiting in my bedroom. In my bedroom! My stomach did a flip-flop at the thought, and I realized perhaps my stomachache wasn't a total ruse.

Malcolm tucked me into a bearlike hug, planting a kiss on the top of my head. I have to admit it felt quite nice in his arms. He was such a gentle soul that I felt comforted by his close presence. Comforted but not safe. I glanced behind him, so sure a demon or that Collector thing would pop out and snatch us both.

"Sorry to end the night this way, but I should go in," I mumbled, giving him a gentle squeeze and pulling back.

"I had a wonderful time tonight. I'd like to spend more time with you."

I looked up and nodded, smiling as best I could. He leaned down for what I thought would be a peck goodnight. He gave me a soft closemouthed kiss, pulled back a second then leaned toward me again. This time, he pried my lips apart, slipping his tongue in tentatively. It was such a shock, I didn't resist. I mean, I had given all the signs I'd enjoyed the night and would welcome a little affection.

Still, I stood there, letting him kiss me. Doing nothing may have given him the wrong impression, because his lips pressed harder, then he gave a soft moan as his tongue plunged in with sloppy earnest.

"Oh, Gen," he whispered across my lips, diving back in for more full-on tongue thrusting.

His other hand slid down my neck, fumbled over my shirt, over my breast, stopping to cup and squeeze. What the hell! Didn't I say I had a stomachache? Not that I really did, but come on. I eased away, breaking contact and pushing his hand away. The whole event lasted all of maybe twenty seconds but felt way longer.

"Good night, Malcolm."

Before he could say or do anything else, I slipped through

the door and locked it shut, leaning against it. Pressing the back of my hand to my lips, I took a deep breath. The apartment was ghostly quiet. Mindy had texted me while we were at the movies that she would be out late with Dave. Though the place was silent, I was not alone.

I crept toward my room like someone going to the hangman's noose. I hoped Jude hadn't seen or heard what just happened on the doorstep.

Walking closer to my bedroom, I sensed him there. My VS recognized the hard strength of his presence, wrapped in flame.

My mind drifted through the different sensory signatures I'd discovered. Kat felt like warm waves on a sandy shore. Those lower demons felt like needles prickling along my spine. The Dungeon master, Dommiel, exuded a penetrating fear before intense pain, if that made any sense. Danté was the ice man with a capacitating gift to freeze with a burning touch.

But Jude. He was all heat and steel and rock-solid, bone-melting beauty. His presence felt like unquenchable fire and impenetrable armor all at once—smothering and burning me with an insatiable need to bask in the nearness of him.

Within his fiery aura, I felt protected, rocking gently within his ship of flame, sure to be taken to safe harbor. I stopped walking, inhaled deeply and blew out a shaky breath, willing myself to be calm before I stepped into the bedroom.

The lights were off. A dark form stood tall and still, his profile silhouetted by the faint light filtering through sheer curtains. A long, sharp line angled against the wall—his broadsword. He didn't face me as I entered. When he spoke, his voice was steady, level, distant. Cold.

"Do you trust me, Genevieve?"

A simple question. Of course, I did. Everything I knew about Jude incited trust. Though the man himself was still a mystery, he'd done nothing to make me doubt his intentions. Having saved my life now several times and having never harmed me in any way, how could I not trust him?

There was a heaviness in his voice, as if this question held the weight of something far greater than I could fathom.

My reply came out low but strong. "Yes."

He continued to gaze toward the curtained window, his frame stiff and unyielding. I stepped farther into the room, standing at the edge of my bed.

"Do you believe I am thinking only of your safety when I tell you to do something?"

Uh-oh. I knew where this was going.

"Jude, listen, I know that—"

"Answer the question." His sharp tone halted the pitiful excuses about to spill from my mouth.

He turned to me then. Though I couldn't see anything but the black outline of his body, I felt the weight of his eyes. Could he see me in the dark? I wondered what other gifts a Dominus Daemonum might have in his arsenal.

"Yes."

He walked toward me, stopping outside that personal zone he so often liked to fill up with all his manliness.

"Then tell me"—his voice monotone, but sharp as a razor—"why do you value your life so little to leave this apartment for what, a romp about town with your boyfriend? You don't seem to comprehend your new reality at all."

His voice was calm but edged with danger.

"I just thought, well, Kat said today… I mean—"

"Do you think I care if you go out with the boy?"

"No. Well, yes. Maybe."

"You're free to do as you please, within reason. If you prefer to spend your time bar-hopping, that's entirely your decision. But understand this, every time you step foot out the door, you're risking your life, your very soul. Is it really worth it to sip beer and hold hands with the boy?"

My mouth went bone dry. He was so pissed.

"Why do you keep calling him a boy? He's twenty-one years old. He's a grown man."

A derisive noise, almost a snort, came from the shadow before me. I felt the touch of shimmering flame he wore like a coat wherever he went.

"Mmm." He inched into my space. I inched back, feeling like cornered prey. "And tell me, how do you know he's a grown man?"

Words dripping with sarcasm. Malcolm was a good friend, possibly more than a good friend. Angry heat flushed my cheeks. "He's…he just is!"

"'He just is.' Excellent definition. I'll have to remember that."

He mocked me. I was glad to have the darkness to hide the smug smile he surely wore and the humiliating flush crawling up my cheeks.

"Well, he's a *gentleman*, that's for damn sure!" I snapped back.

He inched closer. Though my eyes had adjusted, I could only see his outline in the dim light.

"Really? Gentlemen molest women on their doorsteps without invitation nowadays? Interesting. I hadn't realized the definition had changed so much over the decades."

"What? You saw! You watched me when he—?" I broke off, shame and anger making my voice shake. "That's why I went out on my own tonight. I don't want a babysitter all the time!"

Closer still. The backs of my knees bumped the edge of the bed.

"Babysitter? Sweetheart, I'm not sure what mirror you're looking in, but you are by no means a baby any more than that boy is a grown man."

Sweetheart? He'd never called me an endearment, and though I caught the condescending tone, the possessiveness in his voice struck me near dumb.

"Well, what's your definition of a grown man, since you know so much?"

Already breathless, I hoped he couldn't sense my nerves fracturing on multiple levels. The overwhelming sensation of his nearness in the dark was heady, intoxicating. I felt dizzy, wanting to grasp his shoulders for support, but I didn't dare touch him.

"A man," he said, deep voice like velvet, warm breath caressing my cheek, "knows when to take action and when to be still, knows his strengths and his weaknesses, knows control when it is necessary and release when it is essential. And a man"—his voice had dropped deep, throaty, close to my ear—"knows when a woman wants him and how to please her."

Two words popped into my head, and before I could possibly consider the consequences, the challenge shot from my mouth.

"Prove it."

Jude crushed me onto the bed before I could blink, his glorious, hard body caging me in. A large hand hooked behind my knee, bending it as he fitted his body over mine. He pressed lower, his hard bulge pushing into the vee of my jeans.

God! Very hard. I froze.

Long fingers spread into my hair, gently tugging so the column of my throat arched for him. I made a breathy sound as he scraped his stubbled jaw along the soft curve of my neck, trailing warm lips back over the rough abrasion. He tilted my head straight again, grinding against my pussy in one slow movement.

"Ah." A helpless pant escaped my lips.

If I could see his face, he would probably be smiling. I was boneless, mindless beneath him.

I bit my lip to keep any other embarrassing noises from escaping, as if that might help. His hand at my knee slid up along my thigh to my hip, massaging gently. Even through my jeans, his touch seared me to the skin.

"Let go, Genevieve." I still held my bottom lip tightly between my teeth. "Open for me."

God, the man's voice rumbled so low, a rough whisper caressing me in a tangible way, forcing me to obey. I did as I was told. Those lips I'd caught myself staring at entirely too often showed me the difference between the boy on the doorstep and the man on top of me.

Slowly, slowly, his lips urged mine apart with gentle yet determined movements until I tasted the invading heat of his mouth. His tongue came in—exploring, demanding, claiming me as his own.

I'd felt desire before, but not like this. An aching need wrenched at my core, tightening low and deep. His aura of fire singed me from the inside out, waking every sense, wrapping me in palpable longing. A burning tendril reached out, weaving around me, into me, pulling me toward him like the tide to the moon. How did I ever mistake Danté for Jude? I knew in that moment no man would ever come close to him, no matter how long I lived.

I threaded one hand into the hair at his nape, shocked at the silkiness. My other hand moved along his neck to the crook of his jaw, feeling the muscles work as he continued his deep invasion.

I couldn't keep the little whimpering noises from escaping my lips. He responded at once, pressing his erection harder, grinding against me, kissing more deeply, nipping at my lips with his teeth, then devouring me again with heavy intent.

My back arched, a primitive response, pressing my breasts against his chest. The friction wound a knot in my abdomen. He moaned.

Christ! The sound made me want to give him everything, give him all of me. My other leg bent of its own will, inviting and cradling him between my thighs. Right where I needed him.

I rocked up, rubbing my clit along the length of him. His fist tightened in my hair, his mouth coasting along my jaw.

"Fuck, woman," he rumbled, scraping my neck with teeth then licking with his tongue. "You should tell me to stop."

Curling my fingers into the back of his shirt, I rocked my

hips again, moaning at the pleasure of my clit rubbing against his hard dick.

"I don't want to stop," I panted.

For the first time, it was true. I didn't want to wait any longer. I wanted Jude to rip my clothes off and do everything to me.

Plunging both hands under his shirt, I glided my nails to the front and down his ridged abdomen. He bit me at the base of my neck, quickening my pulse and heating my blood. I reached down between us to unsnap his jeans. Before I'd gotten to the zipper, both my wrists were bound above my head.

"Fuck," he grated, his eyes squeezed shut.

Jude froze for a few seconds, panting, still holding my wrists captive. My mind a haze of lust, I wanted to ask why he was stopping but I was also inexperienced and a little shy when it came to sex. I also couldn't stand the thought of me begging him only for him to reject me. Because this definitely felt like rejection.

Though his voice came out calm and steady, the rapid tattoo of his heart vibrated through his chest to mine. He lifted his body an inch, no longer touching but hovering in torturous intimacy. I almost cried out in anguish.

"Proven?"

Proven? What was he talking about? My brain had nearly melted away the conversation before this more than heated interlude. I could hardly form a coherent thought, much less speak, still panting and wanting more.

A throaty laugh. His chest rumbled, inadvertently, or maybe on purpose, rubbing the tip of my breasts, torturing my hardened nipples. I definitely whimpered at that.

He bent his head, keeping our bodies apart, sweeping his lips lightly along mine, giving me a brief, wet kiss, tugging at my lower lip before letting go. He released a jagged breath.

"Don't settle, Genevieve. Don't let strangers grope you on dance floors. Don't allow college boys to fondle you in doorways. Don't waver in uncertainty about your own desires. Even ageless, life is too short to live halfhearted. Know what you want. Endeavor to seize it, and keep it when you do."

The mattress shifted as his weight lifted off the bed. A swift whooshing sound, and he was gone. His heat lingered on my swollen lips, my chest and lower. I curled onto my side, feeling bereft and so very alone.

I'd forgotten all about Garzel and the Collector and Malcolm. None of it mattered as Jude's advice swirled in my mind, specifically the last words he spoke to me.

Endeavor to seize it, and keep it when you do.

"I thought I just did," I whispered into the dark.

There was no answer.

14

"Gen, wake up!"

Mindy shook my shoulder, hissing close to my ear. I jumped awake, positive a demon had found me and broken in. But seeing Mindy's impish smile hovering over me, I knew otherwise.

"What?"

She giggled. "Um, that *extremely* hot guy is sitting on our sofa, said he had an 'appointment' with you this morning."

She'd even done air quotes for "appointment." I glanced at my phone. It was 8:10.

"Damn it," I muttered, nearly falling out of bed. "Mindy, please, please, please ask him to give me ten minutes."

"Oh, Gen. You take your sweet little ole time," she said in her best Scarlet O'Hara impersonation. "I'll be more than delighted to keep the gentleman company."

She shot me a devious grin before prissing out of the room, still in her pink cotton pajamas and white terry cloth robe, her blonde hair twisted in a neat little bun. I rolled my eyes and scrambled toward the bathroom.

After a two-minute shower, I brushed my teeth and towel-dried my hair, letting damp waves fall loosely. Powdering some concealer under my eyes and on the fading bite mark, I noticed the bite had already nearly healed. Kat was right. We do heal quickly.

Come to think of it, I'd never been one to bruise easily or show injuries, even in my early days of learning karate. I'd always thought it was just good genes and lots of vitamins, but perhaps it was something else in my blood—whatever made me a Vessel.

With that thought, I examined the fast-healing wound across my abdomen. The angry red welt had already thinned to a white line, barely puckered on the smooth skin of my stomach. The stitches hadn't even fully dissolved, and the wound had nearly healed.

I brushed a little mascara on my lashes and dabbed tinted lip balm on my lips. I'd done my best to cover up the bags under my eyes from tossing and turning long before falling into a fitful sleep. All thanks to Jude's bit of advice that had me wondering why he seemed to care so much about me, while at the same time rejecting me and finally leaving me in a stupor of sexual frustration.

"Good enough."

I pulled on black workout pants and a white tank with spaghetti straps then zipped on my green hoodie. After slipping on my shoes, I headed into the living room to find Jude filling it up with his massive presence. Lounging on the sofa with one arm across the back, the other casually on his thigh, he seemed too big for the room.

"…but it's really a matter of practice and perseverance."

"Fascinating. Simply fascinating," Mindy said in a rapturous tone.

Fascinating? I've never heard that word come out of her mouth since I've known her, which has been since the sixth grade. I tried not to snort with laughter. She was perched next to him on the sofa in a ball, her chin on her knees, making googly eyes. Much to his credit, he acted quite casual about her overt attentions.

"Oh hey, Gen." All innocence and bright blue eyes.

"Hey."

I glanced at Jude, then away. His gaze fixed on me, making me self-conscious, especially after last night.

"What were you two talking about?" I asked, trying to eat up the awkward silence.

"Workouts. I was curious how Jude kept in such great shape," she replied with a sexy lilt to her words.

Heat crawled up my cheeks, but Mindy kept her sweet smile on like this was a perfectly normal conversation to have. She might've well had asked him how he got so hot and what it's like looking like a sculptured god.

"It was a pleasure to meet you," said Jude, standing and taking her hand, brushing a kiss along her knuckles. How he made this old-fashioned gesture seem normal, I still didn't know.

Mindy tittered. Yes. Tittered! Like from a bad movie where stupid girls giggle like melodramatic morons to something the hot guy says. Did she just bat her eyelashes? I was going to kill her.

"Goodbye, Mindy," I said quickly, shooting her a glare while heading for the door. "Be back this afternoon."

"Okay. Movie night, tonight, right?"

"Yep. Your choice this time."

"Bye, Jude," she crooned sweetly.

I rolled my eyes, following Jude to the curb where he opened the passenger door of a sleek black Audi.

"New car?" I asked, stepping in.

"It's Kat's," he replied, closing the door without explaining further.

He didn't need to. I was a big girl and figured it out pretty fast. Sifting and riding the motorcycle required close skin-to-skin contact. He must regret what happened last night, for whatever reason, and planned to prevent a second occurrence. Damn him.

"Okay, so I want to talk about last night," I said as soon as he backed out of the drive.

I caught the sudden clenching of his hands on the steering wheel and wondered once more why he'd kissed me last night and had gone all cold with me this morning. Was he just trying to teach me a lesson and put me in my place in a macho sort of way? Or did he truly desire me?

He didn't say a word as he headed into traffic, shoulders stiff. I waited a minute, letting him stew, before I continued.

"That demon, Garzel, why did he tell you his name but not his master's?"

Jude visibly relaxed, apparently relieved my questioning was about demons and not the super-hot make-out session on my bed. I might let that slide for now, but not forever.

"One of two reasons. Either his devotion to his master was such that he didn't care about his own well-being, or his master had put him under a spell, a compulsion, where he couldn't reveal the name. It was most probably the latter."

"But if it were the latter, he had no choice but to refuse your demand."

"True." A glance from simmering, dark eyes.

"But then, you gave him to that Collector thing when he couldn't help from refusing you?"

"True. Is this line of questioning going somewhere?"

"Well, I'm trying to figure out how you could hand over a helpless creature to that, that thing, when it wasn't his fault he couldn't give you what you demanded."

"Helpless creature? You do realize he nearly killed you."

"Yes. Of course." Okay, not helpless, that sounded stupid.

"You do realize he has killed many, many others." Jude's icy words made me feel small. If he was trying to push me away, he was doing a damn fine job. "Garzel is a demon. He deserved no mercy."

Yes. He was right, but there was something unjust about condemning a creature, even an evil demon, to an eternity of some terrible fate when the creature had no choice but to obey his master.

This ruthless side of Jude put me on my guard a little more. Perhaps last night was a mistake, no matter that the electric heat between us still filled up the small confines of Kat's car.

"So what is the Collector? That angel-of-death-looking thing."

"Acheron is a soul collector. What we call *endless death*."

I remembered that he'd given Garzel an option—*truth or endless death*. So he had summoned that thing last night to be his underworld assassin.

"When he takes you," Jude continued, "there's nothing but an eternity of sorrow and emptiness, a lifeless agony where the soul has no respite."

"Acheron? As in the river in the underworld from Greek mythology? That's quite a coincidence."

Jude drove down Decatur, the streets rather empty this time of day.

"Not a coincidence. Mythology always has a grain of truth, does it not? Acheron is a river of souls, of sorrow and lament, feeding on unending woe. Some call them soul eaters, not Collectors."

"Nice."

Jude ignored my sarcasm and went on. "I imagine the Greek philosopher who first put the rivers into writing was a Flamma of some kind, knowing the truth of our world and wanting to put fear into the living."

"Wait, there are five rivers in the Greek underworld. There are five of those Collector things out there!"

Jude nodded. "Though they don't all look like Acheron."

"Thank God," I sighed, remembering the sight of the ghastly wraith and the touch of hollow, eternal sadness when it opened its mouth.

"Some of them are far worse. Acheron is rather…docile, compared to his brothers and sisters."

"Docile! Are you fucking kidding me?"

"Afraid not," he said, pulling onto Dauphine and backing into a spot behind his bike.

"Wait. Acheron actually bowed to you before he left. Do you know him? Like on friendly terms?"

Jude shifted sideways in the seat, one hand on the headrest behind me. "No one is on friendly terms with a soul collector, but let us say he and I have an understanding of sorts."

"Of sorts? What sort of sorts?"

"The sort that helps me do my job."

"As a demon hunter."

"That is what I am."

His aura of flame, though not visible, licked around the tight cabin of the car. I caught his eyes flickering to my lips, then up so quickly I might've thought I imagined it. But I didn't.

"And how exactly does one become a demon hunter? You never told me. Do you just sign up to chase down evil for an eternity? Or did you do something naughty and get punished?"

His eyes sharpened, narrowed. Swirls of black glittered with gold. He moved closer, or perhaps I'd moved closer to him. Hard to tell. "Brazen words. You sure you want the answer?"

"I wouldn't have asked if I didn't. I try not to say or *do* things I'll regret."

Whether he got my meaning or not, I couldn't tell. He held me in his gaze for a heartbeat, considering something, then opened his door.

"Kat is waiting," he said gruffly, stepping quickly from the car.

I got out and sidled up beside him as we passed into the alcove leading to his courtyard. "You're really good at avoiding questions you don't want to answer."

"Lots of practice."

"Hmph, speaking of which, how old are you anyway?"

He held open the wrought-iron gate for me to pass through. A cool breeze blew over me, lifting my still-drying hair as I swept by him.

"Old enough to know when a woman is baiting me into an argument I don't want to have."

"Woman? It seems you treat me more like a child most of the time."

Except for last night, of course.

He unlocked the door to his house and stepped aside in a courteous manner to let me go first, reminding me he certainly had lived in a bygone era and had maintained some of its chivalry. I wondered if he'd also maintained some of its brutality as I moved ahead of him up the stairs. He followed very close behind.

"Oh, Genevieve," he rumbled, making something tighten low and deep. "I never mistook you for anything but a woman."

I was then all too aware he had a full view of me from behind walking up the stairs, feeling his eyes on every part of my body, specifically the lower half. I hurried the last few steps and spun around to face him, not seeing Kat in the living room.

"Where is she?"

He stood there, grinning with a scintillating, closemouthed smile on his lips. Those lips. I thought of where they'd touched me last night. Where else I'd wanted them to touch me before he stopped too soon.

A flush of heat crawled up my neck. He blinked heavily, then pointed down the hall to his studio. Pivoting at once, I tried to get away from him before he read all my thoughts. Too late, of course, for he knew exactly the kind of effect he had on me.

What I wanted to know was why the hell he'd shut everything off all of a sudden. In the midst of my inner turmoil, I tried to figure out whether I should even pursue anything beyond the protector/protectee relationship. Jude followed me into the studio and closed the door.

"Hi, Genevieve!" called Kat, wearing all-black workout

clothes that revealed a well-toned yet curvy figure. Her sleek blonde hair, tied in a high ponytail, glistened down her back. If it weren't for the twelve-inch daggers strapped to her thighs, I'd say she was a beautiful, charming young woman. Knowing what she was gave her innocent beauty a lethal edge. She gave a swift wink and a smile to Jude behind me.

Then it hit me. The green-eyed monster inside me spat and hissed, shaking the bars of the cage I tried to keep her in. Jude knew we'd be working with Kat today and didn't want me showing any signs of attraction or that we'd been in any way intimate, which would forewarn his *girlfriend* that he'd cheated on her. Kat must be his girlfriend!

I mean, look at her. Why wouldn't she be? Damn, I felt stupid. What killed me was that he could flirt with me like he did coming up the stairs right before we entered the room with her.

"Are you okay?" she asked with a concerned expression.

"I'm fine. Where do we start?"

I tried some semblance of passivity, but my aggressive nature had stepped to the forefront, wanting to claw her eyes out. But then, she was so fucking nice, I couldn't even dream of actually doing such a thing.

She walked toward me, sympathy softening into a smile. "Well, did you show Jude how well you can shield?"

I shook my head no, remembering my idiocy at letting my guard slip after several beers last night with Malcolm.

"No, she didn't," he said, only a foot behind me. I jumped. Sneaky bastard.

"What! But, it's so wonderful! You have to feel her when she casts illusion, Jude. It's quite lovely."

Okay. Jude's possible girlfriend telling me he had to feel me in any context made my face turn seven shades of red.

He moved to stand in front of me and took my hands, swallowing them in warm, callused ones. He bent his head low to mine. I stared at the floor. Why did he enjoy my discomfort so much?

"I'm ready when you are," he said.

"Really?" I mumbled.

Before he could answer, my mind sped through the Latin phrase of protection as I plunged into my safehouse—waves of golden hair, soft, lilting words, cocooned in dainty arms—then I blasted my VS into a shield around me. Moon-bright stars scattered through my mind, showering me in a protective shell.

Jude's hold tightened. He gasped. Jude gasped? I opened my eyes. Black orbs fixed on me with confusion and surprise.

"Whoohoo!" laughed Kat, jumping in a cheerleader-like way. She knew Jude had experienced what she had yesterday. I'd actually managed to spread the shield much faster than I did with her. "Amazing, right?"

Jude nodded, still staring. I didn't dare look away. I wanted him to feel the fury warring in my veins. He had deceived me with that kiss—more than a kiss—to prove a point, making me believe he wanted me, then snapped it off so easily as if it were nothing. As if I were nothing.

"Amazing," he repeated Kat's words. "The night. So fitting."

"What do you mean?" I asked.

"Your seal. A moon-bright glow in the night. It suits you."

"You could see that?"

"I know," Kat intervened. Jude dropped my hands. "It was like the cosmos had exploded everywhere when I experienced it yesterday. And wasn't I right? She casts the shield in a split second, Jude!" she yelled exuberantly, snapping her fingers for effect. "It's like she's fully aware after only one week of crossing twenty? And she's already casting without saying the chant aloud! It's remarkable."

One week? Was that all it had been? I reeled from all the insane feelings, unable to join in Kat's enthusiastic celebration.

"It is remarkable," Jude agreed, watching me closely, voice soft, gaze intent.

"Come on, then. Let's see what else she has in store. It's time to learn attack mode," Kat said, taking my arm and leading me to the center of the room.

"Before we get started, there's something that demon Garzel said to me. It's been weighing on my mind."

"What did he say?" snapped Jude.

It was so unnerving when he focused on me like that, making me feel like an insect in a jar.

"I was trying to find a way out of there, so I mentioned that Danté had marked me, thinking the demon would back off."

I swallowed hard, feeling a wave of heat shimmer across the room. Kat glanced from me to Jude. His lips tightened into a line.

"Anyway, he said Danté would have to 'mourn my loss' and that his master wanted no challenger."

Silence.

The mood plummeted. Jude shot a look at Kat across my shoulder. She walked past me to stand closer to him, speaking in a low, coaxing tone. "It's a sign. Don't you see?"

She placed a hand gently on his crossed forearms. Jude's eyes remained on me, though the usual intensity faded.

"Jude." Kat said his name as if imploring him to do something.

"Could someone please tell me what's going on? A sign of *what*?"

Kat turned away from the brooding demon hunter as if his silence was what she sought in order to continue. Sympathy was back in her eyes. "The prophecy, the one I told you about."

I nodded.

"I only have part of it, but the portion I know speaks of signs leading to the end."

"You mean the beginning," interrupted Jude.

He'd walked away from both of us, angling his body more toward the wall of practice swords. He seemed to be gazing at something far from this room, perhaps into the future, or the past.

"The beginning?" I asked.

Kat sighed, coming to me and clasping my hands as if to comfort me. The heavy dread permeating the air pressed on my chest. "There are two high demons after you. One wants you for his Vessel; the other wants you dead. We know your would-be killer is another high demon, one of the seven princes of the underworld."

I nodded, though I hadn't figured out yet how she knew this to be true. Jude remained with his back to us. She went on. "This fits the prophecy. Here, read this."

She shot a nervous glance at Jude, then pulled her cell phone from the hip of her workout pants, strapped somewhere between the fabric and her skin. She flipped through her photos, then tapped on one. "Read it."

It took a second for me to realize what I was looking at. The torn parchment of a yellowed scroll bore curving calligraphy with swirling curls and flourishes. Not only was the penmanship difficult to read, but the writing was in Latin. I understood a great deal, but these words were beyond me.

"Kat, I can't understand this. Where did you get this photo?"

"I shot it myself," she said, taking back the phone and enlarging the screen with her thumb and index finger.

"From where? Who has the original?"

"The Vatican."

"The Vatican! As in *the* Vatican?"

"Is there more than one?" She smirked.

I couldn't help but laugh a little as she continued.

"Well, as the keeper of ancient texts, they still only had this one piece," she continued. "The original was written down by a medieval monk, whose most probable name was James of Glastonbury."

"Most probable name?"

"Monks didn't sign their works, whether it was an illumination or whatever, part of the monastic denial of self and all that. I've done a bit of investigating and questioning of Flamma over the years, and there seems to be some debate about the exact time period and the name of the scribe."

"Does that really matter?" I asked, wondering why the long explanation.

Kat was patient. "Yes, of course it does. Because, you see, the prophet must have been a Vessel with the Sight to have given this specific prophecy. And the monk would have trust in the Vessel in order to scribe the prophecy into their holy books, protected for centuries at Glastonbury. Until, of course, Henry VIII—the big, fat polygamist—had so many of the English cathedrals burned or destroyed. Glastonbury being one of them."

"I still don't quite understand how the name of the monk matters."

Kat focused, apparently realizing she'd been rambling, not making any logical sense. "There are three names attached to this prophecy as the monks who scribed the original text. The names were given to me by different Flamma who've been around much, much longer than I have."

"Was George one of them?" interrupted Jude, which earned him a slit-eyed glare from Kat.

She went on. "Simeon of Glastonbury in approximately 83 AD, John of Glastonbury around 197 AD, and James of Glastonbury in 399 AD. It *must* be James in order to validate the truth of the prophecy. The first very Vessel awakened on this earth in 273 AD. Do you see? Only a Vessel with Sight could've passed the vision on to James, because no Vessel had been in our world during Simeon's and John's time."

"Two seventy-three AD," I murmured, disbelieving the fact that Vessels had come and gone all that long time.

I staggered from the weight of it. Kat had already told me that of all the Vessels she had ever known or heard of, there

were two fates for them—premature death or long-term possession by a demon. I shivered at the thought, wondering how in
the world I could ever hope for a different outcome if Vessels
had been around for centuries and none of them had escaped.
Jude had become as silent as a ghost in the corner of the room.

"Somewhere along the line," Kat interrupted my thoughts,
"the prophecy was ripped in half, either intentionally or by accident, so we only have part of it. The first part."

"Okay, just tell me what it says."

I trembled as she peered down at her phone, reading aloud.

*"Beneath the orb that circles round, while hosts of fiends
and foes abound,*
    the Vessel-born shall walk upright, fall from Grace, lose her light.
    *The sinful reign with demon hand, spread wide the Fallen's mighty
band.*
    But I, the Chalice with full Sight, do see the One to cast off night.
    Time will ebb, Time will flow, Light and Dark combat and grow
    a ruthless army of good and ill, to war on Land; humanity kill.

*When wickedness will rule on land, and all seems lost to
mortal man,*
    One Great War shall begin, upon the hour She stands within
    a ring of wordless, mighty breath; amidst the clutch of endless death.

*Two great sons of Morning Star; divided, until death
will mar.*
    One will woo the warrior maid, one will cut her to a shade.
    Two sisters of the Vessel Light, blood to blood, will evil smite.
    Have mercy on the mindless twin, when Wrath is right and Virtue sin.

. . .

SUN AND MOON, EYE TO EYE...

"THAT'S WHERE IT ENDS. WELL, THAT'S WHERE THE PAPER IS torn anyway."

I had no idea what to say, how to feel, what to think, but a trembling had started somewhere in my belly. The Morning Star—I knew the term well enough from Professor Bennett's class. The name for Lucifer before he had fallen.

"Am I the warrior maid?"

Kat nodded. "Yes. That is, I believe so. Also, you'll note the two brothers fighting over her."

"Two sisters of the Vessel Light, blood to blood, will evil smite," I mumbled, frowning. "What does that mean?"

"I always assumed it meant two women with the gift of the Vessel, sisters in their connection to the unique power."

"Blood to blood, will evil smite," I repeated. "Does that mean they smite evil together or evil smites them? It's not clear."

"No," said Jude standing right behind us. I jumped, spinning around. Damn, he did it again. "It isn't clear. I will agree, Kat, there are events tying the prophecy to the present, but there's still much that is uncertain. Let's not make too many judgments based on what we don't know."

He said this with such finality, there was no arguing. I didn't dare. And neither did Kat. I sighed.

"One thing's for damn sure."

"What's that?" asked Kat.

"I want to know how to defend myself, and I want to know now."

She smiled wickedly.

"Well, what the hell are we waiting for?"

15

When casting the shield of protection, you needed to settle into a place of peace. Not so for the cast of battle, as Kat called it. There was no sweet, rhyming Latin phrase either. Only two words to call on this power.

"*Flamma intus!*"

I channeled the *flame within*, the power emanating from my core, double-punching Kat in the abdomen with the heels of my palm, then kneeing her to the floor. A pulse of white light brightened, then dimmed as she slid across the room all the way to the wall, on her ass.

The words gave me supernatural strength. Or perhaps the strength was already there and the words simply summoned it forward. Not sure.

Kat laughed but rubbed her bum with a grimace as she stood. We both panted from the last hour of exertion. Jude watched us without a word, leaning against the wall, arms folded.

"Well, you've mastered the casting, Gen," she said, taking a deep breath. "But you need a stronger opponent to test it further. Jude?"

His eyes flicked from Kat to me, still stoic as the moment we walked in here.

"Wait, what?"

Me? Fight Jude? She had to be joking.

"Gen, I'm quite formidable, I'll admit, but I doubt you'll be attacked by someone of my build or stature. It'll be someone much bigger, like Jude. Lower demons choose the big guys to possess for a reason, and all high demons choose a strong masculine build to shift into."

Jude hadn't moved, his eyes roving up and down my body. My sweaty tank clung to my torso and loose hair stuck to the side of my face. Having redone my ponytail twice, I tightened it once more as he shoved off the wall.

"Give her a weapon."

Kat pulled a dagger from a sheath at her thigh, walking toward me.

"I thought we were practicing without weapons today."

Jude started to circle. A primitive part of me stiffened.

"A demon won't give up when you throw a few punches, even with the casting power. You need to cut them."

"But I could hurt you."

His mouth tipped up into a mocking smile. "You could try."

His shoulders rounded in a relaxed posture. Muscled arms swung just barely at his sides. He was in no way threatened by me. He probably found this comical.

"No sifting," I warned.

"No need."

He continued to stalk me with slow precision. Kat handed me her dagger. It was heavier than I thought.

"It's too big," I said, feeling the weight of the twelve-inch blade.

"Oh, I think you can handle it." A dark mischievous look. Wait. Were we still talking about daggers?

Heat flushed my cheeks. He circled. I pivoted. Kat disappeared into the corner.

"No power this time, Genevieve." His tone was heavy and dark with promise. A tingle shivered along my skin. "Let's see if you can deliver more than karate moves."

"You don't think I can cut you?"

An eyebrow lifted. Still smiling. Still circling. Arrogant ass.

"I can," I gritted out, widening and squaring my stance.

Sparks of gold glittered in his eyes, a predator honing in on its prey. He stalked closer, then stopped two feet from me, speaking in a husky tone. "Prove it."

My heart jumped, hearing my own challenge thrown back at me. Last night. Scorching kisses, whispered words, rough hands, soft sighs.

My gaze strayed to his lips. One corner quirked up into a knowing smile. He was taunting me right there in front of Kat.

What kind of game was he playing? Anger flared in my gut. I lunged, swiping out at his chest.

Grabbing one of my wrists, then the other, he twisted me around, pulling me tight against his body, my arms crossed and bound in front of me. Completely immobile in less than a second.

Okay, that was embarrassing.

"Too predictable." Warm breath close to my ear. I shivered. A short rumble of laughter in his chest. "Again?"

I struggled. He released me at once. This time, I was the one doing the circling. Leaping left, then dodging right, I ducked under his outstretched arm, slicing as I went. I popped up behind him.

Jude glanced down at the tear along the side of his white T-shirt. A small drop of blood seeped through the fabric. He laughed, stripping off the T-shirt and tossing it to the side.

"Better. Again."

My concentration scattered to the winds at the sight of his bare chest. Cords of muscle and tight, sinewy limbs flexed in preparation for the next attack. Black swirls and barbs of Celtic interlacing ink traced over tight pectorals and down his chiseled abdomen. My mouth went bone dry. A shift of his upper body gave me a glance of a feathered wing inked across a powerful shoulder blade.

Concentrate, Genevieve.

I fought the urge to shake my head as if dizzy from intoxication. For that's truly what I was, imagining what it would feel like to have his beautiful body against mine, skin on skin. Trying *not* to imagine what it would feel like.

"Anytime you're ready," he said, smirking.

Damn him.

"You know," I said, thinking to take a different approach, "a demon will attack me, not the other way around. Why don't you attack first?"

"As you wish."

Oh, shit.

He lunged low. I twisted out of reach, leaping right. He changed position, shot out his leg, tripping me to the floor. I landed on my stomach and pushed up an inch before being summarily pinned by two hundred plus pounds of hard muscle. *Oh.* Very hard.

A whisper against the shell of my ear: "Mmm. Close, but not quite. Again?"

"Get. Off!"

He obliged. Another haughty laugh. "The key is to not become distracted or let your anger control you. You must find a way to get the better of your opponent, no matter if you're outmatched in size."

Before I'd even rolled completely over, I clipped him behind the knees. He buckled to the floor as I leapt, swinging my body over his. I straddled his chest, pulling his head to the floor with my left hand knotted in that pretty hair of his, exposing his throat and thrusting the point of the dagger beneath his chin.

"Like this?" I hissed.

A genuine broad smile lightened his face, making me more breathless than I already was. Amber and gold shimmered in his irises, nearly cutting out all the black. Nearly. His hands were on my hips.

"Exactly like this." He squeezed my hips.

"Whoohoo!" Kat cheered, reminding me of the girlfriend present.

I popped up, not offering him a hand. He didn't need one anyway.

"Genevieve, you've got it, my friend." Her friend now. Great. "Combining that with the battle cast, you'll be dynamite. Let's say we go for a test run tonight."

I found it difficult to maintain my pissy attitude with Kat's enthusiasm filling up the room.

"What kind of test run?" I asked, handing her the dagger.

"You know, let's go hunt some demons, get you in a fight, see what happens."

"Is this the way demon hunters train?"

"Yes," two demon hunters replied in unison. I rolled my eyes.

"I'm not going to that damn Dungeon place."

"I wouldn't take you back there anyway," Jude admitted, making me wonder at the statement. "We'll go somewhere easy, where lower demons hang out. Tartarus."

I frowned. "Wait, that place I first met you at? In the business district?"

Jude nodded. I felt sort of stupid, realizing now he wasn't there just checking me out that night, but actually hunting his usual prey.

"I think the name of the place makes them feel more at home. I've never gone there without catching a demon or two."

"Sounds good," said Kat, walking toward the door. I followed with Jude behind me. "I'll meet you guys there about nine o'clock."

"Shouldn't I have a weapon?"

Kat stopped and leaned down in the hallway. "Here, take these," she said, unstrapping the sheath from her left leg.

"No," interrupted Jude. "I'll have something that suits her better. Go on in."

He gestured toward one of the closed doors next to the hall bathroom. As I walked in, Kat touched his arm.

"Jude, can I talk to you a minute?"

He waved for me to enter the room and followed Kat farther down the hall. I heard her say "speaking of George," then I was lost in the splendor around me.

A wall-to-wall showcase gleamed with sharpened stainless steel crafted in a forgotten age. I didn't need an appraisal to know these weapons weren't made in the here and now. Some were roughly made, some finely so.

Artisans of old must've forged the one like a medieval war sword with a thick blade and handle-less hilt. There was another, seemingly as ancient—a long, thin saber with an ornate T-handle embedded with red jewels. Were they rubies? There was a set of powerful blades with simple hilts. Square Crusader-like crosses circled the tips. The metal didn't glint like the others. Possibly iron.

How old was he?

I practically choked when my eyes slid to the last case where a four-foot-long claymore stretched the entire length of the blue-velvet-backed case. My dad's all-time favorite movie was *Highlander*. I'd watched the hero Connor MacLeod decapitate his enemies with the long Scottish sword a hundred times. The mere thought of Jude wielding such a monster made me shiver.

I faced away from the wall, realizing the room held antiques of every kind. On a small mahogany writing desk stood an ivory vase painted with the goddess Artemis on the hunt, the finish crackled with age. A feathered quill pen stood in a pewter rose-shaped inkwell. The gray feathers were frayed from use, the hollow quill worn smooth from the hand that had held it.

Were these relics of Jude's past he could not part with? What sentimental attachment could he have to these things? Had he written love letters with this quill? To Kat or some other woman?

I moved around the desk, past a huge ornate armoire to the wall behind. And my heart stopped beating altogether.

I stared into a painting of a midnight pool where a golden goddess floated in death. Garments spread wide like an angel's wings. Pale wrists bound at her waist. Yellow hair fanned in a rippling halo. I could almost hear the water lapping, trying to pull her down. Her expression—no fear, no pain. Only tranquility touched the unblemished perfection of her ethereal face. A luminescent aura shrouded her in death, promising the peace she so deserved in the afterlife. No eternal darkness for this fair maid. Above the pool, hovering in shadow, stood a guilty figure, the executioner, fleeing the scene.

I had no idea tears streamed down my face until Jude appeared silently at my side.

"What is this?" I asked.

I barely noticed he'd changed into a dark blue T-shirt and his leather jacket.

"Le Jeune Martyre."

"I know damn well what the painting is!" I nearly choked, swiping angrily at my cheeks to rid any sign of weakness. "I mean, how the hell do you have this painting in your house? A replica of the very one my mother painted shortly before she died!"

"This isn't a replica. This is the original by Paul Delaroche."

I blinked in confusion. That was impossible.

"The original is in the Louvre in Paris," I snapped.

"They do have an original by Delaroche, a second the artist modeled after this one. This is actually the first I commissioned for myself."

Hold up. The one in Paris was painted in 1850-something. I'd researched it for a project in high school as I struggled in my angst-ridden teenage years, while still grieving the loss of a mother who obsessed over this beautiful drowning martyr.

"Do you mean you're like one hundred sixty years old or something?"

"No, Genevieve."

Whew. Because that would make him freakishly old. I stepped away from him. His pupils were inky orbs of pitch. No spark of light at all.

He faced the painting. He was remembering. "This woman was the first Vessel ever to walk the earth."

His voice became steady, even, almost too calm. My mind flipped to what I remembered about the history of the painting.

"She was a Christian martyr, according to the history books," I said softly.

"She was that," he agreed, tone thick with disdain. "But she was so much more."

I waited, thinking he wouldn't continue. But he did.

"She was twenty-four when a high demon found her. She'd learned to cast illusion on her own. Actually, the summoning chant we use now was of her own making."

I wanted to interrupt and ask how, why. I thought demon hunters had created the cast of illusion. But he was in a trance. I didn't dare stop him.

"She had evaded the high demons for four years past her awakening. But when he found her——"

I felt heat rolling in waves. The orange shimmer of fire barely caressed his shoulders.

"He used her. Most foully."

I winced at the gruffness tinged with pain in his voice.

"The stain of his evil threatened to steal her very soul, so rather than let him abuse her further, she sought an honest death. She did die as a Christian and a martyr, but she was also a sacrifice so that the damned, pernicious demon Ru'um could not use her as an instrument to do his evil."

The name tingled cold up my spine. I tried the pronunciation in my head. *Roo-um*. I didn't know the name, yet something tugged deep.

"Ru'um?" I asked.

Jude faced me then. The black had not crawled beyond his irises, but I knew he ventured too close to the edge.

"You know him by another name. Danté."

I sucked in a breath, unable to move or make a sound. He wasn't speaking of a history handed down to him by others. He was speaking of memory, his memory, of a past pain lodged deep within him. My heart raced.

"Do you mean that, that you knew this Vessel?"

A single nod.

"She was my duty to protect, and I failed her. So she died."

Soft, soft words. I felt the blood drain from my face. Two things threatened to make me faint on the spot. One, there was no doubt whatsoever that Jude had loved this woman, still loved her fiercely. The pain of her loss was written in every line of his chiseled face. And second, Paul Delaroche's painting was based on the Christian martyr in the era of Emperor Diocletian around 300 AD. Jude was seventeen hundred years old!

Those eyes—inhuman, otherworldly, unnatural and mesmerizing beyond reason—paralyzed me into a statue. I didn't move a muscle as one side of his mouth quirked up in a sad sort of smile. He brushed a long finger along my jaw, then pulled away, as if touching me now caused him even more pain. My heart clenched into a tight ball.

"Do you see, Genevieve, why I protect you?"

I nodded, biting my bottom lip and refusing to cry. He needed to redeem himself, pay for his past failure to save the first Vessel of Light who still held his heart in a gilded cage, locked away from the likes of me. He needed to avenge her, especially since the high demon Ru'um was the same one stalking me. I felt sick.

"Can you take me home now?"

He stared at me with that haunting sadness for a moment more then went to the wall of steel and iron, pulling open a drawer hidden away in the shelf at the bottom of the case. He held out what appeared to be a pile of straps with two small sheaths.

"It's a vest. You loop it across your chest and shoulders like this," he said, gesturing how to pull it through the arms but without offering to touch me and show me how. No need to get too close, I suppose. "The sheaths fall flat to your ribs."

"What goes in them?" I asked, trying to sound businesslike.

Before I could even finish the question, he'd pulled out two sleek silver daggers, black-handled and beautiful. The blades were only an inch longer than the handles, but sharp as razors.

"The distribution of weight makes it easier to wield. Much more accurate if you should need to throw them at your attacker from a distance."

I thought of throwing those Chinese darts with Erik, wondering if Jude had some sort of telepathy to know about my hidden talent. I nodded, sliding both weapons into their sheaths.

He ushered me out of the room. The door closed with an audible snick, shutting his pain away from the world and prying eyes like mine. Ironically, the sting of this discovery made me want him even more—to hold him, comfort him. But that was Kat's job, not mine.

We walked in silence down to the street. Of course, Kat had left her car for him. A girlfriend does those kinds of things. A girlfriend does all kinds of things. Like kissing him good night, tucking him into bed, tucking into bed with him, kissing him good morning.

"What?" asked Jude, opening my passenger door.

"What do you mean, what?"

"You made a sound. What were you thinking about?"

The hell if I'll ever tell you!

"Nothing."

We rode all the way to my apartment without saying a word. Jude didn't seem to be brooding or anything, just thinking. I was doing my damnedest not to think of the man next to me in bed with Kat. Of course, my stupid mouth doesn't always listen to my brain.

"Kat is very beautiful."

A sidelong glance. Dark eyes glimmered with gold. "Yes."

Hmph.

"She's pretty tough, too," I admitted. "Good warrior, I'll bet."

"Yes."

"And smart."

"Very."

So last night's kiss was just what? Proving he was the big, bad alpha male after that argument about Malcolm? Boys versus men? Point taken.

He obviously regretted it, knowing he'd misled me with some pretty strong signals. I let out a huff as we pulled up the drive, opening the door and slamming it shut, practically stomping like a child to the door.

"Genevieve, is something...?"

"What time are we meeting at Tartarus?" I snapped, rounding on him at the door.

He wore a quizzical, I'm-not-amused expression. Like I cared. What reason did he have for that look of censure? I was the one being led on, the one being kissed, then dismissed, and on top of that having to take lessons from the goddess girlfriend.

"I'll pick you up about eight thirty."

"No."

"No?" One dark eyebrow shot up as he pushed into my space.

I don't think so, Mr. Hotness. I backed to the door.

"Mindy and I were supposed to have a girls' night tonight, so I'll have her with me."

"That's not a problem. I'll pick you both up."

"No, Jude. Listen, Tartarus is only a ten-minute drive. If you really think me completely incapable of making that short jump without your constant guardianship, then by all means follow us, but I'm driving *my* car with *my* best friend."

I sounded snippy and petulant. I didn't care. I needed space. Badly. He must've seen something in my eyes, because he stepped away from me.

"Fine. Nine o'clock sharp. Don't be late," he commanded, low and menacing.

I opened and closed the door in his face just about as fast as I'd done to Malcolm the night before. I doubt that had ever happened to him. Ha!

I stormed into my room and tossed my net-o-daggers on the table.

"Ohmigod, ohmigod, ohmigod!"

A little blonde cannonball launched into my room and knocked me to the bed in a tumble of squealing excitement.

"What, Mindy, what!"

Thankfully, she was laughing, or I would've thought something was terribly wrong. She waved a black-and-gold embossed square of cardstock in my face so fast it was a blur.

"What is it?" I asked, still stewing from Jude.

She stood up on the bed, hiding the expensive-looking invitation behind her back. Clearing her throat and straightening her shoulders, she gave me her best British accent, which was horrendous.

"Ms. Drake, you and I shall be shopping for very expensive formal gowns, as we are cordially invited to"—she paused, taking a deep breath and screaming the last—"the Crescent City Masquerade!"ss

She squealed again and thrust the invitation in my face, bouncing to sit beside me while I read. I scanned to the date and place—October 31st, Oakwood Plantation.

"What! How did you get this?"

"It so happens that my mom's boyfriend, Bill, who I thought was pretty worthless up until now, had an extra invitation, which counts for two. So, hello, my lovely date. We're going to the freaking Crescent City Masquerade!"

This was one of the most posh balls in town outside of the elite Mardi Gras balls. A formal masquerade at a plantation house with full orchestra, the rich and beautiful of old New Orleans glittered of an elegant bygone era. Mindy had shown me pictures of the last time her mom went with a friend a few years ago. Extravagant, lush, and gorgeous.

"Can you believe it, Gen? First, your dad offers the trip to New York, and now this! It's like we're blessed or something."

Blessed? Doubt that. My jailer hadn't said if I could go to New York yet. Of course, that's because I hadn't asked his permission. And now I'd have to ask him to go to this. I wanted to scream.

And though I was the one withholding my thoughts about him and Kat and that bone-melting make-out session that wouldn't stop replaying in my mind, I couldn't stop being pissed off. He shouldn't be coming onto me when he was with someone else, and I needed to make that abundantly clear.

"So how should we celebrate?" Mindy asked excitedly.

"You know what?" I finally returned her smile, pretending to be thrilled as she was. "Let's go out to Tartarus."

Mindy was the one always dragging me out, not the other way around. Tonight, I had a few demons to hunt, and I planned on telling Jude no more touching or kissing. The she-devil inside me whispered that it couldn't hurt to look my best when I gave him the news.

As tough as I pretended to be, my ego wasn't unbreakable. And I knew that as much as I wanted Jude, I wouldn't ever be the *other woman*. When I gave myself to a man, I wanted to be his only one.

A knot twisted in my chest at the very thought of pushing such a man away, but I had no other choice. Still, I could dress my best and show him what he was missing. Couldn't hurt, right?

16

"Daaamn, girl!"

I smiled to myself, knowing I'd turn a few heads tonight, hoping one in particular would snap his neck and get a crick when he did. Dark red skinny jeans, black V-neck top that hugged just right and square-heeled black boots fitted to the thigh. The only jewelry I wore was my St. George medal, falling below my collarbone. My nerves were jittery, but at least I looked the part of demon bait.

The bite mark had faded entirely. I straightened my hair, making it fall in sleek lines to the middle of my back.

The dagger vest fit snugly on the outside of my top, the blades at angles along each side of my rib cage. I'd summoned the cast of illusion but was still anxious about whether it would work even though I felt the power humming along my skin. Since Mindy hadn't said anything about the weapons strapped under my breasts, apparently I'd done it right.

"Not too much, huh?"

"Are you kidding me? I love it when you dress like that. Here, try this lipstick. It'll go perfect."

Mindy was makeup lady extraordinaire, always equipped with the perfect blush, gloss, or eye shadow for any occasion and any outfit. She was right. The burnished mauve shade on my lips made my skin glow even brighter.

"See?"

"Did I say you were wrong?"

"Come on. Let's go!"

"You're lookin' pretty hot yourself, Min."

Sporting a silky silver minidress with black cowgirl boots, Mindy would draw them like flies. I'd have my hands full watching out for her.

In middle school this bully Dennis used to taunt her, *"Mindy stuffs her bra-aaaa, Mindy stuffs her bra-aaaa."* That asshole even tried to see for himself if it was true, copping a feel in the hallway.

Fortunately, I was taller than even the eighth-grade boys at the time, so I stepped in, punched him square in the nose and threatened to beat every boy who messed with her again. My heroic feat had the desired effect.

On the downside, the rumor of me beating the snot out of the scariest middle-school bully also frightened away any boy who might've been interested in me for years. Hence, my lack of boyfriends throughout high school.

For some reason, her sweet-n-sexy demeanor coupled with her small stature lured all kinds of losers, thinking to take advantage. Good thing she had an Amazon for a best friend. And now, thanks to my demon-hunter duo, I had a few more moves and weapons with which to do some damage.

I locked the door of the apartment. Mindy started singing one of her made-up songs she tended to create when she was super giddy, twirling her wristlet around in the air. "Min and Gen, hittin' the town, dancin' all night, and messin' around!"

I laughed as we strapped into my 380ZX and I zipped out of the driveway into traffic. Damn, it felt good to be behind the wheel again. For some reason, it seemed like forever. I checked the perimeter for Lord of Protection. No sign of him.

"So, what happened with you and Malcolm last night? You never told me. Was he a good kisser?"

"Mindy, *please*." I did *not* want my thoughts wandering to that whole incident.

"Oh, don't you *please* me. Give me the details."

"It was fine."

"Fine?"

Mindy twisted in her seat to stare me down. I hated when she did that, trying to read my face. She was good at it.

"Oooooo, what happened?"

I realized I was blushing. It had nothing to do with Malcolm and everything to do with the hunk of man who came into my bedroom afterward, pressed me into my mattress, kissed me senseless, and made me want to do a lot more.

"Nothing. I mean, we had a good time, had a few beers."

"Aaaand?"

She waved her hand, palm up, trying to pull the information from me.

"And, yes, we kissed."

"Oooooo, where?"

"At the front door."

"That's not what I meant." She gave me a devious smile.

I punched her lightly. "Stop it. To be honest, Min, he was a terrible kisser."

"Oh, nooooo! But he's such perfect boyfriend material. A bad kiss can ruin everything!"

And a good kiss can melt your brain into mush. Not to mention what it can do to other parts of the female anatomy.

"Well, you can always teach him."

"Very funny. It's just, I don't know, I'm not feeling the chemistry."

"Uh-oh. Then break it off now and try to keep it friendly."

"Yeah. Well, I haven't talked to him since last night, and he's texted me like three times 'hoping I had a good time', as he put it. I don't know what to say. I don't want to lead him on, you know?"

"Take it from me. Do it fast and quick, like ripping off a Band-Aid. Trust me, it's better if you're up-front."

"Yeah, you've had a lot of experience with breakups. You'd know."

A sweet giggle. She knew I was teasing, even though it was true. "I can't help it. I like boys."

"Yes, I'm well aware of that addiction of yours. Here we are."

I found a good spot under a streetlight, not in a dark alley where David had parked us last time. Moron. I could feel the music pumping from the entrance. The big-and-beefy bouncer stood on duty again.

"Hey, there, Sunshine," I said cheerily, passing him my ID. "You still here?"

He glanced at my license, then handed it back between his index and middle finger, raking dark eyes up and down.

"Still here." Nice deep Conan-like voice to match the physique. "I'll be glad to go wherever you go when I get off."

I was about to give him a flirty no thanks when Mindy pinched me and pushed me through the door, saying, "She'd love that!"

"Mindy," I warned, glaring over my shoulder as we made our way inside. "He's not my type."

"The problem is, you don't really know your type, Gen. You spend too much time turning boys into your friends instead of a boyfriend. You need a man, and you need to get laid."

I huffed. "Wow. I'm that desperate looking?"

"Not desperate. Just hungry."

Turning away from her impish smile, I tried to remember why I was really here and tried to ignore who I was so hungry for.

We must've come on goth night. This crowd preferred dark monotones. Florence and the Machine's "Heavy In Your Arms" pulsed slow and intense. Mindy made a beeline for the blue-lit bar.

I reached out with my VS, not sensing the presence of Flamma. Glancing up at one of the metal cages on the edge of the dance floor, I saw Kat swaying gently. She winked at me, then looked away. I realized then that I wouldn't detect Flamma or demons if they were casting illusion.

She wore skintight gray pants and a white blousy top. Of course, daggers were strapped to her thighs, but I couldn't see them until I focused very hard on breaking through her glamour.

I marveled at how the casts worked. What you saw and were able to penetrate depended not only on the strength of the caster but also on the strength of the one trying to break it. Non-Flamma couldn't break through a cast even if they knew it existed.

"Appletini, please," Mindy called to the smiling bartender.

"Oh no you don't," I whispered. "No way am I carrying you out of here like last time. Two Killians, please."

"Ugh. Okay, mother hen. Hey! There's Jeff from psych class."

She sauntered over to a guy standing with two others at the end of the bar. I'd actually seen one of them somewhere on campus before, but couldn't think where.

I waited for our beers, then joined them. Mindy laughed heartily at something Jeff said when I walked up.

"I know! I think the professor's half-crazy herself. Jeff, this is my best friend, Genevieve."

"Nice to meet you," he replied with a smile. "These are my roommates, Matt and Isaac."

Matt gave us a friendly nod and went back to a conversation with the brunette on his left. They seemed like nice guys. Jeans and T-shirts. No frills. The kind of guys who made me feel comfortable. Why couldn't Mindy date a guy like Jeff instead of Dazzling Dave?

"Let's go dance!" screamed Mindy, pulling Jeff with her.

Isaac didn't move, keeping his back glued to the bar. I nodded to the floor. "You wanna go?"

"Uh no. Not much of a dancer."

I decided to stay put too. I could scope out the scene better from here.

"So, did you get all of the information you needed on *Paradise Lost*?" asked Isaac.

I scrunched my eyebrows together, then remembered. He worked at the library. I'd seen him a few times on study nights with Malcolm and Mary.

Isaac had bright blue eyes, framed behind thin, silver-rimmed glasses. He was cute and nice.

"That's where I know you from. Yeah, we got everything we needed. That was for a test in Renaissance Lit."

"Ah," he nodded. "Professor Bennett?"

"Yeah." I smiled, though it didn't put the guy at ease. I tried to figure out why all the tension, glancing down as I took a swig of beer. Oh, my attire. I looked like I was going to kick ass and take names.

Well, I planned to do exactly that once I found myself a demon. I hadn't thought of how my aggressive, albeit sexy-as-hell, getup would affect anyone else, especially Mr. Librarian. "Bennett. He's such a douche."

Isaac laughed. Nice sound. Nice guy. I wished I wasn't scaring the crap out of him.

"He is definitely that. Smart as hell, but he's got the god complex of a lot of professors."

I tried my friendly smile. He seemed to relax a bit. "So, I know this sounds like a line, but do you come here often?" he asked.

"No." I laughed. "Mindy brought me here on my birthday not long ago for the first time. Not my normal hangout."

"Mine either," he said, relaxing further.

I almost laughed. I felt like I was trying to gentle a timid dog closer to my fingertips for a morsel of bread. We fell into comfortable conversation for several minutes when I sensed *him*.

I scanned across the bar, spotting Jude in the same shadowed corner where I'd first seen him, gazing at me with heat and flames. How he didn't set me on fire with that raw, burning gaze I'm not sure. And yes, like a moth to the light, I couldn't help myself.

"Be back in a minute, Isaac."

I set my beer down and walked into the throng on the dance floor as Tool's "Sober" began thrumming slow and steady, vibrating through my chest.

People sort of swayed and bobbed heads rather than danced as the hypnotizing cadence rocked the place. Sweat and perfume mingled as bodies pressed close. I wove slowly through the crowd, catching Jude's fuming gaze as white spotlights swiveled over us to the beat.

I wouldn't be intimidated. At least, that's what I told myself. I walked tall and strong, grazing by dancers, pushing through them. The whole while, Jude melted me with his black stare.

By the time I cleared the last obstructing person to the small space he occupied, my heart hammered at a painful speed. Still, I held my chin high, never breaking eye contact. That would be a sign of weakness. Not tonight.

His voice scraped on that gravelly level. "What exactly do you think you are doing, Genevieve?"

His eyes dropped to my breasts, exposed more than usual in this top. The effect was palpable. He might as well have grabbed my blouse and stripped them bare.

"What do you mean?" I tried to act casual, though it sounded like a frog was caught in my throat. "I'm meeting you here for demon-defense training. That was the plan, right?"

"You know exactly what I mean."

A rough hand wrapped around my nape, hauling me closer.

"I'm afraid I don't," I snapped with a little bite. "Why don't you explain it to me?"

"With pleasure."

His other hand gripped me hip, and he pressed me back into the shadowed corner behind him. His thigh pushed between my own. I tried desperately not to moan, barely succeeding. He kept his chest from touching mine, as if that barrier was too dangerous to cross. The whole while, the angry beat and words of "Sober" pounded into me.

I glared up at him, willing myself not to melt.

"Dangerous girl, aren't you, Genevieve?" He stroked his thumb under my top and along the skin at my waist. "Let me explain to you very clearly what I mean. Dressing in this fashion with a body like yours gives off a certain signal to men, which I could care less about. What I do care about is the signal you're sending to me, for it is quite clear this *is* for me."

His hand rose higher under my shirt, wrapping my waist, thumb grazing my ribs.

I pressed my hands to his rock-hard chest. "Stop it. You have no claims on me, Jude."

"Don't I?"

"*No.*" Emotion made my voice quiver. "I won't be the other woman to your girlfriend, Kat. I'll never be second to anyone."

His expression shifted. A ghost of wicked humor crossed his face, then was gone.

"There is nothing, has never been, and never will be anything between Kat and me but a history of expelling demons to the underworld."

"But, well then…why did you regret last night…what we did in my bedroom?"

"I have no regrets in my life but one. Maybe two. Last night was far from a regret and far less than what I wanted to do."

I sucked in a breath.

"I don't understand," I struggled to say, wedged in by the heat and muscle of him hazing my senses, his thumb still coasting gently over bare skin. "I thought you didn't want me."

"Untainted hands, heart and body. Do you remember me telling you about that?"

I drunkenly nodded as his thigh brushed between my legs again.

"When I see you like this, touch you, I'm quite willing to go to hell for a taste and drag you down with me. Both our souls be damned. I'm restraining myself not for any gallant reason. Burning awhile in hell is a small price to pay to quench the burning I have for you. But"—he leaned closer, lips brushing my ear—"what I won't allow is any possible opportunity for that filthy fuck Danté to get his hands on you. You are *mine*, Genevieve. And I will have you. Do you understand my meaning now?"

I think I stopped breathing halfway through his speech. I couldn't move. I should've been more shaken by the callous way he tossed our souls aside, but his hand wrapping my nape came up and fisted in my hair, forcing me to look up into his feral gaze.

"I left last night because I was on the verge of losing control and fucking you senseless."

I couldn't speak. But it seemed he still hand plenty to say.

"I had to know what was possible, what I could do to you without putting you in danger."

"What?" I whispered, barely audible over the music. Had he like researched or asked someone how far we could go sexually or something?

"Do you understand?" he asked, voice husky, warm breath close to my lips.

I was caught in the storm of his eyes, walled in by flickering flame, unable to say a word. Not sure of anything anymore. Only that I never wanted him to stop touching me.

"And so there's no misunderstanding whatsoever, you can warn the boy, or not, that if he dares lay a finger or even thinks about putting his lips on this skin," he rumbled darkly, grazing his thumb along my throat, his ravenous gaze dropping to my neck, "then he won't even remember his own fucking name when I'm done with him. Am I being clear enough now?"

I nodded dumbly. A hard wall of chest pressed against the softness of mine, pushing me against the brick. A whimper escaped me. No way could I keep my senses in check when Jude had me in his arms.

"Say it, Genevieve."

Sultry, whispered words as his thumb lifted my chin, my mouth closer for his taking. Yes. I wanted very much to be consumed by the flames of Jude. Yes. I wanted him and only him.

"Yes."

A fierce melding of lips and tongue. He branded me, making damn sure I knew where he stood.

God, the heat of him. My VS hummed through my veins, as if inviting the man to set me on fire.

"Wider," he whispered against my lips, pulling my chin down and pushing my thighs farther apart. The sensation nearly drove me mad. My fingers dug into his broad shoulders, willing him to crush me right through the wall.

"Yes," I breathed. "Yes."

He made some sort of satisfied rumbling sound in response, angling my head for better access, tangling a hand in my hair as he swept his tongue in deeper.

"You'll be the death of me," he whispered, trailing scorching nips and sucking kisses along my jaw to the base of my ear and down my neck. That was quite an admission considering how long he'd been alive.

I threaded a hand into the hair at his nape as his mouth tasted and melted me into a liquid, pliant creature. Something stirred not just between my legs, because my pussy had started throbbing the second he touched me, but farther up around my heart.

He knocked on a door slammed shut and bolted tight long

ago when the one I loved most in the world had left me. I felt my hand trembling on the knob, wanting to open it. For him.

Jude lifted the hand from my waist and cupped my breast, his thumb brushing soft circles around my nipple, teasing. I moaned into his mouth, pressing closer. The same hand continued moving lower until I felt the distinct downward slide of my zipper.

I muffled his name, breaking the kiss, wondering what the hell he was doing right here on the dance floor.

"Shhh. Easy." He continued to open my jeans. "No one can see us."

That's when I realized while my body was on fucking fire with lust, I also felt his shield of illusion.

"You can make us invisible?"

"They can't see us," he reassured simply again. "I need to touch you," he murmured. "Can't stand it another second. Open your legs for me, baby."

So when he shoved my jeans a few inches down my hips, I did as he commanded and spread my legs wider. Right there on the fucking dancefloor. But like he said, no one seemed to see us.

"That's my sweet girl," he murmured against my lips then slid his hand inside the front of my panties.

His middle finger glided along my slit straight to my entrance where I was drenching my panties.

"Fuck, yes," he rumbled deep, whispering against my lips, "My girl needs me."

He stroked that one long, thick finger inside me then back out, circling my clitoris slow and gentle.

"Jude," I begged, digging my nails in deep and rocking my hips forward, knowing I was spiraling toward an orgasm embarrassingly fast.

"Need your eyes open, beautiful," he grated. "Need to see you come."

I stared into the glittering dark of his eyes, hardly a speck of gold within. He held me captive with his gaze and his hands and his fierce will.

Music blared and lights flashed and people sweated and danced feet away, but I saw nothing but him. This man who held far more than my life in his hands. My heart tripped faster as if knowing she was in trouble too.

"Jude," I cried on a whisper, still rocking against him, needing him to work me harder.

"Let go," he commanded, flicking my clit faster before he plunged two fingers inside me.

I bit down on my bottom lip, stifling the cry as I came on his fingers, collapsing against him, pressing my forehead to the center of his chest. I continued rocking my hips in small thrusts, fucking his fingers through the orgasm, moaning at the pleasure of his thumb pressing against my clit.

He wrapped an arm around my waist to hold me up and against him, his thick fingers still buried inside me, his big palm now cupping my mound. I gripped his shoulders tight, my pussy continously pulsing around him.

"That's my girl," he murmured against my temple, massaging the heel of his palm against my sex.

When I'd caught my breath and stood straighter, leaning back against the wall, he finally removed his fingers from inside me. But I didn't expect him to hold my gaze and raise those glistening fingers to his mouth then suck them clean.

He hummed masculine approval, while I stared in shock. Before I could say a word, he reached down between us, zipped and snapped up my jeans then rested his hands on my waist.

The song ended, moving into another. A moody new release by Billie Eilish. Jude squeezed my waist, exhaling a heavy breath. He pressed his forehead to mine for a second before pulling away with a smug grin on his face. Completely satisfied with himself. Well, maybe not completely satisfied, I thought, feeling his hard dick against my hip.

"Now that we're clear on where we stand, how about you go

hunt us up a demon?" He could pretend to be all casual about what had just happened, but his chest rose and fell fast enough.

"Okay," I said, pushing him a little farther away. He let me. "Are you okay?" I asked, glancing at the obvious bulge in his jeans.

"No. But I'm better now that I've tasted you."

My face flushed with heat. I'd never had a guy say stuff that bold to me.

He lifted his hand to cup my jaw, tracing my bottom lip with the thumb he'd used on me. Strangely, the smell of myself on him only spiked a new swirl of heat low in my abdomen.

"I can't wait to put this beautiful mouth to work," he mused, his voice rough and deep, "but that will have to wait."

I squeezed my eyes shut. "Please stop saying stuff like that to me."

I'd never had a man talk so blatantly about giving him a blow job before. Or about *tasting* me, for Christ's sake.

The throbbing heat that had started up again between my legs told me that some part of me sure as hell liked Jude's dirty talk.

"Open your eyes, Genevieve."

I did.

He smiled, amusement teasing his perfect mouth. "You're going to have to get used to it. I've been alive too long to play games or be coy about what I want. And I mean to have you, Genevieve. Then I'm going to fuck you in every possible way." He paused. "When it's safe."

He tilted his head, probably calculating whether my supersonic pulse was due to fear or desire. It was mostly the latter.

Gulping hard, some insane part of me was curious to know, so I asked, "If I didn't want you to pursue me, would you stop?"

"No." A sharp, definitive reply. "But I'd give you some space till you realized you were meant for me."

The adrenaline rush from the orgasm and Jude staking his claim seemed to give me courage to say exactly how I felt.

"And what if there's no need to pursue me? What if I'm already yours?"

I thought I'd seen all of Jude's dark expressions by now. But I was wrong.

He stared at me with such heavy-lidded hunger, it transformed his godlike face into a primitive creature. One who was ravenous and needed to feed, sighting in on his prey.

He threaded his long fingers into my hair, sculpting them against my skull then tilted my head farther back, thumbs at the hollows of my cheeks. I wrapped my hands around his forearms.

Dropping his head, he licked my upper lip and swept his lips across mine then whispered against my mouth. "Then it's done. I'll live for you, and I'll die for you." He bit my bottom lip till it stung then licked a drop of blood away. "That's a promise."

"Jude," I whispered, overwhelmed by such a vow. "That's—"

He crushed his mouth to mine, stroking his tongue deep before sucking mine into his mouth. On a rumbly growl, he lifted away, pressing his forehead to mine as laser lights spun around us.

"Let's go get some demons."

Swallowing hard, the metallic taste of my blood in my mouth, I straightened, feeling strong and sure and powerful in the arms of Jude. "I'm ready."

"Good girl." A big, smoldering smile.

My pulse thrummed in my throat. After I took one step out of the shadowed corner, a tight grip on my waist pulled me back. He swept my hair to the side, trailing his fingers along the lower back of my neck. Gooseflesh rose all over. He did that on purpose.

"If you don't see me, don't worry," he whispered in my ear. "I'll need to move around and stay hidden. Casting illusion won't help. The demons around here will know me on sight."

"What about Kat?" I asked, glancing at her slim silhouette still in the cage. "She'll surely draw attention."

"She doesn't work this region normally. The local demons won't know her. I'll be watching. If you see a demon, lure him outside. I'll follow and back you up."

"Who says I'll need backup?"

A squeeze lower on the hip.

"I'll be watching," he promised. "Just to be sure."

"Stalker."

Warm lips on the slope between my shoulder and neck made me jump.

"Stop that," I hissed. "I've got to concentrate. I'm going now."

He smacked my butt as I walked away. Yes! *Smacked* it.

I stumbled a step forward and moved quickly into the crowd, glaring over my shoulder to see a grinning demon hunter, bloated with ego and the knowledge of just how much control he already had over my body. Among other parts of me.

"Oh, sorry," I said, bumping into a couple by accident and moving on.

When I glanced back, Jude was gone. But not really, which gave me a sense of relief. As I found my way back to the bar, Jeff, Isaac, and Mindy were downing shots of tequila.

"Yayyyy! Come on, Gen! Come do one with us!"

"Somebody's got to get you home in one piece," I assured her, hoping she wasn't going to get puking drunk. "Y'all have fun, though."

They licked salt off their hands, clinked shot glasses, downed them and shoved lime wedges into their mouths.

Mindy made an especially sour expression, scrunching up her cute face. Bright blue eyes widened as she clapped her hands. "Whoohoo! Another one, boys!"

Leave it to Mindy. A party girl if there ever was one. I'd lost my beer or the bartender had thrown it away, so I sidled up to get another.

"Killian's?" he asked.

I nodded, fishing in my pocket for some money. Just as I did, a prickling of needles stung along my spine.

"Let me get that for you, sweetheart."

I turned to the eerily familiar voice on my left and looked up into the blood-red eyes of Fabio.

Once I'd gotten over the shock of him standing there with a stupid-ass grin spread on his face, I gave him a bright smile in return.

"Well, hello there, handsome. You know, you should totally get some contacts to hide those. It may just be me, but that's really not an attractive eye color."

"Doesn't matter in a place like this, sweetheart. They all think I *am* wearing contacts. The joke's on them."

"Aha, ha, ha, ha." I laughed in an exaggerated tone, then added dryly, "Pretty funny."

He scowled. "How's your stomach?"

"Oh, awesome. Good as new. Next time, don't be such a baby. You should really actually *try* to hurt me. How's the nose? Didn't heal quite right, from the looks of it."

"Still got that smart mouth, don't ya. Bet you'll lose the attitude when I take you to Master."

"You mean Danté? Oh, he doesn't mind."

Yes, I was feeling quite cocky. His scowl changed to suspicion. I peered past him and saw the other guy who'd been with him at the dojo that night lurking to the side. He looked as menacing as ever.

"He said you might not resist." Fabio was trying to figure me out.

"Oh, he did, did he?"

Wow, one kiss and a kidnapping to Dracula's Castle and I was suddenly willing to hand myself over, body and soul. Danté was quite sure of himself. I suppose that comes with centuries— no, millennia—of seducing others to debauchery. I shivered and screwed my courage into place.

"Well, what are we waiting for? Let's go."

I stepped away from him, heading for the door. A quick glance over my shoulder. Sure enough, he followed with his partner and three others in his wake. From the looks of it, they'd found the new recruits recently. They were sort of dazed and shifty-eyed, reminding me of the guy Garzel possessed at the jukebox.

Luckily, Mindy and the boys were kicking back another round of shots, completely oblivious to me sneaking off. As I made my way through the crowd, I noticed Kat slipping out of the cage. I squeezed past Sunshine at the door and others trying to get in.

"Hey, beautiful. Leaving so soon?" he asked, frowning at my odd escort.

"I'll be back," I called with a wave. "No worries."

Beside me, Fabio latched on to my arm. His expression deepened into an ugly scowl.

"You know, I don't think Danté would want you manhandling the merchandise."

"I don't trust you." He yanked hard, pulling me close to his side.

I cursed inwardly, waiting for my moment. The mean-looking one took the other side with the new guys flanking us. The night had grown cool and windy, blowing my hair behind me. I wished I'd sacrificed a little style and worn it in a ponytail to keep it out of my face.

Two of the new recruits were dirty, oafish, and in a blind

stupor. The third was skinny and unkempt. Greasy hair clung to his face and neck under a black skullcap.

I wondered if they'd found these guys from one of the homeless dens under the interstate, feeling rather sympathetic in spite of the fact they wished me harm. The humans didn't, but the demons did. Now, Fabio and his buddy were another story. Jude had said they were fused to their human hosts, so all bets of mercy were off.

My nerves stretched, suddenly feeling alone with five determined demons marching me farther away from the comforting sound of music pumping and people babbling outside Tartarus.

They walked me nearly two blocks. The only sounds were boots on pavement and horns honking in the distance of the hip-hopping Quarter. I couldn't sense Jude or Kat at all, putting me on edge. My stomach tightened. For a second, I feared Fabio might sift out with me, but Jude had told me lower demons have limited power. They couldn't do that.

Taking a deep breath, I centered my VS and touched that inner place. A shimmer of starlight responded, making me smile.

"What's so funny?"

Fabio glared, veering me down a side street toward a black SUV with tinted windows.

"You are. You and your thug crew just crack me up. Could you get a more obvious kidnapping vehicle? You could've gone old-school with a white van and tin-foiled windows, I suppose."

"That's about enough," said Fabio, gripping my arm tighter.

"Yeah, you're right about that," I muttered, wrenching my arm free and spinning around to face them.

I pulled the cast of illusion back inside myself, revealing the daggers strapped at my ribs. Fabio snickered. His buddy circled to my left, straight-faced. The other three drones followed behind me. I remained motionless, squaring my posture, eyes on Fabio.

"Little kitty cat wants to play, you see that, Bor?" He took a step closer. "I thought you were being way too cooperative," he grunted with a sneer.

"Ooo, cooperative is kind of a big word for you, isn't it? Don't hurt yourself."

"I'm going to make you shut that smart mouth."

"Ready when you are."

I gritted my teeth, dagger in hand. So predictable, he lunged straight for me, bulky arms reaching out, though he moved faster than I remembered.

"*Flamma intus!*"

I slashed my dagger across his abdomen. A pulse of white light rippled out of my chest, down my arm, flinging Fabio back onto the pavement and knocking his head against the brick building. Eyes wide with shock stared back at me as a dark line seeped through his gray shirt in the same place as my own wound.

"Payback's a bitch, isn't it?" I glared.

Stunned still for a second, the mean one lunged for me. I spun, swinging my boot up and punching out with power simultaneously.

My VS obeyed the summons without repeating the words, though my blow missed. He ducked and clipped me from behind. I fell forward, scraping my palms on the pavement, and rolled sideways as he lunged again. I slashed in an arc, my dagger cutting across his face. He screamed and stumbled backward.

Suddenly, two viselike grips pinned my arms. I'd put my back to the newcomers by mistake. Instinct had me yanking to free myself.

"Hold her!" yelled Fabio, grim-faced, marching forward.

I crunched my boot on the foot of the scraggly guy to my left. He screamed and let go. As I swung to punch the one on my right, someone grabbed me from behind around the waist, pulling me tightly against his sweaty, foul-smelling body.

The mean one. Panic shot through me, strong and potent. I

tried to elbow him at my back, but the other minions had a tight grip on both forearms.

"So, the Vessel has learned a few tricks," Fabio grumbled, touching a finger to the bloody spot on the back of his head.

I stopped struggling, took a deep breath and summoned my power. A weak pulse thrummed in my core. I closed my eyes to focus, inhaling a deep breath.

A squeezing hand clutched my throat, snuffing out the pulsing light at once. Fear startled my eyes open to see a leering Fabio, sinister eyes glinting with rage.

"Not so smart now, are you? Master gave me a little something extra to deal with you."

I choked out a laugh, sensing someone else on the wind.

"You won't be laughing long, sweetheart."

"Neither will you," I promised.

His eyes narrowed. "Why is tha…?"

Blood gurgled in his throat. He coughed metallic-scented spray across my cheek as a sword blade ripped through his chest from behind. The besmeared tip exited the left pectoral at an angle. Dazed, Fabio peered down, gripping the blade with a shaking hand as if to shove it back through.

Jude had sifted in mid-thrust. Fabio was skewered before anyone even saw the demon hunter ringed in red-orange flames with death in his eyes.

He chanted low in the demon's ear as the life-blood drained away. At Jude's command, the creature began shriveling inward. Clawing and convulsing on the pavement, it shrieked, gurgling crimson from its mouth. I couldn't feel sorry for the demon, but I pitied the man who'd fused itself with the beast.

Eyes hooded, Jude continued to whisper an expelling chant to the thing at his feet. Fury consumed the air, brushing against my skin, my face, the emotion so strong I felt that if I reached out, it would flay the skin off my bones.

Instead, a moon-bright beam reached out from within by instinct, coating my skin in luminescent light. A shield against the rage pouring from Jude as he broke the man and demon in half.

With a final wail, the human host crumpled to a lifeless heap. Legs and arms twisted at unnatural angles, the neck lolled completely parallel to the shoulder. Smoke swirled up, dissipating in the scattering wind. We'd all frozen to watch the scene in horrific fascination. Fabio's buddy had let me go and now slowly inched away.

"Hello," came Kat's casual voice from behind.

The demon took off in one direction. The two oafs scattered, but the scraggly one fell to the pavement a few yards away. Well, no. His human body fell, but a three-foot, bony creature with sagging gray skin squeezed out of him. I felt a crackle of Flamma energy as the little demon cast illusion, disappearing into the night. Its human host lay unconscious as I'd seen happen to all the others when the lower demons vacated the premises.

All the while, Jude stood over the broken body of Fabio, eyes closed, breathing heavily. His aura of fire licked in angry waves, caressing his shoulders, flaring in arcing bursts high above him. Something was wrong.

"Jude?" I stepped cautiously forward. "Are you okay?"

He labored to catch his breath, his chest rising and falling in quick succession. He gripped his sword, a rough iron-made weapon, in a tight fist. The tip rested on the pavement, dripping dark red into a puddle at his boot.

An acrid stench of sulfur and something else—rotten and putrid—lingered around the distorted body of what was Fabio. Even worse, a malevolent presence moved in the space around Jude. Darkness, tangible and breathing, skirted up the front of his body, almost petting him.

I heard a snap and shrill cry behind me but couldn't tear my eyes away from Jude. Recognizing the distinct sound of a demon's painful exit when ripped from its host by a Dominus Daemonum, I realized Kat had taken care of Fabio's friend.

"Jude?"

Nebulous mist hung in the air for a second longer before settling onto his chest and torso, fading away. The broiling flame of light wrapping his body dimmed, seeping into the taut shoulders, broad back and slightly bent form of my demon hunter. Golden-orange fire evaporated and vanished altogether.

It was as if he simply sucked the elements back into himself. Jude unclenched the fist not gripping the hilt, cracked his neck, then peered at me with irises drenched in obsidian. Not a glimmer of gold.

"Are…are you okay?"

My voice shook. He wiped the flat of one side of the blade on his jeans, then the other, sheathing it in the scabbard across his back.

Kat marched directly toward Jude, gripping his jaw, and forcing his eyes down to meet hers. She leaned so close, I thought she was about to kiss him. If he hadn't just staked an unmistakable claim on me back in the bar, I would've been jealous. But Kat examined him. For what, I don't know. The inspection took all of three seconds before he pulled out of her grasp.

"Take care of it," she murmured in an uncharacteristically grave tone, then spoke to me when I stepped closer. "Good job, Genevieve."

"Thanks," I muttered, feeling strangely like an interloper.

"We better get back to your friend before we have to scrape her off the floor of Tartarus. And trust me, you don't want her on *that* floor." The lightness was back in her voice as she swished back in the direction of the club, blonde braid flying as she tossed it over her shoulder, "You might want to dim the lights too. Don't think we can explain that away."

I glanced down at my arms, shimmering with a faint white glow. Closing my eyes, I willed the stars to pull center, orbiting the core where my power spun and beat to the rhythm of my heart and the flow of my blood.

"Here," said Jude.

He untucked his black shirt, wiping my forehead, left cheek and nose. Fabio's blood. The pained expression Jude wore concerned me.

"What just happened?" I asked, voice shaky.

"I thought it was fairly obvious. We beat the hell out of a pack of demons."

He had flipped my palms up, brushing lightly to remove dirt and a bit of gravel. I winced.

"That's not what I meant. What happened after?"

"You were wonderful. You kept calm under pressure."

"I didn't feel calm at all, and I wasn't wonderful. I got myself completely pinned in. Now stop evading, Jude."

"Your mission was to scrounge up a demon to battle. But no. You corralled five of them and faced them with courage."

"I was scared shitless. Now tell me what I sensed hovering around you after you killed Fabio."

I gestured to the heap without looking at it. The sight was pretty revolting. My stomach squeezed with nausea.

"Does this hand hurt much?" he asked, seemingly unconcerned with my manic quesitons.

I shook my head. He twined his fingers through mine and led me away toward the club. "Jude."

A heavy exhalation of breath. "Let's get you home."

My own sigh nearly matched his. Would I ever win a battle with him? "Okay."

Kat exited the club with a sloppy, stumbling Mindy on her arm when we made it to the door. Sunshine glanced at us, me in particular next to Jude, giving me the oh-well-your-loss shrug.

Doubtful, Sunshine, but I had to admire his confidence.

"Hey, Gen!" squealed Mindy with blurry-eyed giddiness. "This is my new friend, Pat!"

"It's Kat."

"Yeah, that's right. It's Skat."

I shook my head. "At least you're a happy drunk, Min."

We hadn't parked far. Kat and I managed to get her there.

She weighed next to nothing between the two of us, even when she leaned with her whole weight.

"Who's drunk? Where we goin'? Bourbon Street? Whoohoo! Let's go to Pat O's!"

"Um, that would be no."

She turned to Kat, ignoring my refusal. "You like Hurricanes? They're awe-ssssome."

Yeah, that's what she needed, a sixteen-ounce drink of rum, vodka, gin, amaretto liqueur, triple sec and grenadine syrup. Like I wanted to clean up pink puke all night.

"Here we are," I said, unlocking my car with a click and opening the backseat.

Mindy crumpled in and started to sing, "Here I am—rock me like a hurricaaaaane."

"Looks like you've got this," said Kat with her winning smile. She sifted out in a quiet snap.

"I'll drive," said Jude, taking my keys. I didn't argue.

Mindy fell into silence on the ride home. So did I. Jude, laconic as always, said not a word.

The plan had gone relatively well, considering I did demonstrate my use of Vessel power, though weakly. Still, none of us were remotely hurt, and I finally got those two thugs out of the picture.

Then again, there was apparently an endless supply of weak-minded people who could be used for possession. But what disturbed me most of all was the undeniable presence of evil lurking around Jude after he killed Fabio. He didn't want to talk about it, and now I wasn't so sure I did either.

Jude pulled up the drive, parked, then tossed the keys to me. "I'll get her for you."

He lifted Mindy from the backseat and followed me to the door. Her blonde head rolled. She had to force it upright to see her carrier, slowly focusing on his face. "Well, hello, there."

She looped her arms around Jude's neck—a pretty, though highly intoxicated, doll in his arms.

"Hi." He smirked at me as I passed in front of them. Mindy got that glassy-eyed gaze.

"Hey. Are you Batman?"

I couldn't help but laugh as I jiggled the key into the lock.

"Do I look like Batman?"

"You totally look like Batman." Note for Mindy. Tequila and beer—not a good combo. "You'd look soooo hot in a mask and cape," she slurred, staring dreamily up at him.

"Please ignore her drunken blathering." I pushed open the door.

Mindy waved a hand around her ears like she was shooing a fly.

"Don't mind her," she whispered outrageously loud. "Do you have a Bat Cave?"

"Of course I do," he replied with such sincerity I had to choke back another laugh. "But I dare say, it may be a bit cold and dark for a sweet little thing like you."

I led him into her bedroom and pulled back the pink rosebud coverlet.

"I wouldn't mind," she said, her head thudding against his chest. "I like bats."

Jude placed her on the bed while I pulled off her boots and tucked her under the covers.

"Night, Gen," she murmured, rolling over. "Night, Batman."

I clicked the door shut behind us and walked back into the living room. When I turned around, he stood right behind me, gazing with those fathomless eyes.

"I've never seen your Bat Cave," I teased.

He eased forward, sliding large hands along my waist. "I'll be more than happy to show you," he whispered, leaning closer.

"Aren't you afraid it will be too cold and dark for me?"

"Genevieve." His face lost all trace of humor, suddenly bracketed with harder lines. He pulled me into a tight embrace flush against him.

I'd expected something teasing and sexy, not what he said with such seriousness.

"I will keep you close and warm, and you will be my light."

I gulped at the formal and tender vow. How do you respond to a something like that? Simple. You don't.

I laid my head against the hollow of his neck, wrapping my arms around his waist, pressing myself closer. His arms were bands of steel, molding my body to his.

We stood there in silence, feeling the warmth of each other, languishing in a new, fragile intimacy. My mind closed off the world as my senses reached out to record everything—the expanse of his large hand against the small of my back; the heady, masculine smell of him; the steady beat of his heart. Unbidden, my mind opened a vision in the space of a heartbeat.

A line of torches flickered gold light on the faces of warriors smeared with blue Wode at the verge of a wood. Among them, Jude peered from the shadows, the fire dancing over his still features.

Hatred lined the planes of his face. Menace sparked in the bright amber-gold of his eyes. This was no demon hunter, but a man—one filled with such focused loathing that it etched every hard angle of cheek, jaw, nose, and brow. Face fixed on something in the distance, he waited like a statue. Long black hair with war braids at the temples framed the hardened face of a warrior with murder on his mind.

A fierce-looking man to his left bearing a scar across nose and cheek muttered deep and low, "Tá anseo cinniúint, mo dheartháir." *Something lurked in the shadows behind them, swathed in night, wrapping them in cold wind. Jude's stony expression remained fixed, then he gave an almost imperceptible nod, his eyes aflame with torchlight. His voice so deep and low, I almost didn't hear his terse response.* "Aye."

I jumped, reeling back to the present. My pulse pounded wildly in my head. I had no idea what the man had said, but the words must have been some form of Gaelic. I had taken a Celtic mythology class last year with a professor obsessed with linguistics. We'd read stories not only in partially translated Gaelic but also listened to them in the original tongue. The vivid vision struck cold against my heart.

Jude pulled me back, fixing a searching gaze on me. No amber, no light—only the darkness of night. His brows bunched together, though he hadn't seemed to sense me having the vision as he did the time before.

"Are you all right? You're shaking."

I glanced down, my voice proving him right. "Just a little tired." I pulled farther away.

He frowned. But I forced a smile.

"I suppose I should tuck you into bed now." His voice dropped to the tone that made my pulse race like wildfire.

"Um, I'm not so sure that's a good idea."

My hands had moved to his chest of their own volition, fixed firmly on the strength of him. Even with the thread of desire stretching taut and threatening to snap, I was afraid of what I saw tonight—both the evil entity hovering around Jude's body on the street and the murderous man I saw in the vision.

"Perhaps you're right."

Without warning, a rough hand cupped my face, tilting it upward. He melted his lips over mine, licking in with gentle strokes, moving with such intense purpose my knees threatened to buckle.

Jude encircled an arm around my waist, holding me up and pressing me close to feel every hard muscle straining against my soft curves. When I realized I'd changed my mind and was about to ask him to jump into bed with me, he drew back, letting my lower lip slide gently from between his teeth.

A slow, slow smile touched the darkness of veiled eyes, reminding me with a shiver how many years this man had had to perfect the art of seduction.

"You're very bad," I breathed.

The corner of his mouth quirked up for a fleeting second. "I think you'll find," he whispered, nipping at my lower lip with gentle teeth, "that I'm very," warm tongue tracing his bite, "very good."

I let out a jagged breath, unable to disguise what he did to me.

"*Very* bad," I repeated.

A squeeze on the hip. Mischief shining in ebony eyes.

"Goodnight, Genevieve."

Then he sifted and was gone.

18

Though I most definitely needed a cold shower, I scalded myself with steaming water for twenty minutes, running through the events of the night.

My powers had responded at will, except when Fabio had grabbed me. What had he meant by his Master giving him something extra?

After defeating the demons, watching Jude being held within a circle of flaming light and sinister darkness, then hauling my wasted best friend home, and finally ending with a toe-curling kiss, I'd forgotten all about Fabio's final threat. Until now.

Utterly exhausted, I toweled off and slipped into sweatpants and a tank top. After blow-drying my hair and walking back into my bedroom, I realized how chilly the apartment was. Apparently, the cool front the meteorologists had been promising us had finally arrived.

I padded down the hall and switched on the thermostat to the heater for the first time this season. I brought Mindy a glass of water and two Advil, setting them on her nightstand, but she was out cold. Blonde waves pooled on her pillow and lips pursed like an infant, making a soft wheezing sound as she always did in deep sleep.

I unfolded the quilt at the foot of the bed, draped it over her, then quickly shuffled back to my room and crawled into my own bed.

"Brrrrr."

The heater had kicked on, stirring the cool air. I tucked into my goose-down comforter up to the chin and rubbed my cold feet back and forth to get the circulation flowing. Again, I drifted through the night's trials, landing on the man whose lips made me melt and arms made me feel safe as the edge of sleep took me to another place.

Or so I thought.

At first, I thought I was in a dream. Shrouded in darkness, I stood in the middle of a lifeless forest. No insects chirping, no small rodents scrambling to nests, no night birds echoing calls.

Leafless trees with craggy branches and trunks of gray encircled me. I stepped with bare feet to the nearest one, touching the tip of one finger to the trunk. The sooty form instantly crumbled, evaporating into an unseen wind, whisking away the ashes. The brush of wind felt like a whisper, an echo, not the strong gust I've felt before a storm.

A curling gray mist wreathed my ankles. A silken black nightgown with thin straps clung to my body and fell just above the knee. I watched in tranquilized fascination as tendrils of thick mist crawled upward along my pale skin.

Cool fingers of vapor caressed the lean muscle of my calf, dipped behind bare knees, smoothed over my thighs, hips, waist, whispered over my ribcage, cupped my breasts, lingered there and finally curved over my shoulders. The intimate sensation made me gasp in surprised pleasure, despite a gnawing feeling that I shouldn't be here, that I didn't want to be here. The conflicting emotions frightened me.

Mist wrapped around my wrists, tugging me along a path out of the dead woodland. From the line of ghostly trees, my bare feet touched black sand. This was no dream. My soul had sifted to this place.

Whereas my senses were slightly dulled without my physical body, my emotions were heightened, feeling everything pass through me, leaving a mark within. I'd felt this sensation before. Fear flooded my veins.

Before I even saw the black fortress, I knew it was there. Danté had beckoned, and my soul had obeyed—my own blood betraying me through his will. The mist had vanished, but there was no need for a guide. I knew where to go.

A slow-burning dread whispered through me as I stepped to the gate, spikes of iron jutting sharply upward. I didn't look up, knowing there was nothing but a murky void hovering above the castle.

The guardian crouched in the cliff face near the gate—a skeletal creature with white-watching orbs and decayed flesh pocked with gaping wounds where red spiders crept to and fro. He motioned to the gate. I knew what to do.

My mind struggled against the pull, yet the compulsion to move forward was too strong. I touched the cold black iron. It obeyed and swung open.

I walked across smooth black stones toward the Gothic arch framing the door. Yellow-eyed shapes watched from the battlements. Who were these creatures? I wondered for only an instant before some force pulled me onward.

Crossing under the archway of stone demons carved in every niche and shadow, I placed my palm upon the gargantuan black door. It creaked open at my touch.

The familiar golden interior beamed before me. Crackling fire in a large fireplace cast golden light on the black velvet sofa and chaise lounge. Crystal chandeliers sparkled among the grand room, filling the chamber with a pleasant glow. A whisper in the air or in my head called me forward.

My name echoed from deeper in the castle. The cold prince called me. A skitter of raw fear ran down my spine.

"Genevieve."

I lifted a silver candlestick from a sable-wooded table and

walked back into the foyer with a nonexistent ceiling. The black-stoned stairs spiraled up and up and up into nothingness. My name rode the wind again. I followed, unable to do anything else.

Winding up the staircase, I stopped on the second floor, which had only one door—a mirror of the arched Gothic entry of this place. With no door handle, I flattened my palm to the wood. It opened without hesitation.

Crossing the threshold felt akin to stepping into a lion's den, where the predator lurks in shadows. Though hidden, I knew he was there. Watching. Stalking.

Beyond the deep foreboding, an irresistible lure drew me farther in. I marveled at the bedchamber with its four-poster, king-size bed covered in white silk sheets fitted against the far wall to the right. Gold satin pillows piled high against the black lacquer headboard. Luxurious softness welcomed me, making me want to edge closer.

A fireplace equally as large as the one downstairs in the great hall breathed warmth with popping, lively flames tipped an unnatural blue.

A burgundy mantel framed the fireplace in an amorphous pattern, appearing to me like many-shaped eyes watching me. I stepped closer, feeling something tickle beneath my bare feet. A white fur carpet of some kind spread in front of the hearth.

I set my candlestick on the mantel, realizing I must've been mistaken, because the ornate design appeared only to be uniquely made in odd shapes. There were no eyes. Everything had a dreamlike quality, or rather like a nightmare, though I knew this was neither.

Standing in its own cozy niche, illuminated by varying-size candelabras, was a dining table. Fine white china, shining silver-ware and a pair of polished goblets were set for two in perfect alignment at the head of the long table. Lifting a silver goblet, I stared into the smooth surface seemingly too perfect to be real. My own reflection frowned back at me, a pale mirror of myself.

The ghostly vapor returned, wrapping me in a cold embrace. Misty coils materialized into bronzed, masculine arms wrapped around my waist. The solid form of a man pressed against me from behind. His head bent into my hair, his voice more concrete against my ear. Not an echo but so close I startled in surprise.

"Genevieve, you look so beautiful for me."

My heart raced from fear, though my head tipped back, offering the vulnerable column of my throat.

Why did I do this? I didn't want this.

"Oh yes, my sweet."

A mouth that scorched like frost-burn sucked at the pulse in my neck. Cold fire lit me up inside. All the same, sensual pleasure doused the pain from second to second. One of his hands smoothed over the black silk, across my abdomen and pelvic bone, sliding down the side of my thigh, fingers inching up the fabric.

I tried to speak, to scream, but nothing happened. Thoughts of protest flitted from my mind, chased away by an icy wind. Why couldn't I focus? I wanted him to stop.

"Skin like milk," he whispered against my shoulder, sliding down the thin strap of my gown, planting another burning kiss.

Silky-smooth fingers found naked flesh under my hem, sliding across the curve of my upper thigh, sloping down. Something screamed inside.

"St-Stop!"

I whirled, panting heavily, skirting around the table to put something between us. A sharp pain stabbed me for that second of rebellion against his will.

He was so beautiful—a golden god with rainstorm eyes. In a crisp white button-down and black tailored slacks, with tousled hair, he seemed like a rich playboy, not a demon prince. He smiled crookedly as I lifted the strap back onto my shoulder, sidling closer to one of the place settings.

"You're right, of course. Dinner before dessert. Come," he said, gesturing to the place setting before him. "Sit."

I shook my head, trying to keep my feet from moving, willing them to stay in place. For a moment, they did. His cold gaze fixed on me.

"Come," he commanded. I gasped, for my body moved without my consent toward the chair he'd drawn out for me. "Sit." And so I did, like a robot on remote command.

He seated himself at the head of the table to my left, smiling genially. "Now then. That's better. Let us get better acquainted."

He snapped open a white napkin and placed it on his lap. From a shadowed corner, a creature appeared I had not seen when I came into the room. I jumped in my seat.

"Don't mind Claudius. He's simply here to serve."

Dressed in the livery of a Victorian footman, the gargantuan zombie-like creature poured red wine into silver goblets. I leaned away from him, feeling unexplainably terrified of the lumbering thing. His ashen skin caved in around the eyes and sagged in hollow grooves underneath the cheekbones.

I shuddered when his eyes fixed on me—pale yellow and full of misery like a hopeless caged animal. He set the bottle on the table, then slunk from the room.

"There now. Drink."

Danté lifted his glass, took a swallow, and gestured for me to do the same. I still couldn't find my voice, but I was able to shake my head.

He angled his head in a curious way. "What is it? Do you think I would poison you?"

"No," I managed to say. "Possibly."

He tossed back his golden head, glossy hair falling away from a lovely lined face, and gave a full throaty laugh.

"Do not fear, my darling. I am not trying to trick you like Persephone with the pomegranate. This is simply"—he gestured wide—"our first date." He winked and sipped from his goblet. "I would certainly never poison my crowning jewel. Besides, your soul cannot be poisoned. Not that way, anyway." He gestured again and commanded, "Drink."

This time, I found that I couldn't resist the compulsion. I lifted the silver cup and took a sip, the liquid burning sweetly down my throat. How could my soul sense things in a physical manner?

"I don't understand," I said, staring at the wine to avoid him. "I'm not really here. How am I tasting this?"

"Oh, you are really here, Genevieve. Your soul is your essence. You can feel sensations with just your soul. However, it is less, shall we say, intense than when the body and soul are one." His voice dipped low and sinister. "All in good time, my sweet."

I glanced at him, wishing I hadn't. His gaze roved over my shoulders and farther down to my breasts. I felt beyond vulnerable in nothing more than a negligee, sitting at Danté's dining table, suffering under his burning gaze. A touch of anger flared inside me.

"Stop calling me that. I am not yours."

Stormy eyes met mine. "You will be, Genevieve. Make no mistake about that. And when you are, I'll be more than happy to teach you what it means to be mine."

The threat, laced with menace, made quite an impact. My hands trembled in my lap. I tried to understand how my soul reacted in physical ways without the body, but there was no time for that.

Right now, I needed to find a way out of here. I closed my eyes, trying to center myself and reach my Vessel power. In a deep, dark tunnel, a pinpoint of light glimmered.

"I had hoped we'd have a pleasant dinner together."

His voice jarred my eyes back open. A flash of crimson when he blinked. I flinched. He blinked again, his eyes returning to cloudy blue. The candlelight flickered, gilding his features to fine gold. The paradox of beauty hiding the beast made me shrink farther away.

"Be a good girl, Genevieve," he warned, ice in his voice.

Claudius entered with a platter, serving slices of rare roast beef and herbed new potatoes onto our plates. This all felt so surreal.

"You eat roast beef and potatoes?" I asked, leaving my hands in my lap. The idea struck me as odd, even ridiculous.

He forked a piece of bloody meat into his mouth, wiping delicately with his napkin.

"I eat whatever I want. I can have whatever I want. And so will you, my dear. Whatever your heart desires will be yours. You need only ask."

"Whatever my heart desires?" I asked, knowing full well my meaning hung heavy in the air. My heart's desires leaned toward the protective steel of a dark demon hunter.

He straightened in his chair and picked up his glass of wine, swirling it in circles. "I know you're infatuated with the hunter. It makes no difference to me. On the contrary, it may serve me quite well."

"How is that?" I asked, feeling more emboldened than before.

Something stirred when I thought of Jude, something strong and fierce. But the glare I received in return cut my breath away. He set his napkin and goblet on the table, holding out his hand to me. A piano began to play a melancholy tune from somewhere beyond the room.

"Shall we dance?"

"No," I said emphatically, shaking my head.

"Oh yes. I think so."

With those words and a flash in his eyes, my body betrayed me again, rising from the seat and joining him in front of the fire.

He pulled me close, holding my right hand out in his left and pressing his other to the small of my back, moving me in a waltzing dance. The perverted façade of civility was revolting.

Everywhere his body brushed against mine felt blistering cold. I went rigid in his arms.

"How are you making me do things I don't want to do?"

"Why, Genevieve. You wound me. Here I thought I was being the perfect gentleman. Isn't this what young ladies desire? Dinner by candlelight? Dancing with a devoted suitor?"

I couldn't even laugh at how ludicrous he sounded. "Most women prefer to be asked, not abducted from their beds."

"I didn't abduct you, my sweet. I simply called. And you came."

"I would never come here of my own free will. It's the blood, isn't it? Is that how you control me?"

Unperturbed, he continued leading me in a slow waltz on the fur carpet. His expression remained stoic. Placid and amiable, as if we truly were in some Victorian mansion and I was his willing lady, content in his arms. The reality was disturbingly the opposite.

"It's always been my understanding that women rarely know what they truly want. Their betters, specifically their lords and masters, must gently show them the way, sometimes with a firmer hand. Only then are they content to follow their true destiny."

"My destiny is not tied to you," I said with a shaky breath.

His expression hardened to sharp planes. "There has never been a Vessel without a demon lord, and I will most certainly be yours. Be sure of it."

I shuddered. A masculine whisper, a familiar chant, shivered through the hollow halls, then faded quickly away. Danté smiled as if he hadn't heard the whisper or as if it were perfectly normal to hear hostile voices echoing in this vast, bleak fortress.

"Don't worry, my sweet," he whispered into my hair, "you'll become accustomed to my touch. We have eternity to discover each other in every way."

"Never," I bit out through clenched teeth.

A throaty chuckle as he bit the lobe of my ear. I cried out, unable to pull away.

"So fiery. I like that. It will make things more…interesting. The end will be the same nevertheless."

"You are so sure of yourself," I challenged, doing my damnedest to put a few inches between us. His compulsion to have me against him was so strong the effort to resist caused spine-numbing pain.

"Yes. Once a Vessel has succumbed to me, there is no going back."

"But I will never succumb to you," I said, trying to thrust out of my mind the fact that he'd had Vessels before. What happened to them? "And Jude will never let that happen."

"Ah, but see, that's where you're wrong." His chilling gaze froze me in place. He stopped swaying to the music, coiling me tightly in his arms, his touch like a cold-blooded serpent constricting its prey. "Your hunter will deliver you to me on a silver platter. He can't help himself. So tempting, vixen that you are."

His face was a hairsbreadth away, smiling at some secret of his own. A loud banging reverberated throughout the castle. Danté's eyes slid sideways to the hallway, a sinister smile spreading wide.

"I hear you knocking, but you can't come in," he said in a singsong way that raised gooseflesh along my skin. "Oh, my sweet, you're cold. I apologize. Perhaps I should get you under the covers."

He started for the bed with a viselike grip around my wrist.

"No!"

The very thought sent me into hysterical panic. I struggled, despite the compulsion threatening to break me in half as I tried to bend away.

Furious pounding echoed from the outer door, growing louder and more violent.

Danté laughed, whether at my vain struggle or at the one

who I could guess was banging for entrance to this macabre place, I wasn't sure.

I punched toward his throat while trying to wriggle out of his grip. He slid sideways in a fluid, sinuous motion, tackling me to the white fur rug. His strength far surpassed his demon minions.

Spreading his body on top of mine, he pinned my wrists above my head, leering from blood-red eyes. He smiled, all sharpened teeth and elongated canines. My heartbeat sped in terrified alarm, the rabbit once again caught so easily by the cat. His cold aura scraped against my skin.

"You think I care about the hunter's fixation on you? It's so perfect, it's almost poetic. I'm amused just thinking of it," he said, laughing between serrated teeth. "I know you want him. There's no doubt he wants you. The fallen are forever looking heavenward. It's so obscene."

He paused to run his tongue along my neck. I bucked to push him away. That wicked laugh again before he pierced me with a bloody gaze.

"Please, with my permission, take him to bed. Go for a nice long ride. Then you'll be perfectly ripe for the taking. I don't mind sharing, just that one time. One time is all it will take," he gloated, "and you'll be mine forever."

He bent to kiss me. I twisted away violently, disturbed at his body pressing intimately against mine.

No, not my body. Just my soul.

Just my soul?

I struggled insanely to get free. The pounding ensued down-stairs, growing louder and louder. Danté nuzzled my neck in a grotesque action of playfulness. I realized I was crying, petrified and panicked. Then something tingled inside.

I shut my eyes, searching in the dark. There it was, a glimmer of white, sparkling silver deep within. I called to it, praying the words of protection in my mind. A swish of silky blonde hair brushed my cheek in memory. Swathed in my mother's embrace, she cooed soft words from long ago. Shining, beating brighter, a moonbeam pulsed out and out.

The enraged pounding downstairs grew more relentless, rebounding through the castle. Sharp pain in my wrists as Danté repositioned and bound them both in one hand. I battled to regain a hold on my power, but he was too strong, overriding my thoughts with his dominant will and piercing pain.

He gripped my jaw, snapping my face toward him. "Open your eyes, Genevieve!"

The compulsion to obey him tore a streak of pain through me when I refused, a whip licking bare skin. My power was building, growing from that inner place.

He pressed his lips against mine, grinding to try to open my mouth. My scream muffled between our mouths, I wrenched my face away. His free hand roved my body and squeezed as he hissed in my ear.

"I'm not done with you yet. Open your eyes and look at your master."

I couldn't, I couldn't. I'd never get away if I did. Burning pain seared down my spine, the penalty for fighting his will.

"Ahh!"

"It hurts, doesn't it, sweetheart?" His voice had lost every ounce of civility, now only the grating of a monster. "I can make it worse. Much, much worse."

An agonizing sharp stab bowed my back. I screamed. He chuckled.

"Open your eyes." A sultry command, like the voice of a lover.

I did, peering into the blood-red gaze of a true monster. Tears streaked hot from my eyes, slipping into my hairline.

"There now. Relax."

I stopped struggling. The pain ebbed when I obeyed his will.

"That's my girl." He pecked a light kiss on my cheek, pressing his body harder against mine. I stiffened. "No need to fear. We'll wait for our first coupling when your body and soul are one." His grin cut a sinister line across his beautiful face. "Now, as for your soul, I believe I will take a taste."

His lips pressed to mine and pried them open. When his tongue swept in, my mind folded inward. The sensation of being flipped inside out melted over me. I tried to suck in a breath, but no air came, as if I were paralyzed, as if I'd lost all control of myself. Then…

Darkness. Nothing but infinite darkness. I could breathe again. So cold here. But I wasn't alone. He followed me. No. He brought me here. His presence—a web of tangible evil wrapped me in his net. If I moved, he sensed the motion, following with stealth. His cold breath brushed the back of my neck. His voice was a hollow echo in this place.

"Mmm… You're even lovelier on the inside." Panic gripped me hard. He was inside me, his ghastly essence strangling my soul, taking hold of me from within. His voice, a sibilant whisper, breathed close to my ear, "So many delectable memory scars."

A flickering of light, then I stood in my mother's studio. I was nine years old, braids in my hair, eyes wide and staring at the horrifying canvas before me, the paint still wet. In a vast ocean of blue, nude bodies of dead women and children floated on the waves, bloated in death, hungry shadows lurking beneath them. In the sky, a bright golden sun shone in mockery of the floating dead. My mother stepped from her washroom, drying her hands.

"Sweetheart, I didn't hear you come in." She stepped behind me, resting one hand on my shoulder as we both gazed at the horror in oils. She brushed a hand down my back, a soothing gesture of hers. I trembled before her artwork. "Remember, death is always waiting for the innocents. Waiting to reach up and pull us down to the world below."

"Lily! What are you doing?"

I spun, finding my father in the doorway, his expression dark, his posture tight.

"Just showing our daughter my latest work."

He stormed across the studio. "You are never to show her this so-called art of yours."

"Why keep her from the truth? Evil lurks. I want her to be aware."

"Are you crazy!"

I pressed my hands to my ears as the arguing escalated to shouts. I backed to the doorway till I was outside and running from their raging voices.

Darkness again. Coldness seeped through me.

"No," I whispered, still shrouded in night, constricted by ropes of Danté's making.

"There are so many to choose from," he hissed. "How about this one?"

Another fluttering of light, and I stood in the hallway of my middle school, opening my locker. Brenda Blakely hovered a few feet away with a gaggle of girls. I'd beaten Brenda for the last spot on the girls' soccer team the week before. One of her friends whispered something inaudible.

"I don't know," replied Brenda. "Her mom jumped off the Mississippi Bridge. Who could she possibly bring to the Mother/Daughter Tea? She's probably crazy too. Like mother, like daughter."

They giggled. I slammed the locker door and walked away, refusing to let the burning tears fall.

I never did go to the Tea. Never even mentioned it to my dad. One of many events I'd forego because she chose to step off that bridge.

The black enveloped me for a split second before I was once more standing inside a painful memory. "No," I said the second I realized where I was—the cemetery where we'd memorialized my mother with a stone marker. The swirling eddies of the Mississippi had never borne her body up. We were left engraving her name in marble and visiting this empty plot next to where my father would one day lie.

I was sixteen and had come home a day early from a beach vacation with Mindy, knowing how depressed Dad could get near their anniversary. I'd found empty beer bottles and old photograph albums open on the kitchen table. But no Dad. I'd waited for hours, but he'd never come home. I'd called his friends. No luck. Seeing the evidence strewn about the house, I'd finally found him here, stretched out in front of her headstone.

"Dad."

He jerked up, eyes rimmed with red. He burst into tears. Never had he shown such emotion in front of me. Never had I seen my strong father reduced to such despair. I knelt down and hugged him. His shoulders shook with sobs.

"Why wasn't I enough for her?" he cried, heartbreaking anguish in his voice.

"Dad, no. She loved you. She did." Hot tears welled in my eyes.

"But not enough," was the desolate reply.

My soul screamed and ran from the memory, remembering that I'd also felt I was never enough. She chose death over us.

"No more," I whispered into the pitch black. Malevolence skated along my skin, petting me. "Please. No more."

Invisible arms wrapped me in an embrace. I held still, unable to fight or struggle, wanting only the peace of mindless oblivion.

The sensation of folding inward again and falling fast through an even darker hole made me nauseous. I gagged as if someone were choking me, the stranglehold of Danté releasing my soul then…candlelight.

I lay beneath him as before. He still had my wrists pinned with one hand, laughing down with undisguised mirth. "Your fear is a powerful aphrodisiac." His other hand roamed down my ribcage. "Just imagine when you are good and mine, the pleasure we'll share." The painting of the floating dead flashed to mind, and I realized what it would mean to be a Vessel for a demon prince. Not only would I be forced to commit his atrocities, I'd be corrupted into relishing the evil deeds.

"No," I said, jerking my arms, testing his hold.

"No?" He stilled, his fangs elongating. "I grow rather weary of that word." Hard lust glinted in his eyes. His hand clasped the top of my gown and ripped, tearing it down the middle.

"No!" I screamed, wrenching one hand free and grappling to push him away. He was too strong.

A flash of sharp fangs. His teeth sank into the tender hollow of my neck below my jaw, penetrating me with frost-numbing pain. He groaned with sick pleasure, sucking at my neck viciously. A strangled scream reverberated against the walls. My own.

The pounding on the outer door snapped me away from the brink of insanity. Danté had violated my mind, my soul. He'd take no more.

Amid the cesspool of potent fear and pain I was drowning in, a flicker of light, a tattered thought, buoyed its way to the surface, up to the moon-brightness.

He would not take all of me. He would *not* take all of me. Righteous fury flared into a building burn as my lips said the words.

"*Flamma intus.*"

With a blinding flash, my Vessel power exploded in a burst of silver white. Danté flew off me and crashed half across the dining table. China shattered, silver scattered, and a candelabrum knocked to the floor, snuffing out the candles. He stared with wide, gray eyes, half-dazed, bewilderment plastered on his face. His fierce expression, hard and dangerous, jarred me into action.

I leaped to my feet and sprinted out the door, not caring that the torn gown fell half off my body and flew behind me in torn strips.

Practically stumbling down the steps, I scraped bare feet and toes on the cold stone. I followed the hammering echoes—down, down, down. It was only one flight of stairs, but a chill wind brushed my back. No!

Leaping the last few steps in one bound, I made it to the giant black door, which swung backward at my touch.

There on bended knees was Jude. Fists tightly clenched and

so, so bloody. His head snapped up, black gaze tormented with despair and helpless rage.

Bursting onto his feet, he took in my state of undress as I teetered on the threshold of the door, dazed and terror-stricken. He grabbed me by the shoulders, gaze flicking behind me, and yanked me roughly into his arms, holding me close.

A gust of cool wind slammed the massive black door with a resounding boom, but not before I heard the distinct, smug sound of lilting laughter.

19

Sifting through space, Jude crushed me in his arms, no chance of letting go and losing me in the Void. Iron-clad armor covered me like a blanket of steel. In a state of shock, I held on and kept my eyes closed, oblivious to any motion sickness that normally twisted my stomach when sifting. I squeezed my eyes tight, trying to erase the images of Danté. Impossible.

I don't know how long we sifted, but when the sensation of falling had stopped, I opened my eyes to see my body, still as death, tucked safely in bed, one arm hanging over the edge. Jude quickly laid my spirit literally on top of my still, solid form. Darkness behind closed lids for a split second before I opened them and sucked in a lungful of air. Whole again.

That elusive feeling of transparency had vanished. Back in my skin in my own room with Jude standing above me, I sat up and burst into tears. Abruptly, he had me on my feet in his arms. Panicked, I pushed away. He pulled me close and sifted out again.

What? Where is he taking me?

I beat and shoved, trying to break free of his tight grasp. My hair whipped wildly. The dark Void sucked at me when I put distance between myself and Jude, drawing me toward windy oblivion. I almost wanted to go. He manacled my wrists, yanking me toward him.

"No!" My scream echoed in the abyss.

Gray shapes blurred past, some drawing closer, as if curious, whispering. I kicked and punched, managing to free one hand. Jude spun me by the other wrist, pinning me against him, my back to his chest.

The vacuum released me, and we were standing in Jude's living room.

"Let me go!"

He did. Still, I spun with force and cuffed him under the jaw with the heel of my hand. He didn't resist or restrain me as I rained blows on him, one very hard across the cheek.

I don't know why I hit him. My mind knew it wasn't his fault, but my body didn't care. The fierce hatred boiling to the surface needed release. And he was there, standing and taking it when I needed something to beat.

I finally took several steps away from him, my chest heaving in gasping breaths, hot tears spilling down my cheeks.

"Why did you bring me here? I want—"

"Genevieve, it's safer here."

Jude's voice was thick with emotion I'd never heard before— his words tight and hard. I didn't give a shit. My body started shaking, teeth chattering with grief and anger thrumming through my veins.

"Safe?" I choked on a laugh, my sardonic tone biting the air. "Safe? I'm not safe! Not here, not with you! Not anywhere!"

His eyes, devoid of all color but the darkest pitch, glared with seething anger. Tangible rage beat off of him in a misty, black aura. This only incited me more.

"How, Jude? How did he get to me? You promised," I sobbed, "you promised he couldn't soul-sift me again."

He stepped toward me. I took a giant step back, bumping against the fireplace, where something poked my shoulder. I jumped at the carven image of the writhing dragon that wrapped the wooden mantel.

My mind shifted, seeing another one, deep red with amorphous eyes…feeling the white fur carpet against my bare back…the bronzed creature looming over me with a sinister grin. Disgust and horror permeated every fiber, though I felt no bruising on my wrists or neck, no memory of Danté's dark invasion. I sighed a shaky breath, trying desperately to forget the visceral image and feel of him invading my mind and soul.

"He's grown in power," Jude began, his own breathing labored. "My cast of protection should've kept him at bay. But somehow, he circumvented it. I'm—" He paused. His gaze dropped from me to the floor as if he couldn't stand to look at me, his bloody fists clenched. "I'm sorry."

"Sorry doesn't even begin to touch how I feel." Voice trembling, I added, "It doesn't matter anyway."

"What?" His shoulders squared to rigid stone. His gaze was the same.

I ignored his question, unable to keep Danté's hateful threats from spewing from my mouth. "You know, he talked about you."

Jude moved closer. There was nowhere for me to go. I tipped my chin up defiantly.

"What"—his voice grating like steel on stone—"did he say?"

"He told me you would be the one to deliver me to him— body and soul. 'On a silver platter' were his exact words."

If black could burn, there would've been fire in his eyes. The darker shadow hovering around Jude swelled outward. "And how would I go about doing that?"

He edged closer, now only a foot away. My pulse raced.

"He said you'd seduce me because you couldn't help yourself. He even encouraged me to do it, to, how did he put it? 'Take a nice long ride.'" Bitterness leaked from every word, but I couldn't stop. "Of course, he'd only let you fuck me the one time, because that's all it would take to 'taint' me before I'd become his play toy forever."

Jude gripped my arms, squeezing long fingers into bare flesh. "Do you think I would do that?" he asked, voice vibrating with fury.

I shrugged. His fingers clenched tighter.

"Fuck you and leave you for him? Is that what you think I'd do?" A vein pulsed at his throat that I'd never noticed before, but of course, I'd never seen this Jude—completely, absolutely consumed with burning hatred. It might have even matched mine.

My heart pounded furiously against my ribcage. I wanted to scream, but my instincts pulled me into a morbidly calm place. "Let go of me, Jude," I enunciated softly. My eerily gentle tone spun him into madness.

"I couldn't get you out!" He released me with a jerk. "I couldn't fucking stop him!"

His fists came down in a thunderous crash on the mantel behind me. A resounding crack split the dragon down the middle, his jaw stretching in a grotesque yawn.

The silent aftermath made my quiet words even more cruel.

"No. You couldn't," I said, watching him try to regain control with his palms splayed on the wall above the mantel, his head bowed between broad shoulders. "And neither could I. Not until he held me down and possessed me, forcing me to relive my most painful past, showing me how easily he could take me and do what he wanted."

Jude flinched, jerking upright, frozen in place. Horror bent his features into fearsome, hard lines. Whatever stormed inside of him was nowhere near what raged inside of me. But the truth cut deep, and I knew we would both bleed from this wound for a long, long time.

I walked away, went into his bedroom, and slammed the door behind me, locking it. Though he could sift in any time he wanted, I knew he'd get the message.

I stood in front of a mirror on the wall, staring at my reflection, hardly recognizing myself. Red-rimmed eyes traveled directly to the spot at my neck and shoulder where Danté had savagely bitten, seeming to suck the life right out of me. Nothing. No blood, no gaping wound, no puncture marks of any kind.

My fingers traced over the unmarred skin. I gazed as if hypnotized by my unblemished reflection, to my wrists where he'd bound me. How could I bear no trace of what he'd done?

But, of course, I did bear marks. You just couldn't see them. I felt scraped and scarred on the inside where he'd poked tender, precious memories. He stirred old heartbreak and laughed at my pain. He toyed with me.

He would do worse if he ever had me truly in his grasp. The only way to stop the staggering pain he'd whipped through my body was to succumb, give him what he wanted. I knew now why other Vessels surrendered to their demon hosts.

My confident hope that no demon could ever possess me crumbled under the memory of Danté chaining my body and mind. I feared whether I could hold out if he caught me again. Would I then become his possession, a Vessel of darkness?

I jumped at the furious, bellowing yell and the sound of splintering wood, crashing glass and toppling furniture outside the bedroom door. I crept to the corner behind the bed, sank down, curled into a ball and wept for something precious that was irrevocably lost.

I AWOKE IN SEMIDARKNESS, JOLTING UPRIGHT WITH A GASP, NOT knowing where I was. Nestled into the clean softness of Jude's bed, under the covers, I was surprised he'd come in after all and tucked me into bed. The house was ghostly quiet. Had he left me here alone? Panic washed over me, sweat beading along my hairline.

He'd left his closet light on. I pushed out of bed and walked to it, wanting something more over my tank. I thumbed through his closet—leather and denim jackets galore, black slacks, a long trench.

"Someone's afraid of color."

Everything in monotones of black, gray, and brown. Wait. Except in the back. My hands brushed the delicate garment of soft yellow, my pulse quickening, for I knew what it was before I took it from the rack. My pretty blouse, the day Danté had disguised himself as Jude and forced himself on me the first time.

I'd tossed the bloodstained top in Jude's trash, not wanting a reminder of that painful bite. But Jude had washed it clean of any mark of him, no blood at all, then kept the delicate blouse tucked neatly with his clothes. He'd even found and sewn the buttons ripped away by Danté.

Fresh tears slipped down my cheeks, but I swiped them away. Could Jude wash me clean? A darkness hovered inside where Danté had smothered me with his evil spirit, mocking memories I'd hidden from everyone. Even myself. Hands trembling, I put the blouse back, a fresh wave of loss burning inside.

I found a navy-blue hoodie and slipped it on, completely unable to imagine Jude wearing such a thing. Perhaps the great Master of Demons must travel in disguise sometimes. The hoodie dwarfed me, which was exactly what I wanted.

When I opened the door, I stood staring in shock. I'd forgotten about the violent crashes and noise I'd heard before I fell into a weary sleep. The mantel had been ripped from the wall, now in a heap of splintered fragments of wood. An ugly patch of unpainted, exposed brick framed the fireplace. Both lamps were shattered into tiny pieces on the floor. His over-stuffed chair was embedded halfway through the large window overlooking the courtyard.

A slight breeze squeezed through the shattered glass, making a soft whooshing sound. Other than that, everything was still and quiet.

I peeked down the hall. The door to his room of weapons and antiques was ajar, but no light emanated through the crevice. I stepped in quietly, not seeing him. Still, I sensed him here.

Treading on light feet, I found him sitting underneath the painting, "Le Jeune Martyre." Back against the wall, slumped forward, knees drawn up and one bloody hand gripping the wrist of the other. His head bent, he didn't seem to notice me.

As I passed the writing desk, I turned on the Venetian lamp. The click snapped Jude's head up. He regarded me for a second, then glanced back at the floor. I sat silently in front of him, crossing my legs yoga style. The rage now subdued, I needed some answers.

"Why couldn't you get inside that place?" I asked.

He didn't reply at first, and I thought perhaps he'd fallen into some sort of trance, but finally he looked up at me.

"He used a blood cast to keep me out."

"A blood cast? He used my blood to keep you out?"

The idea struck me cold, knowing it was my fault I'd let Danté get close enough to bite me. Of course, I thought he was Jude at the time.

"Not yours, Genevieve. Mine."

What?

"Your blood? How did he—"

He shook his head and exhaled in an exasperated way, seeming to rouse from a deep reverie. His head fell back against the wall.

"I can't believe a mistake I made so long ago would come back to haunt me now. Now when—." He stopped and gazed at me, his features shadowed in the semidarkness. "I have so much to lose. The irony is laughable."

But he didn't laugh. Simply gazed at me as if he couldn't believe I was still sitting there before him.

"What do you mean irony?"

A brief pause.

"At the time, I cared about absolutely nothing. Not my blood. Not my body. Not my soul. And now, I—" He stopped. I'd never heard Jude so much at a loss for words. He whispered so softly to himself, it could've been the voice of a child. "So this is the price of a devil's bargain."

He lapsed into silence again, but I needed to know.

"Jude, why did you let him take your blood? Did you know he could use it for a blood cast?"

His eyes closed in a sign of resignation, looking almost ashamed.

"Actually, no. I knew blood casts could bind people to demons, but I never knew it could block someone out of a demon's domain. It was such a long time ago." He paused, shaking his head with a snort of sad laughter. "I gave my blood willingly as a trade to save her." He nodded upward. "He'd said it would save her. Fool that I was, I believed him. He used my blood to summon me on occasion, to torture me, and manipulate her."

More pain creased that noble brow. I wanted to trace my fingers along those frowning lines and wipe them away. But I didn't.

"So you sacrificed yourself for her, though he lied."

"I never thought of it as a sacrifice."

No. He wouldn't.

"You loved her very much, didn't you?"

He lifted his head. "Of course, I did. She was my mother."

"Your mother?" I'd assumed the woman was his wife or lover, not his mother. "But, she was so young. You said you were responsible for her. How could you be?"

A heavy sigh. He tilted his head against the wall behind him. "She married my father when she was thirteen years old. I know. Seems young to you, but at that time, it was commonplace. I was born the same year. As a Vessel, she expelled demons for several years, until she was twenty-four. That's when Danté found her."

His voice dipped dangerously low.

"I'll spare you the details, but suffice it to say, she refused to become his"—he glanced at me meaningfully—"his slave. She begged my father to kill her before Danté could take her away. Danté had already threatened to kill me and my father if she didn't bend to his will. So my father did as my mother wished. He bound her hands, drowned her in a pond near our home, and then hanged himself from the nearest tree."

I gasped, glancing up to the painting above his head. The man in shadows wasn't simply her executioner. He was her beloved, Jude's father. Tears pricked my eyes, realizing the extent of Jude's grief. Jude and I shared the same feeling of abandonment, though his outweighed my own.

"And what happened to you?" I asked, voice breaking.

"Me? Danté sold me into slavery to a Celtic war party not long after. I was twelve years old, on the cusp of manhood. Again, that probably seems young to you, I'm sure, but then I would've been nearly a man. I was big for my age, so I was summarily sold into fighting another man's battles as another man's property."

His lips compressed. I knew this was all he would tell me for now. My heart ached—for him, for myself.

"Jude, I'm—"

His gaze locked on me—intense and burning. Nothing I wanted to say could possibly come out of my mouth.

Jude, I'm sorry. Sorry for you. Sorry for me. I'm broken. I'm furious that you couldn't save me. I hate you for it. I need you to hold me. I want you in the worst kind of way, but I'm terrified to let another man touch me. I'm falling into a dark place, and I don't want to go. Please, don't let me go.

Jude reached out slowly, hands gripping my waist in a gentle hold, and pulled me across the floor to him. Barricaded between his legs and arms, he buried his head in my hair, resting his forehead against my shoulder, and I felt…safe. My heart quieted.

I'd been in Jude's arms many times at this point, but I hadn't felt the gentleness of his touch, not like this. His hands fisted in my hair and the back of the sweatshirt, clutching me to him. No words were needed. He knew my soul-deep anguish.

I wrapped an arm across one shoulder, cupping the back of his head to cradle him against me. We didn't say anything but simply held each other for some time. When he pulled back, he wore an unreadable expression, everything hidden once again. He traced his thumb along my cheekbone before pulling both hands into his lap and looking at them. I held them palms down.

Dried blood caked in brown splotches and scratches on both hands. Rough abrasions with skin scraped clean off from the tip of his pinky fingers all along the outer edge of both hands to his wrists. Knuckle bones exposed white on the middle and forefingers. I flipped them. A gash ran along the fleshy part of his left palm.

"Let's get this cleaned up," I said.

In the bathroom, he ran his hands under the water, still silent.

"Where's your medical kit, that one you used for my stitches?"

"Bottom cabinet," he said, scrubbing his hands clean.

I found it and opened it up, searching for gauze or bandages or something. Jude dried his hands on a towel, then slid the kit closer to him on the counter. I watched as he took the stitching needle and thread and, without anesthetic, closed up the gash on his palm with seven perfectly spaced stitches.

"That doesn't hurt?" I asked as he snipped the ends expertly. I realized then he moved with the deft swiftness of an expert who'd done this countless times.

Having set aside the stitching tools in the kit, he fixed dark eyes on me, the whites now showing but no sparks of amber in the irises. The air was heavy with too many things said and too many unsaid.

"Genevieve, you do realize I would never jeopardize your safety. For any reason."

It wasn't a question.

"Yes," I replied honestly.

"He won't be able to soul-sift you again," he said, holding my gaze.

"Why not?"

"He may have some power over us with the blood casts, but I have connections of my own, more powerful than him. He'll *never*—listen to me—*never* be able to soul-sift you again."

"There's a way to keep him from soul-sifting me." My voice quivered with an accusation. He answered my question before I could ask it.

"Yes. I didn't think it would be necessary to go to such extremes. My protection cast should've been enough. But I—" He caught my gaze in the mirror. Pain bracketed his eyes and mouth.

"But what, Jude?"

He leaned sideways against the counter. "Danté could never break through my cast of protection before. He was never strong enough to beat me."

"But he is now," I added, unable to hold my tongue. The truth was that his opponent had bested him. He'd underestimated Danté's strength, and his error had cost me dearly. But while Danté had invaded my heart and soul with his malevolent essence, he hadn't taken me in every way. My Vessel power made sure of that.

Jude gripped the edge of the counter with one hand, white-knuckled. "Apparently. But there are others stronger than him."

"Friends of yours?"

"A friend. Yes." He sighed and crossed his arms, shoulders drawing tight. "He'll help us."

Us. Jude saw this as *our* problem, not mine. I should be grateful for that. He had made a mistake. A big one. I needed to accept that and move on. Allowing him to wallow in his misery only hurt us both. I blew out a breath and leaned with one hip against the counter.

"Jude, can I ask you something?"

A sharp nod.

"How did you know he'd soul-sifted me? I mean, how did you know to come for me?"

He paused. "Honestly, I'm not certain. I was lying in bed. I felt a tremor, a disturbance, and somehow I knew you needed me."

I frowned, wondering how that could be possible. "What does that mean?"

"I'm not sure, but I can tell you this. No matter what, I'll always come for you," he said softly, tucking a lock of loose hair behind my ear, then pulling his hand away, fixing me with a look that made me breathless. "Always."

I gulped hard, unable to speak.

"I'll be damned," he added, "more so than I already am, before I let him take you again."

More so? I gazed up at his beautiful face hardened by grave determination, such depth of feeling etched in every line. I needed this man beyond reason, and I couldn't explain why.

"Would you do me a favor?" I asked softly.

"Anything, Genevieve. Anything," he said with such emotion I thought my heart would break in two.

"Kiss me."

I wanted Jude to erase the memory of the demon's lips, so rough and cruel against mine. I wanted the sensation of touch from someone who cared about me. I wanted...I wanted Jude.

He stared as if memorizing my face. Obsidian eyes lingered over cheek, brow, nose, lips. He hesitated, then cupped my cheek, letting the tips of his fingers edge into my hair. Leaning down, he brushed his lips lightly against mine. As he coaxed a soft kiss from me, I met him with tenderness. He didn't deepen it but only showed me with feather-lightness that I was still his.

"So strong, my Genevieve," he whispered against my lips. "My warrior woman."

I'm not sure if he knew what it did to me when he claimed me in such a way. I shivered from head to toe.

"Cold?" he asked, planting gentle kisses up my cheek, across closed eyelids.

"No."

"Scared?"

"Yes."

He paused. Words so soft. "I'd never hurt you. Never."

He made his way across my brow and descended, giving me assurance of my safety and of his feelings for me. He angled his head and pressed in a little deeper, barely opening his mouth. After the slowest, most languorous kiss I'd ever experienced, he lifted away, pressing warm lips to my forehead.

My heart hammered against my ribs, partly from fear, partly from desire. I pressed my cheek against his chest, wrapped my arms around his waist, and listened to his own heartbeat racing. A wave of relief swept through me.

Fear hadn't ruled me. One stitch closed a seam in the fracture caused by the demon prince.

I mumbled low, lower than a whisper, "Thank you."

20

The trickle of water calmed my nerves. I stared at the frozen figures of Eros and Psyche, wrapped in a passionate embrace. Psyche had fallen for Eros blindly, not knowing the man, the god, who made love to her every night in the dark. When she finally saw his true form, she lost him, forced to wander and seek him out across the heavens, the earth, and the underworld. I wondered at this as the slow, waking sounds of the city rose with the gray morning light.

Knees tucked under my chin, I listened to the world coming awake—a pleasant, comforting sound. Two larks flitted and chirped on the stone wall surrounding the courtyard. On Dauphine Street, a car door opened and shut, then the engine started and was gone. The distant murmur and shuffle of vendors opening booths at the French market rose over the wall. Someone laughed. It all seemed so strange, but soothing at the same time. My personal troubles didn't keep the world from turning. Funny, but that actually made me feel better.

"Good morning." Kat walked toward me, bright smile beaming.

"Morning," I replied, but not as brightly.

In faded jeans and a gray peacoat with her platinum hair

twisted in a messy bun, she appeared so much younger than she normally did in her kick-ass attire. She sat next to me and slid a white baker's box across the stone bench. "I thought you'd want some breakfast."

I tried to smile. She opened the box to a tempting assortment—chocolate éclairs, bear claws, cinnamon twists, chocolate-glazed donuts.

"Oh, come on. Chocolate always makes a girl feel better." She picked up an éclair and took a bite, smiling encouragingly.

"He told you?"

She nodded, setting the pastry down, and sighed.

"He told me that Danté soul-sifted you last night and that he'd…possessed your soul before you could get away."

Her eyes dropped, then met mine with a knowing look. More green than black, they held empathy. A horrible thought struck me.

"Danté's taken you before?"

She shook her head. "Not him. Another." She stared at the fountain. "He kept me for a long time and possessed me in every way possible."

Something shifted inside. This bad-ass beautiful woman reeking of confidence and I-don't-take-no-shit attitude had been through an ordeal even worse than mine—dominated and humiliated through pain and shame for the sick pleasure of another.

"How are you holding up?" she asked, her tone sharp.

"Barely."

She wiped her fingers on a napkin in the pastry box and stared at the bench a minute, stalling, it seemed.

"I'm sorry, Gen," she said awkwardly. "I'm just glad Jude was able to get you out of there before he could do worse to you."

"He didn't. I got myself out."

Her eyes widened. "Really?"

I nodded.

"Your Vessel power saved you? That's awesome!"

I nodded again with a shrug.

"Holy hell!" She stood up, pacing in front of me. "Don't you see? Don't you get it?"

"No. What?"

"It's a sign!" She sat down, taking one of my hands and squeezing. "You're the one, Gen, the Vessel in the prophecy! I know it now! Like, I'm absolutely sure of it!"

"What do you mean? What does that prove?"

"Are you kidding me?" She stared, incredulous and wide-eyed. "You're not even fully awakened, and you fought off a demon prince, older than earth, who controls your soul with your blood, and you fought him off in his realm where everything must obey him. As far as I know, it's never been done. I mean, even I couldn't get out on my own. I needed—well, never mind." She shook off the persistent memory marring her face. "I'm certain. You are *the* Vessel."

She was right. I suppose it was pretty incredible, knowing the power he wielded up until the moment I blasted him.

"Oh man, what I would've done to see his face."

I couldn't help but smile, remembering Danté's wicked eyes widening with confusion.

"It was pretty awesome," I admitted.

"I bet it was." She laughed.

"Kat." I turned serious again. "When I was there, everything, I mean, it was just my soul, but it felt so… I don't know how to explain it."

She nodded, scooting closer on the bench. "Yes, I know what you mean. Our souls, even outside of our bodies, experience emotion and sensation the same as if body and soul were one. But," she said with a grave gleam in her eye, "our bodies complete us, giving us the power of physical form. When we're whole, we're more than body or soul alone. It's difficult to put into words, but just know"—she paused, giving my hand a squeeze—"it will fade. You will heal. And you'll be stronger than before."

I believed her, despite the ache sitting on my heart. After all, she knew from experience.

"Kat, can I ask you, well, did Jude save you when you were…taken?"

She shook her head. "No. It was someone else." A frown creased her pretty brow, and she wouldn't meet my gaze. "It took a very long time for him to get inside the lair of Damas. By the time he came for me, I'd lost all my hope."

Pain tightened her features and pinched her brow. I stayed quiet a moment longer until I couldn't help but ask, "Why did it take so long?"

"He has a deep lair, well-guarded."

"So, this Damas, he's one of the princes?"

A curt nod.

"You said deep. Deep in where?"

She gave me a puzzled look. "In hell, of course."

I flinched. How did I not realize I'd been in hell that whole time? Black fortress in a lifeless void, demonic creatures on watch, serving their lord and master. I laughed at my stupidity, but my heart opened to a wonderful realization.

"You mean I saved myself from the clutches of a demon prince in hell? On my own?"

"Yeah! That's what I'm saying. You're so awesome." She gave me a gentle shove on the shoulder. "You're my hero, Gen."

We both laughed. Though the wound was still raw and fresh, Kat gave me hope. She'd been through worse and survived to be this vibrant and strong warrior. So could I. Hammering broke up our girl-power celebration.

"What's he doing?" Kat asked, peering up at the second-floor window where Jude nailed plywood over the broken window from the inside.

"Oh, he's, um, cleaning up."

"Cleaning up or remodeling?"

"Well, I imagine he'll be doing a little of both."

"Yikes," she said, eyebrows raised. "I'm actually surprised his house is still standing."

"Why do you say that?"

"Genevieve. Seriously?"

"What?"

She scoffed. "Listen, I've known Jude the better part of two centuries, and while he's generally an intense guy, I've never seen him so smitten before. For anyone."

"Smitten?"

"Smitten. Fixated. Obsessed. Bewitched. Whatever you want to call it, he's got it bad."

I felt a warm blush crawl up my cheeks. I glanced at my watch nervously.

"What's up? You late for something?"

"Actually, I will be soon. I've skipped tons of classes since, well, since I met you guys. Mindy is even harassing me about ditching so much class, and she's not exactly the studious type."

Kat smiled. "I wouldn't worry about that. Take a little more time off. You deserve it."

"Are you kidding?" I asked a bit sarcastically. "Go home and lie in bed where I can be alone with my thoughts all day? I don't think so."

She nodded. "Touché, my friend. Well, you can't go without a bodyguard."

"Yeah, I know but—"

"Jude!" she yelled up toward the house.

The man being summoned popped into existence before us, sifting in a snap. Ripped jeans, stained T-shirt, flexed arms, and hammer in hand, he looked like a walking advertisement for Studs-R-Us.

"Down, boy," protested Kat with her hands up. "I didn't do it, whatever it is."

The corner of one side of his mouth twitched. His eyes fell on me, totally unreadable. He seemed to be having difficulty dragging his gaze from me as Kat informed him she was taking me to class.

"I can take her," he said, dark eyes still fixed.

"I'd rather Kat took me," I said, adding quickly, "I need to go by the dojo after class, and it'll be easier to introduce Kat to my dad rather than have to explain, well, you."

I gestured my hand up and down the length of him. Again, his lips almost pulled into a smile but didn't quite make it.

"Why would I be difficult to explain?"

"Well, I don't bring boys, I mean, men, home or to work, and Dad's really protective, so it would just be easier to bring my new friend Kat along so I won't get the third degree."

Kat looped her arm through mine, giving me a cheesy grin with her new title as friend. I wondered if she had many, or any, for that matter. Then I realized that she probably didn't, besides other demon hunters, who were most probably all men. Men like this stubborn slab of steel in front of me. But Jude nodded, finally agreeing, proving me wrong for once.

"Your father has some sense. I like him," he grumbled. I rolled my eyes. "But, Kat, I want check-ins every hour on the hour. And if you so much as think there is company in the vicinity—"

"I know, I know. Sift out ASAP. No problem. I got this."

He gave a tight nod, moving forward as if to embrace me, then seemed to change his mind. He touched my cheek lightly with the back of his knuckles and withdrew.

"I'll see you this afternoon," he said, then sifted back upstairs.

AFTER DRIVING TO MY APARTMENT WHERE MINDY WAS STILL passed out from the night before, I took a quick shower and changed into jeans and my Witcher sweatshirt. Glancing down at Geralt of Rivia looking badass as ever, it hit me that he bore a strong resemblance to Jude, if he had black hair instead of blond.

I took my time getting dressed, meandering around, fetching more Advil for Mindy and putting it by her bedside. Procrastinating.

"So," Kat said as we backed out of the drive in her car, "why don't you want to go to your Lit class again? I thought you were all into that ancient literature and stuff."

I watched the joggers doing laps through City Park as we drove by.

"I'm not ready to deal with Malcolm."

"Malcolm? Was that the guy with you on the Riverfront that night?"

"Yeah. He's a friend. Well, he was. I don't know. We were friends, then I went on a date with him, and now I've changed my mind. Ugh. Just so awkward."

Kat laughed.

"What?" I asked.

"Oh, nothing. I'd forgotten about this kind of stuff, not that I ever actually dated in my youth. We more or less did the London Season, went to balls, and if you danced too many times with one gentleman, then I suppose that was construed as leading him on as you've done to poor Malcolm."

"Thanks. That makes me feel so much better."

"I'm here to help," she said, giving me a huge grin as she swerved into a parking spot.

"You know, I can't even imagine you in the Victorian era. You just seem to scream twenty-first century."

"I'm very good at adapting." She winked conspiratorially, locking the door with her key fob as we walked toward campus.

"I have no trouble believing that at all. Geez, the men must've been impressive at those balls. All dashing and dapper in their swallow-tailed evening dress?"

"Hmmph," she grunted. Her eyes swirled darkly. "Some, yes. But, a gentleman of the gentry in evening dress is the perfect mask to hide the wolf beneath. They weren't all dashing and dapper."

We walked along the outer buildings.

"Did you ever marry one of these flirtatious Victorian men? One of the dashing, dapper types?"

I regretted the question as soon as it spilled out of my mouth. I could've kicked myself. Her expression turned wistful.

"Yeah. Sure did." Her eyes grew distant and cold with no further explanation. "I'll meet you right here afterwards."

I nodded, ducking into the building. When I glanced back, she'd opened one of those romance novels with a bare-chested hottie on the cover. She was a conundrum, Kat.

I was a little nervous about Latin class after nearly a two-week hiatus. Fortunately, Professor Minga adored me, which made it all that more difficult to outright lie to her, saying I'd had some lingering bug that kept me bedridden. I easily jumped into the lesson, translating a passage of Cicero. Mary was seated at the desk next to me.

"Where have you been?" she whispered as I opened to the passage I was assigned. "Were you really sick?"

I shrugged. "A little," I half lied, for I had gotten quite a few injuries recently. "I've had some personal stuff to deal with."

Mary accepted that excuse with a nod, focusing back on her work. She wasn't the nosy type.

I took a deep breath and read Cicero's words. As I started to scribble the translation in the margin beneath the passage, my hands began to shake. How could I possibly have returned on this day to translate this specific passage? I couldn't go beyond what was already translated, but just stared down at the words.

Professor Minga stopped by my desk, pushing her spectacles up on the bridge of her nose. Kind, pale blue eyes examined me.

"Is there a problem, Genevieve?"

"No, ma'am. I was just thinking about this passage. Is this correct?"

"Read it to me."

So I did.

"*Be sure that it is not you that is mortal, but only your body. For that man whom your outward form reveals is not yourself. The spirit is the true self, not the physical figure.*"

"*Perfectus.* It seems time off hasn't made you rusty at all. Why the frown?"

Professor Minga didn't mince words. She said what she thought, and I liked that.

"I was wondering about the meaning of what Cicero is saying here. About the body and the soul."

"Ah. Yes. Well, Cicero was a pagan like the rest of the Romans, but he also had high ideals and believed in an afterlife. He often professed that man's deeds on earth determined the goodness or foulness of his soul and thus affected them in the eternal realm. Here, he is concerned with eternal death if the mortal man abuses his soul through his physical form."

"Do you believe that, Professor? That the soul can be eternally damned if it is damaged?"

Her nose twitched as she pushed her glasses up another half inch. My heart was in my throat, waiting for her answer.

"In my mind, that would depend upon the person's intent in doing the damage. Sometimes we are injured regardless of what we say or do. Am I right?"

She had no idea how right she was. I sighed with a sense of odd relief at her cryptic words.

"Right," I agreed.

She nodded with satisfaction. Her duty done, she moved on to Mary.

My question, of course came from the ghastly thought that Danté could've damaged me permanently last night, opening old wounds I'd all but forgotten. Wounds that stirred fear and anger in my heart. The body and soul are separate entities, one reflecting the other.

I thought of Jude. His body was beautiful to the extreme. Did it reflect his inner self? Or keep his true self hidden?

I packed up and found Kat right outside the building on a bench where I'd left her, engrossed in her romance. Her expression of deep concentration made me laugh.

"Is it a good story?"

She popped up as we headed back across campus. "It's so thrilling," she squeaked. She pointed to the title on the cover. "*Captain Sparr's Captive*. I mean, there's this pirate, Captain Sparr, you see. And Violet, that's the girl, she's on a voyage with the British troops to the new colonies in America when the pirates attack. And when she's captured, oh my gosh, the captain keeps her captive and—"

"Kat! You're blushing *so* bad." I laughed. I'd never seen her stumble over her words.

"I can't believe people write stuff like this!"

"Okay, Kat. You actually witnessed the sexual revolution firsthand, right?"

"Yes, but, I don't know. There's something about reading the words combined with your own imagination that's so intense! Oops," she said, pulling out her iPhone vibrating in her coat pocket. "Every hour on the hour, that man."

"What's our orders? Back to his house pronto?" I asked as lightly as I could.

"No. He wants us to meet him at Drago's for dinner after your karate class," she said with a question in her voice.

"Drago's?"

I was taken aback, wondering why he'd want to meet there. Drago's was a four-star restaurant in the Riverfront Hilton over on Canal Street. While Kat texted him back, I glanced down at my frumpy attire. I was definitely not dressed for the occasion. Kat snorted when her phone vibrated a response.

"Smart-ass," she mumbled.

"What?"

"I asked him why we're meeting there. His reply was 'to eat'.

Dinner reservations for six o'clock, and don't be late are his orders."

I smiled. Playful Jude was back.

"Well, I'll have to go shower and change from the dojo. I can't go there like this."

"Neither can I," she agreed, waving to her faded jeans with a trendy rip at the knee. "What time does your last karate class end?"

"Five o'clock, but I can get Erik to cover for me so we can jet a little early. He practically runs the dojo with my dad."

"Cool. Well, let's go kick some karate butt. Well, you can, anyway. I've got a date with Violet and Captain Sparr." She winked and waggled her eyebrows suggestively.

As it turned out, Erik called in sick, but thankfully, Dad took the class for me. He fell in love with my "new friend" Kat. But who wouldn't? She put on a particular smile, the one I'd dubbed her Victorian-coquette smile, and he melted like butter. My dad was a sucker for a pretty face. With a hug and a kiss and assurances that I would be careful going out (with my demon-hunter friend), we were off.

At my apartment, I dressed in black slacks, a green silk top that billowed away from my torso, and modest heels, a weak attempt to be more invisible. Kat angled her head to the side and put me in my place.

"Gen," she said with a sad sigh, "dressing like a secretary won't hide who you are. You're a Vessel. You're stronger than you think. You'll be stronger yet." She put her hands on my shoulders. "Trust me. One of these days, you'll be able to turn assholes like Danté into ash with a glance."

I straightened. "I wish that day were now."

"Soon." She pushed me back toward my closet. "Now go put something on that says, 'I'm Genevieve Drake, bitches.'"

I stopped in front of the mirror next to my closet, seeing self-doubt weigh me down like a heavy cloak.

There are pivotal moments in every person's life. Take this

path, and you will become this. Take that path, and you will become that.

Like the day I returned to school after my mother killed herself. The mean girls of fifth grade whispered in a corner about how I'd end up crazy and suicidal just like my mother. I had two paths—retreat or stand tall. I chose the latter, thrusting my tiny fist in their faces and threatening to punch their pretty little noses crooked if they ever talked about me or my mother again. It was a pivotal moment.

After that, I became less afraid because I chose to become less afraid. I realized that we are the choices we make, not just what the world chooses to make us. Even though I still had to face the Brenda Blakes of the world, I always rallied myself and remembered who I was.

This was one of those pivotal moments, and I knew it. Does Danté win and rule me with fear and hatred? Or do I keep myself whole? I stared in the mirror at the timid blue-eyed girl, not recognizing her. I inhaled sharply and lifted my chin a tad higher.

"Right."

I pulled out the black dress I'd bought on a sale at Saks, but had never worn. It fit elegantly against my body to the knee, but not tight. Classy. With semi-high heels, I felt…pretty. Confident. I left my hair down with a quick, natural application of makeup and stepped back into the living room where Kat waited.

"Much better," she said with a wink.

We then ran by Kat's hotel in the Quarter. Three outfits later, she wore a tight red dress revealing a hell of a lot more than mine as if she were dressing up for someone in particular. Somehow, I knew she was.

21

At five fifty-six, Kat careened up to the valet of the twenty-nine-story Hilton overlooking the Mississippi River.

"I would've sifted us here, Gen, but it's best not to do so in public places. Freaks people out when they see someone appear out of thin air."

"I'm sure it does," I agreed with a smile, getting out of the car. "We made it. Don't worry. Why are you worrying? You're so fidgety," I said as we were swallowed by the giant, glass rotating doors.

"No reason," she replied, swinging her sleek ponytail behind her.

We walked past the front desk in the lobby toward the restaurant entrance.

"We have a table under Jude Delacroix," I told the smiling hostess.

"Oh yes. They are waiting for you."

She swished toward the quiet din of clinking glass and murmuring voices. I shot Kat a look as we followed.

"They? Who else would be with him?"

Kat's shoulders straightened and stiffened. Her green-black eyes narrowed into slits. "I'm going to kill Jude."

"Why?"

The hostess led us past the open-air kitchen, where fire licked through grill grates around thick steaks and oysters on the half shell. I could feel the heat radiating more from Kat than the kitchen as we zigzagged to the far back corner.

"I *knew* it. Damn it," she grumbled.

Jude sat facing out with his back to the corner, definitely a defensive move. Next to him sat a breathtakingly handsome man he engaged in conversation.

Chestnut hair glinted reddish-gold in the candlelight. He had a fine physique nearly matching the height and breadth of Jude's, and a beguiling, dimpled smile. Both men stood as we approached.

The stranger gazed at us from striking, aquamarine eyes, hinting at secrets untold. He wore a crisply starched shirt the same shade as his eyes, creating a dazzling effect. He seemed to know how to dress and hold himself to the best advantage. He appeared to be in his late thirties, but I knew better. My Vessel Sense had amplified, pulsing brightly the moment we stepped into the restaurant.

Appearances were often deceiving as of late. I forced through the Flamma barrier of protection, seeing the distinct hilt of a sword strapped to Jude's back. Always prepared.

The hostess nearly wilted as we drew nearer the two men. Jude, dressed all in black from head to toe, the top of his Celtic tattoo revealed in the open triangle of his shirt, didn't seem to notice. When his smoldering met mine, my knees wobbled.

"Good evening, ladies." The stranger greeted us with the most charming English accent, very 007-ish with a mischievous grin.

"What are you doing here?" Kat asked nastily.

"My dear Katherine. So delightful to see you. And aren't you absolutely stunning," he crooned, pulling out a chair for her.

She glared at him, getting ready to spit fire or something. A rather attractive shade of pink began crawling up her neck to her cheeks. Jude came around to pull my chair out, rested his hand under my elbow and leaned down to my ear.

"How are you feeling?"

"Fine," I replied quietly.

He leaned even closer, his fingers sliding up my arm to rest on my shoulder, his voice husky with emotion. "Genevieve Drake, you are the most beautiful woman I have ever laid eyes on."

His lips brushed the shell of my ear. Intentionally or accidentally, it didn't matter. The effect was the same. Coupled with the sensation of his hands and lips brushing my bare skin, his words made my knees buckle.

I knew I wasn't the most beautiful woman he'd ever seen. He'd been alive for centuries. Still, the fact that he seemed to believe it was enough to make me blush. The smug sparkle in his eyes told the truth. He knew exactly what he did to me. Dangerous man.

"Genevieve," he addressed me louder, "may I introduce George Draconis."

I nodded.

"You are Flamma," I stated matter-of-factly. "A Dominus Daemonum."

"Yes and no, my dear lady."

"George is our commander," clarified Jude. "Our leader."

"Oh!" I was a suddenly surprised that Kat had been so rude to her own boss. Surely there was something I didn't know. "So you're the master of the Master of Demons."

"At your service." He bowed as regally as possible over the dining table. "Clever girl, Jude."

"More than you know," he added as the waiter arrived.

Our waiter opened a bottle of pinot noir and poured us each a glass. Definitely not the wine connoisseur, I could still recognize this wasn't the cheap stuff.

"We took the liberty of ordering for you ladies," offered George.

"Of course you did," Kat snapped.

"I hope you don't mind, dear Katherine."

She took a very unladylike gulp of wine. I quirked my eyebrows at Jude, wondering what I was missing, but he simply smiled boyishly over the rim of his wineglass.

"So, is Draconis a Greek name? Is that where you're from?" I asked.

"Ah, not quite. I chose the name myself, as I was born without a surname."

Old like Jude, this one.

"And when might that have been?"

"Two hundred seventy anno domini."

I almost choked. Yes, Jude was born not that much longer after him, but the truth struck me like a slap in the face every time. These two men were both centuries older than me, making Kat a blooming daisy in spring with her two hundred years of time on earth. Hell, with that metaphor, I'd be a seed on the wind or pollen in the air, not even in soil yet.

Our waiter served our salads, so I sipped my water, recovering while the young server offered fresh cracked pepper. We waited in silence till he was gone.

"So, why Draconis?" I asked. "Do you have a thing for dragons?"

George's eyes twinkled with amusement. Kat squirmed next to me, and Jude watched from the sidelines as if this were an entertaining tennis match.

"Well, I don't have a thing for them, so to speak, but I do want to bury each one of them in the darkest abyss imaginable."

"Oh. Of course," I said, sipping my wine as I realized dragon was meant simply as a symbol for demons.

"You're actually already quite acquainted with George," said Jude with one of his enigmatic smiles that made my insides puddle into goo.

"Uh, no, I don't think I am."

Jude's eyes dropped to my neckline, where the medal my mother had given me normally hung around my neck. Instinctively, my fingers went there, but I hadn't worn it tonight as it didn't go with the dress. When my brain processed what he was implying, my jaw dropped open. Jude smiled wider.

"Wait a minute. George Draconis, George the Dragon. You're…don't tell me you're…you're *the* George, as in—" My voice squeaked as I stammered like an idiot.

"Well, George the Dragon Slayer was a bit of a mouthful, so I shortened it for convenience."

"You're Saint George!"

I'm sure my eyes were as wide as saucers as I tried to internalize this rather startling news. Kat nonchalantly poured herself another glass of wine and started chugging.

George laughed. "Well, I wouldn't exactly call myself a saint. Not in the strictest definition, that is."

"You can say that again," mumbled Kat next to me, tearing into a piece of bread. He ignored her little quips. Actually, he smiled broader each time Kat made a comment.

"But, you are a saint. I've been praying for your intercession and protection for years."

"And you were heard," he said, tipping his glass up to me in salute, his eyes sliding sideways to Jude so fast he probably thought I didn't catch it. But I did.

"Wow," I said, falling against the back of my chair. I could hardly believe I was sitting in a Riverfront restaurant, drinking wine with a bona fide saint—the very saint my mother had sworn would protect me.

I don't know why I was so surprised after all I'd seen lately. He certainly didn't appear like I imagined a saint would. More like a dashing movie star out on the prowl. My curiosity compelled me out of a starstruck stupor.

"So, how did you become the leader of the demon hunters? And did you really kill a dragon?"

Jude chuckled. He seemed to be enjoying my childlike candor, smirking behind his glass of wine. I turned my attention back to George.

"Oh, darling, dragons don't actually exist."

I rolled my eyes. "Geez, you sound like someone else I know."

Jude's leg found mine under the table, sliding against my bare calf. I ignored him, shooing his leg away. Persistent though he was, George had my unwavering attention. He swirled his wineglass, watching the burgundy liquid as he prepared to tell his story.

"After I died in 303 AD, I—"

"Wait, wait, wait," I stopped him, leaning forward. "After you died?"

His sparkling sea-blue eyes reminded me that he was different from Jude and Kat, lacking the telltale swirling of black in the irises. He might be their commander, but he wasn't exactly one of them.

"Yes, well, when I was martyred by order of Emperor Diocletian, I was given the opportunity by a higher power," he said, glancing upward, "to serve here on earth. Like you, Genevieve, the whole thing came as quite a shock to me that demons and angels were, in fact, fighting battles right here among mankind. So I thought, why the bloody hell not? Given back my body, ageless now as my dear friends here"—he gestured, sweeping the table with a large hand bearing a silver signet ring on his index finger—"I became the 'master of the Master of Demons' as you so eloquently stated."

"I see," I said, taking a sip and relishing the warm burn of potent pinot noir down my throat. "That legend of you slaying the dragon takes place in the medieval period. Was any of that accurate?"

"There is always truth in legend." He smiled. "That was quite a beast, and he did favor the appearance of a dragon, I must say."

"A demon then?" I asked, completely riveted.

"Demon spawn of Damas, actually. That bastard sets all kinds of abominations on humanity. Pardon my profanity."

My eyes flickered to Kat, but she appeared completely engrossed in her salad, as if she hadn't heard a word. I knew that she had.

"Demon spawn? Yes, Jude mentioned something about that once."

Jude merely nodded, his expression grim. At that moment, platters of char-grilled oysters and plates of filet mignon with sides of marinated portabella mushrooms and baked potatoes were set neatly before us.

George leaned to Kat's side of the table. "You do still prefer your steak medium rare, do you not, Katherine?"

She glared at him and commenced to eating the mushrooms. I'd never seen her so aggravated. Once the waiter disappeared again, I continued the conversation.

"There are many kinds of Flamma, then," I added. "More than demon hunters and Vessels."

"Oh yes," agreed George. "Many."

"Like?"

"In addition to demon hunters, there are angel hunters, guardian angels, guardian demons, sentinels—"

I put a hand in the air, closing my eyes for a second and setting my wine down.

"Okay, wait. Explain to me what an angel hunter is. And all the rest of what you just said."

"Eat, Genevieve." Jude nudged me. I realized then I was the only one not eating. I started cutting a piece of steak, my knife sliding into it like butter.

George set his glass of wine down. "While you are familiar with demon hunters, angel hunters are the counterpart— soldiers of the underworld seeking out angels to destroy. Of course, the only ones they are ever able to find here on earth would be the guardian angels, and they're more cunning than most demons."

"So, guardian angels actually exist?" I asked, forking a bite of juicy steak into my mouth.

"Yes, of course. They don't fly around all day, granting wishes. But they hear the call of a human in need. The humans who still belong to the Light, that is."

"What do you mean?" I asked, taking my refilled wineglass from Jude.

"People tend to take one path or another, correct?"

I nodded.

"Those who follow the Light have guardian angels watching over them, guiding them, sometimes even saving them. Let me ask you something, Genevieve, have you ever almost done something that could've been disastrous, but an inexplicable feeling made you make another decision?"

Instantly, I thought of my sophomore homecoming when Greg Myers wanted me to go with him to the after-party. He hadn't been drinking or anything, but something made me refuse him at the last minute. I couldn't figure out why; it was a bone-deep feeling that I shouldn't go. Greg Myers fell asleep coming home from the party, drove off the road, and hit an oak tree, flattening the passenger side of his car into a pancake. He escaped with a broken nose and a concussion, but I would've been killed on impact had I been sitting next to him. I snapped from the memory, simply nodding to George.

"Just as there are guardians of light, there are guardians of darkness. These are lower demons, with which I believe you are familiar, guiding humans further into debauchery and sin."

"They also fuse with some humans, as Jude told me."

"Yes. And sentinels are actually humans who've either made a deal with the devil, or actually, one of the higher demons to be precise, or with an angel. They use their influence to sway humans for good or ill, depending on who they serve."

"But, why would any human serve a demon?" I asked, folding my napkin and setting it on the plate.

"My dear, there are any number of reasons a man or woman would walk the path of darkness. Fame? Fortune? A lover they desire and cannot possess? The reasons are endless. Sentinels tend to be quite dangerous, for they are invisible to the radar of other Flamma, still being human."

I sat back, my head swimming. I thought of something else.

"Then there are the Collectors, like Acheron," I added.

Kat perked up at that. George's eyebrows rose. "So, you know of the rivers? You've met Acherontis?"

"I, we"—I glanced at Jude whose expression revealed nothing—"bumped into him. So, are they Flamma of light or darkness?"

"Neither," interjected Jude, breaking his long silence. "They serve no one but themselves and anyone who will barter with them. They want only one thing—to feed."

"Yes," agreed George, a frown creasing his high brow, "a rather dismal version of purgatory, I must say."

"Except, of course, souls in purgatory actually get out," added Kat in her snippy manner.

I sighed heavily, dumbstruck with all the images spinning through my head.

"Come, Genevieve," said Jude, rising. "Let's get some fresh air. We'll meet you two on the river-walk."

George nodded, fixing his brilliant blue eyes on Kat. Jude placed my hand into the crook of his arm. He took his jacket from the back of his chair and draped it over my bare shoulders. I glanced down before we walked away and saw a mixture of both resentment and longing swirling in Kat's eyes, which had darkened more black than green.

There was little light by the streetlamps along the riverfront, but I didn't care. I felt no fear with Jude at my side. I actually felt somewhat empowered after today. What I'd learned of Kat had taught me to hope, to see beyond my internal wounds. Meeting

George reminded me that there are many others out there fighting the same good fight against these ruthless demons. I was not alone.

The salty, musky smell of the river blew in gentle gusts. Water lapped in a steady rhythm against the levy. Warm with wine and safe alongside Jude, I stopped to take in the city lights glistening on the water. A gray pall obscured the moon, like a pasty smudge on a charcoal canvas.

Propping my elbows on the railing, I faced away from the river. Jude rested his hands on my hips beneath the jacket, drawing me close. A breeze caught his hair, lifting and obscuring one eye. I swiped the lock away so that I could see him clearly. Before I drew my hand back, he grabbed it, pulling my wrist toward him. He pressed a lingering kiss against the delicate skin where blue veins crisscrossed under pale skin.

"Did you have a good day?" he finally asked, pulling me gently against him.

I rested my palms against his chest, knowing exactly what that question truly meant. *Did Kat help you? Are you okay? Did you miss me?*

"Yes," I answered truthfully to all of the questions in my head.

"Good."

His arms wrapped around me, pulling our bodies together as one, and his jacket fell away. His lips rested against my skin just below my ear. He didn't move, caress, or kiss. Simply kept still, inhaling my skin. We stood there, feeling the nearness of each other. The sensation and warmth of intimate touch without aggression or fear stitched a few more seams in that wound inside me.

"I hope this is okay," he whispered into my ear. "I needed to touch you."

"This is more than okay."

My heart had started her erratic beat; the one she made

when Jude wrapped around me like this. A hand pressed harder against the small of my back, clutching.

"Genevieve," he whispered, a hoarse plea.

"I know."

My body was already responding. I lifted my face up to his, needing him just as badly. A second later, his mouth found mine, prying my lips apart, moving in a sensual rhythm, his tongue sweeping in.

Salt and wine and Jude invaded my senses. I let out a small breathy cry, unable to keep it in. Molding my mouth to his, I slipped my tongue in to taste all of him. A low moan from this splendid man, and my heart skittered away, mingling the emotions of fear and desire. Desire was winning. He spread long fingers into my hair along my temples, cradling me close, kissing me harder.

Some internal warning made me pull away. He let me.

A flutter. A flapping. I glanced to the railing, thinking a pigeon or gull had landed nearby. Staring fixedly from lifeless eyes was a large sable raven.

Jude stiffened. A swirl of black shadow radiated around both of us. Hot fury billowed. Jude's guttural voice was deep and terrifying.

"Dommiel."

Jude gripped my arm, thrusting me behind him, and unsheathed his broadsword in one swift movement. As Jude swung his sword in a deadly arc, the raven flapped once into the air before silver clipped its wing, sending the creature cawing and tumbling across the pavement.

Ebony feathers spiraled and fluttered into the air. Droplets of black blood spattered the walkway, spraying in wild profusion as the injured bird flip-flopped in panic, creating a morbid Jackson Pollock-like painting across the stone.

"Dommiel! *Aperio!*"

The power in Jude's voice shook the air. A black shroud of menace enveloped him in a dark mantle, brushing against my skin, chilling me to the bone. I gasped. Malevolent whispers echoed in the mist, reaching out to me.

Kill…cut…maim…slice…devour…pain.

"Aperio, Daemonum." Jude's grave command to "reveal" made the hair on the back of my neck stand on end.

The injured creature choked out another caw, obeying him at once. Talons elongated and thickened. Feathers ruffled and vanished. Wings stretched, and the fat, round body grew into a man's torso. Beak shortened, black eyes widened, and bled into red.

Within seconds, there lay the nude form of Dommiel, clutching at the stump of his arm, severed above the elbow and bleeding black. His dismembered limb lay closer to me, the silver skull ring decorating the lifeless hand.

It twitched. I jumped away.

Before Dommiel could even roll to his back, Jude was there, planting a boot into the man's injured shoulder as he shoved his blade through the demon's chest, piercing flesh to the pavement beneath with a definite clink of steel in stone. Staked to the ground, Dommiel writhed in agony, bleeding out from several wounds. But a high demon couldn't die. Was Jude simply torturing him? His misty cape draped over him completely. There was no sign of his other aura of fire and flame.

What was going on? My heart raced into panic mode.

"I warned you, Dommiel," said Jude, death in his voice.

The demon gaped, now in his human form, looking like a man except for the red eyes and canine teeth. He sucked in air, still clutching his mangled arm that was bleeding black.

"I didn't come to hurt her! I promise," he pleaded, sounding much less sinister than my last meeting with the lord of The Dungeon.

"I don't care about your motives. My word is absolute."

I hardly recognized Jude's voice, leaking such menace that I stepped back and gripped the cold railing for support. He whipped out a razor-sharp stiletto, glinting in the streetlamp, and leaned closer to the helpless demon awaiting more punishment, defiance in his gaze.

Jude's back was to me, but I knew darkness veiled even the whites of his eyes.

"No! Please, don't! I have information," he stammered, his feet scrabbling against the pavement helplessly. "I'll give it to you. I fucking swear!"

George and Kat sifted onto the scene in a blink. George's

amiable expression had vanished behind a fierce mask, blue eyes glittering like exploding stars.

"Damn it, Jude!" shouted Kat. "I told you to take care of it!"

Seemingly unaware of either of them, Jude had gripped Dommiel by the throat, leaning forward to do something terrible, though I didn't know what.

"He's fallen into the Black. You take care of the demon," ordered George, "and meet us back at Jude's place. Come, Genevieve," he said, holding out his hand to me.

Instantly, I obeyed. There was something in George's voice that made me move, a promise of protection in those startling eyes. By the time I reached him, he had yanked Jude to his feet, and then we were sifting. Sifting fast. My stomach roiled as shapes streaked by in one long blur of gray. My high heels were yanked from my feet, flying into nothingness.

We reappeared on solid ground in a quiet grove of oaks. Dizzy and nauseated from the sift, I fell back against the sturdy trunk of a tree. I leaned behind it and lost the contents of my stomach. I shifted from one bare foot to the other on the cool ground.

George guided Jude to the center of the grove and thrust him to his knees. Jude didn't protest. I could see his profile clearly. He stared down, hands at his sides, completely docile. Yet the misty shroud circled him still, whispering. George began to chant, not to Jude but out to the world itself, his arms spread wide. I couldn't make out the words.

A gibbous moon peeked from behind the cover of clouds, filtering through the oaks strung with swaying moss, casting moving shadows around us. It felt as if the night itself were alive. Cicadas buzzed incessantly. An owl hooted nearby. Gray clouds swallowed up the humped moon once again.

Arms still raised, George's body began to shimmer with brilliant light, then all was still and quiet. Not a sound. Not a shadow flickered. Even George's whispered chant had died away.

Gooseflesh prickled along my skin. I'd felt this sensation before, this feeling that the world had frozen, and I was being sucked into a soundless vacuum.

My eyes darted to every shadow, waiting for wraithlike Acheron to emerge from one of them. But he didn't.

The clouds opened, allowing the moon to reveal herself again. One beam shone through the foliage directly in front of Jude. The moonbeam brightened and brightened. Thinking I was imagining things, I gripped the rough bark of the trunk for support. The beam shimmered, morphing into a transparent shape.

George backed away, his stony expression showing a brief glimpse of revulsion before fading into passivity. My breath quickened. An eerie pulse of dread emanated from the form appearing by slow degrees.

Gossamer limbs and silken hair solidified into a creature of fearsome beauty. Floating in a gown of translucent white, the pale silhouette of a voluptuous woman's body touched the earth before Jude.

Pearlescent arms and spidery-long fingers reached out to him. I gasped, but there was no sound. All was drowned, except for the voices hovering around Jude in the inky mist, growing louder.

Slit…slash…eviscerate…gut…devour…annihilate.

The air reeked of loathing—doubling, tripling, continuing up the scale until I crumpled to my knees. I pressed my hands to my ears, trying to block the painful swell of evil pouring from both Jude and the ghostly creature.

My Vessel power beat within my breast, pushing against the tide of hatred lapping against my body. The ghastly being, vaporous gown billowing in soft, slow curls, cradled Jude's face in her hands, demanding that he look up at her.

He remained silent, obeying her will. White orbs narrowed into slits. Pallid lips creased into a sinister smile. I wanted to remove her hands from him but was crippled by the heavy malevolence rippling in the air. I couldn't move. I screamed for Jude but made no sound.

Jude raised his hands, palms out, like an invitation to the creature. She wove her long, slender fingers through his, gripping him hard, pulling him to his feet and against her translucent body.

With a resounding crack, a powerful ripple hit the air. Her head snapped back. Her mouth gaped wide. The voices of vile souls inside her screamed.

Images flashed in my mind—bloody death, twisted limbs, mangled bodies. The weight of primal hatred threatened to crush me down into the soil.

The white woman inhaled the black aura surrounding Jude, sucking it into her mouth and nose like smoke through a flue.

Within seconds, she had finished her grisly meal and vanished with a silent flash of blinding light. The screaming voices died with her sudden disappearance.

I could hear myself again, gasping for breath, the hangover of emotion overload so familiar to my encounter with Acheron. George was at my side, helping me to my feet.

"Just breathe, Genevieve. The feeling will pass shortly."

I could care less about how I felt, peering past him to Jude. As I raced across the clearing, he stood and spun to face me. Then I froze.

"Jude. Your eyes."

Amber gold, devoid of swimming pools of black, glinted with unnatural luster. A thin dark ring outlined the shining irises, but that was all. These were the eyes of the man in my vision, yet the hatred was gone.

"What, what happened? Who was she?"

"Her name is Stygos, also known as Styx."

"A Collector," I said, knowing she was one of Acheron's sisters. Styx, the river of hate.

"Yes," he nodded.

"But, what was—"

"It's the Black. She feeds not only on souls but on the residue that accumulates in demon hunters."

"Residue of what?" A chill tingled up my spine.

"Each demon I cast out leaves something behind. A piece of him clings to me, to my soul. It builds up over time until I must purge the bulk of it. I'm afraid it built up rather quickly this time."

Golden eyes shimmered bright, even in this dark grove. I stepped closer, placing a hand on his arm.

"Does it hurt?"

"Yes." He cupped my face with one hand, caressing my cheek with his thumb. My heart broke a little, realizing the constant battle warring within him. The Black, the residue of evil, always growing and building, smothering his soul bit by bit. Those whispers of malevolence made me shudder. How could he possibly listen to those voices all the time?

"But why? Why does this happen?"

He shrugged as if it didn't matter. "It's part of my penance, Genevieve. I am Sisyphus," he said with a wistful smile, "and this is my hell."

What a terribly morbid joke. And yet, not a joke. I hadn't felt the tear escape until his thumb brushed it away distractedly.

"Jude," I whispered, wanting to say something, anything to comfort him.

No words would come. How could he endure such pain all the time? For hundreds of years! The thought was unfathomable. I felt sick again.

"No tears for me," he said, so close I could feel warm breath against my face, amber eyes bright and mesmerizing. "I don't mind bearing a small burden of hell, since it's giving me another chance at heaven."

He leaned down, pressing his lips to my cheek where the tear had fallen. I placed my hand on his jaw, tiptoeing to brush a soft kiss on his lips. Not one of desire, but one filled with all the compassion spilling from my heart.

Our lips came apart reluctantly, as if neither of us wanted to let go. The look shining in those unnatural eyes beckoned me closer. He touched his forehead to mine.

I felt a rope tying me to this man, knotting us together and drawing tight. Being tethered to Jude made me feel stronger, as if I could weather any storm.

"Come, you two," said George, startling me. I'd nearly forgotten he was there. "We're too vulnerable here. I told Kat to meet us at your place."

I noticed he'd used her nickname. Jude pulled away slightly, clasping George's shoulder.

"Thank you, friend."

The charming George reappeared, tension gone from moments before.

"Of course." He smiled. "Wouldn't want my senior man falling down on the job, now would I."

George winked, then sifted out. Jude pulled me into his arms. I'm not sure what he saw in my eyes, but something made him stop abruptly. His expression softened. Could he see what I truly felt? Were eyes truly the windows to the soul?

"God, woman." He pulled me tight. "You will most certainly be the death of me."

His armor of protection shielded both of us as we sifted into his house. George and Kat were seated on the sofa together, talking heatedly. They broke apart on our sudden appearance. Kat scooted away.

"Jude, you are the most stubborn man I have ever known. Didn't I tell you to deal with the Black last night?"

Last night? It felt like eons since he'd destroyed Fabio into a crumpled carcass of burnt bones.

Apparently, the Black had a way of taking over, guiding a demon hunter beyond the necessary means of destruction. I had wondered what caused Jude to lose control like that. I couldn't imagine what he'd planned on doing to Dommiel before George pulled us out. I shivered.

Jude guided me to the overstuffed chair, which was, thankfully, no longer embedded in the window. He picked up a brown fleece draped over the back and wrapped it around my shoulders.

He sat down before I could then pulled me into his lap. Rather than feel awkward, it was natural. I burrowed into Jude and the warm blanket. He leaned back, holding me around my back, his hand on my waist. The other hand slid under the blanket and wrapped my bare thigh under my dress.

"Yes, Kat, I should've listened to you" Jude replied, "but no harm done."

"Tell Dommiel that," she snapped.

Jude sobered. "He got no more than he deserved. I'd already warned him to stay clear of Genevieve. It's his own fault." He shrugged nonchalantly.

"What other payment might he have received for disobeying you had we not arrived in time?" Kat asked. "If you removed him, another less cooperative high demon may have taken his place."

Unruffled, Jude shrugged nonchalantly.

Jude had tidied up the splintered wood and shattered glass from last night's tirade, but there were still signs of his raging temper. No one remarked on that or the plywood-covered window or the bare hearth with exposed brick, but I saw George observing with a smile.

"Let him alone, Katherine."

Back to her formal name. *What was their story?*

"Oh, you two always side with each other!" she exclaimed, throwing her hands in the air.

"What *did* you do with Dommiel?" Jude asked pointedly.

Kat straightened with a superior air, flipping her ponytail, and crossing her rather shapely legs. George's eyes wandered down the length of them.

"I made a deal with him, which you were certainly in no mind to do."

"What kind of deal?"

"His measly life, or rather a stay of expulsion back to hell, in exchange for very important information. Thanks to me, we now know which high demon wants Gen dead."

She paused for dramatic effect. It was very effective. I sat up straighter, breathless. Jude didn't move, but the muscles in his shoulders and arms tightened around me.

"Well?" I blurted. "Who is it?"

"Bamal, High Demon of New York. Dommiel's orders were to do surveillance, not to kill."

"Surveillance? Why the sudden change? Did he say?" asked George.

"That, he wasn't privileged to know."

"Wait," I interjected, "isn't New York your territory, Kat?"

She nodded. "Yes. But, I've never laid eyes on him. He stays cloistered in his lair, coming out only either in shape-shifting form or in possession of his Vessel."

I sank farther into my chair. I'd forgotten Kat had told me there was a Vessel in New York. Poor woman. My mind conjured up Danté, leering over me.

Jude pressed his mouth to my temple, a comforting gesture. Interesting that George nor Kat found our cozy seat together in the chair odd or strange. I suppose they both knew we were… what were we exactly?

"Who's covering for you now, Katherine?" asked George.

"Dorian. He's assured me nothing unusual has happened, not since I left anyway," she answered in a much more professional, and less hostile, manner than she used with him before.

"Dorian's covering his province as well as yours?"

George's devil-may-care expression faded behind an austere one. I suddenly had no doubts about his capabilities as leader of the demon hunters.

"He's had no trouble," she assured him. "I only left New York at Jude's request because of, well, because of Genevieve and the odd circumstances surrounding her."

I realized that while George was their commander, he gave them leeway to make decisions on their own. There was trust in this hierarchy. I liked that.

"And what's so odd about my circumstances? Besides being attacked by demons on a daily basis, I mean."

Kat smiled. "That's just it, Gen. Vessels aren't usually attacked, as in, to be killed." The clarification made me a little uneasy, but she went on to avoid that awkward pause. "They're collected by high demons to harvest their power, to use as weapons for darkness."

"So something unusual did happen before you left New York?" I asked.

"There have been a number of high demons, barons and dukes, coming and going to his penthouse residence. No princes, but lots of courtiers of the underworld."

"Is this so odd?" I asked. "Wouldn't demon princes always be surrounded by them?"

"No," said Jude. "High demons are territorial and extremely paranoid of anyone usurping their power. If he's gathering them to counsel, you can bet there's a big reason."

"But let's just say I'm the one in this prophecy, why would they want to kill me?"

The three of them glanced at one another before Kat looked at me. "You're right. I think it is because Bamal wants to a player in fulfilling the prophecy. Bamal thinks you're the one as well, the Vessel mentioned. Do you remember, the prophecy said, 'Two great sons of Morning Star'? Bamal must see himself as one of these two sons in the prophecy, and Danté as his other rival. He's been trying to destroy you, while Danté has been seeking you for his Vessel."

I tightened the fleece around me, ignoring the prickly sensation of fear tingling down my spine.

"Danté?" asked George. "Who the devil is that?"

"Ru'um," clarified Jude. "He's going by Danté these days."

"What a pompous prick. So now he thinks he's Danté Alighieri, creator of *The Divine Comedy*? That's a laugh."

"But why the sudden change?" I asked, repeating George's question from earlier. "If Bamal thinks I'm this one in the prophecy, why would he tell Dommiel to just do surveillance? What is he watching me for? Waiting for? To kidnap me instead?"

"That would make sense, actually," said Kat. "The prophecy mentions a face-to-face sort of showdown, Vessel to Vessel. Perhaps, Bamal thinks you're supposed to challenge his Vessel."

The thought of fighting another woman to death sent a chill up my spine.

Kat tapped her high-heeled foot nervously. "No matter the reason, I need to start doing surveillance of my own when I head back, which needs to be soon."

"I agree," said George. "What we really need is a way to draw him out or other minions he may have in play. Dommiel is a local high demon, and we've taken him out of the equation. Have we not, Katherine?"

"Yes. He'll stay out of it now."

George nodded. "Then if he's serious, he'll send some of his own demons."

Jude leaned forward. "He has. There was one the night I met Genevieve. And another, Garzel, a lower demon who attacked her in a local bar. Of course, that was before this incident with Dommiel. It seems Bamal has changed tactics since then. You're right, George. We need to set a trap. Someplace public that would also offer a way for his demons to stay hidden. They'll know we're watching Genevieve closely, so they'll be cautious."

I cleared my throat, shifting sideways in Jude's lap so I could see him.

"I know of a place," I said, twisting the frays of the fleece absently. Three pairs of eyes turned to me. "Mindy and I are invited to the Crescent City Masquerade coming up. It's exclusive but will be very crowded, and of course, it's a masked ball. Anyone could stay hidden."

"When were you planning on telling me about this ball?" asked Jude with more humor than anger in his tone.

"Just now," I said with a straight face. "But like I said, it's exclusive. I have no idea how you'd go about getting tickets."

"Oh, don't you worry your pretty head about that," said Jude. "I'll get in."

The corner of his mouth twitched. He either wanted to kiss me or spank me. A flash of heat shot through my body at the thought of both.

"That sounds perfect," said George. "When is the ball?"

"Halloween night."

"Perfect is right," said Kat with a snort. "The freaks will be out in droves."

"High-society freaks," I added.

Kat rolled her eyes. "And on that note, I'll bid you gentlemen good night. It's late. We can strategize for the ball tomorrow."

She walked over and pulled me out of Jude's lap who let me up reluctantly. Kat gave me a super-tight bear hug. "I had a blast today, Gen. You're the bee's knees. I'll be your babysitter anytime."

She winked at me and, with a fleeting glance at George, sifted out.

I stood there for a moment, smiling.

"We mustn't overlook Danté," added Jude quietly, standing behind me. "He's gained in power, George. The very reason I summoned you."

"Right. Of course. Come, Genevieve, sit here," he said, taking my hand gently.

I sat, folding my hands together in my lap. Jude settled back into the chair we'd shared a minute before, his hands clasping the arms. A gloomy expression clouded his features, and he looked like a king getting ready for battle.

George leaned forward on the sofa, elbows on his knees, hands loosely clasped in casual masculinity, exuding confidence. He gazed intently at me with those hypnotizing eyes, glassy-clear like the Mediterranean.

"Genevieve," he said, voice dipping to a deep tenor, "Jude has made me aware of certain situations, about the blood cast and Ru'um's predilection for soul-sifting. I can give you the power to prevent this, but it will come at a small price, if you're willing."

I nodded, mouth gone cotton dry, waiting for him to continue.

"A transfer of power requires that I lose a little of my own, which is not too great a price to pay for peace of mind that you're safe," he said, glancing at Jude.

Somehow, I knew he was minimizing the cost of his loss of power. I was beginning to see that the Flamma of Light were as covetous of their power as the Flamma of Darkness.

George tapped my knee with an index finger. "However, you're a Vessel. I know that you're aware why these high demons covet you. Vessels are just that—vessels of power. The high demons want what you already have for their own, but your capacity to hold power is endless, be it power of dark or light. If I pass you my own power, we will be forever linked. Do you have the Sight?"

I nodded, quivering a little now. I refused to look at Jude, for the only visions I'd seen so far were painful visions of him.

"I thought so," continued George. "I don't know how we'll be linked exactly, meaning I don't know what visions you'll see of mine—whether they're from my own past or demons I've destroyed or even my own future. A Vessel's Sight is boundless in every meaning of the word. I cannot promise that the visions you inherit will be pleasant. I cannot even predict when they may visit you. But," he paused with a sly smile, "I can promise you that with this power, your soul will be sealed to you. No

Flamma will be able to pull it from your body unbidden. Only you will have the power to release it, should you wish."

"That sounds fair enough," I said, letting out a breath I hadn't known I was holding. Though I was well aware visions could be painful to experience, it was a small price to pay to keep Danté or any other demon prince from taking me again. "So what do I need to do?"

"Nothing, actually. Just keep still. This may seem a little strange to you, but transfer of power takes place through a kiss."

Wait a minute, Saint George was going to *kiss* me? Like, on the lips? In front of Jude!

My inner voice was running ninety miles a minute. Surprise and something like fear must have shown in my face. Jude nodded in reassurance, though his expression remained tight. And very grim.

"Genevieve, don't be afraid." George gave me his charming laugh, complete with wide smile and adorable dimples, making me blush further. He covered both of my hands in my lap with one of his. "It's not that kind of a kiss. All right?"

Rather than frighten me, his touch was comforting. He waited with eyebrows raised for my consent.

"All right."

"It will feel a little odd, but it won't take long."

As in my-man-watching-another-drop-dead-gorgeous-man-kiss-me-on-his-couch odd? My heart fluttered. Not in the same way Jude made my poor heart race, but she was definitely gearing up for warm-up laps.

I was stiff as a board. George gave my hands a reassuring squeeze to make me relax, but it didn't work. As he shifted his upper body toward me, I closed my eyes, unable to watch him draw closer. A hand gently cupped my cheek, tilting me at a small angle. I could feel Jude's gaze burning into me, no matter that he'd actually asked George to do this.

Soft, warm lips touched mine, slightly apart. He didn't move in a sensuous motion. Thank God! But his hand drifted to the nape of my neck, lightly pressing us together. The pressure of his lips felt soothing. With a sudden shock, my VS jolted awake, flashing in a burst of stars.

Our mouths tasted each other more urgently, his tongue sliding over mine, lost in a moment of sensation. His power replied with a burning waterfall, a cascade of energy pouring over me from the tip of my head to my toes. Talk about a kiss that makes you melt. Fiery power draped through my torso and limbs, penetrating through bone, muscle, and singeing along my skin—a symphony of energy meeting and connecting us to one another.

Although the kiss wasn't sexual, it was sensual and intimate, a bonding of another kind. My VS hummed, absorbing the power as my own. I'd forgotten that we were kissing in that extraordinary moment of light and power. Coming back to myself, I realized my hand had curled tightly, clutching his hand in my lap. Electric-hot, his mouth pulled from mine slowly with the slick, wet sound of lips parting.

"Genevieve." He grinned devilishly. "Talk about seeing stars."

I exhaled an unsteady breath, leaning away from him. My whole body thrummed with power.

"I'm not so sure you're a saint anymore."

He tossed his beautiful head back in a laugh. Jude rose stiffly, pulling me to stand beside him. I could feel the strain in his body, tight like a rubber band. I hoped he wouldn't pop.

"I'm sure it was a wonderful experience for the both of you," Jude bit out with painful effort and a sardonic lift of the brow. "Much obliged, George, but she needs her rest."

In other words, *get out.*

"A lovely creature, your Vessel," he said, clapping a hand on Jude's shoulder and giving me a wink. "Keep her close."

"I intend to," was the curt response.

Before George had even sifted out, Jude's lips devoured mine in a bone-melting fusion of tongue, heat, and breath. I knew what he was doing. Marking me. Not like Danté. No.

Jude spread his scent with mouth, hands, and body—a primal need to imprint me as his own overpowering every other impulse.

If I'd tried to resist, it would've been futile. As it was, I didn't want to. I wanted even more than he gave. After kissing me senseless, he pulled back, piercing me with lion-gold eyes.

"*My* Genevieve."

A throaty whisper against kiss-swollen lips. He held me against his body with a steel grip, the hard lines of him promised protection. And pleasure. He started a slow descent down the upward edge of my jaw, nipping softly at the tender flesh of my neck. I couldn't say the word as my body tipped into a pool of sensation, swallowed whole by Jude. But my response pulsed loud and clear in my mind.

Yours.

Suddenly, I was on his bed with his hard body pressing me into the mattress. Crazed with lust, I thrust my hands under his shirt, moaning at the feel of smooth skin over taut muscles.

On a groan, he popped up onto his knees between my open thighs. Holding my gaze, he unbuckled his belt, sliding the belt out of the loops with a resounding snap.

Jumping at the sharp sound, I said, "I thought we couldn't..."

I lost my words, waiting for him to continue and unbutton his black pants.

Instead, he lifted the other end of his belt then said, "Put both of your arms straight out."

Confused, I still thrust them forward. He wrapped a figure-eight with his belt, pulling tight to be sure they were secure then wrapped and buckled the ends around a decorative bar in his intricate headboard.

"What are you doing?" I asked in a rush, twisting my wrists on instinct, finding them securely bound.

He devoured me with his gaze and unbuttoned his black dress shirt with impressive speed. He tossed it aside then his undershirt, effectively punching the air from my lungs. The Celtic cross with its dark ink and sharp barbs rippled beneath flexed muscle, especially when he lowered his body over mine, propping his weight on his forearms.

Hovering his face close to mine, amber gaze molten fire, the lion present and hunting, he murmured, "I can't fuck you, any part of you without putting you in danger." He ground his hard cock between my thighs, his warm chest pressing to mine. "But apparently I can kiss and touch you without breaking the rules."

Breathless, I managed to ask, "Who'd you find that out from? George?"

"Mmm," he murmured in assent, lowering his mouth to my neck and licking my pulse. "Didn't think I'd ever have to ask him the details of a Vessel's boundaries."

He lifted my dress, knuckles trailing up my thighs and stomach as he revealed more skin, pushing the thin fabric up to my neckline. Then he reached under my back to unsnap my bra.

"You didn't think you'd ever date a Vessel, I guess." I was nervous chattering.

"Date." He huffed a small laugh. "We're well beyond that phase, Genevieve."

After unclasping my bra, he lifted the cups up to expose my breasts. A deep rumble vibrated from his chest to my stomach where he rested between my legs. His gaze was on my breasts as he mounded one, lightly pinching my nipple into a peak.

He glanced up at me to catch my reaction, but I couldn't take that intense stare. My head dropped to the mattress on a moan as he held my breast and circled the nipple with his hot tongue. Then he sucked—hard—drawing a wet line with his tongue to the other and repeating his attentions.

"God, Jude," I muttered, rocking my hips against his torso, needing friction.

Then he was dragging my panties down my thighs. I couldn't help but open my eyes, heart pounding at the sight of him, sitting back on his knees, his gaze on my pussy.

After he tossed my panties aside, he circled his long fingers around my ankles, lifting them to plant my feet on his bare shoulders.

When I tried to pull them away, feeling utterly exposed, he held my ankles against him, his chest rising and falling quicker.

"Don't hide from me," he rumbled, meeting my gaze as he smoothed his palms over the tops of my thighs. "I want all of you, Genevieve."

He dropped one hand between my thighs, the other cradling a knee to keep my foot planted. He stroked two fingers along my slick slit.

"Even the secrets at the heart of you," he murmured and planted a biting kiss to the inside of my knee as he thrust two fingers inside me.

My hips came off the bed on a whimper. I bit my lip, while eagerly thrusting up for more.

"You're so fucking beautiful," he whispered, stroking and curling his fingers slightly, brushing against the bundle of nerves inside me.

"Ah!" I cried out at the pleasure, raising my hips to meet his shallow thrusts.

Then he lay down on the bed, his head between my legs, my knees gripping his shoulders, and he opened his hot mouth over my clitoris.

"Fuck!" I screamed, jerking on my wrists that were bound too tightly to pull loose.

"That's it," he murmured gently, licking a circle around my clit while pumping his fingers a little faster. "Take your pleasure from me, Genevieve." A suckling kiss on my tight nub that had my vision hazing. "Because I'll be the *only* man to ever give you pleasure."

The possessiveness in his voice and in his hands had me spiraling closer to my climax and breakneck speed. He reached up with his free hand and gripped my breast possessively, pinching my nipple lightly.

That did it. I screamed his name as I came, undulating beneath him then suddenly tightening every muscle, curling my toes. He opened his mouth over my pussy, lapping up the juices as more slid out with his slow-pumping fingers.

He hummed against my clit, making me jerk, now that it was so sensitive post-orgasm.

When the throbbing dimmed, he pulled his fingers free, pumping one last time, before he climbed over my body and pressed me flat. He took my mouth, kissing me on a guttural groan, rocking his hips against my wet pussy. I was soaking his pants, but he didn't seem to mind.

I couldn't help but rub against the giant steel rod, wishing he could fuck me already.

The irony. I'd waited for the right guy, and now that I'd found him, I couldn't fuck him or I'd become a demon's pet. My goddamn luck.

Jerking on the belt, I huffed in exasperation, "Why the belt? Are there rules that I can't touch anyone else or something? With the whole Vessel boundaries, that is."

He reached up with one hand and unbuckled his belt, freeing my wrists. He took one and pressed a kiss on the reddened underside.

"No." He exhaled a heavy sigh. "That's for me, actually."

I frowned.

"If you touch me," he explained, "then I'll lose control." A swirl of darkness blackened the outer rims of his eyes. "Can't take that chance."

He pressed a quick kiss to my lips then shot off the bed, gaze raking my half-naked body as he gripped his big dick over his pants. Then he turned abruptly for the door.

"Where are you going?"

"To take a shower. And take care of this." He gave his cock a squeeze.

"Oh." I pushed my dress back down to my thighs, inching toward the edge of the bed. "I should probably shower too."

"Don't you fucking dare." He pointed a finger at me, serious Jude scowl in place. "You stay in this room till I'm done."

I fell back onto the bed, smiling while basking in my orgasm endorphins. But also, I was feeling a little guilty about not being able to help Jude get his own.

One thing that I knew for sure about this new world that I hadn't known existed—demons sucked.

The sun. *An orb of fire shrinking in dark water. Plunk, stipple, swipe. My mother brushed midnight blue into churning waves. Facing away from me in bare feet, jeans, and paint-stained T-shirt, she painted a vast gray wall rising upward into nothing. The sunset shimmered, then faded and was gone. I was dreaming.*

"Mother?"

She didn't answer or seem to know I was even there, beginning a new painting on the slate-gray wall. Her brush widened of its own accord as she stroked four stark lines extending out of a black rectangle. She dipped her brush again, a smear of white and splatter of gold.

Dropping the brush and palette to the stone floor with a clack, she reached up to two of the black lines, her fingers curling into the wall around the painted posts. With a hard jerk, she pulled out a three-dimensional bed, dragging it from the flat canvas.

A rhythmic pulse pounded in my head—my heartbeat—as I recognized the form. Decorative gold pillows sat atop a pile of white silk sheets.

"No."

My whisper echoed and died. She stared at me with eyes of crimson, devoid of any emotion, any love or care. Her slender arm lifted, pointing a long finger to the bed. I shook my head.

"No."

Without moving, I was under the covers, sliding under silk, brushing against naked skin. He was here in a sea of white, a shark in glossy waters. Folds of fabric wrapped me in place. I clawed in panic, drowning. He caught me, laughing in my ear, whispering with a satin-smooth lilt, "I knew you'd come back to me, my sweet. Now, we have eternity together."

Smothering in snow-white silk and cold hands, I screamed.

"No!"

Sticky with sweat, I jerked awake in Jude's bed with him lying behind me. It was still dark out the window, so it was the middle of the night or very early before dawn.

"Shh," he whispered. "It was a dream."

Yes. Just a dream. Not soul-sifted. A dream.

A strong hand slid up my arm, squeezing gently, bringing me back to the here and now. After a shower last night, I'd slept in one of his T-shirts and boxer briefs. The heady scent of Jude all around me settled my spirit back into a safe place.

He spooned behind me from behind, having put on pajama pants last night before he climbed in with me. Now that it was quite clear my life depended on keeping my body "untainted," Jude was keeping tight control over himself.

My wrists were a little sore from being bound and my jerking on them to get free last night, but I totally understood his reasoning.

"Do you want to talk about it?" murmured a sleep-husky Jude. "Did you dream of him?"

I cleared my throat. "He can't soul-sift me and can't take me unless I'm tainted, right?"

"No, he can't. Unless you're planning on an escapade of murder that I don't know about, then you're completely safe."

I sighed with relief, but that wasn't the only thing on my mind.

"I dreamed about my mother." Jude's fingers stopped for a second, then continued on their trail back up my arm. "It's the second time in recent weeks I've dreamed about her."

"What is it that troubles you?"

I flipped over. My hand caressed the bare skin of his chest in the dark. I refrained from touching him, curling my hand between us instead. As much as I wanted to touch and caress him, I wouldn't do that and tempt him. It was only cruel when he couldn't get pleasure from me if I did. It was all so fucking frustrating.

My mind drifted back to that dream about my mother.

"Everything troubles me. You said that…when we were in her gallery at my house, you said that she'd gone mad. How did you know?"

His hand had continued its journey around my back, making lazy circles between my shoulder blades. We were pressed close, the warmth and strength of his body cocooning me in safety.

"I've been alive a long time, Genevieve. A very long time. I've witnessed a devastating amount of pestilence, plagues of all kinds. They come, they go, they mutate and come again." He coasted a hand up my spine under my hair and wrapped my nape. "But the disease of madness is the same, never changing, a pattern from order falling into disorder, from constancy into chaos. Your mother's paintings didn't simply evolve. They illustrated her descent from lucidity to desperation to insanity. I don't want to hurt you, but the evidence is quite clear."

I knew he was right and couldn't be angry at his open observation.

"She left us, you know. Dad and me."

He didn't respond, just continued to soothe me with his trailing fingers, waiting for me to continue.

"It must've been madness that made her do it, because I know she loved us. I know that. She loved me. But just…not enough."

Jude's roughened hand brushed the hair away from my cheek, where his fingers curled along the side of my neck, thumb resting in the crook between ear and jaw. He didn't offer condolences I'd heard all my life, like *it's not your fault* or *there's nothing more you could've done* and other phrases I despised.

"How did she take her life?"

He knew for certain that she'd died by suicide without me ever having to say it. I felt the rope binding us to each other tighten a bit more. Our mothers ending in similar fates. My hand found its way to his bare chest. He tensed.

"The river," I answered bluntly. "She didn't leave a note, unless you want to call her version of 'The Young Martyr' a suicide note. The day she completed it, she drove out to the Mississippi River bridge and jumped off. There were witnesses. One of them had videoed it with his phone and posted it on Facebook of all things."

Jude's thumb stroked down the length of my neck, still soothing.

"Did you see the video?" he asked, knowing I was struggling to share this part of my life but needed to do it anyway.

"Yes. My dad had hidden it on a flash drive in her jewelry box that he'd stored in the attic. FB had pulled it down once it was reported, but he'd kept a copy." I swallowed against the memory. "When I was thirteen, I went searching for things of hers, needing to remember, needing to touch her. I watched the video only once and never again. Once was enough."

The video began where she was already leaning out from the bridge's railing, holding on with one hand. Still in her everyday painting garb—bare feet, jeans, and all. Her sun-gold hair had pulled from its knot, whipping wildly in yellow streams as if the wind wanted to take her with it.

People shouted. In the distance, sirens wailed, trying to get to the scene before the desperate woman clinging between life and death made an irrevocable decision.

Someone shouted, *"Lady, don't do this. It's not worth it."* Her face snapped back to the speaker, somewhere near the guy with the phone.

Haunted eyes of a ghost stared straight into the camera. A

sorrowful smile spread across her face before she said her dying words. *"Yes, they are. They are worth it."*

Then she let go. Someone screamed, but she was already gone, disappearing beyond the lens into the muddy depths of the churning river. I never understood her last words, and apparently never would. For who was there to explain them?

Jude's voice rumbled close to me in the dark. "Despite this tragedy, this loss, you have done more than survive, you have flourished. She would be proud of the woman you have become."

When Jude called me a woman, something inside always stood straight up at attention, wanting to be everything he saw in me and more.

I didn't want to talk about my mother anymore. My hand was making its own journey across the hard planes of his chest. I trailed an index finger along the ridge down the middle, wishing I could see the beautiful swirls of ink. However, the darkness made me brave. I'd never touched him quite like this.

"Genevieve."

A warning, low and deep. Oh God, that voice. My fingers splayed across the ridges of his abdomen, tight and tense at the moment.

"Genevieve, what are you doing?"

"Exploring."

My hand flattened across a pectoral. Did he just growl?

"Sorry," I added, snatching my hand back and curling it under my chin. "You just feel good."

A strangled laugh rumbled from him. "More like torture. Think I'd prefer the rack." He took my wrist gently and nipped the fleshy part of my palm, teeth pinching.

"Ouch!"

He kissed where he'd bitten, trailing hot kisses along the inside of my wrist. I made a little moan.

He rolled me onto my back and pressed his body into mine. Even with the goose-down between us, I could feel the hardness of his erection and the source of the aforementioned torture. Quite a sizeable torture device, I might add. My mouth went dry.

"Oh."

"Yes." He chuckled. "Oh."

"Jude, do you think we, I mean, will we ever be rid of Danté?"

"Yes," came the immediate, terse reply. "Why do you ask?"

"Well, I was hoping, wondering if, when——"

"Genevieve, relax and tell me what you're thinking."

I blew out a puff of exasperation, thankful the darkness hid the blush rising into my cheeks. It certainly did make me brave, because I said exactly what I was wondering and never would have done such a thing by the light of day.

"When will we get to make love?"

The man looming above me froze so still I'd have thought he wasn't there were it not for the comforting weight of him on top of me. As usual, my heart hammered an erratic beat. He didn't move, didn't speak.

"Jude?"

"When all the threats are dead or your power outweighs theirs."

"You're going to kill all of the demon princes? All seven?" My tone was flat and disbelieving.

"Yes. Or you'll help me."

"*Me?*"

"Once you come into your full power, you'll be stronger than any creature on this earth."

I laughed. It seemed so ludicrous. Who was I but a young student from New Orleans? Apparently, fate had much more planned for me. It was all still so surreal.

"So," I heaved a sigh, "that means we will get to have sex, hopefully, soonish."

His head fell forward with a choked half laugh, face nuzzling into my neck and hair.

"Why are you laughing? You want to, right? You told me last night—"

"Woman, you undo me," he whispered in a way that made goose bumps rise all over. "The things I want to do to your beautiful body would condemn me to the most everlasting, deepest pit in hell. Do I want to? *Christ*, you have no idea."

He started nibbling my neck slowly. I lifted my chin to give him better access, melting under his hot mouth.

"Yes, I want you," he said, brushing his lips across mine in a brief caress, teasing me, not diving in. He lifted a bare inch. A glimmer of amber eyes pierced through the dark. "I want you in my arms. I want you in my bed. I want to bury myself deep inside you and feel you shatter beneath me, again and again. I want you daily, nightly, repeatedly, constantly, forever. And when I know it's safe to take you, you'd best be ready. If you're not, you'd better run and hide, because it will take a legion of angels and demons to keep me off of you. Even then, you won't stand a chance."

Holy shit! I think my heart just stopped. A silver streak of panic shot through me, but desire and anticipation quickly overpowered that shrinking emotion.

"Oh," I finally managed to say in all my magnanimous eloquence.

"Yes." He bit my bottom lip much less gingerly than before. "Oh." Then licked the entrance to my mouth before falling back to my side.

"Now, be a good girl and roll over before I lose control of myself."

I rolled over. Even so, he spooned snugly up to me, making a grumbling sound. My mind raced away with very naughty thoughts, but I wasn't stupid. I recognized the danger we were both in. If we gave in to temptation now, the consequence would be not only permanent separation from each other, but literally an eternity of hell for me. So, like a *good girl*, I changed the subject to get our minds off the present exquisitely painful predicament we were in.

"Why doesn't Kat have a strong English accent? She was born and raised in England, right?"

I stared at the windows, two blocks of faint light streaming in from the streetlamps.

"Kat has tried to scrub out her life as a human, which included her life as one of the English nobility."

"So, demon hunters aren't human?"

"Not exactly, not anymore," he replied. "Flamma operate in a different realm. You are like us now, even not fully awakened."

I pondered that a moment, wondering when I'd be fully awakened and what that would entail. My thoughts wandered back to Kat.

"Well, why did she want to forget her human life? What happened?"

"I'm afraid those are her secrets to tell. As you meet others like us, you'll find we keep certain things to ourselves."

"No. You're kidding."

He pinched my upper arm as punishment.

"Ow!"

Then kissed it and burrowed closer behind me, one arm banding around my waist. "Suffice it to say, she had a cruel husband. Uncommonly cruel. But Kat's a survivor. Like you."

Like me. Yes, I was a survivor. I'd already survived a mother's suicide and several demonic attacks, including the horrific assault on my soul by Danté. I would survive and continue on.

"So, what's the story with her and George?"

His chest rumbled against my back as he let out a short laugh. "They have a history together."

"Um, yeah. I gathered that. So, they dated or something? Can saints even date? That's sort of weird."

Jude laughed a little harder—a sweet, wonderful sound that made my heart sing.

"Yes, they were together once, around the time she became

one of us. I don't know why they fell out, but it seems they both are reluctant to let go. And George isn't exactly like Mother Teresa. He's more a warrior than an angel of mercy."

"Yeah, I figured that one out tonight."

"What do you mean?"

"Well, I doubt Mother Teresa has kissed anybody like George kissed me."

"Are you taunting me, woman?" he grumbled, squeezing me tighter around the waist.

"Taunting you? Me? Of course not." I paused, suppressing the laugh bubbling up my throat. "But I can't stop thinking about that kiss."

He blew out a breath, sounding like a tire deflating, before flipping me promptly onto my back. I did laugh then, wrapping my arms around his neck, my fingers combing into his hair.

"I knew it had to be done, but God help me, when I saw his mouth on yours, I thought I was going to have to kill one of my dearest friends."

"It wasn't *that* kind of a kiss," I laughed. "Didn't you hear him say that?"

"Yes, I know. Since it wasn't a real kiss, then I'm sure it wasn't any good," he said as a statement not a question.

"Hmmm, well, I wouldn't exactly say that."

"Wicked wench," he muttered before fully possessing me with his mouth, smothering anything else I might say. My body arched for him, a soft moan escaping.

"Jude," I murmured when he let me breathe, "you have nothing to worry about." I pulled his head down, angling so that I could be the one to nibble at his jaw and the soft patch of skin by his ear. He drew in a sharp breath between his teeth.

"Genevieve…Genevieve, what are you doing to me?"

He sounded desperate, like a man on the brink. His hand clutched at my hip. Even through this damn comforter, I felt his warm hand squeezing that spot that made me tighten in low, wonderfully feminine places.

The well of emotion in his voice threatened to ignite us both into flames. I was playing with fire, and hell if I didn't want to get burned, but the consequences of giving in to the heat of Jude could result in Danté having possession of me.

Never. I needed to take the reins. I was pushing Jude too far.

"You like to say my name," I said, combing my fingers softly through the back of his hair. He said my name often, and sometimes his voice lilted like a reverent plea. I'd often wondered about this but never had the courage to ask. Until now. "Why is that?"

Breathing labored, he fell onto his back. I snuggled closer but not too close, wrapping one arm across his waist. He urged me up so that his left arm pillowed my head. When his chest finally rose and fell in a steady rhythm reflecting in-control Jude, he spoke.

"Did you know that Genevieve is the name of the patron saint of Paris?"

"No," I murmured encouragingly. Jude rarely spoke of his past, especially his life in France. I understood this as a small gift.

"When Genevieve was seven years old, Saint Germanus, the bishop of Auxerre, prophesied her future greatness. She promised to become consecrated to God, and so she did on that very day and again when she was fifteen years old. In 451, when Attila the Hun threatened to overtake the city of Paris, promising to pillage and kill all those inside, young Genevieve implored the inhabitants not to abandon their homes but to pray and have faith that God would save them. I was there, in the crowd, and she seemed to understand something that no one else could."

"And what was that?"

"That good will prevail if you maintain faith despite the odds. Paris was my city to protect at the time as a Dominus Daemonum, so I had no plans to leave regardless. But she, a young girl with unwavering faith shining in her eyes, put me to shame. Many people were furious at her outright blind faith, as they called it. Some wanted to stone her. Others fled in fear during the night."

"I imagine you put a stop to the stoning," I said, wrapping my arm more tightly around him.

"I did," was his curt reply, but I heard the smile in his voice.

"And did Attila the Hun pillage the city?"

"No. She led a group out to the ramparts of the city before daybreak. I was there too, watching. In the face of the enemy, armed with spears and bloodlust, she led the faithful in prayer as the morning light swept over them. That night, Attila led his army south to Orleans, and the city was saved."

"Was she, was she a Vessel?"

"No. She wasn't Flamma of any kind. She was simply a woman."

Why would he tell me this story?

"So, you like my name because it reminds you of the nun who saved Paris?"

The words sounded flippant, but I didn't mean them to. A slow rumble of laughter vibrated beneath my cheek where it lay on his chest.

"I like your name for many reasons." His hand played with strands of my hair that spilled down his arm pillowing my head. "Because it reminds me of a woman who had faith in the impossible when all signs threatened bloody death. Because it is French, a name that speaks to me in my native tongue. But most importantly," he said, shifting and lifting my chin. Our eyes met. He hesitated but finally dove ahead and said what seemed perched on the tip of his tongue anyway. "Because it is your name, the name of the woman who shines a light in my darkness; the woman who will save me from my worst enemy, despair; the woman who currently holds my jaded heart in her very lovely hands."

He went still. His pulse sped up, pounding in his breast beneath my hands. He was afraid. Of me, and how I would respond to such an open declaration. Trusting me with this vulnerable part of him made something precious open inside. I propped myself on my elbow, weaving my fingers through his available hand, pulling our clasped hands to my lips, grazing a kiss on his knuckles.

"Well," I whispered softly, "I promise to be very, very careful. I've always been known to have capable hands."

"I bet you have," he replied at the somewhat teasing statement, pulling me closer.

But the kiss that followed wasn't filled with heated passion or bridled lust. Rather, it was one of adoration and blooming hope for the both of us, the bonds weaving in and around our hearts pulling a little bit tighter.

25

"But I just don't know! I mean, the Jimmy Choos make me taller and make my calves look *amazing*. But then I'll be able to dance better if I wear these. Whaddya think? Stop reading that magazine and pay attention to me!"

Mindy was on what I call an out-on-the-town high. It starts at the break of dawn with her run to Starbucks for caramel macchiatos with extra shots of espresso for both of us.

The grooming stage occurs before lunchtime, though she refuses to actually eat lunch on these days because it'll give her a "pooch" and ruin her attire for the event. In reality, she never has a pooch, but I get sick of arguing this point. Grooming consists of showering, shampooing, and conditioning her hair using all kinds of high-end products, shaving pretty much everything, and finally painting nails and toes if she hadn't already gotten a professional mani/pedi for the occasion.

From this moment on, she flounces around the rest of the day in her robe, stressing about the details of her wardrobe. We were currently at the obsessing-over-accessories and yelling-at-Gen-to-pay-attention phase of the day.

"Oh, definitely not the Jimmy Choos," I said with serious finesse. "What if you meet this super-hot guy and the shoes make you taller than him? Some men find that emasculating. Plus you won't even be able to dance with him if he can get over the fact that you're taller than him."

Of course, Mindy was very petite, and even in those five-inch heels, she'd still be shorter than the average guy. But if I didn't have some kind of input with a crafty explanation, she'd start fussing that I didn't care and we'd go rounds about that.

"You're so totally right. Why didn't I think of that? Okay, awesome. I'm going to start my hair. Gen! Go get in the shower! I've gotta do your hair too, for goodness sake!"

Then she vanished in a whirl of blonde hair and terry cloth. The clock on the microwave read 4:00. She was right. I should start getting dressed if we were to be on time for the limousine picking us up at six. A freaking limousine. Leave it to Mindy's mom to take us in style.

I wandered back to my room to take a shower, catching a glimpse of my midterm on my nightstand. Malcolm had brought it over earlier, and I'd had to give him the very unwelcome and difficult news that I wanted to just be friends.

After an awkward hug, he handed me my midterm he'd picked up for me since I hadn't been to class in two weeks.

Picking up the paper again, I frowned at Professor Bennett's scrawled handwriting beneath the C-: *Ms. Drake, while your intellect is evidently superior, your reasoning as to why demons actually do exist and plague humans in the literal sense is preposterous. Were it not for your definitive remarks on the matter, your grade would have been much higher. As it is, I cannot reward faulty logic and reasoning, no matter how well-crafted it may be. In addition, attendance to class would not go amiss.*

"Pretentious ass," I muttered, throwing the paper on the coffee table and stomping to my bedroom. "Well, I certainly do hope you're never in need of a demon hunter, Mr. Bennett, because you can't use mine. I'll stand back and watch, debating with you whether the thing trying to crawl inside your body is actually real or not."

I turned on the scalding water, letting my concerns about

bad grades drift away, focusing on more pressing matters. Like fighting actual demons that *did* in fact exist.

After a long steamy shower, I stepped out in a much lighter mood, realizing Mr. Bennett couldn't help the fact that he was a grade-A moron. I almost felt sorry for him with all of *his* "faulty logic and reasoning."

Wrapping a towel around myself and tucking it under my arm, I stepped out of the bathroom and nearly jumped out of my skin.

"Ack! Jude!" Pressing a hand to my chest, I hissed, "Don't ever scare me like that."

In charcoal slacks and a snug, light gray sweater that hugged every delicious part of his upper body, he leaned casually against the doorjamb of my walk-in closet directly across from the bathroom. With arms folded and one leg crossed as well, propped up at the ankle, he looked like a model on display.

His eyes, molten gold ringed with obsidian, made a slow, slow progression down my body and back up. My hair snaked in wet trails across my bare shoulders and down my back. I shifted, self-conscious of my near-nudity. When his eyes made it back up to my lips and stopped for what seemed like a fucking eternity, I lost the ability to breathe.

I cleared my throat to get his attention. "What, what are you doing here? I thought we were meeting at the ball."

Finally, his eyes lifted to mine, smoldering and dark and knee-bucklingly sexy. Yet, he didn't move toward me. Not an inch.

"I brought you a gift."

His voice was rough as bark, rubbing a sensuous promise against my skin. When Jude was steely and hard like this with slow, deliberately calculating eyes, my body turned to jelly. I had no idea how I was still standing under his heated gaze.

"Oh?"

I gathered my dripping hair over one shoulder and used

another towel on my counter to squeeze it dry, trying not to notice that he watched me with predatory eyes.

"I would love to do that for you," he nearly whispered.

I paused with my head at an angle, gazing up at him.

"Then why don't you?"

A slow shake of the head. I'd never seen him bite his lip like that, but when he did, my whole body shivered in response, wishing he'd come closer. I took a step toward him.

"Stay where you are, Genevieve."

A rough, sultry command, but a command nonetheless. He kept his stance casual, but all his muscles locked tight.

"What's wrong?"

"Nothing will go wrong as long as you keep your distance in that flimsy piece of fabric that's supposed to be covering you."

"Something wrong with my towel?" I teased.

The towel stopped higher than midthigh. I had long legs.

"Nothing at all, love." That endearment made my stomach flip. "But the thought of what's under it makes me want to misbehave."

I swallowed hard, knowing his resistance was as thin as the fabric barely covering my body.

"Where's my gift?" I asked with my attempt at a smile.

He nodded toward the bedroom. I walked over, seeing a strappy thing lying across the bed. I picked it up. It was made of fine black leather with a single sheath for a beautifully made dagger.

The blade was razor sharp, thin, about eight inches in length. The thicker hilt, fitting perfectly in my palm as if it were made for me, bore a sinuous design of two lovers locked in rapture. The male lover bore wings. My heart pounded harder. I knew this design, knew it well.

"Eros and Psyche. It's lovely," I murmured, wondering at my beautiful yet practical gift. "I don't get how this straps on, though."

Jude had moved closer, hands in his pockets. He truly was

trying to keep from touching me. I lifted the soft leather straps, trying to figure out how they'd cross my chest.

"It goes on your thigh, Genevieve." My eyes jumped to his. "From the looks of things, it'll fit just right." His gaze lingered on my legs, or rather, the very tops of my legs, seeming to measure the straps with his imagination.

"You think so?" I teased. "Should I try it on to be sure?"

Otherworldly eyes flared fire-bright.

"Don't you dare." His threat wasn't menacing, but breathed all kinds of danger. The kind of danger I seriously wanted to get into. "I thought it best you have protection that was easily concealed. Remember, no casts of illusion tonight. We want the demons to find you."

"Do you think Bamal's men will know how to find me?"

"Oh, yes. They'll be there. Without the cast of illusion, you burn like a bonfire."

I was thinking the same of him. Illusion or not, Jude was a constant burning flame.

"It's kind of funny, but I'll have to focus to not use my VS tonight. It seems to snap on without my even thinking about it."

"VS?" he asked, one eyebrow raised.

"You know, Vessel Sense. Sort of like spidey sense."

"Ah." A smirk lifted his beautiful lips almost into a full smile. "Why, what do you call it?"

"I don't," he replied, matter-of-factly.

I rolled my eyes. Of course not. He was too serious and practical about such things.

"Do you want to see my dress so you can find me at the ball?"

"I'll find you." A rough promise as he stepped closer, hands still in his pockets.

I froze like a statue, the anticipation of his touch an exquisite torture all its own. But he didn't touch me. He stopped an inch from my body, leaning down toward my neck, his breath skimming my skin. I waited for the kiss of lips. It didn't come. His whisper caressed and tormented.

"Vanilla and—what's the floral scent?"

"Cherry blossom." I reddened at that, especially when I received a full smile for the response and all its implications—sweet, innocent and bursting with flavor.

"Mmm. Perfect."

Jeezum crow. I was about to crumble, and the man hadn't even touched me. Embarrassingly, goose bumps rose all over.

"Are you cold, Genevieve?" I nodded, breath catching, refusing to admit it had anything to do with the temperature in the room. "I want nothing more than to warm you right now. But my hands on your body at the moment wouldn't be prudent."

Then I felt a soft, warm caress of lips on the slope from neck to shoulder—so sweet and too quickly gone. I whimpered.

"It will be worth the wait. Trust me, love." He took a step back, removing his luxurious heat. A shimmer of amber in fiery eyes. "Oh. And the weapon wasn't the gift."

He nodded toward the bedside table, winked at me, then sifted out with a snapping whoosh.

A blue velvet box with silver-metallic ribbon sat on the table. I instantly tore off the ribbon and opened it, never having been prissy or patient with wrapping paper.

"Oh, my."

On a delicate silver chain in a thin but decorative silver setting was a perfectly round, unbelievably beautiful opal. I pulled the necklace from the box, holding the weight of the jewel in my hand.

The iridescent stone was colored with blue and lavender waves. There was a small square of cardstock on the inside of the jewelry box. I snatched it up, thinking it was a note from Jude. But it was the stamp of the maker with small print reading "Crystal Opal from Lightning Ridge in New South Wales, Australia."

"Wow," I admired, gazing at the gem again. There was something so familiar about the transparent markings—crystal white opaqueness swimming with smudges of blue and purple. Then I realized what it resembled.

"The moon! How lovely."

I went to put it on and saw something inscribed on the back. In delicate script were the Latin words: *Mea luna in tenebris.*

"Oh, Jude." I clasped the necklace securely around my neck, butterflies flitting around as it settled beneath the hollow between my collarbones. "Mea luna in tenebris," I whispered to my reflection.

My moon in the darkness.

And he was my guiding star. If he only knew.

26

"A Roman empress and an Egyptian queen. Girl, we are so going to be the hottest chicks there."

Mindy never lacked for confidence, but I had to agree we looked pretty damn good. Mindy wore a silvery-white, flowing chiffon dress that draped perfectly on her petite body, scooping across her breasts and hugging slim but nicely curving hips. She did indeed look like a Roman patrician. Her strappy matching sandals were way better than the ginormous Jimmy Choos.

My golden gown—sweetheart cut and strapless with corseted boning—hugged my waist and hips, then dropped straight to the floor. The burnished fabric shimmered with lighter flecks like gold dust, giving a dramatic effect under the light. A gold cuff in the shape of a snake with a ruby-red eye coiled around my upper arm.

"And now for the final touches," said Mindy, passing me my mask.

Her cat-eyed mask was satin white with silver swirls, embellished with wispy feathers. Mine covered more cheek and nose in the Venetian style—gold under black lace studded with small white rhinestones. This one touch of silver enhanced the crystal opal hanging below my throat.

"They're here!" squealed Mindy, shoving her phone into her small white pouch-purse that hung from a silken rope around her wrist.

We stepped out into the driveway, where a black stretch-Mercedes limo awaited. The chauffeur already had the door open. Mindy laughed, bright blue eyes twinkling, as we scooted in.

"Good evening, ladies," said a dapper gentleman stretched out with casual grace next to Mindy's mom.

"Oh, girls, don't you look gorgeous!"

"Thank you, Miss Donna," I said, doing my best not to catch my heel on her burgundy dress.

"Hi, Bill. Thank you so much for the invitation," said Mindy, bouncing closer to her mother.

"I'm delighted, Mindy. So, should I call your friend Cleopatra, or does she have another name?"

"Genevieve Drake." I smiled.

This very cheesy introduction would ordinarily rub me wrong, but Bill seemed to be a genuinely nice guy. Attractive too. In a sharp, black tuxedo and with that indefinable blue-blood poise, he was a stunning older man. Miss Donna complemented him with her petite, fair features, slightly aged with laugh lines at the eyes.

"And you are Mister…?"

I dragged out the Mister, hoping he would fill that in. Gentleman that he was, he did.

"Mr. Bridges, Genevieve, but please call me Bill."

"Yes, Gen. He prefers Bill."

"I do believe I will be the envy of the ball with the three most beautiful ladies there."

Mindy and Miss Donna laughed in unison. I smiled at Mr. Bridges, I mean Bill, as he passed us each a flute of Cristal champagne. We toasted and sipped as the city faded behind us, embarking farther into bayou country toward La Blanche Plantation Home where the Crescent City Masquerade was held each year.

On the final rural tract, the limo followed behind another one onto a long, paved drive. Passing under a canopy of centuries-old live oaks and through a line of torches lighting the path, I twisted around to see limousine after limousine filing behind us.

Mindy squeezed my hand in girlish giddiness. My stomach flipped in fear and excitement for two different reasons—that I was bait for Bamal's assassins and that my demon hunter would be here among the masked men. The idea sent a thrill of anticipation through me.

The chauffer opened the door, and we followed Bill and Mindy's mom up the outer steps into the throng of New Orleans' finest. The gowns on these women were stunning. I leaned over to Mindy.

"I'm glad I let you convince me to charge the more expensive gown now."

She nodded and winked behind her pretty mask. The antebellum home was a Greek revival, complete with two stories of wide verandas, and gardens that wound for acres beyond the home. When we walked into the main foyer, I thought we'd stepped back in time.

Candelabras burned everywhere, bathing beautiful people in ethereal light. Servants in full tuxedos and black masks greeted the guests with a choice of champagne or wine. Mindy picked up two glasses of red wine and passed one to me.

"Cheers," she said, clinking her glass to mine.

"Mindy, come here, dear," called her mom, waving us over into the main ballroom.

The room was mostly an open dance floor, the orchestra set up on the far end. On the outer rim of the stage and dance floor were alcoves draped with curtains of red velvet and gold trim, partitioning off private sitting areas.

I scanned the room, searching for Jude, but didn't see him.

I'd know him with or without a mask. There was no mistaking that man.

"Mindy and Genevieve, this is Mr. and Mrs. Clark and their son, Nathaniel."

The Clarks nodded graciously in greeting. Nathaniel, a tall, russet-haired guy about our age gave us one of those smiles that put me on edge, brushing a kiss on the top of my hand. Hooded hazel eyes assessed from behind a navy-blue mask. His lips lingered longer on Mindy's hand with a wider smile. A wolf in sheep's clothing, this one. But the wolves here were camouflaged in designer Italian formal wear and plastic faces.

I remembered what Kat had told me. *"A gentleman of the gentry in evening dress is the perfect mask to hide the wolf beneath."* Too true, Kat.

"Ladies, let me show you to our private area," said Nathaniel.

Apparently, Mindy's mom and Mr. Bridges had already agreed to share a private space with the Clarks. Who was I to argue even if the guy gave me the creeps?

He swaggered slowly toward the middle of the room, gesturing toward an alcove where the curtain was drawn to the side. I saw that you could either keep the entrance open with a drawstring or close it for a more private party. We stepped into the small space furnished with three round tabletops spread with white linen and red roses as well as a sofa to the back.

"Whoohoo! Look at this, Gen."

"Nice, isn't it?" commented Nathaniel. "We can bring in bottles of wine from the bar to avoid trips back and forth."

"Sweet," said Mindy. "This is my kind of party."

Nathaniel's wolfish smile showed teeth as he watched her bend over the table to smell a vase of roses. I noticed hazel eyes dipping to take in the revealing view when Mindy leaned over.

"Well, take it easy, Mindy. We don't want a repeat of our last night out," I said, bumping her to stand upright.

"Stop your frowning, Gen. We've got a fabulous designated driver tonight."

The DD wasn't what I was worried about.

"Don't be concerned. I'll take care of her," said Nathaniel.

Now, *that* was what I was worried about.

"May I have the first dance, empress?" he asked, offering her his hand.

I cringed at his cheesy line. But Mindy smiled and took his hand.

"I hope to have a dance with you as well, Genevieve."

I nodded tightly, trying to smile. I didn't like him but couldn't be rude either. He was the son of Mindy's mother's friends. We were their guests.

And what was he doing that other guys didn't do on a regular basis? Ogling pretty little Mindy was a regular pastime for most guys in her vicinity. It was the cold hunger in those hazel eyes that made me nervous. I might be oversensitive due to recent events in my own life, suspecting every man when it was unwarranted. But still.

"Relax, Genevieve," I whispered to myself, downing my wine in two gulps and strolling out to find another.

An orchestra of strings played at the front of the ballroom along with a modern band onstage. In sleek black suits, two men played electric guitars in accompaniment with the classic instruments. The drummer wore black slacks and a white T-shirt, his hair a wild mess. A statuesque redhead in a floor-length green gown stepped up to the microphone. Her hair draped in shining waves over one shoulder. Were it not for the full-sleeved tattoo on one arm, I'd have thought she fit right into the mix.

I liked this touch of incivility in the room. It made me more comfortable. As she began to sing a soft, melancholy melody, I drifted farther across the hall. The effect of violins and cellos in harmony with the electric guitars was haunting and lovely.

I drew closer, seeing a server holding a tray of red wine. I knew I should refrain from drinking too much, but I needed a bit more liquid courage.

My VS tingled with Flamma present. Jude, Kat, and George were here somewhere, but there were others as well.

I took a glass and sipped lightly and slowly from the sidelines. The myriad of masks had a fantastic effect in the dimly lit room while the ghostly melody echoed through the grand hall.

Vibrant colors, curving shapes, glitter and satin, all enhanced the beautiful dancers under crystal chandeliers. Then there were others. Strange and bizarre masks—animalistic, suggestive of large cats, predatory birds, and ravenous wolves—adorned the more eccentric.

Nathaniel spun Mindy close by. She tossed her head back, laughing.

"He should be wearing one of those," I said to myself, thinking of the slit-eyed wolf mask I'd just seen.

"Who should be wearing one of what?" came the feminine voice next to me.

I jumped, then relaxed. "Kat! Oh, thank God."

She wore a formfitting gown in leopard print, a feline mask framing green eyes swimming unnaturally with eddies of black. Her platinum hair spilled over her shoulders in crimped waves. She was breathtaking.

"Damn, Kat. If you're trying to blend in, it'll never happen."

"All in a day's work, my friend. Just trying to fit in with the nobility." She said the word "nobility" as if it were something contemptuous that might bite. Who knows? Maybe it would.

"Has George seen you in this dress yet?" I grinned.

Her head snapped to mine. "What do you mean? Who cares if he sees me?"

"Oh, I think you care very much, Kat."

She huffed out a breath, gulping her pink champagne. "Is it that obvious?"

"Yeah. But he's got it bad too. The way he looks at you."

"Really?"

Her austere gaze transformed to something more vulnerable. My heart hurt for her. I wondered what had happened between them, but this was certainly not the time or place to get the details.

"Without a doubt," I assured her.

She swigged the rest of her champagne and placed the empty flute on the tray of a passing server.

"So, have you seen any demons?"

She asked this so casually I would've found it funny if it weren't for the fact that they were here to kill me.

"No. But I feel them."

"Yes. They're definitely here. At least three, maybe more," she calculated, scanning the crowds. "Bamal knows you have protection now, since his last two lower demons were expelled. He'll have sent higher demons this time, some of his dukes or earls, so be careful. They can shape-shift. And sift you out of here."

"Awesome. I feel great now," I said, a tremor quivering down my spine.

Kat glanced at me and smiled. "Gen, you've got the leader of the demon hunters, the oldest and strongest demon hunter there is, and me here for your protection. You're covered, girl. Don't fret."

Jude was the oldest demon hunter? I didn't realize that. I wondered for the hundredth time how one became a demon hunter. This secret was guarded, hidden for dark reasons, I was certain. But what?

"Have you seen Jude?" Kat interrupted my thoughts.

"No. Not yet."

"Okay. I'm going to mingle. You should move around. Let the demons see you. We need our bait out in the open."

"Terrific. A lamb in a den of wolves," I said, tossing back the rest of my wine.

Kat grinned at me, appearing even more like a cat with

narrowed green eyes. She glanced at my dress for a second and let out a feminine laugh.

"Just you wait till the alpha gets a look at you in this."

I knew she didn't mean George, making me wonder why she considered Jude more dominant. Of course, I knew who was more dominant but found that intriguing, as George was their leader. I shivered, peering out across the crowd.

"On that note, I'll go mingle. Here goes the little lamb."

Kat laughed and stepped toward the crowd.

"Kat, wait," I stopped her. "What about Danté? Could he be here too?"

She shook her head definitively. "No. Now that George has given you his power of protection and Jude plans on keeping you untainted, though I'm sure it's killing him, you're safe." She grinned.

"Stop that, Kat!"

She let out a throaty laugh. "Anyway, Danté will have to come up with some other plan. I'm sure he's scheming, but he's less powerful than Bamal and some of his other brothers."

"Seriously?"

He seemed pretty damn powerful to me. I shuddered, remembering how easily he made me his puppet.

"Just get out there. You have nothing to worry about."

With a wink, she pressed her way through the socialites laughing near the stairwell and headed toward the balcony on the second floor overlooking the ballroom.

"Let's go, little lamb," I muttered to myself, steeling my spine and sauntering out into the open.

While many men admired my passing, they were just men. My VS was sensitive, able to penetrate casts of illusion quickly. I was progressing in power.

I focused to keep my cast of protection from wrapping my body—barring other Flamma from seeing me. Forcing myself to wander through the throng, knowing demons were here, made me feel vulnerable on a painful level.

I circled around the dancers, seeing Mindy and Nathaniel, his hand sliding over her bare back in circles as he whispered something in her ear. Mindy smiled. She seemed to be having fun. Perhaps I'd misjudged the guy.

The singer pulled my attention to the stage. Her voice harmonized with the violins, crooning out a melody of love and redemption. The music tugged on my heart, luring me closer.

I paused near the orchestra, feeling the music vibrate through me, when a hand wrapped around my forearm. In swift reflex, I elbowed back into the ribs of my assailant. I heard an "oof" then felt a large male pressed close behind me, pulling me toward him. My free hand was going for the dagger when a familiar voice halted me.

"Rumplestiltskin," he whispered.

"What?" I asked, dumbfounded.

"Your code word, Genevieve. Rumplestiltskin."

I vaguely remembered our conversation eons ago about using a code word to avoid startling me. Too late. How this man made the name of an evil, twisted dwarf sound sexy was beyond me.

Before I could even think of a snappy comeback, his arm wound around my waist, his hand flattened against my stomach and pulled me back into a private alcove, red velvet curtains sealing us in. No one occupied this one. No one but Jude. And me.

He spun me around. My hands went to broad shoulders clad in a fine, obviously expensive, jacket. The simple black mask he wore perfectly framed eyes of flame and accentuated sensuous lips now curling into a smile as he drank me in.

"Do you approve?" I asked lightly.

He traced my bottom lip with a callused finger. I parted my mouth farther for him. His eyes brightened impossibly more.

"Yes," he said, trailing his finger down my chin, dipping along my throat, over the hollow to where his gift hung for the world to see. "I like you wearing this."

"I like me wearing this too."

His finger trailed ever lower, horizontally crossing over the slopes of my breasts, skimming along the line of the fabric. I closed my eyes, unable to handle the heat in his eyes, my breath coming quickly.

He tipped up my chin to take my mouth, and I opened for him instantly. Waiting.

"Genevieve."

His hands scaled down my sides, burning through the fabric.

"What?" I panted, eyes still closed.

One hand stopped on my hip with a proprietary hold; the other drifted to the small of my back.

"You're giving in to me so easily."

"Should I be a tease instead?"

I opened my eyes to see a smug smile spread wide just below the line of his mask.

"You give a man all kinds of ideas when you melt in his arms, all soft, beautiful curves and bitable skin. All obedient."

My hand wove into the hair at his nape. I let my ring and pinky finger tuck beneath his stiff collar, caressing the sensitive skin beneath. He shivered. That was a first.

"Jude, I only melt for you," I said in all earnestness, sweeping my eyes down, then looking up through long lashes. "And I'm only obedient to you."

He took my mouth, crushing me close, kissing me deeply, tongue and teeth clashing in a maddening frenzy. His hand at my back lowered more, curving over my ass, pressing me up against his pelvis. His evident arousal made me moan.

He broke from my mouth, sliding hot, lingering kisses down the side of my neck, scraping with his teeth. Down, down. His hands pulled me against the hardness of him, his lips leaving a hot, wet trail along the top of my cleavage. The hand he had on my hip moved up to cup my breast, his thumb rubbing a tight circle over the silk.

I moaned, my nipple tightening to a peak. Then I arched

into him and felt flames ignite me into an inferno, dazed by sheer sensation as orchestra music and whirling dancers laughed just beyond the red velvet curtain. It would be so easy to let go here and now. I couldn't think anymore, encased by a seductive wall of heat.

"Jude. Please," I breathed, my hand clutched in his hair, pressing him closer.

I didn't even know what I was begging for. Did I want him to stop or go on? Though I couldn't see his aura of flame, it burned me nonetheless, in a sweet, lapping caress.

My mind reeled, forgetting everything but him—strong arms, caressing hands, imploring mouth. I was well beyond thinking clearly, wanting him so badly I didn't care anymore.

Sensing the danger, Jude slid his hands away from sensitive curves to my waist, pinning me in place against him but not with the crushing force as before. His mouth found mine again, sweeping more gently, slower, softer.

He sipped at my full lower lip, pulling his body an inch from mine, bringing me down from a rapture that had nearly consumed us both. I was dizzy, heart pounding like a frightened rabbit's.

"No," he said, voice deep and husky and out of breath. "I don't want you to be a tease, though I do believe abstaining is going to kill me."

I sort of laughed, unclenching my hand in his hair, moving it to his shoulder. "I thought you said a gentleman didn't fondle ladies in doorways, or perhaps behind curtains, in this case."

A self-satisfied grin quirked his beautiful mouth.

"I never professed to be a gentleman. That was an assumption on your part."

"Oh, well, in that case, let me go find one."

I pretended to pull away. He snapped me back against him.

"No man of any kind will fondle you or do otherwise ever again." It was a promise, not a threat. He planted a tender kiss on my forehead and held me there. "I would love to take you out onto the dance floor, hold you in my arms, and show every man here that you are mine and no other's."

"So, why don't you?"

Lion-gold eyes captured me. His hands drifted to my hips and squeezed, but not in a seductive way this time. Protective. Possessive. After a long moment, he blinked and broke the connection.

"Bamal's demons will know me on sight. I need to keep my distance if we are to lure them into the open."

I nodded, taking a deep breath and letting it out. He evidently had no desire to keep his distance, nor did I, but we had a mission tonight—to capture Bamal's henchmen and negotiate a deal with the high demons in his employ. I didn't ask Jude what that entailed. Honestly, I didn't want to know.

With my mind on present problems, I pulled out of his arms. "Well, I better get back to work then."

He cupped my face with large, warm hands, gazing into my eyes for what seemed like forever. His thumb brushed my cheekbone. "Be careful, Genevieve."

I smiled, tiptoed, and planted a swift kiss on his lips. "You too."

I slipped out of the curtain and skirted the perimeter of the dance floor, returning back to Mindy, hoping she was in the alcove.

"Genevieve."

I turned to find Nathaniel looking down at me, having removed his mask. He was handsome, a strong jaw and steady, arrogant gaze telling me he was used to getting what he wanted.

"May I have this dance? Mindy's sitting this one out."

I was pretty sure Mindy forced him to ask me to dance to make sure I was enjoying myself. If she only knew I'd enjoy myself better without Nathaniel's attentions.

"Sure," I replied, taking his offered hand.

Normally, I would've refused politely, but I needed to be in the open. Perhaps a spin around the dance floor would tempt the demons to come out so the others could find them. Thankfully, Nathaniel placed his hand on my waist in a respectable way, gracefully taking my other hand to guide me around the dancers. I was in no mood to fend off roaming hands.

"Are you feeling well?" he asked. "You appear flushed."

Crap. Evidence of Jude's caresses were all over me, in the pink of my cheeks and probably in marks along my neck and chest as well. Pale skin revealed everything.

"Perhaps it's the heat."

"Ah. Yes." His lip twitched. I couldn't tell whether he was mocking me, perhaps having seen me reappear from someone else's alcove and put two and two together, or whether he naturally seemed like a snide ass all the time. "It is a little warm in this crush of people."

He led me along, spinning smoothly between the couples. Though I didn't let on, a prickle of unease warned me that I was being observed.

"So, you and Mindy go to school together at Loyola?"

"Yes." I nodded with a smile, glancing over his shoulder to try and find who was watching me. "Are you in school?"

"Tulane."

Condescending smile. How did Mindy fall for these guys? I found myself wishing Dazzling Dave would make a sudden appearance.

"So what's your major, Genevieve?"

I gave a tight smile at the go-to question every guy seemed to ask. "English literature."

"And what are your plans with your degree? English teacher?"

He said English teacher as if it were a disease. It made me want to slap that smug look off his face. "What's your major, Nathaniel?"

"Business."

"And what are your plans with your degree? Take over Daddy's business?"

Ouch. Where did that come from? Seems my tongue had a mind of its own tonight.

A flash of anger sharpened those hazel eyes, then the shadow was gone. He smiled coolly. "Yes, actually."

"Pardon me, but may I cut in?"

I glanced over my shoulder to see George smiling charmingly at me. He gave Nathaniel a curt and cold nod, swinging me out of his arms without an answer. As George spun me around, I glimpsed Nathaniel's dark expression before he walked off the floor alone.

"George, you're my hero."

He laughed, his dimples and bright eyes revealing how gorgeous he was. The candlelight cast a reddish glow on his chestnut hair.

"I am ever endeavoring to be the hero, Genevieve. It's so nice to hear that I'm doing a fine job of it."

I laughed at that. "But should you be seen with me? Won't the demons recognize you?"

"No, I doubt it. I tend to stay out of the fray. Most demons don't know what I look like. They only know me by name. Still, we'll keep this dance short and sweet to be certain."

I glanced up, feeling a sudden sinister tug in my core.

"Oh God. George, up there." My voice came out in a whisper.

He followed my gaze to the balcony. Two men, dark-haired and dressed in all-black tuxedos, wore identical cold expressions. They stood like stone glaring down at us—me.

Their wicked glares were fixed unwaveringly. I was definitely their prey. I reached out with my VS, touching on an aura of menace seeping down from the balcony area. My eyes flickered to the stairwell where Jude was already making his way up the stairs.

"And, abracadabra. There they are."

George spun me expertly to the far end of the dance floor near the stairwell, sweeping a kiss on the top of my hand and ascending the stairs. George and Jude could catch the demons faster if they sifted, but then this place might erupt in chaos.

I backed away, walking toward our alcove, glancing nervously around. I saw another man standing behind the stage looking out. My VS homed in on him. He was identical to the two at the top of the balcony. Wait, they weren't there anymore. Neither were Jude and George. The three demons could've been triplets. The one behind the stage turned away from me.

A statuesque blonde in leopard print leapt from the shadows. Kat grabbed his shoulder, and they both sifted out. No one noticed.

I reached out with my VS, sweeping the dance floor, the stairs, the balcony. Nothing. I didn't feel Flamma anywhere.

"Wow."

Just like that, they sifted out with Bamal's demons to a safer place for negotiations. They'd told me the plan. Once they identified the demons, it was a simple step to take them elsewhere and deal with them. I inhaled a deep gulping breath, my heart pounding.

Still afraid, I swept the area again with my Vessel power. All safe. Relief washed over me. I couldn't believe our luck or that I'd escaped a near-death experience. I suppose it wasn't too shabby having this badass trio of protection.

I walked back to the alcove to find Miss Donna and Mrs. Clark whispering over some sort of gossip.

"Miss Donna, have you seen Mindy?"

"Oh yes, dear. She and Nathaniel headed out for some fresh air."

Fresh air? Yeah, I bet. I ambled back out into the ballroom, laughter and music swelling as the night wore on. Mindy had been flirting with this guy since we got here, but I knew she wasn't the cheating type. She might let Nathaniel think he was getting somewhere, but she and David were still an item.

The problem was, I also knew Nathaniel's type. He owned lots of things. He was the kind of guy who believed wealth equaled power, and power meant the world could deny him nothing or no one. Panic seized me. Mindy had been knocking back quite a bit of champagne. I made my way to the main foyer in longer strides.

"Excuse me," I asked one of the statue-like waiters at the door, "have you seen a small blonde in a white dress with a tall guy?"

He nodded down a darkened hall along the front of the house. I hurried along the marble floor, the click-clacking of my shoes sounding hollow on the walls. The hallway wrapped around to the back of the house. Turning the corner, a set of French doors stood ajar.

I pulled off my mask and stepped out onto a patio. Moonlight spilled brightly, casting blue shadows on the pavement and lawn. A damp chill settled in the air. I walked with careful steps over slate stones, around a gurgling fountain, and scanned the shadowed garden. There on the third step was Mindy's white purse, a lipstick having spilled out.

"Oh, no."

My heart sank. Then I heard her. A scream, cold and piercing. *Mindy!*

My breath caught in my throat as I ran, losing my heels in the grass turf. The muffled voices came from the right where a maze of hedges stood tall and black under night's cloak.

My gaze darted to a small luminescent shape in the grass, white and wispy—Mindy's mask. Then her stifled cry again. I heard her beg, "Please."

I ran as fast as possible in my damn dress. Fear and panic spiked an adrenaline rush through my limbs. I drew closer to the sound of a struggle. A thump, then silence. A tearing sound.

I rounded a tall hedge to find Nathaniel on his knees, his jacket tossed aside as he worked on getting his pants open. Underneath him was my unconscious best friend, her hair pulled loose, her white dress ripped up to her navel, and her legs sprawled obscenely.

Not Mindy. Not Mindy. Not Mindy! Red filled my vision. Rage a burning brand on my heart. Not thinking, I launched myself onto him, cuffing him across the head and scratching at his face.

"Get off of her! You bastard!"

He shoved me back and stood quickly, his pants half-open. I lunged at him again. Pure, raw rage spurned me on, but he was a big guy. He hauled his arm back and hit me full across the face, sending me spinning to the grass.

Dazed and seeing spots, I nearly lost consciousness myself, faintly hearing his sinister reply in that condescending tone he used on the dance floor.

"You want me first, baby? I'm more than happy to oblige."

My head buzzed from the punch across the head. I felt my body being flipped onto my back. Hard, cold hands fumbled up my dress. My instincts launched me out of the stupor.

I struggled, jerking my knee up toward his groin. He narrowly blocked me. This was the worst position to be in for defense—on your back with someone much larger than you clambering on top. I couldn't punch out, so I grabbed his hair and yanked. He gripped my throat and slammed my head against the ground.

"You wanna play rough? Not a problem."

He fumbled with his pants with one hand, the other tight on my throat. I bent my leg up so that the slit in my dress opened. A look of confusion crossed his face, flushed hot with anger and lust. He thought I was inviting him to continue.

Panic retreated. Hatred—cold and stealthy clamped down on me with a venomous bite. My fingers slid along my thigh. Nathaniel stared stupidly, starting to grin, feeling triumphant in a sure conquest. I refused to let my gaze shift from his as my right hand found the dagger. Before he could register what I held, I put the ball of my left hand behind the hilt and thrust the dagger hard and deep up into his chest. I stabbed only once, but he slumped forward instantly on top of me.

Trembling with fury and fear, I shifted his weight off, flipping and sliding out from under him. Pulling out the dagger, slick with blood, I put it back into its sheath, my movements robotic, the acrid taste of hatred still bitter on my tongue.

I'd hit him directly in the heart. A pool of crimson spread across his white tuxedo shirt on the left side of his chest. His eyes and mouth gaped wide in a frozen expression of shock, unmoving.

Dead. He was dead. So quick, so fast.

I sat back, staring at my hands in horror, shining wet and near black under the moonlight. An uncontrollable quivering shook me from head to toe. I hadn't intended to kill him. The thought of what he was going to do had driven me into a madness of fury. My breath came out in quick white breaths, the temperature dropping rapidly.

A billowing, cool mist floated around the body, Mindy, and me. I whimpered, bloody hands in my lap, shaking uncontrollably. It wasn't a natural mist.

The dread making my heart hammer with violent force inside my ribcage grabbed hold of me with icy fingers.

"No," I cried, like a child in the dark.

"Mmmmm, my sweet." A sinister whisper, so horrifyingly familiar, rose from the coalescing shadows in the gloom. "Blood-stained hands. My darling is so wonderfully *tainted*."

A wicked laugh I knew from the darkest of nightmares snapped my chin up to see Danté walking sinuously toward me, the supernatural mist curling around his legs in a cold caress.

What had I done?

The sparkle of triumph in ice-gray eyes taught me a new definition of fear. I couldn't move, paralyzed in shock, as he drew closer with slow, deliberate steps, sliding through the mist like a serpent.

"Wrath is an awfully deadly sin, my sweet."

"What do you"—my breath was coming out in quick white puffs, the temperature having plummeted in minutes—"mean by that?"

I knew the answer, but still, I thought, hoped that maybe I was in a nightmare, that this wasn't real. When you talk to the monsters in your dreams, they sometimes go away. The beautiful monster crouched right in front of me, his golden hair glinting silver under the moonlight.

"But I-I was defending myself, my friend," I protested, trying to justify what I'd done.

Danté shook his head back and forth as if to chastise a naughty child.

"Tsk, tsk, Genevieve. You cannot lie to a supreme liar. I felt it," he cooed, eyes shining darkly, "I can still feel it now. Pure unbridled loathing pumping through your lovely veins. You didn't want him to simply stop. You wanted him dead for what he would do to you and to her. So the savage beast called Revenge seduced you to do her bidding. And, oh, my sweet, you did it so well."

Untainted heart, hands, and body. Oh God. I could feel the malevolent sin of hatred and murder wrapping around my heart, clouding my Vessel power to a dim glow.

This was what it meant to be tainted, to let the darkness in. It crawled into the very corners of my being, whispering. The trembling in my hands spread to the rest of my body.

"Thanks, friend. Much obliged." Danté spoke to the corpse off to my right.

I refused to look at those sightless, accusing eyes. Something in the prince's voice spread a chill straight through me.

"You knew him," I whispered, tears stinging my eyes.

"Oh, yes. Nathaniel and I made a little deal, and I must say he kept up his end of the bargain."

"What bargain?" My voice came out in a hushed whisper, the truth dawning slowly in a cold, sickening wave. I'd been tricked, trapped.

"Nathaniel, being the lusty fellow that he is"—he paused, laughing—"was—had a predilection for petite women. I promised him a most succulent peach and that he'd never go to prison for it. In return, he only had to be sure you would find them together. He didn't mind voyeurism, rascal that Nathaniel was and so you see, he kept his end of the bargain, and so have I. He's certainly not going to prison."

I squeezed my eyes shut. I thought I was going to vomit. Then I heard Danté's voice much closer.

"You are the most stunning creature, Genevieve." My eyes snapped open. He had edged much closer, lifting the braid along the left side of my face, and smoothed it along his smiling lips. After a second of gazing, he dropped it lightly. "So unbelievably beautiful with fresh sin painted thick on your hands."

I gazed down at them, quivering in my lap, covered in

Nathaniel's blood. Danté picked up my wrist delicately. Truly, I was in shock, for I could do nothing but watch as he elevated my hand and drew my bloodiest finger into his mouth, sucking it clean in one long motion and staring into my soul.

"Your sin tastes so good, my sweet. Like a decadent dessert." His mouth quirked into a wicked smile. "Or perhaps an aphrodisiac."

That got me moving. I fell back, scrambling on my backside closer to Mindy.

What was I thinking? I couldn't get away. Before I could even think what to do next, Danté lunged forward, grabbed my ankle, and yanked me hard. The friction with the ground hiked my gown up as he pulled me toward him.

Frantically, I clawed at the grass and pushed my dress down at the same time, cold blades of fear spiking through my veins. He had both ankles now, hauling me back bodily, then pressed his full weight on top, pinning me facedown to the cold earth. He grabbed my forearms, keeping them still, and laughed in my ear.

"Hmm, this seems pleasantly familiar." He ground his hips against me and nuzzled my neck. I struggled to no avail, nearly choking on my own fear.

"You're right, my sweet. This is no place for an amorous encounter. We don't want Nathaniel over there watching. Let us go where we can have some privacy."

Then we were sifting. Clutched tightly from behind around the waist, I felt the suction and weightlessness of the Void. The roiling nausea gripped me at once as we descended. Gray shapes blurred around us. I closed my eyes to quell the nausea, but nothing would help. It wasn't the Void that had my body revolting; it was being once again in the arms of sadistic Danté. I murmured a prayer the second before I felt my feet on solid ground.

Spinning away from him, I backed against a wall. I didn't

recognize this room but knew from the heavy air and slate-gray walls that I was in Danté's castle.

The room was carpeted in plush burgundy. The furnishings were sparse—a four-poster bed covered in red silk sheets, an ornate vanity with brushes and hair combs displayed, and a standing wardrobe near a changing screen.

I stared wide-eyed at the bed, my heart sinking at the metal chains and cuffs linked to each post, heart pounding painfully. I skimmed over the wardrobe, trying not to see the abundance of sheer nightgowns in varying lengths. A fire crackled in a black-manteled fireplace. I shuddered at the sight of the white fur rug, identical to the one in his bedroom. I swallowed hard.

"Here we are, darling. This is your suite. Shall we get you into something more comfortable?"

He snapped his fingers. A wraithlike woman in a maid's uniform appeared from nowhere, holding a slip of a black night-gown, the exact same one I wore the last time Danté had soul-sifted me. The night he'd possessed my soul and had nearly—

Calm down, Genevieve. Think. Think.

Danté propped one arm on the mantel, the other hand casually in his pocket as he watched me. I needed to leash this fear and think of a plan to get out of here. He hadn't seen the weapon strapped around my thigh, or he would've taken it. I forced my expression into a blank slate, covering the inner turmoil bubbling in my gut.

"Come on, darling. While I do so like the Egyptian-goddess charade, it's time we made this official."

Danté leaned casually against the fireplace, but the hard look of lust in his gaze warned me he was at the breaking point. I gulped, staring at the zombielike creature with haunted yellow eyes like his slave Claudius, who I noticed was guarding the door. The zombie maid moved closer with the silky garment outstretched in her hands.

"I'm not changing in front of you."

I was surprised, impressed how confident I sounded, the trembling gone from my voice. Danté managed a half smile.

"The blushing bride. Of course."

He gestured to a changing screen in the corner near the bed. I took the nightgown and vanished behind the screen, which bore a tapestry of seven dragons, some roaring, some sleeping, some breathing fire. The seven princes.

I slipped out of my ball gown, removed the snake cuff on my arm and touched my fingers to the opal. I lifted and kissed the back of it where Jude reminded me who I was—the moon in the darkness, *his* moon in the darkness. The blood cast between him and Danté would keep Jude from saving me. I had to save myself.

I closed my eyes, clenching the opal, cool in my palm, a comforting talisman giving me the strength to do what must be done.

"Hurry, my sweet. I grow impatient."

Bastard. I've got something for you all right. I slipped the black gown over my head, the silky clinginess more abrasive than when I was soul-sifted here. I reminded myself that I was here, body and soul, more powerful than before.

Readjusting my strap and sheath to be sure it was hidden but in perfect position for my reach, I stepped out from behind the screen.

Danté stood in the middle of the room, bare-chested, wearing only black silk pajama pants. Man, did he have an obsession with silk.

"Ah, Genevieve." His gaze brightened with open hunger, meandering over my body, making my stomach churn. "Like mother's milk." I quelled the sickness with the thought of my dagger buried in his heart.

He disgusted me. I smiled. The golden demon sauntered closer. My heart skittered in a panic, but my mask stayed in place. I even managed an alluring light in my eyes. How? I don't know. Something still and quiet guided me now. The horror and fear muffled by purpose—the fervent need to punish this beast and to avenge myself and everyone who came before me.

"I don't want an audience," I said with dark sensuality, glancing at the maid and Claudius.

"Your wish is my command."

Without saying a word, the two vanished into the walls. Literally.

The door to my bedroom remained open. As he drew closer, I knew that I'd have to kiss him. I couldn't let him put his mouth near my neck. He might bite, drain my blood, and weaken me. I needed my wits and strength. I needed to be in control.

"There now," he whispered as if trying to quiet a frightened animal, slipping his arms around my waist to my back. "Isn't this more pleasant than last time?"

I managed a small smile, anxious because his arms blocked me from getting to the dagger. He must've sensed it.

"Shhhhhh. It's all right. We can go slow, my sweet. I can be gentle when you're a good girl."

His finger tipped my chin up. I marveled at how absolutely beautiful he was in perfect hard lines. The paradox was staggering, knowing what this mask of perfection concealed. I forced myself to be absolutely still as he leaned down to me. Cold breath, cold lips pressed hard, prying mine open. My body wanted to reject—kick, bash, slap. I kept steady, my mind calm.

"Oh, my sweet. I can't wait to crawl under your skin again."

Terror gripped me hard. He meant full possession, a violation of body and soul, one that would surely send me over the edge into madness. His slow affection transformed into something raw, rough.

This was the Danté I remembered. His right hand pulled up the hem of the gown, squeezing my thigh opposite the dagger. I still couldn't reach my weapon.

Take control, Genevieve.

As his hand drifted higher, I grabbed his wrist, pulling back to pierce him with sultry eyes.

"The bed," I ordered.

"I thought you'd never ask."

He grabbed my hand as if I still might try to get away. A liar knew a liar. He might not have fully believed me just yet, but the one fatal flaw of so many men was ego. Vanity was an awfully deadly sin.

He tried to ease me back onto the bed. I shook my head, pushing him onto his back instead. His eyes sparked brightly, like lightning in a winter sky. Evidently, he was pleased with my idea. He spread himself out across the red silk, one arm propped casually behind his head, arrogant smile wide and confident. I crawled on all fours, up along his body till my knees straddled his pelvis. Running my hands slowly along his abdomen up across his chest, I did my best to lull him into a stupor. I leaned my upper body over his, moving closer as if to kiss him. But I didn't. He'd gotten all the kisses he was going to get out of me.

His eyes closed. I continued to pet, rubbing my hands back over his chest and down his torso. As I braced myself with one hand on his abdomen, my right hand unsheathed the dagger, raised it high, and plunged it violently into the left side of his chest.

My body flew with a supernatural push, knocked clear of the bed onto the floor. A gurgling shriek of rage had me scrambling to my feet, still clutching my dagger. Danté stood at the edge of the bed, staring at the wound seeping black blood. I'd hit him exactly where I'd hit Nathaniel, yet there was no real reaction. No fatal reaction.

Liquid crimson eyes pierced a chill straight through me. He laughed. I stood, legs apart, ready for him.

"I have no heart, Genevieve, so there's no need to go for the vitals. It will do you no good."

I watched as the wound slowly closed, healing instantly, though black fluid streaked across his chest where his fingers had touched. He circled toward me as I inched toward the door. He held out a hand, curling his fingers as one might summon a child.

"Come to me now. No more games."

When I didn't obey, he vanished, sifted directly behind me. I elbowed him hard enough to crack something and spun, swiping out with the dagger.

"*Flamma intus!*" I screamed, beckoning my VS that had felt dormant since I'd killed Nathaniel.

A dim flicker of inner power hummed down my arm and through the razor-edged steel as I sliced across his face, from ear to lip. He howled. I ran.

Disoriented, for I'd never seen this hall, I sprinted, bare feet slapping hard on the slate floor, not knowing how to get out. There were doors randomly placed along the hallway. I ran toward one, throwing it wide, and halted.

Creatures that might have once been human were chained to the wall by different limbs. Eyes yellow, hollow, seemingly lifeless glanced disinterestedly at me. They were in various stages of starvation. One small creature was no more than skeletal bones with a thin layer of papery gray skin. What was this? A torture chamber? No. It was cold punishment. A place to punish disobedient slaves who could not die. This was hell, one small room in one realm of it.

I ran again, knowing Danté was close behind. The hall seemed an endless path into gloom. I saw another door and thrust it open, screaming as one foot fell into endless air. The shock made me drop the dagger, which clattered to the stone floor of the hallway as my body swung over the abyss. I gripped the doorknob with both hands and clung to the edge of the entrance with one foot.

I hung over impenetrable darkness falling away beneath me. The cold emptiness of a deep gulf stretched wide and far. Using leverage and my foot still crooked on the edge of the door, I managed to pull myself back into the hallway, slamming the door shut.

"Genevieve." An echoing, singsong whisper. "I do so love a chase, but I'm in no mood anymore."

I grabbed my dagger and kept running, now in a frantic state to find the stairs or some other way out. Sweaty strands of hair clung to my temples and neck.

A large door stood at the very end of the hall, the walls narrowing toward the iron-studded entrance. A special room. A way out?

Opening more cautiously this time, I entered a vacant space, gray stone on every side, with six tall, rectangular windows—three on the left, three on the right. Wait. No. They weren't windows exactly. I walked up to the first on the right, peering inside.

Through the glass, I saw a cathedral-ceilinged room, walls and floors of white marble. A long red carpet led to a throne of shining silver with clawed feet and arms. There was a second smaller one molded from sparkling gold. There was no one sitting on either throne, but two muscular, blackened demons with ghastly yellow eyes stood on either side, staring straight ahead, oblivious to me.

The glass separating the room I was in from the other moved, shimmered. I lightly touched one finger to the surface and drew back. Ripples blurred the image for a few seconds, then righted itself. My finger felt wet but wasn't.

I moved to the next one. The room was pitched in darkness, and though I could see nothing, I sensed something there. I shuddered and moved on to the third. Another vast room with Gothic ceilings and ribbed vaulting canopied a throne. This one had no carpet at all centered down the hall, and there was only one throne—tall and wide, carved of deep mahogany wood with a pointed arch at the head. Black velvet draped behind the dais where the throne stood. This was definitely for royalty.

"Throne rooms."

My head swiveled to each doorway. Six of them. Six princes,

brothers of Danté. The seventh throne room would be in this castle somewhere.

"Yes, my sweet," said a bitter, cold voice behind me.

I spun to see Danté in the doorway. Smeared with black blood on his chest and a dripping gash on his face, he darkened the door like the demon prince he was. The wound on his face festered in a red welt and didn't seem to be healing. My VS power. While my power had been mostly blocked by my foul murder, smothering what light she normally gave me, she'd still come forward when I summoned.

My pulse staggered a beat as Danté moved into the room. I glanced at the entrance to the throne room right next to me. Danté chuckled.

"If you think to find mercy or sanctuary with one of my brothers, you're sadly mistaken. I will show you far more mercy than they ever would. When I'm done. Step through one of those doors and find out for yourself if you don't believe me."

Don't panic. Stand your ground.

"No more games."

His voice was an ice blade cutting the air. He wound black wire around his fists, pulling the wire taut and snapping it in a loud crack. I jumped. He smiled a monstrous smile—all serrated teeth, promising pain.

"Do not fear, Genevieve. I have no plans to strangle you. But, oh, darling, I will bind you." He sauntered casually into the room, making his way carefully closer, red eyes piercing the dark. "I will teach you to behave, my sweet. It may take a few days, weeks, months, perhaps, but you will learn obedience. Willful fillies must be broken by their master's hand. It will only hurt a little. Now come to me."

"I will never give in to you. *Never!*"

"We'll see about that."

I was against the wall, shaking from terror and rage. My hand holding the dagger trembled, but I held it aloft. He was out of his fucking mind if he thought I'd let him bind me willingly. He came closer, not even trying to hide the menace in his eyes.

A ghastly, high-pitched shriek pierced the castle walls in an explosion of anguish and agonizing woe. My dagger clattered to the floor as I pressed my hands over my ears, sound sucking from the room. Danté swiveled.

"Cocytus. What's that bitch doing here?"

That was the last I heard as a string of curses spilled from Danté's mouth. Evaporation of all sound but the shriek of cold-blooded despair screamed through the halls, coming closer. Something close to fear skittered across my captor's immaculate face. No longer immaculate with the angry gash searing one side.

Cocytus. The River of Lamentation. Soul-eater of woe. She came closer still. I could hardly stand it, a deep sorrow creeping into my bones. Danté threw down the black wire he carried and started for the door when she swept into the room, floating above him.

Banshee-like in a tattered gray cloak, wisps of cloth billowing, framing a grisly white face with wicked, black eyes, she screamed again, spreading skeleton arms wide. I collapsed to the floor, tears streaming down my face from the painful pressure of despair.

Danté approached, drawing his arm back. I have no idea what he was about to do, because she cried out again. Her jaw yawned grotesquely, until I saw fire burning in the cavernous gulf. Her mouth gaped unnaturally wide. Something crawled over her tongue.

In a millisecond, a man spilled out and landed on his feet. An aura of flame burned him into an entire being of fire. Flames arched behind him, forming a blaze of huge wings as he drew a massive claymore from the scabbard strapped to his back.

"Jude."

Danté took a giant step back and stared. Jude circled, his

muscles rigid and taut. Cocytus floated, undulating in the corner like a spider spinning a web, but there was no web. She stopped shrieking, watching with ink-black eyes—a spindly predator awaiting her meal.

Flames of light simmered and rippled around Jude as he circled his prey, who'd straightened himself in an arrogant stance, gesturing wildly. Jude's back was to me, but as he moved, his head swiveled in my direction.

I gasped. In Jude's dark gaze, I saw only death. It was all for him, for Danté. An all-consuming fury intent on its prize.

Danté said something to Jude. The vacuum of sound eased. I heard sporadic words—*luscious…inevitable…like her…so sweet.*

Jude's aura of fire licked brightly as he clasped the claymore with both hands, his knuckles stretched white, centering the blade upright. He spoke to Danté. Though I couldn't hear the words, I read them on lips I knew so well, now tight with promise.

For Genevieve.

The massive sword swung around in a wide arc, cutting the air in a long sweep, cleanly slicing off Danté's head, which bounced twice and rolled across the floor, hitting the wall.

Cold gray eyes widened in shock. The head's mouth opened and closed like a guppy, gasping for air. Danté's body fell to its knees, black blood dripping down chest and back. But Jude wasn't through.

Rage blazed fiercely in a flaming halo of red, orange and gold, framing his lithe body, taut with strain on the edge of triumph. He plunged the claymore straight through the decapitated body. Rather than pull the sword straight back out, Jude ripped upward through chest and neck, his mouth open in a soundless scream.

The fiery blaze dimmed with his victorious stroke. Jude walked to the wall, picked up Danté's head by the hair and tossed it in the air toward Cocytus as if he were simply lobbing a ball.

She opened her mouth and gulped the head like a bird swallowing a worm. I should've been sickened, but I wasn't. I felt something entirely different as Cocytus leaned over the rest of her gruesome meal and Jude sheathed his sword, stalking in long strides toward me, something desperate in his eyes. I leaped into his arms.

He gripped me with such vicious need, I lost my breath and nearly fainted. I nuzzled my face into his neck, breathing in the safety and smell of Jude. His steel armor of protection clamped on to me. I didn't even need that. Being in his arms was enough.

He held me and held me and held me, his lips pressed to the crown of my head, his arms a vise of possession.

Cocytus shrieked softly, sated, floating out of the room and away to wherever soul-collectors went. Sound came back to the room. I could hear my own breathing coming fast. Jude's too.

"Are you okay? Did he…?" he breathed into my hair.

I pulled back.

"No," I said, knowing what he was asking. "I'm okay. I'm all right."

He stared down with such intensity, I thought he meant to melt me on the spot.

"Oh, Jude. Your eyes."

A cloud of obsidian, barely sparking with flinty gold, gazed down on me.

"A small price to save you."

I ached, thinking of what it must've been like in the belly of Cocytus, what despairing souls must've rubbed their dark essence onto him.

He grabbed my hand with an iron grip. "Come. I can't sift within these walls. Let's get out of here."

"I thought you'd never ask."

As soon as we were in the hall, Jude lifted me into his arms. I could easily walk but wasn't arguing with him. A man on a mission—protection of his woman foremost in his mind—he found the stairs easily, walking straight down, glancing warily in case one of Danté's slaves attempted to stop us. I'd love to see them try.

Once outside the castle and beyond the gates, I clasped my hands behind his neck, feeling the elation of safety in Jude's arms. My eyes slid shut, reveling in the warmth spreading inside. A few more steps and we sifted. The Void didn't bother me this time. Nothing bothered me at this point.

When I opened my eyes, we were in Jude's living room. He sat on his overstuffed armchair with me securely on his lap. He positioned me upright then pulled off his shirt.

"Lift up your arms."

I did. He pulled the black nightgown over my hips and up over my head. Jude then slipped his shirt over my head. As I put my arms into the sleeves, he hauled his arm back to throw the gown.

"Wait!"

I used the gown to wipe the black blood spatter along his neck and cheek, then handed it back to him. He threw the balled-up gown across the room into his mantel-less fireplace, where it immediately ignited into flames. I reminded myself to ask about his power to start fires later. Right now, I really didn't give a shit.

He pulled me close. I braced one hand on the top of the Celtic cross that stood strong up to the hollow of his throat. That hard edge of anxiety and fury was fading now that he knew I was truly safe. Still, he didn't seem ready to let me go.

His eyes were so fixed on mine, I couldn't breathe. An emotion deeper than anything I'd ever felt washed through me, bone-deep. When he spoke, the words struck me dumb.

"I was in the midst of battling Bamal's men when I felt a tremor of danger. Something foul pierced my soul. I thought Bamal or some other evil had shown up on the scene. Then I knew…it was you. I felt you. My heart felt you. My heart felt yours." His warm hand cupped my cheek. "I'm so sorry. By the time I sifted, you were gone."

"Hush. You weren't too late." Our lips met. A soft, tender kiss. "I'm here." Another kiss. "I'm safe."

"*Mon coeur,*" he whispered against my lips, stroking. Gentle caresses. Soft. Comforting.

He'd never spoken to me in his native tongue. He had kept his childhood in France locked away from me. But now, he was opening that door of secrets. Slowly.

"Mon coeur," he breathed again, eyes imploring, wanting, needing.

I nodded, kissed him more deeply, whispering, "Yes."

And my heart was his.

It had been ten years since my last confession. I'd given up on the idea of forgiveness when my mother abandoned me through suicide. But today, I'd needed it.

Jude had refused to let me turn myself in or try to explain to the police that Nathaniel's death was self-defense.

Rather than argue with that steel-willed man, I ignored the fact that George surreptitiously made Nathaniel's body fall into the bayou. Not very saintly behavior if you ask me.

While Kat propped Mindy up near the patio, George had given Mindy a persuasion cast, which conveniently made her think she drank too much and split her dress falling down the garden steps.

The only thing I could think to do to rid myself of the guilt was go to confession. For the most part, it had. Even now, as I walked away from the confessional, I could feel the cloud wrapped around my VS start to dissipate, letting the moon-brightness shine through. I touched my fingers to the opal at my neck as I stepped up to the candle votives at the entrance.

I dropped a dollar in the offertory and lit a candle on the row of soft-burning candles beneath Mary's statue. I knelt and remembered my mother, feeling more tender than ever toward the woman who loved me and left me.

Kat had returned to New York, needing to do some serious surveillance on Bamal. While I missed her, I knew she was only a sift away and would be back frequently for training sessions. George returned to wherever he lived too.

I discovered that negotiations with Bamal's demons revealed little. The three high demons were supposed to deliver me alive to the demon prince of New York. Great.

We get rid of Danté, and now this one. But Bamal wasn't Danté. He had other motives. Kat thought it had something to do with the prophecy. Of course, Kat thought everything had something to do with the prophecy.

I crossed myself and walked out of St. Louis Cathedral into Jackson Square. Jude's tall figure faced away from me on the other side of the wrought-iron fence in the garden. I ambled past the art vendors spread out on the pavement and stepped through the gate. Jude was talking to someone.

The man he spoke to was tall with blondish-brown hair, wearing casual gray slacks and a crisp white shirt. Good looking but average in appearance except for an indefinable glow. No one seemed to notice, but my VS went crazy as I sidled closer, pumping out a beacon of recognition. Though I didn't know him, my VS recognized him.

"But, is this..." Jude stammered.

Jude never stammered.

"Is she—"

"My dear friend," said the glowing man, "I do believe you already know the answer to that question."

With a beaming smile that was both compassionate and enigmatic, he nodded and walked past Jude. The man stopped right in front of me, peering down with impossibly green eyes. Okay, let me amend my former statement, better than average in appearance. *Way* better.

By now, I'd become accustomed to my VS picking up on a

signature in supernaturals I encountered. The man standing before me exuded a suffused power so great I felt that if I could breathe it in, my chest would burst.

"Good day, Genevieve," he said with a nod in a deep, melodious voice. "Do take care of yourself, won't you?"

I blinked rapidly. All I could do was nod in agreement as he exited the garden and disappeared into the crowds of Jackson Square. My ability to breathe slowly coming back to me as he slipped farther away.

Jude stepped up beside me.

"He was an angel, wasn't he?" I said more than asked.

"Archangel. His name is Uriel, the creator of our kind."

"What?" I looked up at Jude as he linked his fingers with mine. "I thought that was George."

"No. George was commissioned, shall we say, to serve as our leader, our trainer. But Uriel, he's the one who makes us what we are."

There was a bittersweet tone in his voice, mixed with fervent gratitude. He blinked, and the spell was broken. He peered down at me with a classic, mischievous Jude grin, planting a quick kiss on my hand. "I'm hungry."

"Me too. Where shall we go?"

I glanced around the square, thinking of the dozens of famous restaurants within walking distance.

"My place."

"Jude, you can't cook," I said, watching his lips curl. "Can you?"

"Genevieve, do not attempt to penetrate the mystery that is me. You will never know all my secrets."

I loved playful Jude.

"Well, I'll definitely discover whether you're a good or a bad cook."

"Mmm," he mused. "Do you like strawberries and whipped cream?" he asked, pulling me along the side street toward Dauphine.

"That's dessert, not lunch."

"So it is. I like dessert."

His eyes skimmed from my eyes to my lips then farther south. He kept me close as we walked along. Even in broad daylight, he watched the shadows. The shadows of Danté's lair still lingered in my mind, but I no longer had nightmares.

Jude had once told me he'd gladly go to hell for me. He went twice. He even traveled into the bowels of a Collector, mingling with condemned souls and staining his own in order to save me.

And save me, he did. In so many ways.

No matter the darkness in his eyes. No matter the secret sins in his heart. No matter the stains on his soul. I vowed one day I would save him too.

THANK YOU SO MUCH FOR READING THE BEGINNING OF JUDE AND Genevieve's story! Jump into book two, SEALED IN SIN, where a new player jumps into the game!

SEALED IN SIN, EXCERPT:

The moment he entered the room, all my senses rose to full alert. The man packed enough heat and power in his aura to melt a girl into jelly. A mere glance from his dark eyes or slight touch from rough hands, and I was lost.

I focused on flipping the pancakes on the stove, still trying to figure out how to tell him about our trip to the House of Hades, the near-miss with Gorham, and the brief and strange meeting with my guardian angel.

Kat preferred asking forgiveness rather than permission, or just omitting the admission of any sins altogether. But I had trouble lying, though I seemed to do it often as of late. I especially had trouble lying to Jude.

"Want some brinner?" I asked, plopping another dollop of butter in the pan.

"Brinner? What might that be?" He leaned with his back against the counter next to the stove, splaying one huge hand on the countertop, watching me pour the batter into the pan. How did this man make watching me cook a sexy thing?

"You've never heard of brinner?" I glanced at the door to make sure Mindy was out of earshot. "For someone who's been alive nearly two thousand years, you don't know a whole lot."

He slid a finger down my forearm. I nearly dropped the spatula. He leaned closer, his chest brushing my shoulder, voice dropping several decibels. "Educate me."

And just like that, my heart slammed into my ribcage, my thoughts scattering to the wind. I stared at him, knowing my eyes were no longer hungry for pancakes. He pressed warm lips, a feather-soft kiss, to the slope between my neck and shoulder. "Genevieve?" Another press of lips higher up my neck, melting me into goo.

"Hm?" Eyes closed, I welcomed a third kiss just under my jaw, relishing the heat pooling in lower places.

"Your brinner is burning."

"Oh, dammit!"

I snapped open my eyes, grabbed the smoking pan, and thrust it under the water faucet in the sink. A hissing crackle spit up more smoke.

"There goes brinner."

"You've made more than enough already."

He motioned to the ten-high stack with a smirk. I couldn't even think about eating now. Not after that kiss. And not with this guilt weighing me down.

Something registered in his gaze. He reached out his hand. "Come here."

From his expression, I wasn't sure if he planned to give me a hug or a spanking. I wouldn't mind either. Taking his hand, I let him pull me into his arms.

The familiar molten-steel illusion that Jude cast when we touched immediately locked on to me.

Flamma cast illusion to trick their enemies' eyes and demonic senses. There were no enemies in the kitchen of my apartment, but Jude couldn't help himself. Whenever he touched me, his armor coated me in a snap. As if he couldn't control protecting me at all times.

He circled one hand around my waist to the small of my back, hooking a thumb in the elastic of my pajama shorts.

I stared at his collarbone, admiring the visible part of his full-torso tattoo poking out of his black T-shirt. The top of his intricate Celtic cross entwined by thorny vines became extremely interesting all of a sudden. He tipped my chin up, forcing me to meet his dark gaze.

I didn't say a word, though I'm sure my conscience screamed loud and clear.

"Tell me."

ORDER **SEALED IN SIN** TODAY!

EXTRA SCENE: JUDE'S POV

Did you wonder what happened to Jude when he disappeared after Dante pretended to be him with Genevieve in his alcove? This is what happened in his point of view after he left her in his home.

Red. Red. Red. Blood pounded through my veins, pushing me over the edge. That fuck had his mouth on her skin, her lips. When I find him, I will crush him into nothing with my bare hands.

He marked her. That mother fucker!

No matter. She will never be his. Never. I will cast my soul into oblivion and him with me before I let that happen.

Her lips were swollen from more than one kiss. She thought it was me. How much had she given to him before the asshole revealed himself? Her mouth, parted, wanting.

Oh, Genevieve. The danger you're in. Hell and damnation.

Black clouded everything. I couldn't cage the rage.

I sifted to his gates and roared my arrival, the black castle looming in the gray haze. Pointed turrets stabbed upward into the constant night of this place. Gleaming yellow eyes of watchmen stood on the battlements.

"Where is he!" My voice shook the crumbling wall surrounding his castle.

Cassius dangled gaunt, skeletal limbs from his perch. He sat twenty yards up the precipice of black-rock facing beside the iron spires of the gate pointing into the gloom.

"Now, now, Master of Demons. He is not at home at the moment. And you know you are not allowed here. So take your little temper-tantrum and just be on your way."

My black glare made Cassius draw up his bony feet in case my wrath was turned on him. The spindly red spiders that kept him company crawled somewhere in his ribcage and an opening at his throat, hiding from the likes of me. Good.

"I want that fuck in front of me. Now!"

"We all want lots of things, Demon Hunter. I would like to be free of my perch. I've paid the price for my sins for long enough," he said, eyes glowing white, "but I can't have what I want. Just as you will not have what you want."

I laughed, feeling the rage slip just a little.

"I will have what I want. Soon enough. Here's a gift for your Lord and Master, Cassius."

I grabbed two bars of the gate, ignoring the searing pain of its touch, wrenching the entire left side from its hinges. I bent each spire inward upon itself, releasing the fury through the stabbing pain, until I finally held a mangled ball of black iron.

"You'd better stop, Demon Hunter!"

Cassius stood now on the edge of his precipice, pointing and shaking a gray, bony finger. I stared at the pathetic creature, grinning.

"Tell Goldie Locks to stop hiding and come out to play."

I launched the ball of unnatural metal. It arced and smashed into the wooden Gothic door, splintering the black facing, leaving a gash a foot wide and deep. Cassius' shrieked.

I gave him a withering glare then sifted through time and space until the smothering black cracked and diminished. I could not go back to Genevieve with death on my mind, fury in my heart, and violent desire pumping furiously through my blood.

ALSO BY JULIETTE CROSS

Vale of Stars Series

WAKING THE DRAGON

DRAGON IN THE BLOOD

DRAGON FIRE

HUNT OF THE DRAGON

Stay a spell Series

WOLF GONE WILD

DON'T HEX AND DRIVE

WITCHES GET STITCHES

ALWAYS PRACTICE SAFE HEX

Vampire Blood Series:

THE BLACK LILY

THE RED LILY

THE WHITE LILY

THE EMERALD LILY